FALLOUT

A PROSECUTION FORCE THRILLER

LOGAN RYLES

SEVERN RIVER

PUBLISHING

Copyright © 2025 by Logan Ryles.

All rights reserved.

No part of this book may be reproduced in any form or by any electronic or mechanical means, including information storage and retrieval systems, without written permission from the author, except for the use of brief quotations in a book review.

Severn River Publishing
SevernRiverBooks.com

This is a work of fiction. Names, characters, businesses, places, events and incidents are either the products of the author's imagination or used in a fictitious manner. Any resemblance to actual persons, living or dead, or actual events is purely coincidental.

ISBN: 978-1-64875-646-7 (Paperback)

ALSO BY LOGAN RYLES

The Prosecution Force Series

Brink of War

First Strike

Election Day

Failed State

Firestorm

White Alert

Nuclear Nation

Fallout

Full Dark

The Reed Montgomery Series

Overwatch

Hunt to Kill

Total War

Smoke and Mirrors

Survivor

Death Cycle

Sundown

The Ian Hale Series

Line of Fire

Path of Terror

To find out more about Logan Ryles and his books, visit

severnriverbooks.com

*For Lisa—one fantastic editor.
Thanks for everything.*

1

Somewhere in Azerbaijan

Screams echoed down a concrete hallway. Reed registered them through his left ear—the only ear that still functioned. His right was so clogged with dirt and blood from an RPG strike that it was now useless. He couldn't see. He was blindfolded. His wrists burned from metal shackles that bound them to an invisible ceiling. His toes barely touched the ground. His mind slipped in and out of consciousness, merciful oblivion overtaking the constant, searing pain that ripped from one end of his body to the other every time that oblivion failed.

But despite the useless ear, the blindfold, the pain, the semiconsciousness...the screams always radiated through. Desperate, shrill, and female, they were blended with the deeper howls of men. Reed recognized Corbyn's irate British cursing, mixed at times with the defiant shouts of Wolfgang and occasional bear howls from Ivan.

They were all in pain. They were all suffering. Reed fought to lift his face toward the clink of metal chains over his head, but invisible weight pinned his chin against his chest. It was difficult to breathe. He attempted a shout, but his throat was too dry. Consciousness wavered again. Welcome darkness offered a momentary release...

Then a door opened. Reed heard it as the electronic beep of a lock followed by the creak of hinges. Boots thumped across concrete and curt orders were given in words Reed couldn't understand. A light blazed on, so bright it hurt Reed's eyes even behind his blindfold. Somebody jabbed him in the ribs and Reed gasped.

"*O oyaqdır*," a voice snarled.

The light beamed down directly against Reed's face. The blindfold was yanked away but the pressure holding his chin down remained. Reed couldn't see anything. All was white, so bright there was no difference whether his eyes were open or closed. His good ear rang.

Boots tapped against the concrete. A body approached. Reed still couldn't see it, but he could sense its warmth. From someplace beyond the white light a voice spoke in heavily accented English.

"Who are you?"

Reed didn't answer. He couldn't get his mouth open far enough. The weight bearing down on his skull kept his chin rammed against his chest.

The voice returned, this time in that unrecognizable foreign rumble. Hands reached up around Reed's head, and like a concrete block lifting off his skull, the weight was removed. Reed inhaled like a free diver returning from the depths, nearly choking on his own tongue. His head rose off his chest and he detected vague shadows beyond the lights. A rubber hose passed between his lips and a surge of water rushed his throat.

Reed choked. He gulped. Half the water spilled down his throat. The stream kept coming. When at last it was removed, he heaved and blinked.

He was fully awake. That merciful oblivion had faded completely. Hanging from the chains, every muscle, every joint in his body screamed in pain. The toes of his boots slid across the concrete. He kicked and fought for footing, breaking into a gargled shout.

The shadow on the other side of the light closed in. A face appeared—dark and narrow, with cutting eyes and flashing bright teeth. A hand grabbed Reed by the jaw. Fingers dug in. The dark man shook Reed's head until Reed choked again.

"*Who are you?*"

Reed saw the man's lips move, but his mind failed to attach the voice to the face. The room around him wavered. His senses were disjointed, his mind unable to connect the dots.

The best he could manage was to regurgitate a prepackaged line.

"I told you," Reed choked. "We're a reconnaissance team...sent into Georgia. We were monitoring Russian military activity on behalf of NATO."

It was the same story Reed had stuck to from the moment he was first thrown in this pit—repeated loudly enough that hopefully his team could hear. It wasn't a perfect story, and not exactly a truthful one either.

But as the memories slowly returned to Reed's disoriented, exhausted mind, he knew in his very bones that the actual truth—that he and his team worked at the behest of the Central Intelligence Agency—could not be divulged.

Not after what he witnessed in the back of that Russian semitruck only moments before a mushroom cloud exploded over northern Azerbaijan.

Reed struggled for air as the strain on his arms constricted his lungs. The dark face smiled, looking like a vulture right before it dives into a bloody meal.

"One Russian," the face said. "One English woman. Three Americans. *Some reconnaissance team.*"

Reed didn't answer. He breathed through his teeth and fought to replay the events in his mind. Beyond the light, behind the pain. Past the disorientation of aching muscles and that ringing ear.

Back before the gunfire. Back before the screaming RPG that hurtled him into a ditch. Back to those chaotic moments in an Azerbaijani valley, locked in a gunfight with Russian Alpha commandos while Russian and Azerbaijani fighter jets danced and fought in the pitch-black skies overhead.

Reed had slaughtered the Alphas. Together with his team, they had captured the primary semitruck forming the core of the Russian convoy.

And what they found inside...they couldn't defeat.

Reed closed his mouth and stared the man right in the eye. The dark face drew closer. The fingers dug into Reed's face, so hard that lancing pain raced into Reed's skull. He didn't so much as blink. The man shouted, a blast of spittle spraying Reed's mouth.

"What do you know about the bomb? Who really sent you here?"

"We were sent by NATO," Reed repeated. "The bomb was Russian!"

The man didn't buy it. Reed saw the steel flashing across his iron gaze. He released Reed's face and hit him hard in the jaw. The world spun. Reed's boots slipped free of the concrete and he kicked for balance. He was swinging from the chains. His shoulders burned, his lungs constrained. He barely felt the impact of fist against jawbone. It didn't even matter.

Hands closed around his torso from behind and pressed him forward. The light returned, and the dark face with it. The man closed in, and from down the hall a fresh shriek of pain ripped into Reed's good ear.

The dark face smiled. "Do you hear that? That is your team. I know you are their leader. I can see it in your face...the desperation. The responsibility. How you are *failing* them."

Reed's stomach tightened. He fought the chains but could barely make them rattle. His own bodyweight was too much, his muscles too exhausted.

"I will rip them apart," the dark face said. "One piece at a time while you listen...until you tell me the truth." He leaned close. "*Who are you?*"

Reed gathered what little moisture remained in a dry mouth, pooling it on his tongue. He spat straight into the face—a dirty, slimy spray.

The face recoiled. One light toppled to the ground with a crash. Fists landed in Reed's stomach and the wind left his body. He heaved and choked. He swung from the chains.

Then another command was barked in Azerbaijani. The beating stopped. The face returned, one hand wiping the spit away. The vulture smile stretched.

"You don't want to talk? Very well. Then you will *listen*."

Boots thumped. The lights cut off. The hinges groaned. Reed shook the chains and shouted. His voice was little stronger than a dry rasp. The lock rattled again.

Then the screams redoubled. Louder than ever. Howls echoing down the hallway in multiple different voices of desperation. Pleading—begging.

And not stopping.

2

The West Wing
The White House

The weapon detonated nearly six thousand miles east of Washington, DC, but the shockwave of its blast was being felt at the seat of American power in ways Acting President Jordan Stratton could have never imagined. It wasn't just the fear, the predictable military posturing, the demand for answers from the media, and the scrambling of an administration already shaken to its core by the disablement of its Commander in Chief, Maggie Trousdale. Stratton had faced a plethora of geopolitical turmoil since accepting the vice presidency, and even more since Maggie descended into a coma and left him alone at the wheel.

Stratton knew what headwinds felt like. He knew how rough seas could shake the country to its core. He was familiar with the bite of salt winds blasting into his face. But this was different. It was worse than when Maggie was shot. Worse than when America was lured into military action in South America, or when radical Islamic terrorists successfully distributed potent chemical weapons across the city of Baton Rouge, killing thousands.

This was even worse than when a nuclear weapon had been detonated in anger for the first time since the Second World War, smashing the

Panama Canal and sending the American economy into a tailspin. That blast had ripped around the globe barely two weeks prior, and already it felt like a distant memory.

Because generations had been born and buried since hellfire was unleashed at Hiroshima and Nagasaki, but in the space of only fifteen days, *two* bombs had detonated on opposite sides of the planet, shattering a paradigm of supposed security and thrusting the Free World into a new geopolitical reality. The planet had officially gone nuclear.

And worst of all...nobody knew who was responsible.

"Mr. Vice President, I have Majority Leader Whitaker's office on the line. They'd like to confirm your ten o'clock appointment."

"Reschedule it," Stratton barked. "We'll meet next week."

"We've already rescheduled it, sir. Three times."

"So do it again. I don't have time to coddle Congress."

The aide blinked behind large, round glasses. She was twenty-something, probably barely out of college, but she looked ready to drop. Likely, she hadn't slept in days.

Stratton understood. He hadn't either.

The aide disappeared and Stratton snatched the phone off his vice-presidential desk. Despite the uncertain condition of President Maggie Trousdale that had thrust him into the position of acting president, Stratton rarely used the Oval Office. He liked to be deeper in the West Wing, near the heart of the action.

At least, that was the theory. Now the action was starting to swamp him.

"Jill, get in here." Stratton snapped the command and hung up. From outside the heavy oak door, the voice of turmoil echoed down hallways and reverberated out of cramped offices. Aides, cabinet members, military officials, political advisors. Everybody was in overdrive, and had been for days. Everybody was exhausted, tense, and breaking apart at the seams.

Stratton was used to that. What he wasn't used to was the lack of control. The ship was fragmenting, things were happening without his knowledge or consent. Departments were scrambling and acting autonomously.

It was chaos...and it felt like a time bomb.

The door creaked open and White House Chief of Staff Jill Easterling stepped in. Her face was pale, eyes rimmed with red. She carried a notepad and a pen and took her seat across the desk without a word.

"I just got off the phone with Carrie," Stratton said, referencing the ambassador to the United Nations. He spun the monitor of his computer around, revealing a *New York Times* article—*US Ambassador States Trousdale Administration Is Ready for War*. "What the *hell* is this?"

Easterling blinked, seeming to struggle to pivot her mind to the problem at hand. She shook her head. "I'm sorry, sir, this is the first I'm hearing of it."

"You and me both. Did Carrie go off script? I specifically told her to *deescalate*. We don't even know where these weapons came from. We're not even close to being 'ready for war.'"

"She's likely just riffing off your speech, sir. Projecting strength."

"That's my job. Her job is to follow orders."

"I don't disagree. I'll speak to her."

The phone rang again—a page from Stratton's secretary. He breathed a curse and mashed the speaker button.

"*What?*"

"Speaker Holland's office is calling—"

"*Take a message.*"

Stratton hung up and ran a hand through unwashed hair, once deep black. Now rapidly turning gray. It wasn't the lack of sleep that wore on him most. It was the lack of options. The lack of control. He felt like a cow pressed into a loading funnel, being pushed rapidly toward the mouth of a trailer.

Only, maybe it wasn't a trailer. Maybe it was a cliff, or a sledgehammer straight to America's forehead.

"Do you believe it, Jill?"

Stratton didn't have to clarify his question. The *New York Times*, the *Washington Post*, the *Chicago Tribune*, CNN...they were all asking the same question. News had leaked. Suspicions were piqued. The one word on everyone's lips was the same: *Russia*.

Was Moscow behind it all? The sponsor of terrorism, the puppet master of attempted Presidential assassinations and nuclear attacks? The White

House had only first begun to suspect as much just days prior, and already word had leaked. The media knew.

Rumors ran like wildfire through a country already reeling from a spiraling economy, skyrocketing prices, and intoxicating amounts of fear. The worst of it all was that Stratton didn't actually *know* much more than CNN did. Intel was scarce and contradictory. The truth elusive.

The consequences world-ending.

"I don't know, sir," Easterling said. "It's difficult to fathom."

Stratton couldn't disagree, but his list of alternative theories was growing shorter by the second. He pivoted across the desk with an impatient retort ready on his lips. Then he stopped.

Easterling wasn't even looking at him. She was staring at her legal pad, right hand trembling just a little over the page. Eyes bloodshot.

"What's wrong?" Stratton said. The question came out a little harsher than he intended.

Easterling looked up, mousy face pinched into a grimace that seemed to be damming up a tidal wave.

"I'm sorry, sir?"

"What's wrong with you, Jill?"

"I'm...I'm sorry, sir. I just got a call before I walked in. A personal thing. I'm okay."

"Personal? What are you talking about?"

Easterling's voice descended into a dry whisper. "My father just died."

Something like a hot knife sank into Stratton's gut. He wanted to curse and throw something, or maybe just ram his head against the wall until blackness overtook him. It wasn't just frustration or weariness. It was disbelief.

How could one more thing go wrong?

"I'm sorry," Stratton said. "I'm very sorry."

Easterling wiped her eyes. She lifted her chin. "I'm here, sir. I'm still here. What do you need?"

It was an absurd question. At any other time, in any other context, Stratton wouldn't have wanted or accepted anything. *Go home*, he would have said. *Be with your family.*

But not now. Jill Easterling might be the only dependable soldier Stratton had left, and he needed her more than ever.

"I need you on the phone with Secretary Gorman. She's got to tell Carrie to step it down. Our message to the UN is to remain calm—America isn't rushing into anything. This won't be another Iraq or Vietnam."

Easterling nodded, but she didn't get up. Stratton thought he knew what she was thinking.

"What if..."

"It really is Moscow?" Stratton finished.

Easterling didn't answer, and Stratton reached for the phone.

"Then we're gonna need flawless intel. Martha? Get me Director Aimes."

Dr. Sarah Aimes hadn't left Langley in three days, showering at the facility gym and catching catnaps on her office couch in between meetings. She took the call from the White House and told the acting president exactly what she knew —which was nearly nothing. The moment the bomb detonated in Azerbaijan, the CIA went into overdrive searching for answers, but they were blinded not only by the ensuing chaos but also by a deeper and even more sinister reality.

The Prosecution Force—the off-the-books black ops team Aimes had personally deployed to the Caucasus only days prior to the detonation of a nuclear weapon by as-yet-unnamed aggressors—had vanished. She'd lost all contact with them just as the mushroom cloud rose over northwest Azerbaijan. The CIA's operations directorate had been unable to reestablish communication.

One moment the Prosecution Force was operating on the ground at the Georgian/Azerbaijani border...and the next, it was simply gone.

"I want updates every eight hours," Stratton said. "Even if you have nothing, I want to hear it."

"Understood, sir."

Aimes hung up and simply stared at the phone. Across from her, Silas Rigby, her deputy director of operations, sat with iPads and notebooks spread across the conference table, his tie tugged loose and his hair disheveled. He hadn't slept either, and hadn't showered. He smelled like a gym rat, but Aimes had stopped caring.

Only one thought swirled in her head over and over, like a broken record turned up to full volume: *Who dropped the bomb?*

Nobody had, in truth. It wasn't dropped at all. It was carted into Azerbaijan aboard a semitruck, but somebody was responsible. Somebody wanted an escalation of already white-hot tensions in the Caucasus. With Russia's recent total occupation of Georgia, tens of thousands of ground troops gathering at Azerbaijan's northern border, Baku and Moscow seemed poised for war.

But why?

"What now?" Rigby was the first to voice a question after the phone call ended. He'd caught most of it. He understood the implications, regardless.

Aimes's gaze snapped over the desk. She didn't need to consider the question for long. Only one answer made sense. "We need eyes, Silas. Whoever you can find, whatever you can throw into the region. We need facts, ASAP."

Rigby stood. "I'm on it. I'll update you in two hours."

He turned for the door.

Aimes called after him. "Silas?"

"Ma'am?"

"Moscow, also. I need intel from Moscow. Pull out all the stops. Whatever assets we have, put them to work."

"Understood."

Rigby left, and Aimes stared at the door—a little dazed. A little disoriented. A lot unsettled.

It was a feeling she'd never experienced since joining the CIA, and certainly not since ascending to the directorate. A feeling that left her as helpless and vulnerable as a turtle crossing a freeway. Cars rushing. Horns blaring.

It was the feeling of being in the dark. The feeling of the greatest intelligence-gathering agency in the history of the planet being left totally, completely...blind.

3

Goranboy District, Azerbaijan

Turk and Lucy escaped capture by the skin of their teeth. As Turk led the way through waist-high grass across the floor of a mountain valley, the storm of gunfire erupting behind him redoubled in ferocity.

It was coming from a detachment of Azerbaijani infantry, and it was all concentrated on the overturned Russian Tigr that the Prosecution Force had used to flee the blast site of the second nuclear weapon to detonate in the past two weeks. They'd cleared the initial shockwave and witnessed the glow of the mushroom cloud through the truck's rear windows. They had survived.

But then the Azerbaijanis had arrived, and with a massive Russian army gathered on Azerbaijan's northern border, there was little patience for the intrusion of an unidentified Russian military vehicle. The Azerbaijanis responded with force. With Ivan Sidorov behind the wheel of the Tigr, the Prosecution Force attempted to evade them. The Tigr ended up rolling down the side of a hill.

Kyle Strickland and Kirsten Corbyn, the team's pilot duo, were both knocked unconscious. Wolfgang was pinned to his seat. Ivan wouldn't leave.

Reed had survived and remained in command. His orders to Turk had been clear and absolute: *Take Lucy, find communication, contact Langley. Now.*

It had taken something stronger than courage and deeper than conviction for Turk to leave his team—and his best friend—huddled in the back of that Tigr as the Azerbaijanis closed in, but Turk had done it. Not because he was afraid to fight, or afraid to die, but because he knew in his very bones that Reed was right.

The Prosecution Force had lost contact with Langley some time before the bomb went off, and in the intervening minutes, they had made a lethal discovery. Langley *must* be informed. As soon as possible. Whatever the cost. Turk was in the best shape to get the job done. Lucy was badly shell-shocked and in no condition to fight.

So Turk had led her through the valley and up the next hillside. He'd stood with tears in his eyes and looked back as an RPG raced toward the open back doors of the Tigr. It detonated just outside.

The rifles firing from the armored interior of the truck had fallen silent in that moment. The Azerbaijanis had closed in.

What happened next to Reed Montgomery and his broken team was anyone's guess, but it weighed on Turk's mind like a muddy boot crushing down on his skull. Pressing every other priority away...every one, except one.

Contacting Langley.

From a hilltop some ten miles from the site of the overturned Tigr, Turk finally slumped to his knees amid a stand of poplar trees and allowed Lucy to slide off his back. He'd carried her, along with a loaded AK-12 and a backpack containing only the most rudimentary gear, for most of the desperate flight through the dark. Morning had come as a still gray light growing gradually brighter in the east, and still Turk wouldn't stop. He avoided roads and stuck to the brush, punishing himself with thorns and briars that tore at his filthy combat pants and shredded his arms. Lucy clung to his back like a child, eyes wide, breath whistling through her teeth.

Not speaking. Not crying. Not making any sound. It was as though she were dead, but still somehow breathing. It had happened during the plane crash that preceded the blast, and Turk couldn't imagine that the nuclear detonation had helped. Lucy was shell-shocked like a World War One soldier stumbling through a trench. Her mind was deadlocked. Her body functioning only to the degree of most basic necessity.

She was useless to Turk for any combat or mission-centric purpose, but he couldn't leave her behind. He'd left enough people behind.

Setting Lucy at the base of a tree, Turk dug through his backpack, past a bottle of water and a spare AK mag, right to the bottom, where a pair of Russian military binoculars lay. He'd taken them from the body of a Russian kid in Georgia.

An innocent man, probably. A conscript of Moscow, sent to a faraway land to prosecute a political ambition he very likely cared nothing about. And now he was shot dead, just like so many others before him and, if Turk wasn't badly mistaken, a lot more yet to come.

Cradling the rifle, Turk advanced to the tree line and scanned the valley behind with the binoculars. There was a road and a pair of villages that Turk didn't know the names of. A mountain range in the distance, and the sun rising to about the eight or nine o'clock position. Cars appeared like dots on the two-lane, seeming to crawl their way across the horizon.

None of them looked military. There were no aircraft in the sky. All was shockingly quiet, given the momentous act of terror that had shattered the peace of this place only fifteen or so hours prior. The people had to know.

They would be panicking. They would be glued to their TVs and computers, desperate for an update. And so was Turk, but unlike the villagers at the bottom of the valley, he wasn't desperate to *receive* an update, he was desperate to *deliver* one.

Looking back to Lucy, Turk found her sitting with her knees bunched up to her chest, arms wrapped around them, swaying softly. Mouth open, eyes wide. Not making a sound. The anguish he'd felt the night before bubbled up in his gut, and his free hand began to tremble. Tears threatened to break through, mixed with maddened desperation.

What had he *done*? Abandoning Reed to the teeth of a lion. Leaving him to die. Running like a coward, prioritizing his own life...

Langley, Turk. Langley has to know.

It was the last direction Reed had given him. His next mission. His number one priority. Enough to keep him going a little while longer.

Back at the backpack, Turk took inventory of his supplies. The single bottle of water, about fifty rounds of ammunition, the binoculars, a pocketknife, and not much else. No food. No medical. No navigation. Most importantly of all, no communications equipment.

He and Lucy could survive in the hills for another twelve hours before the thirst set in. He'd need more water by then, and food. Those needs could be met if he could only contact Langley, but reaching around the globe into the offices of the Central Intelligence Agency was easier said than done. It wasn't like Langley had a 1-800 number or a contact email address. The secure messaging devices the Prosecution Force had used to communicate with their handlers in Virginia were long gone, fried by the EMP released from the bomb.

So what was his option? What was the next step?

Turk twisted the cap off the bottle and took a long pull. He wanted to wash the grit out of his eyes, but there wasn't enough of the precious resource. He moved to Lucy instead and extended the bottle.

"Here. Drink some."

Lucy didn't even look up. She continued to rock on her haunches, knees pulled into her chest, eyes staring dumbly ahead.

"Lucy." Turk shook her by the shoulder. Lucy looked up, but she didn't make eye contact. It was as though Turk was invisible.

"Drink," Turk said, lifting the bottle to her lips. Lucy swallowed twice, then turned her face away. Turk capped the bottle and turned to the tree line, rifle in hand. He marked the distance to the next village.

Three miles. Maybe four. Very little cover stood between him and his destination. He would need to wait until nightfall before he attempted the trek. Then he would leave Lucy hidden in the poplars and venture into the village. His objectives would be supplies first, then communication. It might take a while to find a cell phone programed in English, or a computer with a satellite internet connection he could use. In the meantime, he and Lucy had to stay alive.

Yes. He would wait for nightfall. Not a moment later. The village might be overrun by Azerbaijani military by then, all moving north to confront the insurgence of Russian ground forces already occupying Georgia. It was a mission that could very well get Turk killed.

But he would go, beyond any doubt, because it was Reed Montgomery's last order.

Langley *had* to know.

4

The Kremlin
Moscow, Russia

Russian President Makar Nikitin hadn't slept in nearly forty-eight hours, but he had never felt more alive. From the Operations Center buried inside the Kremlin—the Russian version of the White House Situation Room—Nikitin had monitored his military's total capture of Georgia, unfolding like the first act of a stage performance.

First, Georgian President Giorgi Meladze went missing—a mystery as yet to be solved, although Nikitin certainly knew the truth. By standing order of that missing president, Georgian Defense Forces were directed to cooperate with Russian peacekeepers deployed into their country under the guise of a WMP recovery mission. The nuclear weapon that radical Islamic terrorists had detonated in Panama two weeks prior had been sourced from a forgotten Cold War weapons stash in Georgia...or so Moscow claimed. The deployment of Russian forces into Georgia wasn't an act of aggression, but a security measure.

By the time the Georgian Defense Forces finally awoke to the imminent occupation of their entire country, it was much too late. There would be no long battle lines drawn, no lengthy artillery campaigns that dragged on for months the way the special military operations of Ukraine had dragged on. It all happened in the blink of an eye.

At one moment Georgia was free and independent...and the next? She was under total control of the Russian Federation, with fifty thousand battle-hardened of the Ukraine offensive already occupying strategic positions across the country, and tens of thousands more on their way to reinforce them.

That was when the second nuclear bomb went off. Not all the way around the world in the Americas, but up close and personal. Right there in northern Azerbaijan, a small weapon. A tactical nuke, technically, but still a nuke.

It shattered the stillness of a calm Caucasus night and sent a mushroom cloud blasting skyward. The Azerbaijanis responded with predictable panic. A full deployment of the Azerbaijani military was underway within hours, all racing northward toward the Georgian border and the ballooning Russian army gathered there.

Rushing right into a trap.

Nikitin congratulated his generals on their success, shaking hands and patting shoulders before departing the Operations Center. Then he was back across the Kremlin, sipping bitter Russian tea and escorted by bodyguards. Headed to his personal residence, where he showered and dressed in a new suit.

He didn't sleep. He didn't need to. Raw energy surged through his veins like the radioactive heat of the nuclear blast from the previous night. His mind was sharp and alert, his body fully charged. He didn't even bother to eat.

There wasn't time. The special guests had arrived in Moscow three hours earlier. They'd been fed, given time to refresh themselves, and now waited in a conference room adjacent to Nikitin's presidential office.

Two men. No entourage. No pomp or circumstance. No press releases or press conferences to be held. This was a clandestine meeting, which had been a trick to pull off, given the identity of Nikitin's guests. Soon enough the secret would leak. The entire world would know.

But by then, it would be too late.

Nikitin paused for a moment to inspect his appearance in a gold-framed mirror just outside the conference room. For fifty-one, he was lithe and strong. His hairdresser allowed just enough gray around his temples to project a tone of age and wisdom, but not so much that he lost his youthful energy. He was a man Russians could respect—a man they could admire, and when appropriate, a man they could fear.

A man the entire world would fear in the very near future.

Satisfied that he looked the part, Nikitin nodded to the pair of FSO officers standing outside the door. They opened it for him. He stepped in with his shoulders back, a subdued smile on his face.

The room was nearly empty—the giant conference table occupied by only two men. One was tall and slender, about sixty years old. Asian, dressed in a conservative black suit.

The second was short and broad, closer to seventy, with a long gray beard and a black turban wrapped around his head. Narrow glasses guarded squinting black eyes. Both men rose as Nikitin entered. Both men bowed.

Nikitin bowed back. He settled into a chair across from his guests. He fit an earpiece onto his right ear and they did the same. Trusted translators in the next room would convert Russian to Mandarin, Mandarin to Farsi, and Farsi to Russian.

Nikitin's smile broadened. He reached into his pocket and clicked open a gold-plated pen, resting it over a legal pad.

Then he said: "Let us begin."

5

Somewhere in Azerbaijan

The torment felt endless. Reed was beaten from his hanging position in the concrete cell, hard fists pummeling his torso while from down the hall the screams of his team indicated much more severe treatment.

He heard electric sparks. The grind of power tools. The bark of angry men speaking in that same unintelligible dialect as the dark face that first spoke to Reed. That face, in fact, had departed, leaving his deputies to carry out the grueling work. They worked Reed over for what may have been minutes, or hours, or half a day.

The questions were all the same. Who was he? Why had he come here?

And most importantly: *What did he know about the bomb?*

To all the questions, Reed only repeated his initial claim: That he was part of a NATO reconnaissance team and that the bomb was Russian. He shouted that statement with every ounce of strength that remained in his body, ensuring that his team heard it.

He knew they heard it, because they shouted the same claim as they were tormented. Even as the Azerbaijanis laid on the pressure, not one member of the Prosecution Force deviated from the narrative.

Individually they dug in hard and endured the misery, awaiting their turn with the jailers while they listened to their comrades being beaten to bloody pulps.

At present, it was Kyle Strickland's turn to suffer. He had survived the plane crash in northern Azerbaijan. Reed knew because Strickland was loud. There were screams, certainly. Inhuman shrieks that burst out of Strickland's throat when the pain overcame them.

But in between those screams, the ex-fighter pilot made another sound. As loud as the shouts. As defiant as a battle cry: he *laughed*.

"Is that all you've got? Man, my fraternity hazed me harder. You better try again!"

Reed admired the bravado. He also knew it was stupid. The tormentors focused on Strickland. They broke him down. The clock ground by for what felt like forever, and by the time the torturers finally departed, Strickland wasn't laughing anymore. He wasn't making any sound at all.

The prison had fallen deathly quiet, only muted gasps breaking between the bars and reaching Reed's one good ear. He hung from the chains, too tired and numb to even notice the burning muscles in his shoulders. Whatever weighted cap had been placed on his head kept his chin pressed down, his neck muscles stretched, each breath a labor. But he no longer cared.

Blackness had returned, but it wasn't the welcome cloak of unconsciousness he hungered for. No. The Azerbaijanis knew better than to drive him into that sweet embrace. They'd kept him lucid, even injecting him with what might have been caffeine. He felt everything, but when a person feels everything, at some stage they feel nothing but a dull buzz.

Reed was chasing that dull buzz, eyes closed, muscles spasming. His throat was so dry it burned when he breathed. His tongue felt like wood, his eyes encrusted with blood and dried tears.

He was alive, technically. But if this continued, he wouldn't want to be. Reed had endured torture and captivity before, many times. Each time soured his value of his own life, driving him closer to the cold reality that he might be better off throwing himself into the depths. Just letting go, shutting off.

Giving in.

"Prosecutor?"

The voice was dry and accented. Reed's eyes fluttered open and he attempted to lift his chin, but he couldn't fight the weight affixed to his head. It kept his face pointed toward the floor, neck straining. He had to take his time inhaling enough breath to reply.

"Ivan?"

"Da."

Ivan's voice was muffled, likely passing through bars and down the concrete hallway into Reed's cell. With one bad ear and another still ringing, Reed couldn't pinpoint the location. But it was impossible to misidentify the accent.

"Are you alive?" Ivan asked.

It seemed a strange question. Clearly, Reed was alive. He'd answered.

Hadn't he?

For a brief moment Reed doubted his own consciousness. His own presence in this pit of hell.

"I'm here," he rasped.

A long pause. From down the hallway somebody moaned. It may have been Corbyn, or Wolfgang. Reed was unable to gender the tone. His ears were too shot.

"You must hold on, Prosecutor," Ivan said. *"We know what we saw."*

Ivan put special emphasis on the words, and Reed understood why. To the Azerbaijani jailers no doubt listening via ceiling mounted bugs, it might have sounded like Ivan was reinforcing Reed's claim that the bomb was Russian. Which, in fact, it was.

But Reed knew what Ivan really meant, and what Ivan was really thinking. The item the Prosecution Force had found in the back of that Russian semi-truck was, indeed, a small nuclear device.

But that device was stamped with *U.S.A.*, and an American flag. Moscow, it seemed, was trying to frame America for the attack, thereby undermining American power in the region, and paving the way for further Russian expansion.

If the Azerbaijanis knew that Reed's team actually worked directly for the CIA, any further truth wouldn't matter. The situation would play right into Russia's hand.

Don't break. You can't break.

The admonition repeated in Reed's mind. It sank into his gut, burrowing into the foundations of his psyche. With both eyes open, Reed gritted his teeth. He braced his toes against the concrete and forced his chin upward with everything he had left.

A chain rattled. The cap affixed to his head resisted the movement. But Reed's face rose. His line of sight traced concrete to a wall, and a wall to a doorway with a grate in it. Dim light shone in the hallway outside. Again he heard that soft moan.

Reed spat blood. Then he shouted into the darkness.

"Hey, assholes! Go make passionate love to yourselves."

From down the hall the moaning broke short. Reed's voice echoed.

Then the faintest hint of a laugh drifted down the hall. Broken and weak. But unmistakably Corbyn's.

"This wasn't what I had in mind," Ivan said.

Reed allowed his chin to droop back over his chest. The weight of the cap was too much. He struggled through another breath.

"Trust me, Russian."

Ivan grunted. He spat. The prison grew very quiet.

Then Ivan said: "Trust me, American. In places like this, the worst is yet to come."

6

Goranboy District, Azerbaijan

Turk was right about waiting for cover of nightfall—it came with a price. By the time darkness descended over the Caucasus, Azerbaijani troops had swarmed the little village at the bottom of the valley and established occupancy amid the hotels, hostiles, and homes sprinkled along main street. They appeared to be some manner of fast infantry brigade, maybe three thousand strong. Besides ground troops armed with assault rifles, there were three dozen eight-wheeled armored personnel carriers, painted dark green with machine guns mounted to their roofs, the Azerbaijani flag printed on their side.

Turk recognized the APCs as Russian, possibly Soviet in design, which he couldn't deny was ironic, because he knew where they were headed—north. To confront Russia. By early the next day this division would be on the front lines of the Azerbaijani/Georgian border, digging in to stave off an invasion.

It was a geopolitical puzzle Turk couldn't begin to make sense of, but even though the Azerbaijani troops presented a challenge to his and Lucy's continued survival, they also presented an opportunity. Fast infantry depend on reliable communication to coordinate their movements. They need radios, GPS, and satellite phones.

All things Turk could repurpose in his mission to contact Langley...*if* he could get his hands on them.

Returning to the poplar knoll where he and Lucy had spent the remainder of the day, he found her exactly where he'd left her, sitting at the base of a tree with her knees pulled up to her chest, eyes wide. Turk had seen shell shock before. ISIL insurgents enjoyed mortars, and they'd used plenty of them during the Iraqi Civil War. Once, a mortar had detonated on the opposite side of a block wall, only feet from Turk's position. In an instant, he couldn't remember where he was. He couldn't remember *who* he was.

Everything was just a buzz, and it had lasted for a couple of hours. But not for over a day, and he hadn't been as completely incapacitated as Lucy now was. Somewhere during the plane crash, the thunder of gunfire, the combat on the highway in northern Azerbaijan, Lucy's psyche had simply snapped. It wasn't a sign of weakness. It could have just as easily happened to Turk himself.

But it hadn't, and now he was left balancing Lucy's survival with the mission at hand. He could only pray that the two wouldn't conflict.

Squatting at the base of the tree, Turk drank half of what remained in the bottle, then cupped Lucy's chin and forced her to drink the rest. She swallowed but she wouldn't look at him. She just stared at a tree, lips parted, tongue moving in soft rhythm. Turk thought she was whispering something, but he had to lean close to discern any words.

"*The Lord is my shepherd...the Lord is my shepherd...*"

Turk withdrew and scrubbed the back of his hand across his mouth. His tongue was so dry in his mouth it hurt to swallow. He stared at Lucy and something deep in his gut twisted—maybe remorse, maybe guilt.

He didn't have time to sift between them. He'd lost enough hours waiting for night to arrive. The pressure of the intel boiling in the back of his mind joined with nightmarish imaginings of what Reed and the rest of the team might be enduring, and together those thoughts were easily powerful enough to propel him toward the next problem.

"Lucy. Look at me."

She didn't respond. Turk cupped her chin again and twisted her face toward him. Lucy's lips continued to move, her eyes as vacant as empty tombs. Turk gave her a gentle shake.

"Lucy. I'm going to be gone for a while. Maybe a couple hours. I'll be back, though. Okay? So you stay put. Stay quiet. Understand?"

"Shepherd," Lucy whispered. "Shall not want."

Turk nodded slowly. He forced a smile he didn't feel. "That's right, Lucy. Just keep praying. I'll be back."

He pushed himself off the ground and reached for the AK. It leaned against a tree a few feet away, but as his fingers closed around the hefty weapon, Turk stopped.

He couldn't take it. He couldn't afford to. There was no way to conceal it, and even though he planned to sneak into the village completely out of sight, there was always a possibility that somebody might detect his presence. Being mistaken as a local villager offered him a better chance of survival than fighting off an entire fast infantry brigade with a single rifle.

Turk was better off leaving it. Maybe he could hope to scrounge up a pistol during his mission.

Returning the rifle to the tree, he pointed at it. Called Lucy's name.

She didn't respond. She was staring off into space again, once more repeating the opening line of the twenty-third Psalm.

Turk gave her shoulder another gentle squeeze, then he was headed back to the edge of the tree line. From the top of the hill he didn't need the binoculars to look down into the valley. The lights of the Azerbaijani military blended with those of the town, painting a clear view of his target. Three miles of hiking through the darkness—hard, hungry, dehydrated hiking. And then he had to find a way to lift vital military equipment without being detected. Return to the hill and contact Langley without his transmissions drawing attention.

Turk looked back over his shoulder to Lucy. He watched her rocking slowly back and forth and he thought of his team. He thought of that bomb in the back of the truck, and the flag stamped into the sheet metal. He thought of war, of radiation sickness, of global cataclysm.

And then he thought of Sinju. Of baby Liberty. His entire world waiting for him back in Tennessee, counting on him to get this right. To come home alive while preventing the next world war.

"God shepherd us all," Turk whispered.

Then he started toward the village.

7

Walter Reed National Military Medical Center
Bethesda, Maryland

President Maggie Trousdale had traveled a lifetime through space and loneliness, lost in a nightmare world of swirling memories and flashing hot pain for what may have been days, or could have been a year. At times it was very dark, and at times there was light. Occasionally she heard voices, and more than once she questioned whether not she was even alive.

Was this Heaven? Or, more likely, the other place. It was dark. It was cold. Then it was hot. The searing pain ripping through her torso reached all the way to her brain and exploded like an artillery shell. She tried to scream and wretch. Heavy hands pressed down on her and muted voices called from the far side of the universe.

"*Give her more.*"

The pain faded. So did the voices, and the light, and all sensation of passing time or even Maggie's own existence. She faded out again into pitch darkness...

She saw Louisiana. Her home state, clothed in bright green swamp foliage, with a war chant echoing in the background. She wasn't walking, she was floating, like a ghost right over the swamp. She recognized the piercing tall silhouette of the Louisiana State Capital, and then she was standing in the middle of Tiger Stadium. It was game day, and the stands were packed with LSU fans. She straddled the fifty-yard line, and a cadence pounded through her head like a drum.

"White eighty! Hut, hut, hike!"

Feet thundered. Maggie turned and saw a monster of a defensive end blasting through a left tackle and headed straight toward her. Panic surged through her system. She looked into her hands and saw a bloody football clutched between her fingers. She stumbled back. She shook her head, confused and desperate.

He hit her—so hard and fast she slammed right into the dirt and sank beneath the field. The crowd cheered from someplace far away. The big DE leaned over her, snarling through his helmet. His face was contorted and disfigured, swollen and purple like a corpse's. When his lips parted, Maggie smelled death, a stench so rotten she choked.

"You dropped the ball," the player growled, sinking thick fingers into her stomach and squeezing. "You let us *die!*"

His face began to melt, like candle wax. Maggie screamed as the pain raced back up her spine. Her head slammed into the field. The crowd roared a vindictive chant.

Everything swirled to black.

James O'Dell heard the screams from down the hallway. He threw down the newspaper he was reading and bolted out of the chair, rushing past Secret Service sentries and barging his way into Maggie's hospital room before anybody could challenge him.

The doctors were all there. The trauma nurses. Maggie lay on the bed with eyes wide open, the first time she'd awakened in nearly two weeks. Sweat streamed down her chalky-white face, and her hands clutched her stomach. She was howling like a dying animal, eyes darting around the room, confusion clouding her face.

"Give her morphine!" O'Dell barked.

The doctors ignored him, but they were already working on her IV line.

The heart monitor next to Maggie beeped a rapid cadence, her blood pressure reading 170 over 100. O'Dell ran to Maggie's bedside and shoved past the medical staff, nearly flattening a nurse. He found her right hand and wrapped it in both of his, squeezing.

"Maggie," O'Dell whispered, his own heart rate spiking. "You're okay. I'm right here."

"Stand back!" the doctor barked.

O'Dell ignored him, descending to one knee and leaning close. There was morphine in Maggie's IV now—or some kind of drug. The beep of the heart machine had slowed a little, and even though she was still panting like a winded racehorse, Maggie's thrashing had subsided. She fell back on the bed, wide eyes fixated on the ceiling at first, face twisted into a grimace of pain.

Then her head slowly rotated. She faced O'Dell, and the fog in her eyes parted. Recognition replaced it.

"James?"

It was déjà vu. O'Dell had been in an almost identical situation almost exactly a year prior, when Maggie surfaced from a coma inflicted upon her by an assassin's bullet. She hadn't died then, but her liver had sustained extreme damage, and the stress of the White House had stalled recovery.

Stalled it, and then derailed it altogether. Maggie's liver failed. She descended into another coma. She needed a transplant. None could be found.

And then one was...although how it came to be available was a story James O'Dell would take to the grave.

"I'm here." O'Dell smiled.

Maggie's breathing relaxed. Her shoulders slumped into the sweaty hospital bed. She still grimaced, but the facial muscles began to loosen.

She didn't look away from O'Dell. Instead, she squeezed his hand. Her breathing regulated along with the tempo of the heart monitor, blood pressure and heart rate descending together back to healthy levels. Maggie's eyes grew heavy, then closed. Sleep overtook her, and the doctor placed a hand on O'Dell's shoulder.

"Give us the room, son."

This time O'Dell didn't argue. He took one last look at Maggie, her broken body stretched across the bed, pasty pale. Then he hurried down a hallway to the private waiting room reserved for guests of the president. He was the only occupant. The lights were turned off. He slammed the door and threw himself into a chair, head descending into his hands, body trembling.

He couldn't close his eyes, as badly as he wanted to. If he did, he would see the faces—two of them now. One a former CIA director, the other a random convict on the bad side of Washington. Both caught off guard. Both confused, temporarily defiant.

And both now *dead*.

O'Dell's heart hammered with a sudden onslaught of anxiety. His breathing quickened and he focused on the pattern printed into the carpet. Tried to unravel the twisting spirals and geometric shapes. Anything to keep from thinking.

This wasn't him. He shouldn't feel this way. He'd done the *right thing*.

He'd protected Maggie.

From his right-hand pocket O'Dell's phone rang. He ignored it and focused on his breathing. In and out. Measured. The phone went to voicemail and the room grew quiet.

Then the phone rang again, and O'Dell snatched it out with gritted teeth. The same number had called twice, and it wasn't a number the phone recognized. Area code 615. Was that...Tennessee?

O'Dell swiped to answer.

"Hello?"

"James O'Dell?" The voice was female and sounded vaguely familiar. It also sounded pretty strung out. O'Dell could empathize.

"Who is this?"

"Banks Montgomery. Reed's wife."

That was enough to warm O'Dell's blood and calm the shivers. Not because there was any comfort in either name, but because just thinking about the Prosecutor was an irritating enough picture to distract his mind from that pair of faces.

"How did you get this number?" O'Dell barked.

"I'm looking for Reed," Banks said, ignoring the question. "I can't get him on the phone. He's been gone for days. *Where is he?*"

Banks's voice edged with increasing panic as the words fell over themselves coming through the phone. O'Dell straightened in the chair, squinting across the room.

"What are you talking about?"

"He was deployed," Banks said. "Don't you work for the president?"

O'Dell's mind froze in temporary confusion. He backtracked to the last time he'd interacted with Reed Montgomery—sometime during the terrorist attacks. Reed had called, wanting assistance from the White House in his pursuit of the man who detonated bombs in Tennessee. Banks had been badly injured by those bombs. Reed was on a warpath.

But O'Dell hadn't helped. Not only because he wouldn't have pissed on Reed if the man were on fire, but also because the White House had cut all ties with the illegal black ops team known as the Prosecution Force. Their utility had been exhausted. They'd become a liability for Maggie Trousdale.

As far as O'Dell knew, that was still the case.

"Your husband doesn't work for the White House," O'Dell said. "I don't know where he is."

"I *know* he was deployed!" Banks retorted. "Don't lie to me!"

"Yeah? Well, he wasn't deployed by us, sweetheart. Check the local whorehouses. Reed Montgomery isn't on the payroll."

O'Dell hung up before Banks could respond. He shut off the phone and tossed it into the seat next to him, already forgetting about Montgomery. The Prosecution Force. Anything to do with the past.

Anything except the two faces. When O'Dell closed his eyes, he saw them both.

8

The Situation Room
The White House

"This is ground zero—three square miles of extensive devastation, with the worst of the blast concentrated inside a region roughly the size of New York's Central Park."

From the end of the conference table, a Pentagon expert specializing in nuclear blast analysis—something Stratton never fathomed he would actually have to consider—used a laser pointer to mark out regions of a satellite map depicting northern Azerbaijan. The site of the nuclear blast still cooling from two days prior was peculiar, to say the least. It was centered along a lengthy highway that ran south into the heart of the country, with a mountain plateau stretching out on either side and mountain ranges rising in the distance. A scenic place, probably, but not a very heavily populated one. In fact, the nearest village was nearly ten kilometers away and had sustained no direct damage from the blast and only minor secondary damage. Those mountain ranges had served as wind barriers, stemming the spread of radioactive fallout from reaching the bigger cities fifty and a hundred kilometers away.

There was no logical reason anyone had been able to imagine as to why a nuclear bomb should be detonated in anger in the middle of a vacant Azerbaijani valley. In fact, there were only two reasonable solutions up for debate.

The first was that the detonation had been an accident, but that didn't really hold water because Azerbaijani fighter jets had engaged with Russian fighter jets in the moments preceding the blast, as documented by CIA satellite surveillance. Also, there was the fact that Azerbaijan was not known to possess any nuclear weapons, and neither was any nation remotely close to its borders.

Except Russia, of course. Which gave way to the second theory, that somehow a weapon had been deployed out of Russia and trucked into Azerbaijan. Very likely, the intended target lay deeper down that lonely highway, but the plan had gone awry and the bomb was detonated early.

That still didn't explain who was responsible, or how a nuclear device could have escaped the protective custody of a nuclear nation. Only hours prior to the blast, Russia had claimed that Georgia was host to a forgotten Soviet weapons depot which included WMDs, and even nukes. That was where the bomb that shattered the Panama Canal had originated, according to Moscow, and the presence of such a dangerous forgotten weapons depot was Russia's justification for invading Georgia.

But if that were the case—if any of that were *actually true*—then why had Russia gone radio silent on the world in the hours following the second unexpected detonation of a nuclear weapon?

"That's enough," Stratton said, cutting the presenter short halfway through a spiel about the exact nature of the radioactive damage and its long-term implications. "We get the picture. What's the military update?"

The Pentagon specialist took a seat, and General John David Yellin, the chairman of the Joint Chiefs himself, assumed the floor.

"Russian ground forces have congregated in the southern regions of Georgia, near the Red Bridge border crossing with Azerbaijan," the general began. "Thus far we're counting at least four divisions of both standard and mechanized infantry, roughly fifty thousand personnel, plus armor and mobile artillery. It's the largest ground force Russia has deployed anywhere in the world since the Ukraine offensives—and most of these soldiers are, in fact, assumed to be Ukraine veterans."

"Battle hardened," somebody said with a grunt.

Yellin nodded. "The most combat-experienced soldiers in the world, as of today. An additional two divisions of standard infantry are moving south as we speak, out of Chechnya and into Georgia. Their target seems to be reinforcing the Russian position in Tbilisi, a tactical foothold."

"The Russians haven't crossed into Azerbaijan?" Stratton asked.

"No, sir. Not as of our latest updates."

"So what are the Azerbaijanis doing?"

Yellin gestured for the map to be adjusted. An aide obliged, panning it south of the Red Bridge border crossing and over the northern half of Azerbaijan. It was mountainous, and largely rural, but what arrested everyone's attention were the bright neon arrows marking troop movements headed north toward Red Bridge.

"The Azerbaijanis appear to have conducted a full mobilization of their defense forces. Infantry, armor, and mechanized artillery are all moving rapidly north as we speak. Some units are assuming footholds in vital tactical regions throughout the middle of the country, while the majority are headed straight for Red Bridge to confront the Russians."

"How many total?" Stratton asked.

"Everything they have. Roughly fifty thousand men—an even match for the standing Russian force, but the Azerbaijanis have over a quarter million reservists available. We expect those to be armed and deployed within the next week, depending on what happens next."

Stratton squinted at the map, arms crossed, seated at the end of the table with the bulk of his cabinet stretched out around him. All eyes were on the map. Everybody was thinking the same thing.

Ukraine. This situation had all the same flavors of impending war. Russian soldiers massing on the border. A Russian president who refused to answer international phone calls.

An overwhelmed nation scrambling to respond...

Except Azerbaijan *wasn't* overwhelmed. Not if they had a quarter million reservists on hand. Russia would need far, far more than fifty thousand troops to seize complete control of the nation, even if they were the most experienced soldiers in the world. What was more, they should be moving *now*. Crossing the river, headed south. Not waiting for the Azerbaijanis to obtain defensive positions, park their guns with muzzles pointed into the valleys, there to rain hellfire on the enemy.

None of this made sense, not to Stratton. Granted, he wasn't a military strategist by any extent, but Yellin seemed confused also.

"What's your read, General?" Stratton pressed.

Yellin bunched thick lips, bulldog shoulders bulging under his uniform shirt. He shook his head.

"I can't see a win for Moscow in this. I don't know why they occupied Georgia—or why Georgia let themselves be occupied—but for Russia to mire themselves in another slogging ground war makes zero sense. Especially with Azerbaijan."

Stratton had to agree. Not just because every ground war was, at its rotten core, a senseless endeavor. But also because he assumed Azerbaijan to be a Russian ally.

"Secretary, will you refresh my memory on Russian/Azerbaijani relations?"

The question was addressed to Secretary of State Lisa Gorman, who sat a few positions down the length of the table, busily working on an iPad. She looked up quickly and removed her glasses. Stratton noted black hair that was turning increasingly gray, almost as rapidly as his own. The last thirty-odd months had not been kind to any member of Maggie Trousdale's cabinet.

"Relations between Baku and Moscow have been traditionally civil over the past few years," Gorman began. "President Elchin Rzayev is an autocrat and as much a de-facto dictator as Nikitin is, but the two men haven't butted heads to our knowledge. There was some dispute about oil pipelines a few years back. Some cultural tensions, I'm sure. Rzayev isn't known to be an easy man to deal with. He's obstinate and proven to be violent with opposition. Azerbaijan is reliably ranked as a very poor respecter of human rights. But again, these are small-picture problems. Nothing Russia should want to start a war over."

"What about natural resources?" White House Chief of Staff Jill Easterling said. "Something Russia might want to take by force."

Gorman passed that question to an aide.

"Azerbaijan is rich in oil and natural gas," the aide said. "Some valuable minerals and ample agriculture. Useful resources, but nothing Russia is short on."

"It's military strategy," Yellin said. "This isn't about natural resources. With control of Azerbaijan, Russia holds most of the Caucasus land bridge, encircling the end of Turkey—a NATO ally, I might remind you."

Gorman shook her head. "That doesn't make sense either. Russia would still need to invade Armenia to directly threaten Turkey. Azerbaijan is out of the way. Why bother?"

"If they successfully seize Azerbaijan, they won't *need* to invade Armenia," Yellin retorted. "Yerevan will fold like a cheap lawn chair. Armenia will be annexed."

"If control of Armenia was the end game, wouldn't it still make more sense to directly invade?" Secretary of Defense Stephen Kline entered the conversation with the next question. It was logical and concise, as usual with Kline. "Why bother with Azerbaijan?"

"We're missing an ingredient," Stratton cut back in. "We can't solve the formula with insufficient information. Lisa, where are we with Moscow?"

Gorman shook her head. "They still won't pick up the phone, sir. We've had zero contact with the Kremlin, and we aren't alone. I've spoken to London, Paris, Berlin, Brussels...the Russians are stonewalling everyone. Their embassies are dead silent."

"So we kick down the door," Yellin growled. "You don't get to steamroll a sovereign country and then ghost the planet."

"Except...what are we going to do about it?"

It was Kline again, and his latest observation brought a cold chill over the room. He'd said the quiet part out loud, and Stratton felt the impact in his very gut. It was like the moment misted glass shatters, and you clearly see what lies beyond. The telescope comes into focus. Perfect clarity arrives.

"They're testing us," Easterling said. "They want to see how hard they can shove."

Kline nodded. His chair squeaked as he pivoted toward Stratton. "Whatever Moscow's intentions in Azerbaijan, this has nothing to do with the Caucasus. Russia's end game could be far more drastic. The Caucasus might just be their way of testing our strength."

A president in a coma. A nation reeling from terrorist attacks, rampant panic, skyrocketing inflation, and tumbling markets. Half of its international trade strangled by the loss of the Panama Canal.

The situation replayed through Stratton's mind and he knew—for the first time he knew. Beyond any shadow of a doubt. None of this had been coincidence. He might never be able to prove it, but there were puppet strings behind the curtain, and they had wrapped a noose around Washington's throat.

"Madam Secretary, maintain pressure on Moscow," Stratton said. "You keep that phone ringing until they pick up. Coordinate with our allies and call for an emergency NATO summit. If Russia is pushing, we have to push back."

"A military stance would send the strongest message, Mr. Vice President." That was Yellin, predictable as ever. But for once, Stratton couldn't disagree.

"Do what you can with the Fifth and Sixth Fleets, General. Once we've spoken with NATO we can discuss what a larger military response would look like, should..."

Stratton trailed off, momentarily stunned by what he was picturing. Had it really come to this?

"Should Russia attack NATO," Kline finished.

Stratton nodded. "Exactly. Thank you very much, everyone. That will be all."

Chairs groaned and papers rustled as the cabinet prepared to depart. CIA Director Aimes lagged behind, advancing to the end of the table where Stratton's attention was still buried in an iPad, sifting through economic reports on the status of the market.

It was bad. He didn't understand half of it. But words like *depression* were being used, and not in a distant hypothetical kind of way.

"Sir, may I have a moment?"

Stratton looked up. The room had cleared. Aimes stood behind a chair to his right. He gestured for her to have a seat and tossed the iPad down.

"What is it, Director?"

"I didn't want to mention this in front of a full cabinet...I didn't want speculation to run rampant."

That got Stratton's attention. "What?"

"I want to stress that none of this intelligence is confirmed. I can't be sure that anything I'm about to say is correct, but..."

"Spit it out."

"The Agency has received independent, corroborated reports out of both Beijing and Tehran. President Chen and Supreme Leader Kazemi are missing."

"Missing? What do you mean, *missing*? They've been lost?"

"Not lost, sir. More like AWOL. Their absence seems to have been concealed. Our usual sources keep pretty close tabs on their locations and we seem to be a few days behind. It's most probable that both men are traveling."

"Is that usual?"

"For Chen? Occasionally. He's been known to take trips to meet with Cho Jong, but since China occupied North Korea after the hypersonic missile crisis, there's little reason for Chen to do so. He could just as easily have Cho Jong come to him. Cho is a puppet, these days."

"And Kazemi?"

"Kazemi never leaves Tehran. Not in nearly a decade. If the Iranians need to deploy somebody, they deploy General Amir Bahrami."

"Leader of the Revolutionary Guard," Stratton said.

"Correct, sir. A useful tool of the regime."

"And yet Kazemi himself is missing?"

"It seems that way."

Stratton didn't have to think very long to come up with a plausible answer. It was staring him right in the face—a missing Chinese leader and a missing Iranian leader. Russia refusing to answer the phone. Massive military action unfolding only a few hundred kilometers north of Iran.

"You don't think..."

"I don't know, sir. I can't know. Not without additional intelligence. But it's deeply concerning. If the Russians are in cahoots with the Iranians or the Chinese—"

"Or *both*," Stratton cut in.

"Or both, yes. It could be disastrous. It could be..."

The start of a third world war.

Stratton kept the thought to himself. He understood why Aimes had elected to reserve this bit of intelligence until after the others left. It was the right call.

"Find them," Stratton said. "Whatever you have to do. Deploy your deep assets and filter the Kremlin. Filter Beijing and Tehran. I want to know what they're up to, ASAP."

9

Goranboy District, Azerbaijan

The town had a name, but Turk couldn't read the sign. It was written in something that looked like a blend of English and Cyrillic...plus something else entirely. He guessed it to be Azerbaijani, and its meaning wasn't relevant to his situation.

Turk's immediate concerns were all about getting up close and personal enough with the military units stationed in the town to lift some vital equipment, and then get himself back out again before being detected. It would have been a difficult mission under almost any circumstances, given his abject lack of gear or support, but Turk did encounter one stroke of luck.

It started raining—hard. Thunder rolled and dark clouds swept over the valley, blanketing Turk's path in inky darkness. It took him half an hour to obtain enough natural night vision to slog ahead, by which time he was soaked to the bone and shivering cold. The fertile ground beneath his battered boots closed up to his ankles, and he was forced to fight his way through waist-high grass, keeping his head down as he closed on the village outskirts.

It had been years since Turk had deployed into the Middle East. Well, there had been one time since, with Reed. A short mission in eastern Turkey that wound up giving birth to the Prosecution Force. But even then, when a bad parachute landing resulted in a busted ankle, and he was subsequently shot in the leg by a sniper, Turk wasn't alone. He wasn't unarmed. He had a solid American M4 rifle in one hand and Reed freaking Montgomery at his back...the only man Turk had ever counted as a brother. His best friend in the world.

It was a strange, gut-wrenching feeling being separated from Reed. Turk couldn't help but feel that if he hadn't held out on the Prosecution Force's last mission—if he had deployed to Georgia alongside the others—the situation he now found himself in might be different. Reed might not have been captured...or killed.

The weight of guilt tugging down on Turk's shoulders was now crushing. More than guilt, it was a sense of failure. Even cowardice. Self-condemnation for not being there when the team needed him most...

It ate at him, devouring from the inside. Stronger than the hunger pains, the sore muscles, the cramps, the cold. This was real pain, and as desperately as he missed Sinju, as much as he longed to hold little Liberty, Turk knew that he wasn't leaving this place until he could make it right.

Whatever that entailed.

The rain in Azerbaijan reminded Turk of a similar thunderstorm in North Korea, during the Prosecution Force's second mission. That thunderstorm had driven the Korean People's Army under cover, allowing he and Reed to slip into Pyongyang with relative ease. This thundershower had no such effect. The Azerbaijani military continued to buzz around the streets of the five- or six-hundred-home village, loading trucks and cramming dinner down their throats. Even as Turk descended to his stomach and wormed his way to the edge of the grassy field, he could detect the urgency in the soldiers' movements. The haste. Maybe even fear.

These guys weren't sprinting for cover to escape a little cold rain. They were on fire to refit, refuel, and move to confront the snarling grizzly bear pacing on their very doorstep. Turk could respect that energy. He understood it.

He only needed to figure out a way to evade it.

Inky black shadows provided a narrow highway for Turk to slide up behind a warehouse on the outskirts of the city. It must have been some manner of food storage facility, because a trio of heavy-duty military trucks were parked out front, and soldiers were busy loading sacks into them. They spoke in Azerbaijani, and Turk didn't understand a word of it. From the backside of the warehouse he blew rain off his nose and pressed his ear to the sheet metal wall. Shifting pallets and clinking rifles joined the voices. If he tilted his head around the corner of the building, dim security lights illuminated an Azerbaijani soldier smoking beneath the warehouse's eaves, officer patches on his saturated uniform jacket. He was armed with a handgun and a flashlight, but Turk saw no radio. What was more, there was little value in overpowering and robbing an officer—somebody who would quickly be missed.

No. Turk needed *something* he could pilfer, not *somebody*. Maybe a truck.

Waiting until the officer was distracted by an unsatisfactory transfer of supplies, Turk sprinted from behind the warehouse and moved deeper into the city, sticking to the darkest shadows and becoming one with the night. His boots glided, they didn't slosh through the running rainwater. He stuck close enough to buildings to shelter from each flash of lightning, and avoided security lights.

The noise of Azerbaijani soldiers grew louder down every street, as did the growl of truck engines and the rattle of occasional tracked vehicles. The soldiers gathered amid the outskirts seemed to be prepping to move out. Traffic congested on the town's main street, with headlights blazing and officers shouting orders.

Turk was almost to the heart of the village before he identified the opportunity he'd been waiting for. It came in the form of a Turkish-built light tactical vehicle, something Turk recognized from occasional appearances in Iraq. A competitor to the American Humvee, the vehicle was called a Cobra and stood atop fat wet tires, parked in an alley just outside a small bakery. Windshield wipers flapped rhythmically as the engine chugged, but the driver and any passengers were out of sight. They'd left the Cobra's primary door open—a sort of hatch in the armored driver's side.

From fifty yards down the street, Turk knelt in the rain and watched the cavalcade of passing vehicles and foot soldiers moving rapidly out of town along the main drag, some troops still packing in their sopping dinner while officers shouted them forward. There was an air of general emergency hanging over the entire affair, which reinforced for him that whatever glimmer of opportunity remained to steal some equipment would soon be gone.

He had to move immediately. The Cobra was as good a target as any.

Sprinting out of the shadows, Turk crossed a small intersection and reached the rear of the Cobra. Unlike a Humvee, the Cobra was built using a steel hull as opposed to a steel chassis. That gave the vehicle amphibious capabilities, but on certain models it also limited the number of doors. This was such a model, with only the primary hatch providing entry—or exit. Circling to the driver's side, Turk advanced toward that single open door with nothing better than his fists as a weapon.

The interior of the vehicle was dark and cold, floorboards wet with rainwater. The oily metal smell reminded him of years in Iraq, but the headroom was even worse than inside a Humvee. Turk had to fold his oversized body into a wad just to get inside, then he was tumbling through the darkness, random metal objects ramming into his ribs and knees.

Radio. Find a radio.

Turk crouched in the rear footwell. Pivoting, he jammed his torso between the front seats and searched the dash.

A distant streetlight joined with a glowing gauge cluster to provide only dim illumination. It wasn't enough to clarify the gear spread across a center console. Turk fumbled through the mess and felt something metal and heavy. Pulling it up to eye level, he was rewarded with a flash of lightning that blazed through the windshield.

It was a handgun—some kind of hammer-fired, steel-framed thing. A Zigana, he thought. A Turkish pistol. Turk pulled the slide and chambered what looked like a round of 9mm. He didn't have time to double-check. Voices rang toward him from outside the bakery. A curt order, a pound of boots. Turk's face snapped back toward the door, but there was no time to flee, and no other door to use. A torso appeared in the doorframe and Turk jammed himself into the back seat furthest from it. Panic rushed his body and he gripped the Zigana against his right hip, hidden from view of the door but only a split second from deployment.

Go away...please go away...

The troops didn't go away. They loaded up instead. The first smelly body clambered through the door without so much as glancing into the darkened rear passenger seat where Turk sat. He loaded into the driver's seat instead, his mouth full of fragrant fresh bread, a loaf of the same cradled under one arm. The soldier wore rain-soaked camouflage and shouted through the bread to his companions. Two more men appeared—the first took the seat ahead of Turk, still not noticing him. The second sat alongside Turk and slammed the door. It wasn't until the engine shifted into gear that the Azerbaijani soldiers finally noticed the man sitting in the pitch-black recesses of the back seat.

The reaction was a lot quicker than the delayed identification.

"*Ey! Kimǝsǝn?*"

Turk could guess what the question meant, but he didn't have time to answer. He didn't have time for anything. The driver's head pivoted, gaze landing directly on Turk. His eyes went wide and he slammed on the brakes. The front passenger writhed to turn around in his seat. In an instant, everybody was shouting. The man to Turk's left kept repeating his original question, coming out of his seat and jabbing a finger at Turk, looking more outraged than afraid.

It was then that Turk saw the sat phone. It was clipped to the guy's chest rig, shaking as the man continued to jab with his finger. It was inches away—

The driver made the decision for him. His face turned from surprise to suspicion a lot quicker than the shouting idiot in the back seat, and he did what all three of them should have done from the start—he reached for his sidearm.

Screw it.

Turk pointed the Zigana backward, toward the cargo bay of the Cobra and whatever unidentified contents it contained—hopefully, not explosives. Then he clenched his teeth and pulled the trigger. Three shots, back to back. Almost as good as a flash-bang in the metal confines of the Cobra. The soldiers ducked on instinct, covering their ears. Turk's own ears rang so loudly he could no longer hear their shouts, but he wasn't taken off guard by the sudden noise. He had expected it, and that gave him just the hint of an edge.

Throwing himself out of the seat, he went for the soldier with the sat phone first. His left hand grabbed the guy by the shoulder and threw him backward while the two men up front continued to flail. With his right hand he slammed the Zigana up and left, smashing it into the guy's unprotected face. Then he was throwing himself over him. Grabbing the sat phone with his left hand and ripping it free. Reaching the door and throwing the latch. Up front the two other soldiers reached for his legs, but a swift kick of his boot landed in somebody's face, and that was enough to free him.

They didn't shoot. He knew they wouldn't shoot. He was escaping right over the body of their comrade. Turk shoved the door open and tumbled out into the mud, face first. An instant later he was rolling left, toward the back of the vehicle. Away from the door.

It wasn't an instant too soon. Gunfire erupted from the inside of the Cobra and bullets whistled out into the dark. Turk detected them as faint pops through his still-ringing ears. Dizziness overtook him as he returned to his feet. He made it to the back of the Cobra, then felt the vehicle shift. It was coming back on him.

Turk threw himself out of the way just as the Cobra surged in reverse. He landed in the mud and rolled onto his back. The Cobra had passed him on the washed-out street and its headlights now bore down on him. He thought he saw the door fly open, then the guy whose nose Turk had busted appeared from the shadows inside the vehicle.

Move!

Turk rolled. An AK opened fire, dumping a short burst of heavy rounds that tore through the dirt and shredded the backside of a woodshed. Turk made it to the corner and slid behind a stack of split firewood just as the rifle chased after him. Wood erupted in splinters on all sides, nothing but that incessant ringing and faint *pop pop pops* marking each shot.

Go! Go! Go!

It wasn't his own voice Turk heard in his head. It was Reed's, hoarse and demanding in the heat of battle. An order to keep him alive.

Turk turned into the darkness, facing back the way he'd come, and sprinted for dear life. Behind him the popping continued. He thought he detected a surging engine, also, and maybe shouts. Whatever the case, the Cobra didn't follow. Turk lost it as he made one quick turn after another, passing a couple of wide-eyed villagers but not stopping until he reached the meadow.

It wasn't until he was nearly halfway to the hill where he'd left Lucy that Turk allowed himself to sink into the grass, desperately panting, sweeping his hands over his entire body in search of blood. He couldn't find any. He didn't think he had been injured. Somehow, he'd escaped that sudden burst of rifle fire.

Turk checked the Zigana next, confirming twelve rounds remaining in the box magazine, plus one in the chamber. He looked back the way he'd come but he didn't see anybody. The field was torn by rain and wind, but darkness prevailed. There were no headlights.

At last he checked the sat phone, and it was then that his heart plummeted someplace south of his boots. The phone still rode in his left hand, clutched tight between thick fingers. But when he pressed the buttons, nothing happened. The screen remained black. He smacked it against his open palm and mashed the power button.

Then a dead battery symbol illuminated across the screen, flashing once. Then vanishing into darkness.

10

Moscow, Russia

His name was Mikhail Orlov, and he received his directives from the CIA in the most mundane, old-school way imaginable—via coded message. Deep in the dusty recesses of the Russian State Library's reference section, Orlov found the communications hidden amid the pages of books that all true Russians revered but nobody actually read. Classics by Bulgakov, Solzhenitsyn, Akhmatova, and Sholokhov. Books of poetry, novels of symbolism and political revolution, and historical accounts of Soviet labor camps. Things that couldn't possibly interest Orlov less, and yet he made it a habit to study them and to appear at the library regularly, even when he wasn't waiting for a message from the other side of the world.

It was all part of the ruse. A delicate dance that blended the ordinary with the routine and the expected, boring the attentions of FSB agents and allowing Orlov a narrow opportunity to do what he did best—sell out his government, one hefty bounty at a time. All in US dollars, of course. Deposited into a Grand Cayman account, there to collect for his eventual retirement.

In the meantime, life was a game of subterfuge, but unlike in the American movies, very little of that subterfuge was fast or sexy. Mostly Orlov drowned himself in routines and boring reading, the watchful eye always looking over his shoulder without appearing to do so. It was a deadly business. Many had died, many more had been swallowed by more sinister fates than simple death. Russia was vindictive in her treatment of spies... particularly *Russian* spies.

None of those thoughts were on Orlov's mind as he drifted down the tall shelves of dusty books, stopping here and there to inspect a random work, sometimes sitting on the floor to flip through its pages for half an hour along his eventual route to the back of the building, where he would retrieve his message. He knew there would be a message, because an unsolicited order of fresh baked bread had arrived on his doorstep that morning. No note, no identity of the buyer, but the address was correct, and the signal had been received.

The CIA had work for him.

It was a Tuesday, and an odd day of the month—the seventh. That gave him a code of two for the second day of the Russian week, and B for the B-side of his dead-drop pickup chart. Options on the B-side included works by Anna Andreyevna Gorenko, better known by her pen name, Anna Akhmatova, an early twentieth-century poet that Orlov had learned to detest. The two code meant that the message would be contained within a dusty copy of *Izbrannoe*, a 1943 collection of poems containing Akhmatova's musings on the Second World War.

The message itself wasn't hidden between the pages, written on a microfilm like it might have been during the Cold War—or rather, the *first* Cold War. That method was too dangerous. If found, the message could be easily deciphered.

No, there was yet another level of concealment. All Orlov found in the book was an old-school library punch card with seemingly random digits printed along the bottom—codes themselves that when decoded provided page numbers, paragraph selections, and Cyrillic letters pulled from select lines.

The process was laborious, made more so by Orlov's boredom with the subject matter. He took his time, ensuring that anyone who passed by would be convinced that he was a true aficionado of Soviet-era poetry. Certainly, he could carry on a spirited conversation of the topic should the need arise. Occasionally, it did.

But not this time. The library was quiet. Orlov was left undisturbed. He wrote the message in his notebook, one letter at a time, using pencil. He didn't bother to read it, flipping through *Izbrannoe* for another hour after he was finished before at last departing the library.

He ventured down the street and took tea at a nearby bakery. He strolled in the park and fed some ducks. He completed a grocery list and collected dry cleaning.

He did all the things an average Russian might do on his day off—unhurried. Relaxed. Possibly under the surveillance of the FSB, although Orlov hadn't observed any tails.

When he returned to his sixth-floor apartment and locked the door, he still didn't rush to the notebook. He unpacked. He played Nautilus Pompilius on his stereo and fed his goldfish.

At last he retreated to his bathroom, collecting the notebook as if by afterthought. He shut the door, and his body language changed. Excitement radiated through his nervous system—a hunger in his gut. There was one part of the message he *had* paid attention to during the decoding process. The part that most concerned him.

The bounty offered—and it was a lot. Twenty *thousand* US dollars, more money than the Agency had ever paid him for intel mining. This job must be big. A portal to more advanced work, perhaps. Or maybe there was a rush order. Maybe...

Orlov read the message and stopped. He started at the beginning and squinted. One of the words was difficult for him to read. It wasn't Russian. It was...Farsi? A name?

Another word was brutally easy for him to read. Any child in Russia could have read it: *Kremlin*. The seat of Russian governmental power, and Orlov's place of work. His duties there as a senior military clerk and dispatch courier were what made him useful to the CIA in the first place. But what the Agency needed this time wouldn't be found inside the military wing of the Kremlin, where Orlov usually worked. If Langley's assumptions were correct, this information would only be found inside the very heart of the Kremlin—a place where Orlov had never ventured, and should he be discovered there without a legitimate purpose, his only possible fate would be immediate arrest and imprisonment.

The CIA wanted Orlov to infiltrate President Makar Nikitin's private offices.

11

Baku, Azerbaijan

President Elchin Rzayev met his top military officials on the second floor of the DSX building—the headquarters of Azerbaijan's State Security Service, a conglomeration of intelligence services and secret policing. The SSS was run by Colonel General Yusif Hasanov, but Hasanov was far from the only member of Baku's government waiting in the conference room. In fact, most of Rzayev's cabinet had assembled around a circular table, all standing to attention as he entered. Doors clapped shut and the room went dark, LCD screens displaying maps of troop movements clustered along the Azerbaijani/Georgian border.

Tens of *thousands* of them. Russia had deployed enough military might to blitzkrieg her southern neighbors, and she had done so in record time. Tbilisi, it seemed, had already fallen fully under Russian control, and neither Armenia nor the remainder of the Collective Security Treaty Organization seemed to have anything to say about it. It was as though the world were blind to the outbreak of Russian military aggression.

And that said nothing of the *bomb*. The weapon had detonated in a relatively rural portion of northern Azerbaijan, and thus far the casualty reports that landed on Rzayev's desk every four hours numbered in the dozens, not the hundreds or thousands. Radiation was spreading, of course. Fallout dissipated eastward, distributed by rainstorms and saturating villages throughout six different provinces.

More would die—not in the short term, but in the years to come as cancer sprang up like a plague, the result of radiation exposure. It was a horrific reality that turned Rzayev's stomach just to consider, yet it was far from his primary concern.

That honor went to the thousands of battle-hardened Russian veterans of the war in Ukraine now gathered at the Red Bridge crossing, only an order away from sweeping southeast, straight for Baku.

"What is the update?" Rzayev demanded.

Colonel General Hasanov answered by default. "Russian forces have increased by ten percent overnight. They've added sixty heavy tanks and an entire division of mobile artillery. Three dozen helicopter gunships landed this morning just outside of Gardabani. The Russians seem to be erecting an operational airfield there. Fuel trucks are inbound, along with munitions, mobile command posts, and food stores."

"Food stores?" Rzayev squinted. "What manner of food stores?"

"Large ones—heavy trucks and rail cars. Enough to sustain the army for months."

Months.

It wasn't a good sign. With only about four hundred kilometers of distance between Baku and the Red Bridge border crossing, a supply post such as the one Hasanov described could fuel an occupying military with ease.

What was Moscow *doing*?

"Any word from President Nikitin?" Rzayev demanded.

"Radio silence, sir," Rzayev's minister of foreign affairs answered. "We've been calling every half hour."

Rzayev advanced to the wall-mounted screens and rocked his head back. All the intelligence was there—not only the Russian troop movements, but the Azerbaijani response, also. Forty thousand personnel, both infantry and armor, hurrying to Red Bridge to stem the incursion of Russian aggression. Additional troops were already deployed to all of Azerbaijan's key military installments, with a meager detachment held back to protect Baku.

"Where are we with the reserves?" Rzayev demanded.

Hasanov stepped back in. "We've issued a full deployment order. By the end of the week we'll have fifty thousand additional ground troops armed and ready to march. By the end of the month, another two hundred thousand."

Too slow. Much too slow.

How could this have happened so quickly? Rzayev knew his neighbor in the far north was a slithering snake, to be carefully watched and not trusted even under the most demanding circumstances. Relying on the collective influence of the CSTO seemed like Azerbaijan's best avenue to enforcing their diplomatic will across the region.

Sparks had flown. Tensions occasionally escalated. But military force? For *what*?

A better question—if Russia planned to invade Azerbaijan, why was she waiting? Every hour that passed gave Baku more time to move troops into defensive positions while calling her three hundred thousand reservists into active duty.

It's a game. It's some kind of game.

Rzayev believed it. He simply couldn't break the code.

"Continue our deployments to Red Bridge," Rzayev said. "Withhold five percent of ground forces to protect Baku. Direct our air forces to maintain air superiority over our key military installations and be available for anti-armor strikes."

They weren't political orders, they were military. But with decades of military service under his belt prior to achieving the presidency, Rzayev knew a thing or two about protecting his country. He remembered well the years of Soviet lordship, bearing down on the Caucasus like the heel of a boot, sucking away the wealth of this place for the glory of Moscow.

Rzayev would be damned if he let that oppression return. Rule of Azerbaijan belonged to him and him *alone*.

"Colonel General, with me."

Rzayev exited the room. Hasanov followed him to a quiet kitchen where coffee machines and teapots waited. Neither man spoke as Rzayev fixed a cup of Turkish blended tea, dark and rich without sweetener. He let it steep and looked to the glass door to make sure nobody else had approached.

Then he turned back to Hasanov. "Where are we with the bomb?"

Rzayev didn't need to clarify which weapon he was speaking of. There was only one bomb on the minds of every Azerbaijani still breathing after the blast. Only one key question.

"Our testing capabilities are limited, Mr. President. It may take weeks to obtain a clear answer on where the weapon may have originated."

"So what about intelligence?" Rzayev pressed. "What are your informants telling you?"

Hasanov shook his head. "Intelligence is limited. We are pressing as hard as we can. It seems the weapon was trucked across Red Bridge shortly before detonation. By whom, we do not know. It would be logical to assume the bomb could have been another forgotten Soviet device lost in Georgia—"

Rzayev shook his head. "Do not be a fool, Yusif. There were no lost weapons in Georgia. Arms dealers and scavengers scrounged up the last Soviet rifle and handgun years ago, let alone any significant WMD. Whatever game Nikitin is playing by blaming the Panama Canal bomb on Georgia, it is a lie."

"So...what then?" Hasanov asked.

Rzayev thought. He sipped black tea. He didn't have an answer.

Nine nations were known to possess nuclear weapons. Any one of them could have, in theory, misplaced one. The most logical answer was Russia herself.

But who had stolen it? Who had detonated it? And *why*?

"Our captives know something," Rzayev said. "I am sure of it. They are not who they say they are. Where are we with the interrogations?"

"We're pushing hard, Mr. President. The prisoners still claim that they are a NATO reconnaissance team and that the bomb was Russian. It is all they will say—when we press for more, we get nothing. They are like iron. If we press much harder, we may kill them."

Rzayev's cup smacked the countertop. He closed in next to Hasanov, his voice lowering to barely above a growl.

"Then you will kill them, Colonel General. Whatever it takes. They must know more. *Make them talk.*"

12

Goranboy District, Azerbaijan

Turk ran all the way to the hilltop where he'd left Lucy. He wanted to turn back—he wanted to dive right back into the village and find a USB-C charger to fit his current phone. Use the Zigana pistol, if necessary. Reach Langley by any means possible.

But long experience with pushing the envelope of combat had taught Turk what it feels like just before that envelope bursts into spontaneous flame. With Azerbaijani troops swarming the village, and more than a few of them looking for the random white man who appeared inside their Cobra, his chances of completing his mission without being gunned down in the process were shrinking by orders of magnitude.

It was too late to go back, and even if he located a compatible charger for the sat phone, that was only the first half of his problem. Then he would need a power outlet. An untold number of minutes left undisturbed while the device recharged, even while dozens of soldiers searched for him.

Another village.

It was the only option. Turk had to get Lucy off the hill and locate another community with a charger cable before being ensnared by the deluge of Azerbaijani armed forces surging northward. His best chance of doing so would be to move quickly, through the dark and the thunderstorm.

It was time to force march.

At the top of the hill, Turk found Lucy right where he'd left her, seated at the base of a poplar tree with her knees pulled up to her chin. The AK remained next to her, streaming with rainwater but undisturbed. Lucy no longer rocked the way she had before. Her lips no longer repeated passages of scripture. Now her eyes simply stared into the darkness, as empty and vacant as the eyes of a corpse.

Looking back over his shoulder, Turk marked the lights of the village and the slow convoy of military vehicles churning out of it. He couldn't see anyone following him across the valley. There was no sign of pursuing infantry.

Not yet, anyway. For the moment, Azerbaijanis had bigger fish to fry.

"Lucy, are you awake?" Turk knelt beside her and gently shook her shoulder. He was so tired he could picture himself crumpling to the ground right next to her. Falling asleep in the rain—something he'd done plenty of times before.

But that wasn't an option. They had to move. Lucy looked up with glassy eyes but didn't seem to recognize him. Turk stood and lifted the backpack. He worked the strap adjustments and loosened them to max capacity. Worn backward with the pack hanging over his chest, Turk squatted in front of Lucy and turned his back to her.

"Come on, Lucy. I'll carry you. Put your legs through the straps."

Lucy made no response. Turk shook her again, but she didn't even notice. Breathing a curse, he guided her petite right foot through the bottom of the right-hand backpack strap, then followed with the second. Lucy didn't fight. Turk pinned her against the tree and heaved with both hands, lifting her up by the hips, and allowed her legs to drop the rest of the way through the straps. All ninety-odd pounds of her descended on his shoulders, and the backpack stretched.

But it didn't break. Turk adjusted her position until the weight was best balanced, then wrapped her arms over his shoulders and around his chest.

"Grab hold, Lucy."

This time she responded. Narrow fingers dug into his shirt, balling it into fists as her chin landed on his shoulder. Lucy's lips were only inches from Turk's ear, her breath soft on his cheek. She was whispering again, so gently he barely discerned the words.

"Though I walk through the valley of the shadow...of the shadow..."

Turk twisted his face to make eye contact. Lucy didn't seem to notice. He looked once back toward the rifle still leaned against the tree, but knew he couldn't carry it for the same reasons he couldn't bring it into the village before. It would draw too much attention. He tucked the Zigana into the front of his pants instead, dropped his saturated shirt over it, then turned for the edge of the poplar forest.

As he broke out to look over the valley below, Lucy repeated her words about shadow. They came as a whisper in his ear.

"*Thou art with me.*"

Turk's eyes rose automatically to the pitch-black sky high above, dumping rain and void of stars. The pit in his stomach widened into a chasm, and he gritted his teeth.

Then he set off into the valley of shadow.

Turk carried Lucy across desolate Azerbaijani farmland for what felt like hours. The rain beat on, now flooding the earth so absolutely that if he departed the beaten farm roads and attempted to cross a field, his boots sank up to his shins in sticky mud.

Twice he fell. Once Lucy inexplicably slipped out of the backpack straps and crashed into a ditch with a shriek. When Turk attempted to refit her onto his back, the right-hand strap snapped, and she fell again. He toppled with her, biting back a scream as his knee landed on a rock.

He was covered in mud, soaked to the bone, and could barely see more than a few yards ahead. As Turk clawed his way back to his feet, he finally abandoned the backpack and what insignificant contents remained, and simply carried Lucy piggy-back. It tied up his arms, hampering his balance and sabotaging his ability to quickly draw the handgun should need arise.

But it was the only option. Turk went on. He bent his back. He sank his toes in like a draft horse. And he simply kept going, across the valley and around the road, skirting the noise of chugging trucks and rattling tanks, and following pointing signs toward the next village.

He wouldn't attempt to rob the Azerbaijani armed forces a second time. They would be ready, and even if he caught them unawares, he couldn't expect to get so lucky as to stumble on a compatible phone charger. He was much more tired than he had been before. His body burned. His mind buzzed.

He thought of Reed—of Corbyn, Strickland, Wolfgang, and Ivan. All either dead or held hostage, which could potentially be worse than death. Turk didn't know much about Azerbaijan but he'd heard that their government was dictatorial and undervalued human rights. With the threat of war on the horizon, the outlook of the Prosecution Force would be bleak.

Turk might be their only hope. He was certainly the only hope of getting critical intelligence back to Langley, and that left him with only one choice—to *keep* going.

"*You're nothing but a mule, Turkman! I've met dogs who are smarter than you, but I'll give you this. You don't stop!*"

The voice of Turk's USMC drill instructor thundered in his head just as lightning broke the sky. It was a voice he hadn't thought of in years, maybe over a decade. But the wind and the rain and the endless miserable mud brought it all back. Lucy's weight was roughly similar to a full combat loadout. His feet hurt just as much as they had hurt during basic training. He was in better shape now than he'd been when he arrived at Parris Island, the famed Marine boot camp, but he was also a lot older. He'd broken a lot more bones, been shot a half dozen times. Dumped down hills, wrecked in high-speed chases, thrown out of airplanes.

But one thing hadn't changed. One thing would never change. He was a mule—he would *keep* going. It was what had saved him when his father died in the first Gulf War. What saved him when his mother succumbed to narcotics and flushed her life away, leaving him to flail his way through high school. What had saved him when the Marines put him through hell, did everything in their power to break him, then shoved a rifle in his hands and shipped him overseas to a place he'd never even heard of before 9/11—Iraq.

One tour. Two tours. Scout sniper training and Force Recon admission.

Reed Montgomery. Sandstorms. Brutal fights and that horrible night when his best friend transitioned from soldier to cold-blooded murderer in the blink of an eye...

And then everything that followed. That brief stint in the FBI. Teaming up with Reed again on the other side of the law. Eventually joining the Prosecution Force. Now this—this slog across another meaningless field on the backside of nowhere.

It was all the same. It was all a grind, and the thing that had never before failed Rufus Turkman would not fail him now—his mule-ness.

He would *keep* going.

Thunder rolled and Turk's right foot slipped. He caught himself before going down, digging in and forcing his way up the side of a hill. Half a mile to his right a roadbed wound through the eastern edge of the valley, but that smooth asphalt wasn't an option. It was chock-full of soldiers. He had to circle wide, using nothing but intuition to plot a course over the next hill, across the next field, and curving back around toward a small village whose existence he only believed in because of the road signs he couldn't even read.

Onward. Next step. Keep moving. Do the work!

Lucy shivered on Turk's back, and he ground on. One kilometer blended into three. The night grew so bitter that Turk's teeth chattered even as he fought his way up another steep hill. He was starving, his stomach cramping. His head felt a little light, as though he'd just knocked back three fingers of whiskey.

He reached the top of the hill by sheer willpower and staggered to a stop, looking down to a plateau that stretched ten or twenty klicks to an invisible horizon. The sky was as inky black as before, but the plateau wasn't. Halfway across it, a cluster of bright yellow light marked the location of another village...

But between himself and that village was more than five kilometers of empty mud. An entire *army* was parked there—several thousand ground troops with trucks buried up to their axles under headlights torn by rain, soldiers scrambling to pull them out.

It was only people. Only chunks of steal driven by diesel. But it might as well have been a hundred-foot iron wall. Turk panted atop the hill, looking across that morass of angry, wet killers, and felt the very hope leave his body. He staggered another step, Lucy clinging to his back like a barnacle. His head went light again and his knees locked. Suddenly, the dizziness magnified. Turk released Lucy with his left hand and flailed for balance. Another three steps toward a tree brought him closer to the edge of the hill. He reached for the trunk. Lucy slipped, obliterating what remained of his careful balance. She tugged him sideways. One foot flew out from under him and he missed the tree.

Then he was on the ground. They were both on the ground, colliding with nothing but wet grass and slick mud. At one moment he was standing and the next he was simply hurtling, rolling and sliding down the hill as though it were a water slide.

Headed straight for that swarm of Azerbaijani soldiers.

13

Moscow, Russia

Among Mikhail Orlov's many duties as a civilian military aide inside the armed forces division of the Kremlin was that of courier. While much of the Russian government's critical communication was conducted the modern way—encrypted emails, secure messaging, or private phone calls—there were still enough old hats inside the seat of Russian federal power who preferred the old-fashioned way. A sealed envelope, hand-delivered across the complex to this general or that government official.

Orlov had delivered thousands of such folders early in his career. Two decades in, he'd ascended far enough up the hierarchy of civilian military officials to have an army of his own deputy couriers at his disposal—albeit a shrinking one, thanks to technology. Those couriers did most of the leg work, leaving Orlov inside his windowless office to answer phone calls and manage logistical tasks. It was in this office, alone with his tea and his dual monitors, that Orlov mined most of the information that the CIA found so valuable. Scraped from reports and what bits of top-secret military activity that fell like crumbs into his lap, Orlov had learned what nuggets the CIA would find interesting, and what they would dismiss with disgust. It was a profitable business. Already he'd saved nearly a hundred thousand US dollars in his Grand Cayman account, more than three years' worth of his current Russian salary.

But the job the CIA had requested this time—the job they were willing to pay twenty *thousand* dollars for—couldn't be managed from his desk or his office. It couldn't be managed with his army of deputies. If it could be accomplished at all, it would only be accomplished in person, and for Orlov to go in person he needed a special opportunity.

That opportunity came at 4:36 in the afternoon, only an hour before Orlov was due to clock out for the day. It was a missive, an old-fashioned yellow envelope enclosing military updates from the front lines in Georgia. The sender was General Yuri Balakin. The recipient was Dimitri Smirnov, deputy chairman of President Makar Nikitin's Security Council.

And the destination? Inside the Kremlin. *Deep* inside the Kremlin, amid the offices of the presidential cabinet. It was exactly what Orlov needed.

"I'll take that." Orlov scooped the missive from the outbound bin before one of his deputies could reach it.

"Are you sure? I was headed that way."

"I need the exercise." Orlov flashed a winning smile. The deputy only shrugged.

Orlov had visited the executive branch of the Kremlin many times before, always under legitimate business. He was familiar with the security protocols and the checkpoints. He cleared them with ease, flashing his government ID and remaining calm. The FSB guards directed him around bends and through corridors, the faded carpet and stained walls growing gradually cleaner and more opulent as he neared the heart of the building, where no expense was spared.

With each step closer to Smirnov's executive office, Orlov's blood pressure spiked just a little bit higher. He could feel it, not only in the pulse of his tightening hands but also in his skull. A steady thump, growing gradually faster with each dripping second. There was sweat also, trickling down his spine. He couldn't blame it on the building's temperature—Nikitin liked it cold, therefore everyone liked it cold. Orlov doubted whether the building was warmer than fifteen degrees Celsius.

But still the sweat ran, because this wasn't like any other operation. Not even close. Besides the greater pay and greater risk, there was also the question of *how* exactly Orlov would complete the mission. The missive was his key into the Kremlin, but beyond that he was on his own. He'd lain awake all night prior trying to cook up a scheme and had failed completely.

The CIA needed one very specific—and very odd, he thought—piece of intelligence. The positive confirmation of two individuals in the building. One Chinese, whom Orlov thought was the president. The other an Iranian man Orlov had never heard of.

Confirm presence on site, the CIA had directed. *Full payment only when presence is confirmed.*

The Agency hadn't specified *how* he was to confirm presence. They hadn't asked for photographs. That left Orlov room to lie, if he wanted to. But a lie, if caught, would jeopardize not only his opportunities for future business but also his personal safety. What was to stop the Agency from revenge-leaking his identity? Letting the Russians eliminate him.

No. Orlov would do his best to complete the job as requested. He would reach Smirnov's office. Turn in the missive. Strike up a conversation with the cute receptionist, Fiana. Flatter her. Get her talking...

And then go from there. Improvise. He was a smart guy, right?

Orlov reached the office. He passed into the reception with a warm smile ready.

Then he stopped, that accelerating heart skipping a beat. It wasn't Fiana behind the desk, it was a skinny man in his late forties with thinning hair and round glasses. The moment Orlov entered, the man looked up, shooting him a piercing stare that seemed to cut right through him.

Orlov swallowed. He couldn't help himself. He flailed internally, then recovered his mental footing.

Focus, Mikhail. Focus!

"Good afternoon...Is Fiana out?"

The man squinted. His nose wrinkled. He looked suddenly like a rat...a *mean* rat.

"Fiana is no longer with the department," the man said. Something in his tone was indicative of a termination, but nothing about his posture invited further inquiry. Orlov opened his mouth to express a compulsory regret, then stopped. The guy was still staring. He still hadn't blinked.

"Can I help you?"

Orlov closed his mouth. His legs felt locked in cement. What was happening to him? He'd lost all his nerve. Or rather, the nerves had overwhelmed him.

Action. Say something!

"You have a dispatch?" The question was finally enough to jar Orlov back to the present.

"Yes, right." He stepped forward. The smile returned. He produced the folder from beneath his arm and extended it. "For Deputy Chairman Smirnov, with compliments of General Balakin."

The receptionist took the envelope without comment and scrutinized the address. Orlov was left standing and shifting his weight, trying not to appear uncomfortable, fumbling for an edge.

"So you'll be taking over for Fiana, then?" he prompted.

The guy spun, eyes still narrow. Orlov had that feeling of being cut through by X-ray vision again. There was so much suspicion, so much hostility.

"Why do you ask about Fiana?" he demanded. "Did you know her well?"

That question was enough to stop Orlov cold. The implication wasn't a difficult one to decipher. He could read between the lines.

"No," he said. "Not well at all. I was just accustomed to seeing her here."

"Well, become accustomed to seeing me. Ms. Popov will not be returning to this office...*ever*."

So there it was. Orlov simply nodded, now completely unable to manufacture an extension to the conversation. It wasn't like he needed one. The subtext was as clear as a neon sign.

Fiana Popov had been a spy, also. Working for who, Orlov did not know and did not need to know. The end of her story was as predictable as the sunrise.

"Sign," the man said, jabbing a clipboard into Orlov's gut. He accepted it. Scrawled his name beside the date and time. The man took it back. Orlov turned for the door, heart thumping again, fresh anxiety leaking into his blood.

He knew the risks. He knew that Fiana Popov, whoever she worked for, was probably an amateur and a fool. She'd made a misstep. He wouldn't.

But suddenly the walls of the old building shrank around him. He needed fresh air. He needed—

"Was there something else?" the man demanded.

Orlov flinched, realizing he'd locked up again. He swallowed over a dry throat. "Restroom?" he managed.

The squinting man jabbed a finger. "Left out the door. Around the corner."

Orlov hurried out of the room. He turned the corner and made it to the men's room, sweating so profusely he was certain the perspiration was visible on his face. His hands trembled. He needed air, needed water. He tugged at his necktie as his shoes clapped across the marble floor. The bathroom was opulent, an executive facility only yards from the cabinet meeting chambers where the president himself, even now, might be working. Just the thought of how deep inside the mess Orlov had progressed was enough to twist his stomach. He cranked a bathroom faucet on and dashed cold water over his face, heaving. Hands trembling. He looked into the mirror and blinked hard, just starting to collect himself.

Focus, Mikhail. Be calm!

Then a toilet flushed. Orlov straightened, face snapping instinctively toward the marble-encased stall at the end of the room, where clothing rustled.

Then the latch snapped, and a man stepped out. A short man. Dark skin. A gray beard. A turban wrapped around his head. The two of them locked eyes, and Orlov's heart lurched.

It was the target—or one of them, anyway. The Iranian, Ali Kazemi.

Orlov didn't move, so taken off guard he didn't know what to say. The Iranian's eyes were somehow even colder than those of the new receptionist. Even meaner. He glared at Orlov as though the man had run naked into a shrine. There was an invisible offense. Silent judgment.

Orlov closed his mouth. Swallowed. And then he did the first and only thing he could think of—he bowed, bending at the waist. Ducking his head. Without making eye contact again, he twisted for the door. He headed back down the hall, away from the heart of the building. Back toward his own branch of the Kremlin, heart hammering.

He'd only confirmed half of the CIA's target list, but Orlov would risk a lie on the other half. The nerves had got the best of him. He kept thinking about cute Fiana Popov, alone in some secluded government pit deep in Siberia.

Screaming as they beat the truth out of her. Only one step from Orlov's own position. One crucial mistake.

No. He had enough. He would report to the CIA as soon as he escaped the Kremlin.

14

Washington, DC

The route between CIA Director Aimes's office and the office of her boss—at present, Jordan Stratton—ran nine miles southeast along the George Washington Memorial Parkway. Nineteen minutes of travel time, according to a GPS, but the drive never required less than thirty, and occasionally demanded the better part of an hour. Aimes had driven—or *been* driven—this way so many times that it felt almost as routine as her regular commute to Langley. As global peril and looming domestic catastrophe multiplied, she sometimes wondered why she didn't simply relocate her operational office to the West Wing.

Maggie Trousdale was a hands-on sort of president. She liked to *see* her people face-to-face. Stratton had picked up the habit. The update meeting Aimes was inbound for wouldn't be an easy one. She didn't have the answers Stratton demanded. Given her preference, Aimes would have shot the acting president an email and returned immediately to work.

Instead she kept her head down for the entire drive, ignoring the congested traffic and zeroing in on her laptop while her driver kept the AC cranked up and the music cranked down.

Things were *not* going well for Aimes. Fifty-two hours removed from the nuclear detonation in Azerbaijan, and there was still no word from the Prosecution Force. Still no intelligence of merit from the CIA operatives on the ground throughout the Caucasus regions. Still no tangible explanation as to *what* was happening.

Radio silence from the Russians. Obscurity from Beijing and Tehran. Growing panic from European allies.

Aimes needed a break—desperately. As if on cue the secure cell phone in her purse chimed and she swiped to answer as soon as she saw the name RIGBY, S. displayed across the screen.

"Tell me something good," Aimes said.

"How about something bad, but at least it's confirmed?"

Aimes winced. She looked up from the laptop. "The Russians invaded."

"Nope. They're still piled up at Red Bridge. The Azerbaijanis are digging in and deploying reserves. It's looking like World War One over there."

"So what, then?"

"We got word from Moscow. Blackjack checked in."

Blackjack. The CIA maintained literally tens of thousands of contacts and double agents across the globe. They all had code names, and Aimes didn't know a fraction of them. But she knew Blackjack. She'd worked with Mikhail Orlov since her early days as deputy director of operations. He was a pig of a man as far as Aimes was concerned, and she certainly didn't trust him. It was all about the dollar for Blackjack—the hunt for a magic jackpot, hence his code name.

But he was relentless. He was hungry. He didn't mind an aggressive risk for an aggressive payout. And thus far, his intelligence had always been rock solid.

"What's he got?" Aimes asked.

"Chen and Kazemi. They're both in Moscow."

"No..."

"Blackjack is positive. He actually saw Kazemi, face-to-face. It's all very covert, but it seems our Chinese and Iranian friends are meeting with Nikitin. Directly, and off the books."

Not good.

The implications of Blackjack's report were impossibly simple, but

Aimes still couldn't bring herself to accept this. How could this be happening? It was like America's every worst fear had manifested into a poison cocktail overnight.

"We're *positive*?" Aimes pressed.

"Blackjack says one hundred percent."

Aimes shut her computer. Her car was pulling up to the executive entrance of the West Wing. In another moment she'd be in the lion's den with Stratton. She was no longer empty-handed.

Deep in her gut, Aimes wished she could be.

"Tell Blackjack to lay low," she said. "We may need more. I don't want him blowing his cover in the meantime."

"Already done." Brief pause. Rigby shifted the phone against his ear. "Does this mean what I think it means?"

Aimes sighed. She cradled the laptop beneath one arm and reached for her door. "We better pray not, Silas."

15

The West Wing
The White House

Stratton was three cups of coffee deep, but the report delivered by his chief intelligence officer landed harder than any amount of caffeine. In an instant he wasn't tired, he wasn't distracted. The brain fog of delirium was gone.

"We're *sure*?" Stratton pressed.

"My source says one hundred percent." Aimes sat across from Stratton in a now cluttered Oval Office. Stacks of paperwork littered the desk, and the stewards had yet to remove a meal tray from a late breakfast. Stratton wouldn't let anybody except a select few cabinet members into the room. He needed silence and insulation from the craziness of an increasingly chaotic West Wing.

"Is he reliable?" Stratton pressed.

"Without a fault," Aimes said. "His intel has always been good."

"And it comes straight from the Kremlin?"

This time Aimes didn't answer. She cocked her head, and Stratton got the message. He waved a hand. "Okay, fine. If you buy it, I buy it. So Chen and Kazemi are meeting with Nikitin."

"Privately and covertly."

Stratton massaged the razor stubble on one cheek, staring at his coffee cup. Contemplating the realities at hand. He would need to call another meeting—bring the secretary of state, the secretary of defense, and the national security advisor in on this. Unpack the problem with the aid of their respective expertise and resources.

But really, did this equation require a rocket scientist? It was obvious.

"He's forging an alliance," Stratton said. "Bringing in the two biggest hitters available to solidify his next move."

Aimes nodded. "It certainly looks that way."

Stratton closed his eyes and breathed deep. He pictured the map in the Situation Room, all those Russian troops gathered at the Azerbaijani border, but not yet moving. Suddenly, it made sense. If Iran was joining the scheme, than Nikitin would wait to spring his trap until the bulk of the Iranian Armed Forces could deploy against Azerbaijan's *southern* border.

Baku was surrounded, and they didn't even know it. But *why*? That was the part Stratton still couldn't understand. What was Nikitin's end game? To seize Azerbaijan, annex Armenia, and dominate the Caucasus?

No. This was bigger than that, Stratton could feel it. They were *still* missing something.

"There's a curve ball coming," Stratton said. "He's about to play an ace."

"I thought the same. Seizing the Caucasus is a flex, but it doesn't do much for Russia's long-term strategic goals as we understand them. Nikitin wants Europe—he always has."

How does this get him there? Stratton thought. And a much better question: *What the hell was the United States going to do about it?*

"I need to speak with Gorman," Stratton said. "We're going to have a punch list of questions for you."

"I have a list of my own, sir. I'll keep you updated as quickly as possible. It..."

Aimes broke off. Stratton cocked an eyebrow. "Yes?"

Aimes flushed, looking suddenly awkward.

"What?" Stratton pressed.

"It would help, sir, if these meetings—"

Aimes was cut off by the chime of Stratton's desk phone. It was a harsh, demanding buzz—a programed noise that only a few numbers could trigger. Stratton glanced to the display and recognized Easterling's number.

Not good—the White House chief of staff would make the walk if it wasn't an emergency.

Stratton lifted the phone. "What?"

"I need you, sir. Right now."

"I'm with Director Aimes."

"Bring her to the Roosevelt Room. You have to see this."

Stratton hung up and pushed himself out of his chair, leaving his suit jacket behind. He gestured to Aimes.

"With me."

The director followed him through wide office doors into the West Wing, directly across the hall to the entrance of the Roosevelt Room. The door was closed. Stratton pushed inside to find the interior dark, the flickering glow of a television set mounted to the top of a rolling cart. Easterling was inside along with a pair of aides from her office. Nobody spoke.

"Jill, what the—"

Stratton broke off as his gaze passed across the television. The face displayed there in 4K definition was impossible to misidentify—a face that Stratton saw in his very dreams. It was Makar Nikitin, standing behind a podium with Russian Federation flags draped behind either shoulder. He wore a dark suit. His face was set in harsh glare lines. He looked straight into the camera and spoke in firm, didactic lines. A script ran across the bottom of the screen, translating Russian to English in real time.

The door closed behind Aimes and the room fell totally silent save for the subdued volume of the television, broadcasting Nikitin's Russian snarl.

"...investigations into the nature of the nuclear weapon deployed into Azerbaijan have yielded shocking results. I am here today to declare this truth to the world, to express Russia's outrage and horror, along with our unequivocal condemnation of these actions. Standing in solidarity with our neighbors to the south, we are ready to do whatever is necessary to ensure the security of the region."

Nikitin paused, and the English transcript caught up. Stratton laid both hands on the back of a conference table chair and waited as ice crept into his veins. He could feel it coming—the curve ball he had predicted. He could see Nikitin winding up like an MLB pitcher. Despite the calibrated anger displayed on the Russian president's face, there was smugness also. A certain level of satisfaction.

Here it came...

"In collaboration with our best nuclear scientists and every intelligence source available...we have determined that the weapon detonated in Azerbaijan was *not* a Soviet-era bomb misplaced in Georgia, but rather an American one."

"*What?*" Aimes and Easterling spoke at once. Stratton shoved the chair out of the way and closed on the TV, his own heart rate spiking, instant sweat breaking out down his spine.

He couldn't believe what he was reading. It didn't compute. Whatever curve ball he feared, this wasn't it.

Nikitin held up a hand, clearly calming the cameramen and reporters gathered for his press conference. He continued: "While we are still uncertain as to the reasons behind this unimaginable event, we can already state with confidence that the weapon used in Azerbaijan was both modern and specially designed, not as a traditional military device but a purpose-built weapon of sabotage, crafted in America and transported to the Caucasus for reasons we cannot imagine. What devilry, what deceit, what twisted machinations have done this we cannot say, but I assure the world, this act of evil will not go unanswered and will *not* go unpunished. Russia stands ready to respond with full force, up to and including nuclear deterrents. I put the world on notice—I put *America* on notice—do not test us. Do not challenge our efforts to secure the region. Russia will not be intimidated. Russia will not be defied."

Nikitin nodded once. Then the press conference ended, and the TV feed transitioned to a Russian news anchor already chattering on as the translator scrambled to keep pace. Stratton grabbed the remote off the table and mashed mute. He turned on Aimes.

"How could he know that? How could he *possibly* know that?"

Aimes shook her head. "It's not possible, sir. It took us weeks to identify the origins of the Panama Canal bomb. He's had less than four days."

"It can't be ours," Easterling said. "Do we even *have* tactical nukes?"

"No," Aimes said. "Nothing remotely close to that size."

"What is he doing..." Easterling breathed.

But Stratton already knew. He stared at the screen and the picture-in-picture image of Nikitin frozen above the anchor's shoulder and measured the anger/smugness in the Russian president's face. He thought back over the months—the long, bloody months.

An attempted assassination. A coup in Venezuela designed to give Russia a foothold in the region. Terrorist attacks funded by an unknown shadow agent. A nuclear bomb that hamstrung America's economy.

And now an unthinkable, audacious claim. A very Pearl Harbor moment that would give Nikitin an excuse to take the next step, even as he solidified alliances with two of America's most powerful and most aggressive enemies.

It was all brutally obvious.

"He's picking the fight," Stratton said. "He's starting a war."

16

Somewhere in Azerbaijan

Reed wasn't sure what changed but something most definitely had. After several hours of abandonment in the belly of the prison, the tormentors returned in earnest. One soldier was stationed in each cell—Reed could tell by the creaking of door hinges and the defiant curses of his team. The man who joined him was just as tall as Reed and every bit as muscular. He carried a club, but he didn't swing it. He simply advanced to within inches of Reed's ear and removed the heavy cap dragging Reed's head down. The man's breath was hot as he whispered in heavily accented English:

"Now you will listen. And you *will* talk."

Then the torture returned. Not for Reed, and not for most of his team. The soldiers began with Corbyn instead, and while Reed could only guess what horrific depravities were being visited on her helpless body, the extremity of the torture was no secret. Corbyn screamed like she'd never screamed before, her voice shrill as it echoed off the concrete and burst through Reed's blood-clogged ears. He smelled smoke, then burning hair. Corbyn shrieked, and the Azerbaijanis laughed.

"Leave her alone!" Reed snarled, struggling to find a foothold with his toes. The tall guy standing across from him grinned, a mouth full of yellow teeth, then advanced to Reed's side again.

"You ready to talk?" he asked.

"I've already talked!"

The man swung. The club landed with a horrific *whump* across Reed's unprotected stomach, and he convulsed. Bile exploded from his throat and his head spun. He lost traction and swung from his burning wrists. His vision blurred and the soldier laughed, swatting him again with the club, this time over the backs of his legs.

"We know you are lying, American. We will shred her one piece at a time. *You must talk!*"

"Hey, assholes!" The next voice that burst through the prison was Strickland's. The pilot shouted from his cell, then a heavy *thump* signaled the land of a boot against flesh. The grunt didn't sound like Strickland. It sounded like one of the soldiers.

"You guys want a real fight? Come try me!"

"Don't..." Reed gasped.

It was no use. Strickland continued taunting the soldiers. Dropping slurs. Daring them to give it a shot.

Within thirty seconds the ploy worked. Corbyn's screams faded. Feet pounded. A door creaked and Strickland's defiant shouts broke short with a heavy thud. One soldier called out in his native tongue, and a cart rattled over the concrete.

Then Strickland got his wish. Reed knew, because the next orchestra of misery erupted from directly across the hall. Strickland shouted through his teeth, gasping as a blow torch erupted to life. Reed smelled burning polyester and imagined a T-shirt melting over Strickland's flesh. The pilot groaned, but when he caught his breath he didn't beg for mercy. He didn't scream.

Strickland laughed—like an absolute psychopath. His voice cracked, but Reed could still make out the words.

"Oh, that's good. Medium rare, boys! Don't forget the marinade."

"Kyle...don't!" Corbyn's panting voice echoed down the hall. The blowtorch cranked up. This time Strickland *did* scream.

Reed dug his toes into the concrete, stopping his swing and snatching his face toward the soldier. He spat, spraying bile and blood, half choking himself but getting a shower of it over the guy's face. The soldier swept with his arm, then swung with the club. Reed was ready. He kicked off the concrete and shot his leg straight into the path of the weapon. Wood glanced off his calf, then his bare foot caught the soldier right in the sternum, hard enough to drive the wind out of his lungs. Reed swung from the chains, metal biting into his wrists. Strickland shrieked and the soldier with the club went down.

"Hey!" Reed choked. "Room service to cell four—I think it's my turn."

The soldier on the floor struggled to regain his breath. His hand found the club, but Reed's toes couldn't grab the concrete. He was still swinging. The guy advanced to a wall and mashed a button. Overhead an electric winch whined. Reed rose another six inches and kicked. He was hanging in midair, no chance of gaining a footing on the concrete. The guy advanced, teeth bared.

Then a voice barked down the hallway. A loud shout in Azerbaijani. In a moment, stillness blanketed the prison, broken only by Strickland's shaking gasps. Boots pounded and the soldier with the club turned to the door.

Reed turned also, quivering with pain as a new face appeared. It was another soldier, but this guy wore a better uniform and a nicer hat. He was an officer, Reed thought. He carried a tablet computer beneath one arm and snapped something at the soldier with the club.

The guy dropped the weapon with a glower, then advanced to Reed's side. He put out a hand and grabbed Reed's shirt, steadying him.

"Get your hands off me!" Reed snarled.

"*Shut up.*" That was the new guy. He lifted the tablet and tapped on the screen. Then he rotated the device so that Reed could see. "*Watch.*"

Reed had to blink to clear his vision. It was difficult to focus on the bright screen. Shapes and symbols blurred and shifted out of place. The volume sounded dim and distant to his clogged ear.

But then he recognized a face. A tall man in a suit, with white, blue, and red flags standing behind him. It was the Russian president, and as he spoke, a string of white letters ran across the bottom of the screen. It was English. Reed struggled to keep up.

"...we have determined that the weapon...Azerbaijan was...American."

Something like a dump truck full of concrete landed in Reed's gut. His body quaked as the officer withdrew the tablet. Stepping close, the man spoke through his teeth in the same heavy accent as his men.

"You see? We knew you were lying."

Reed shook his head, struggling to breathe. "He's the one lying. We're from NATO. The bomb was Russian!"

The officer smiled. "You think so? I will tell you what I think. I think you were sent here by your government to detonate this weapon. I think you want us at war with our neighbors, but now the truth is found out. And you —" He drew even closer, grabbing Reed by the throat and squeezing.

Reed choked, unable to breathe. His body jerked, and his vision paled. The man shook him.

"You will now tell me *everything*...or I will slaughter your team, one at a time."

As he spoke, his fingers tightened. Reed's vision began to fade.

And then the screams returned from Strickland's cell. A horrible, prolonged shriek. The blast of flame. The stench of cooking flesh.

The taste of death itself carried on dank air.

17

Goranboy District, Azerbaijan

Turk landed on his face at the bottom of the hill, and long before he was back on his feet he could already hear the shouts of soldiers in the distance. He wasn't sure if they had seen him or if they were shouting about any number of unrelated military problems.

Whatever the case, despite his bruised back and a right knee that felt badly strained, he was picking himself up on the ground and clawing his way toward Lucy within seconds of coming to rest at the bottom of the hill.

Lucy lay whimpering in a heap, rain beating down on her, blood oozing from her temple. Turk wriggled up beside her, instinctively diving into the grass as a white-hot spotlight flicked over his shoulders.

Oh, the Azerbaijanis had seen something, all right. Even now they were surveying the hillside. The shouts were growing steadily louder.

They were *coming*.

"Come on, Lucy. We've got to go!"

Lucy didn't respond. She continued to moan and held one hand against her head. Turk looked through the grass to see the Azerbaijanis closing in —half a dozen of them on foot, with two more riding in a Cobra attack vehicle. It was from the door pillar of the Cobra that the spotlight swept back and forth along the base of the hill.

The soldiers looked more curious than alarmed, but that could change in a microsecond. Turk had to *move*.

He scooped Lucy up and moved on his knees, half dragging her through the grass. Heading away from the base of the hill, away from the spotlight. The soldiers' voices grew dimmer, and as soon as Turk reached the security of unbroken darkness, he was back on his feet.

"Come on, Lucy!"

He couldn't get her on his back. The best he could manage was to cradle her in his arms like a child. He pulled her close and sprinted into the shadows, right knee barking, lungs burning. He looked over his shoulder and saw the soldiers spreading out. One reached the torn spot where Turk and Lucy had come to rest and pointed, shouting something.

Blood, Turk thought. He'd found blood.

The sloping side of the hill turned fifty yards farther on. Turk followed the curve without thought, cradling Lucy as he plowed into the darkness. He looked back once more, checking for pursuers.

Then he ran headlong into the fence. It was constructed of split rails, about waist high, and Turk's bulk was more than enough to crash straight through it. He tripped, pitching forward and hurling Lucy without meaning to. The two of them hit the mud, and then they were sliding down another hill. Turk tumbled without any hope of breaking his forward momentum. He saw stars, black sky, and then yellow lights. Lucy cried out in pain. Turk slammed into something hard and immovable, coming to a crushing stop.

He lay on his back, blinking upward into the still-pouring rain. Gasping for air. Twisting his face to look for Lucy.

The pair of them lay out in a muddy patch of torn dirt, now flooded with water. The object he'd collided with was a pickup truck—a twenty-year-old Nissan with mismatched wheels. The truck was still and silent, but the yellow glow was coming from somewhere. Turk twisted to locate the source...then he stopped cold.

There was a house, not twenty feet away. More of a cottage, really, standing under the rain with the door flung open. An old man stood in the frame, peeking out with a flashlight clutched in one hand. Before Turk could move, that beam crossed his chest, and the old man called over his shoulder to an invisible companion.

Then he was hurrying out the door, hobbling with the stiffness of bad hips. Turk rolled to his knees and looked back up the hill, checking for soldiers. He didn't see anyone. The old man called out to him in Azerbaijani. The voice wasn't hostile—more confused and alarmed.

Then the flashlight beam fell across Lucy. She lay moaning at the nose of the Nissan, still bleeding from the temple. The old man muttered on his breath and called back to the house. Then he was scooping up Lucy, covering her temple with one hand. He turned back to Turk and tilted his head toward the house. He spoke again in Azerbaijani.

Turk didn't understand a word of it, but he didn't need to. From the top of the hill the sound of the Cobra drew nearer. In another few minutes the soldiers would reach the fence and look down over the house. If they saw anyone, they might trouble themselves to proceed down the hill.

Time to move again.

Turk followed the old man through the mud and into the house. An old woman waited inside, looking roughly the same age as the old man. She cried out at the sight of Lucy and guided the man to a padded armchair. Lucy settled into it, blinking and holding her head. Turk closed the door and stood dripping on the hardwood, a little dazed and disoriented.

But alive. Out of the rain. Sheltered from the Azerbaijani ground forces...at least for the moment.

Outside the house, thunder rolled hard enough to rattle windows in their frames. When it cleared, Turk could no longer hear the rumble of the Cobra. He settled into a hard-backed kitchen chair and the Zigana bit into his stomach. Turk hurried to conceal it before the old man returned to the living room with a towel and a first aid kit.

The man smiled and said something in Azerbaijani. Turk simply shook his head, gesturing to Lucy. The old man settled onto his knees next to Lucy's armchair. In a moment he had the first aid kit open, and then he went to work on Lucy's temple. Clearing. Drying. Bandaging with antiseptic cream. His fingers moved with the easy familiarity of a doctor...or maybe a veterinarian.

The old woman and her husband exchanged a look. Then the old man turned to Turk.

"*Russan?*"

The voice was calm, but this time Turk detected an edge in it. He glanced sideways to the woman and noted the fear in her eyes.

Russan. The man was asking if Turk was a Russian.

"No," Turk said, shaking his head. "Not Russian."

The farmer smiled. "Ah. English."

"You speak it?"

The farmer winced, rocking his hand palm down. "Small. Small English."

"I understand."

Turk leaned back with a wince, allowing himself a glance around the home's interior for the first time since arriving. He sat next to a four-person dining table that had a hand-hewn look about it. The house had an open floor plan, with a simple kitchen to his left and a living room to his right. All the floors were hardwood, the furniture clean but heavily used. The refrigerator looked like something out of the 1970s, and the TV set erected on top of a waist-high bookcase actually featured rabbit-ear antennas. A news broadcast played, the audio turned down low, the video on the screen a rolling montage of war footage.

Smoke rising over Georgia earlier that day…and then the site of the bomb.

Turk looked back to his host, and this time he saw the fear in the man's eyes.

"Who…you?" The man struggled with the words.

"Journalists," Turk lied. He pointed at himself, then at Lucy. Then at the TV. He mimed a camera in his hands, as though he were filming. "Reporters."

The man nodded several times, seeming to relax. He offered Turk a smile.

"Samir," he said, jabbing himself in the chest with a thumb. Then he pointed to the old woman. "Zahra."

"Pleased to meet you. I'm Rufus." Turk patted his own chest, electing his first name over his nickname. He didn't want to deal with the confusion of explaining that he wasn't, in fact, from Turkey. "She's Lucy."

Samir surveyed his medical work for a moment, again seeming to consider. Lucy was back to her deer-in-the-headlights look, lips parted, breathing evenly and not blinking. Not speaking. She looked like she'd survived the nuclear blast firsthand...which, in fact, she had. Maybe Samir guessed as much.

"Tea?" he asked. "Food?"

Turk's stomach growled at the very mention of sustenance. "Please."

Samir said something to his wife and the old lady scurried off with a bowed head. She seemed eager to distance herself from the strangers. Samir tugged his chair back and sat with a grunt. After smoothing his pant legs, he faced Turk again. This time the uncertainty in his face was impossible to ignore.

"You see...bomb?"

Turk's tongue flashed across his lips. He hesitated, unsure what to say. The situation was stable, for the moment at least, but that could change in a heartbeat. If Samir felt threatened or Zahra called the authorities, it most certainly would.

In the end, Turk decided the truth couldn't hurt. It was logical that war reporters from overseas could have arrived in Azerbaijan in preparation for a supposed Russian invasion. Being in the wrong place at the wrong time was all it could have taken to witness that mushroom cloud.

"Yes," Turk said.

Samir's hands worked around a towel lying on the table, knotting and then unknotting it. Turk estimated the man's age, and knew he remembered the Cold War well. The Soviet days. The constant threat of nuclear annihilation, should Moscow or Washington lose their nerve. Those days had faded into a brighter reality of prolonged peace...

And now what? An atomic detonation right in his own backyard?

The Agency. I have to report.

Turk leaned across the table. He drew the damp sat phone from his pocket and rotated the device so that Samir could see the charging port built into the base.

"Do you have a cable for this?" Turk said. "I need to call my bosses."

18

Samir didn't understand at first. Turk had to repeat himself, pointing to the charger hole, then attempting to turn the phone on. At last the old man nodded and hurried from the room. He returned with a cluster of cables, and Turk sorted past outdated landline wires and a decades-old computer power cable before at last locating a USB-C charger with a European wall plug. Samir guided him to an outlet, and Turk plugged the phone in. Ten long seconds dripped by. Then a charging icon illuminated across the screen.

"Are you...soldier?" Samir struggled with the word. Turk looked up from the device. His mind was already spinning ahead to the next problem—his lack of a phone number to call. He didn't know *how* to contact the CIA. It wasn't like they had a 1-800 number, and he didn't have a direct line to the Special Activities Center memorized.

The only option he could think of was one that twisted his stomach, but it might be his only choice.

"No," Turk said. "Reporters."

He repeated the lie, and Samir nodded, but Turk didn't think the old man bought it. From the kitchen Zahra appeared with a plate of warm sausages and dark bread. She offered a timid smile as she laid it on the table. Turk thanked her and helped himself to the bread. It was fresh and delicious.

Samir was carting the plate to Lucy when the phone in Turk's hand buzzed, signaling that the battery had charged enough for him to power it on. His fingers raced over the keys, waiting to see the screen brighten to its home menu...and then stopping.

He knew what number to call. It was, in fact, the *only* number he knew. He felt certain that the love of his life would pick up on the other end, whatever time it might be in Tennessee.

Yet still he hesitated. Not because he didn't long to hear her voice with every fiber of his being, but because he didn't have the time or emotional bandwidth to explain the situation. To reassure her. To justify himself...

Just dial, Turk.

He did, adding the country code and praying that Sinju would pick up.

The phone rang. Turk closed his eyes and waited, picturing his gorgeous Korean wife rushing to the phone. Cradling baby Liberty. Longing for him as badly as he longed for—

"Hello?"

Sinju's timid voice was distorted by distance but clear enough to make Turk's heart jump. Just the sound of her breath over the line made him crazy. He could hear the fear and strain in her tone and knew she hadn't slept in days. That she'd lain awake, wondering whether her husband would ever return. Whether the ugly side of life had swallowed him in the end.

"It's me," Turk whispered.

Sinju gasped. She sobbed. Then she shouted his name. Turk caught Samir watching him and he turned quickly away, scrubbing a tear off his cheek. Sinju's questions were flying thick. All the predictable inquiries about his location, his safety. About what in the world had happened.

Turk wanted to answer them all. He wanted to assure her that he would be home soon.

But he couldn't lie. Someplace in his gut, the reality that he might never hear her voice again was still sharp, cutting deep. He was also short on time. The pressure of his intelligence still burned hot in his mind. Personal desires would have to wait.

"Sinju, I need you to listen."

She grew quiet. Turk switched the phone to his other ear. "I'm overseas. I can't say where. I'm not hurt. I'll...I'll be headed back soon."

"Soon?"

"I need you to do something for me. It's very important. Do you have your computer?"

"Yes..."

"I need you to look up a number—a number for the CIA. Their public access line."

"CIA? Are you in danger?"

The phone crackled. Turk remained calm.

"Just get the number, Sinju. Quick as you can."

From the far side of the globe items shifted and keys clacked. Turk extended a hand toward Samir.

"Pen?"

The old man brought him paper and a pencil. Sinju found the number and Turk confirmed it twice.

"Thank you," he said.

"Rufus? Are you coming home?"

Turk forced a smile. He didn't feel it, but he wanted her to hear it.

"Bet on it, baby. Soon as I can."

A brief pause. "Libby keeps asking for her daddy."

That was more than Turk could handle. His eyes watered and again he turned away from the others, facing the wall. Faded wallpaper peeled at the edges.

"I love you," he whispered. "So much."

Then he hung up before Sinju could answer. He already knew what she would say. He couldn't bring himself to hear it.

Punching in the CIA number, Turk waited. It rang. An automated system answered. Turk mashed zero and barked for a representative. The internal stress Sinju's voice had assuaged was now rushing back in, wearing at frazzled nerves. All Turk could think about was the next step. Reporting to the CIA, requesting backup. Enough muscle to locate and rescue the rest of the team.

"Central Intelligence Agency, this is Officer Spielman. How can I direct your call?"

"Officer, my name is Rufus Turkman. I'm an SAC operative deployed to Azerbaijan. I've lost my team, lost my comms, and I have critical intel to report. I need to be transferred to Director Aimes, immediately."

Long pause. Turk thought the line might have failed. Then he detected the muted laugh.

"I'm sorry, sir, who did you say you are?"

"Rufus Turkman," Turk spoke through his teeth. "Look, I don't have time to explain. I need—"

"What's your officer ID?"

"I don't have an officer ID. Didn't you hear me? I work for SAC. I'm off the books. I need to speak with—"

"I'm sorry, sir. If you worked for SAC, you'd have a direct contact line and an agent ID. This is a public access line, and in context of current events you really shouldn't be prank calling the CIA. It's a federal offense."

That was too much. Turk snapped. *"Federal offense?* I'll give you a federal offense, you dumb prick. The weapon detonated in Azerbaijan was carted across the border by *Russian Alphas*. Do you hear me? Russian spec ops soldiers, but *our flag* was stamped on the outside. We're being framed, Spielman, and if you don't get me on the line with Sarah Aimes *right freaking now*, we may already be out of—"

Click.

The line died. Turk's fingers tightened around the handset. He slammed his hand into the wall and reached for redial.

Then he stopped, his peripheral vision snagging on something from across the room. Turk looked right, suddenly aware that the house had fallen deadly silent. Zahra stood motionless in the kitchen, her face ashen white. Lucy remained in the armchair, but she was no longer staring into empty space. Now she stared at the television set, which was also where the farmers' attention was fixed.

Turk traced their gaze to a flashing news broadcast. He recognized white, blue, and red flags framed in the background, with a tall man in a dark suit taking center stage. The picture quality of the old TV set was poor, as was the broadcast, flickering and distorting at random. But Turk recognized the man as Makar Nikitin, he recognized the voice as Russian, and he recognized a single word of that Russian just as Samir turned wide, terrified eyes on him.

Amerikanskiy—American.

Even as Turk computed the word and assumed an interpretation, Samir confirmed his fears by backing quickly against the wall. The old man's hand fell toward the backside of that waist-high bookcase. Turk's tactical mind slammed into gear and he lowered the phone, extending a hand.

"Don't!"

It was too late. Samir shouted, and Zahra hit the floor. Samir's hand appeared from behind the bookcase with a handgun—a Soviet-era Tokarev pistol, hammer cocking with a snap. The muzzle flicked toward Turk, and Turk's free hand dove for the Zigana in his waistband.

Samir was quick. Turk was just a little quicker. Both guns cracked and Samir's bullet zipped over Turk's shoulder, smacking into the wall. Turk's round was dead on target—not an aimed shot, but an instinctual one, and Turk's instincts had been calibrated not to wound but to kill. A 9mm slug caught Samir dead in his sternum, and he collapsed.

For a long, dreadful moment, time itself stood still. Turk stared in disbelief as Samir's eyes went wide...and then the light faded. The old man hit the floor. The Tokarev fell from his hands. Zahra screamed. Turk looked down to his trembling hand and found his finger still clamped around the Zigana's trigger, ready for a next shot.

He relaxed it. He blinked hard. Then the instincts took over again, and Turk was hurtling across the room. Dragging Lucy out of the armchair and headed for the door, even as Zahra reached her husband's side and fell to her knees. The woman screamed. Turk's eyes blurred. He stopped at the door and looked back once.

The face Zahra turned on him was one of absolute confusion. Total betrayal. Her mouth hung open, her arms trembled.

Then she did the worst possible thing—she went for the Tokarev. Turk saw it happening, but he didn't fire. He slung himself through the door instead, back out into the rainstorm, Lucy stumbling along next to him. They reached the roadbed and dove for cover in the ditch.

But no bullets raced after them. Zahra fired only once...and then Turk heard the second body hit the floor. He clamped his eyes shut in the bottom of the ditch and screamed.

19

The West Wing
The White House

"The Agency can now confirm that Chinese President Chen Lei and Iranian Supreme Leader Ali Kazemi are present in Moscow, having traveled in secret, presumably to meet with Nikitin."

There was no gasp of surprise around the table. In the three hours that had passed since Stratton and Aimes's meeting, the news of a Chinese/Iranian/Russian summit had already disseminated amongst the cabinet. The rows of iron faces now fixated on Director Aimes and her presentation screen had already recovered from their shock.

Now it was dread that Stratton saw in their eyes. A certain understanding of the one thing such a meeting could mean.

"We're not yet certain how long Chen and Kazemi have been present in Moscow," Aimes continued, "or how long they plan to stay. We also can't be certain of the subject of their meeting, but...to read between the lines, the Agency believes it likely that Nikitin may be negotiating a military alliance with Tehran and Beijing."

"God have mercy," General Yellin growled.

A murmur of similar sentiments circled the table. Aimes remained cool and collected, acknowledging the general's comment with a commiserative nod.

"It's not good news, General. Unfortunately, this is not the worst news. If I can direct your attention to the screen, here you see CIA satellite imagery captured this morning over the Esfahan Province in central Iran. It's dark at present in the Middle East, of course, so you'll have to excuse the use of infrared technology. Each red spot depicted here represents a heat signature, in this case an engine. A larger signature equals a larger engine. The big ones"—Aimes used a laser pointer to mark the screen—"are Karrar main battle tanks. Smaller are trucks, armored personnel carriers, and mobile artillery. About three hundred fifty vehicles in total."

"Moving?" SecDef Kline asked.

"That is correct, Mr. Secretary. Northwest, toward Tabriz and the Iranian/Azerbaijani border."

"They're joining the fight," Yellin said. "Nikitin is locking the Azerbaijanis in a pincer move."

"It certainly looks that way," Aimes said. "And the Azerbaijanis haven't seemed to notice. The bulk of their armor and active-duty ground forces are still routing north toward the Red Bridge crossing, with a reserve held around Baku. We can't be sure if there has been an intelligence failure or if they simply aren't concerned about the Iranians."

"They certainly should be," Secretary of State Lisa Gorman interjected. "Tensions between Tehran and Baku are at an all-time high, mostly as a result of Iran's support of Armenia during the Nagorno-Karabakh conflict. Azerbaijani nationalism under President Rzayev has also generated questions over the ten to fifteen million ethnic Azerbaijanis living in northwestern Iran. It's a very similar situation to Russia's claim over the Donbas Region. Rzayev has never had the military strength to challenge Iran, but maybe Iran would challenge him."

"Strike first?" Stratton asked.

"Possibly. It's difficult to say. In all the universe there may not be a more unpredictable entity than the state of Iran. The ayatollah's grip on Tehran is absolute, which basically means that the entire country will dance in whatever direction Ali Kazemi dictates. He's an unpredictable man with a thirst for expansion, and also a clever magician with a penchant for misdirection.

Whatever Iran *appears* to be up to, we really can't assume. Those tanks could turn west and smash into Iraq without warning."

"An unpredictable man with a thirst for expansion," Kline said. "Sounds like Nikitin."

"Or *Chen*," Yellin said. "Don't forget about Taiwan, ladies and gentlemen. Chen Lei has had his sights set on the ROC since he was in diapers. China has no logical interest in a Middle Eastern war. If Chen is aligning himself with Moscow and Tehran, we have to wonder what selfish ambitions are driving that unholy marriage."

"It's no great mystery," Kline said. "It's opportunism, plain and simple. While we're reeling from economic instability, widespread panic, and the loss of the Panama Canal, Russia is willing to push the envelope, and Iran is happy to join. That leaves China an opportunity to exploit our distraction."

Dead silence enveloped the room. Stratton knew everybody was thinking the same thing—asking the question but not daring to speak it. For a rare moment the West Wing felt perfectly still.

In the end it was National Security Advisor Nick West who broke the silence. "Are you suggesting these clowns are about to kick off *World War Three*?"

Yellin pivoted in his chair, flushed cheeks bunched, bulldog shoulders seeming to burst from his medal-laden uniform. He simply nodded.

"Yes, Mr. West. That is precisely what we're suggesting."

With that statement the stillness broke, and a murmur ran through the room. Heads bowed, faces turned. A dozen different private conversations erupted while Stratton stared at the display screen, head spinning.

What was happening? Two weeks prior he'd been entirely consumed by the question of stabilizing a reeling country. Propping up a faltering economy. Instilling confidence in a broken people.

Now war was breathing right down his neck. So hot his skin tingled. He looked at the photographs displayed on the screen and imagined what would happen if those tanks *did* turn west, rolling into Iraq and reigniting a conflict that had lain dormant since the 1980s. Only now there were US troops in Iraq, US military bases, and oil interests.

And *Israel*. The ultimate target of the ayatollah. Stratton could close his eyes and instantly see the world unraveling, almost overnight. Iran—

possibly with other Arabic state support, and certainly with the support of Hezbollah and Hamas—at war with Iraq, Israel, and Saudi Arabia. Russia gobbling up the Caucasus, then quickly pivoting toward an unprepared Europe. China at last moving against Taiwan, ready to erase the last of the old Chinese Republic.

And America—weakened by a broken economy, disabled shipping, terrified citizens, and a fractured White House—caught right in the middle of it all.

World War Three? No. Closer to Armageddon.

"Quiet," Stratton muttered. Nobody reacted. The chatter continued. Stratton sat upright and slammed his hand, open-palmed, across the table. "I said *quiet*!"

The shout brought the cabinet to a screeching halt. Stratton drained his water glass and smacked it down. He glared down the length of the table.

"No more chatter. The general is right. This situation is a breath away from spinning completely out of control, and it's *our job* to stop it."

He turned back to Aimes, who still stood behind the podium with the laser pointer in one hand. "Madam Director, you haven't yet commented on Russia's claims regarding the bomb in Azerbaijan."

"That it's American?" Aimes asked.

"Correct. What do we know about that?"

A shake of her head. "Nothing, sir. As I stated before, it's an absurd claim. To be able to identify nuclear fuel so soon after the blast is a near impossibility. Our sources inside Russia are still sifting through the noise, but my gut tells me it's a smoke-and-mirrors operation."

"It's got to be," Yellin said. "The United States doesn't even manufacture nuclear weapons of that size. It was a tactical blast. We build city-crushers."

"So what, then?" Easterling said. "The bomb had to come from somewhere."

"Likely from Russia," Yellin said. "Just like the Panama bomb. These thugs are manufacturing their own excuses to touch off a war. Even though they can't prove that we manufactured or supplied that weapon, the claim alone will throw the world into a tailspin. How many calls have you received from our allies, Madam Secretary?"

"Nearly a hundred," Gorman said.

"And twice as many from our adversaries, I'd imagine," Yellin added. Gorman nodded.

"Any from *Moscow*?" Stratton said.

"No, sir," Gorman said. "The Kremlin is radio silent. We've called every half hour since the Georgia invasion...nothing. Even the Russian ambassador is ghosting us."

"It's a game," Stratton said. "They want us to panic, and it isn't going to happen. Jill, have Farah draft a statement condemning the blast. Have her deliver it to the press corps. Somebody will ask about the Russian claim. Have her denounce it out of hand and move on to other subjects. I'm talking condescending dismissal. We won't give Nikitin a moment's satisfaction."

"Don't you think..." Easterling hesitated. "The American people would benefit from seeing your face."

"That's exactly what Nikitin wants. He's throwing rocks and hiding his hands. We won't tolerate it. Have Farah draft the announcement and deliver it live before lunch. Lisa, what options do we have to pressure the Russians into communication?"

"Not many, sir. We could channel through the UN, but—"

"The UN is useless. Every time we've attempted to leverage the Security Council, Russia simply vetoes the resolution and smirks from the shadows. I want direct pressure."

Gorman considered. "We could call for a NATO summit, sir. It's a largely symbolic move, but it will rally our allies and underscore to the world that we don't trust Russia's intentions."

"Do it. And, Carmen"—Stratton pivoted toward the secretary of the Treasury—"I want a full salvo of fresh sanctions about Russia, and Nikitin in particular. Anything you can think of. I don't care if it fails in court. Just sling it on the wall and see what sticks."

"Understood, sir. We'll get right on it."

Stratton reached for a pitcher, pouring more water. He gulped it down. Nobody spoke. Maybe they all knew what was coming.

At last Stratton addressed the SecDef.

"What are our options, Steven?"

"I'm not going to lie to you, sir. This couldn't come at a worse time. With drawdowns in Iraq, our ground presence is minimal, and with the loss of the Panama Canal, our ability to maneuver naval assets between Atlantic and Pacific theaters is severely restricted."

"Almost like somebody planned it that way," Stratton said. "What about the Fifth and Sixth fleets?"

"They're in position, sir," General Yellin stepped in. "I can bring us to full alert and put planes in the air on your command. Enough to give the Iranians a second thought about swinging west. Within forty-eight hours we can have Rangers on the ground in Iraq and additional aircraft stationed in the Mediterranean. It won't be enough to fight a war, but it will send a signal."

"Make it happen, all of it. And draft a plan for a full-blown response should either Russia or Iran threaten Turkey."

The room grew still and Stratton pivoted back to the map displayed on the wall screens. He knew everybody was thinking the same thing. He might as well give voice to it.

"It's time to consider the possibility of a Russian strike against NATO."

20

Nashville, Tennessee

Banks only vaguely recognized the Russian president's face when he first appeared on CNN, speaking with a scowl so dark it looked like a thundercloud, but five hours of endless news surfing later, the image was as emblazoned into her memory as that of the mushroom cloud rising against a pitch-black Azerbaijani sky.

There were film reels of Russian soldiers marching south. Cell phone clips of small-arms fire popping across Tbilisi while civilians scrambled for cover. Satellite imagery of Iranian fast infantry moving rapidly north toward the Azerbaijani border. Clips of a White House press conference wherein the press secretary, Farah Rahman, unequivocally dismissed the possibility of an American nuclear weapon detonating overseas, all while announcing a NATO summit and the deployment of additional US military assets to the region.

It was a nightmare. The prelude to erupting war that Banks could feel in her very bones. When she looked out her window, Music City appeared strangely still. No pedal taverns rumbled through the Gulch or down Broadway. The brunch spots beneath her apartment, usually so popular with bachelorettes, stood empty. Even the bars were quiet.

The whole nation was standing breathless, watching the unthinkable unfold. Thinking of their children, their futures. The possibility of a third global conflict that would claim the lives of millions.

But Banks wasn't thinking about any of that. She didn't care about the planet, the economy, the future of the world order, or whose bomb had detonated in Azerbaijan. The one thing that consumed her mind like a drug was an overwhelming fear for her own family. Not just the toddler son who slept on the couch, surrounded by storybooks and building blocks, but the husband that Banks hadn't heard from in days.

He'd deployed...She knew it. He'd gone overseas. To Azerbaijan? To Georgia?

Banks stood in front of the TV with one hand over her mouth and cried as the endless montage of videos played. She looked to a trembling hand and again mashed a button to dial Reed. It was her fourth call in the past half hour.

Just like the first three, the call went straight to voicemail. Reed didn't call back. He didn't message her. She was left with his curt voice demanding a message after the beep.

Dropping the phone, Banks ran both hands through long, unwashed hair and stumbled against the kitchen bar. Lancing hot pain raced through her stomach from the bomb blast wounds still slowly healing. The breath burned in her lungs. Her whole body felt on fire, alive with panic.

How could he do this to her? How could he go *again*? Was he even alive? Why wouldn't he answer?

Banks startled as a bell rang from the apartment's front door. Her face snapped in that direction, and momentary, irrational hope flooded her chest. She pictured Reed, dirty and probably bleeding. Stumbling inside with a mumbled explanation about losing his keys, losing his phone.

But alive. Back in her arms. Banks rotated the bolt and snatched the door open, his name already on her lips.

And then she froze. It wasn't Reed. It was Sinju, Turk's wife, with their baby daughter sleeping on Sinju's shoulder. Sinju had been crying also, Banks could see the tear trails on her face. Without a word she stepped inside and wrapped her free arm around Banks, pulling her into a hug. For a moment they simply stood in the doorway, just holding each other.

When at last Sinju withdrew, she had calmed a little. The iron that carried her through the horrors of North Korea bolstered her shoulders. Her chin lifted.

"He called," Sinju said.

"Turk?"

Sinju nodded.

"Where…" Banks began.

Sinju shook her head, tears bubbling up again. She swallowed.

"He wouldn't say. Someplace overseas. They…they're in trouble, Banks."

It was the truth Banks already knew in her bones. Her lip trembled. The breath in her chest felt heavy, like water.

She pulled Sinju into another hug and the two women cried silently.

21

Moscow, Russia

Mikhail Orlov returned to his apartment after sunset to find another delivery of fresh bread waiting on the doorstep, wrapped in butcher's paper, still hot to the touch. He froze over the doormat and looked quickly over his shoulder, half expecting a smug FSB agent with a drawn pistol to step out of the shadows.

There was no one. The street around the grimy little apartment block was dark and silent, a cold late-summer breeze cutting through his coat and reaching his bones. He knelt alongside the breadbasket and lifted the tag to examine the bakery's name.

The CIA used three different bakeries for signal deliveries. Each corresponded to a communication protocol. This was the third of the three—and the most rare. The name on the tag didn't correspond to an encoded message hidden in a dusty volume of boring Russian poetry, but to a bench located alongside the fountains at the Muzeon Park of Arts, a public park resting along the banks of the Moskva River.

It was a quiet place, this late at night. Popular with smokers and clandestine lovers, and also the only place where the CIA would ever risk an in-person meeting with their Kremlin asset.

Unlocking his door, Orlov stepped quickly inside and transferred the bread to the breakfast table. He stared at it for a while, weighing his options as his heart rate spiked.

This had never happened before. The CIA had organized a structure for in-person meetings but had never actually employed that structure. For obvious reasons, in-person meetings were extremely dangerous. Any FSB agents trailing Orlov would quickly detect a rendezvous with an unknown person—or worse, a known American government operative. Orlov didn't think he was being trailed, but after his most recent mission in the Kremlin, how could he be sure?

He might have raised alarm bells. He might have caught the attention of the wrong people. Even now, they might be headed to arrest him, to drag him away to some pit deep in Siberia where he would freeze to death alongside Fiana Popov...

But maybe that's why.

Maybe the CIA knew he was busted and was ready to pull him. This could be an emergency extraction, in which case he had no choice *but* to respond.

Orlov hurried to the kitchen and removed a false backing inside a teacup cabinet to retrieve the emergency supplies buried there. A Russian passport, a fake Polish passport, and a thick roll of currency roughly equivalent to three months' wages from his government job—both rubles and euros.

Then he was back outside. He walked to the nearest bus station and rode past the park, doubling back to allow himself time to complete a rudimentary SDR—a surveillance detection route. The technique was designed to expose any tails long before he reached his destination, but Orlov rushed it. He made only a token effort to expose a stalker before heading straight for Muzeon.

Now he was certain that he was busted. Orlov had talked himself into it. He'd pushed too hard, dug too deeply at the Kremlin. Running into Kazemi was the fatal move. The FSB was onto him, which gave him hours at most to escape the city and flee to those Caribbean islands where his hard-earned American cash waited.

Orlov reached the bench and settled down to face the choreographed spurts of water erupting from a stretch of polished concrete. Scattered around the park were a few dozen statues and modern art sculptures, including a giant hammer and cycle design bolted to the face of a half globe—a testament to a time not long gone when the KGB, not the FSB, would have been hot on Orlov's heels.

Different letters but the same concept, the same consequences. Orlov had observed the tone of the government in Moscow hardening since Makar Nikitin's hostile takeover five years earlier. He didn't remember the old Soviet days, not really.

But the stories his father told him of Khrushchev's tyranny and Brezhnev's felt eerily similar to Nikitin's developing tactics of free press suppression and the mysterious erasure of his enemies. Russia was not a friendly place. It was not a safe place.

It was a place Orlov was ready to leave.

The CIA contact appeared twenty-two minutes after Orlov reached the bench. He knew, because he'd checked his watch every thirty seconds, almost ready to consider a desperate self-extraction to the Baltic border. Estonia was still within FSB reach, but it was a step in the right direction. His growing panic was overwhelming. He was now certain that black-suited officers waited behind every bush or concealed themselves behind the tinted windows of a nearby van.

He blinked, and the van disappeared. It was never there at all. His mind was playing tricks on him.

"What took you so long?" Orlov spoke as the American operative took a seat next to him, casually lighting up a Turkish cigarette as though time itself were a nonfactor.

"Keep your voice down," the operative replied in flawless Russian with a convincing St. Petersburg accent. It wasn't authentic. Orlov could detect the production of the tone if he focused, but a casual listener wouldn't be any the wiser of the smoker's true ethnicity.

"When do we leave?" Orlov said, gaze snapping around the park. "Do you have a plane?"

The American glanced sideways, dragging on the smoke. He blew through his nose. "What are you talking about?"

"The *extraction*," Orlov snapped.

"What extraction?"

"Aren't you here to get me out?"

"Of course not. Why would I do that?"

Long pause. Orlov's mind skipped. He glanced over his shoulder, back toward the street.

The van still wasn't there.

"What happened?" Now it was the operative's turn to grow hard. "Were you burned?"

Orlov licked his lips. He touched the passports in his pocket.

"I...no. No. I don't think so. I thought something must have gone wrong...because of the emergency meeting."

A soft grunt. The man dragged on the smoke and thumped ash over the sidewalk. "Negative. We have another job for you."

"A job? I just completed a job!"

Orlov's voice cracked, rising above the whisper the two men had been using. The American glanced sideways at him, eyes hard. Shooting him a warning. Orlov swallowed. He forced himself back into his seat.

"If you can't hold it together, I'll leave now," the American said.

"Why didn't you use the dead drop?" Orlov demanded. "This is dangerous."

"Very much so, which should tell you something about our need."

Our need.

Orlov squinted, thinking back to his last report. Kazemi and Chen. He hadn't given much thought to Nikitin's clandestine guests until now. Orlov was about as apolitical as a person could get. He couldn't care less about Nikitin's ambitions, or Washington's. Wars and geopolitical maneuvering were nothing more nor less than an economy for Mikhail Orlov.

But that economy could be a rich one, and now the money-grubbing instincts rooted deep in his soul spoke to him of an opportunity. He smelled desperation on the American—need, like a junkie short on supply.

It was enough to distract him from his previous panic and draw his attention to something a great deal more seductive than the preservation of his own life—the enrichment of it.

"What do you want?" Orlov demanded.

The American smoked silently, dark eyes flicking around the park with easy precision. He had some training. Orlov recognized the location of the park bench as strategic. There was nowhere within a hundred meters where a person could conceal themselves while observing the pair. Parabolic microphones and zoom lens cameras were still a threat.

But that was all part of the risk, and with great risk came great reward.

"We need you back inside," the American said. "Immediately."

"How deep inside?" Orlov asked.

"All the way."

Orlov squinted. The trepidation was completely gone now. He was physically hungry. He could *taste* the payout.

"That's going to be expensive," Orlov said.

"Name your price."

Orlov smiled. "That depends on what you want."

The American faced him. The smoke lowered. There was no amusement in his face, only blunt focus.

"We need to know what Nikitin is up to. Specifically, why he is meeting with Supreme Leader Kazemi and President Chen. We need to know what the content of their discussions are. And we need to know now."

Orlov snorted. "Not even the prime minister could tell you that."

"I'm not speaking to the prime minister. I'm not offering him a hundred thousand dollars, either."

Orlov flinched. He couldn't help it. He sat up a little. It was more money than Orlov ever imagined earning for a single job. Enough to live like a king in Russia...or on an island in the middle of nowhere. At least for a while.

But the taste of opportunity was still too strong. He couldn't resist pushing.

"A quarter million," Orlov said. "Or I don't budge."

"Done." The American didn't even blink. He stood, dropping the smoke and stamping it out. "But you deliver in forty-eight hours. The usual method. We'll be waiting, Blackjack."

The American turned away and Orlov shot another look around the park, checking again for that imaginary van. It was nowhere in sight.

He stood and turned back for the street, content to skip the bus and take a longer route home. Complete a more thorough SDR.

It was worth it now. Worth the time and effort. The next phase of his operation would be more difficult and riskier than any he had attempted before, but the adrenaline would be there to fuel him, the promise of riches waiting on the other side.

Mikhail Orlov could feel the money crinkling between his fingers, and it was more than enough to drive him back into the belly of the beast.

22

Goranboy District, Azerbaijan

Turk believed in crossroads moments. He always had. He knew his mother hit a crossroads moment when she chose narcotics to drown the suffering of losing her husband in war. Turk knew he faced a similar crossroads when he chose to drown that same suffering in the United States Marine Corps.

There was a crossroads when Turk failed to stop Reed from going vigilante on a group of raping murderers in Iraq. Another crossroads when he chose to marry Sinju and start a family. Now Turk again stood at a different sort of crossroads, triggered by his split-second decision to return fire and gun down the old man, Samir.

The wife had called the police. Who could blame her? The village in the valley near Samir and Zhara's country home was alive with blue lights and sirens. The military must have been alerted, also, because they had deployed a Cobra assault vehicle and four troops to the scene. From half a mile away Turk marked the activity of law enforcement and Azerbaijani soldiers only by their headlights. The rain was still pounding. Thunder rolled and occasional lightning flashed. Turk and Lucy had reached a hilltop and once again buried themselves in the woods...

At a crossroads.

Stepping back from the tree line, Turk wiped water from his face and looked back to Lucy. She stood squatted beneath a tree, shivering in the cold, auburn hair dripping water. Her lips moved but no sound came from them. She looked ready to drop, and Turk thought she likely was.

She might drop here. She might die in these hills, and there wasn't much he could do about it. That was all part of the crossroads. Turk had a decision to make. In or out, forward or flee. He could split for the Armenian border and hope to elude the Azerbaijani police, eventually reaching Turkey and hopefully contacting the CIA. He could tell himself he'd conducted his due diligence in notifying the agency of the situation with the bomb, and now it was time to save his own skin. He could even justify self-preservation under the guise of protecting Lucy.

But that would do nothing for Reed, Wolfgang, Ivan, Corbyn, or Strickland. If Turk closed his eyes he could picture their faces, and despite the overwhelming logical evidence that pointed to their deaths, he couldn't buy it.

His heart spoke otherwise. They were alive, and Turk knew they were in trouble. It was another logical judgment. Whoever escaped that overturned Russian Tigr would have fallen into Azerbaijani military hands...and Turk had a pretty good idea what would happen next.

So that was the choice. Left turn for freedom and survival, or right turn to do what Turk *knew* Reed Montgomery would do for him without a second thought.

No. It wasn't a crossroads, not really. Just like joining the USMC and marrying Sinju weren't really crossroads. Turk was a simple man who believed in simple virtues. Right over wrong, loyalty over selfishness, courage over fear. The call of duty was as undeniable to him as it had been for his father in Kuwait.

To hell with it all. There was no decision here.

Headed back into the trees, Turk took inventory of what supplies remained to him. First was the captured Zigana loaded with thirteen rounds of ammunition. He also had a pocketknife and two muddy boots. He had managed to hang on to the satellite phone as they fled the house, but he'd lost the charger. The device now carried only five percent battery life.

More problems.

Turk reached Lucy and knelt under the tree. He gave her arm a squeeze, shaking gently. "Lucy. Look at me."

Lucy's bright green eyes had dulled over the hours since the plane crash. She looked left and right but didn't face him. Turk squeezed again.

"Lucy, I need you to focus."

Still nothing. Lucy was like a zombie, conscious but completely unfocused. Turk forced himself to remain calm. He closed his eyes and breathed through his nose, long pulls like Sinju used during her yoga stretches. It helped to slow his heart rate and clear his mind. He put himself in the boots of the most competent person he knew—Reed Montgomery—and asked himself what his best friend would do. What would Reed say?

Turk opened his eyes. He dropped his tone to a flat bark. "LB. Look at me."

Lucy responded. Her eyes flicked upward, locking with Turk's. Vague recognition was followed by a frown of confusion. She didn't recognize him. His face didn't match the nickname that only Reed Montgomery ever used —letters that corresponded to Lucy's initials.

"Do you hear me?" Turk repeated, mimicking Reed's voice. "I need you to focus, LB."

Lucy's lips parted. She seemed to freeze. Then she nodded.

Turk smiled. "Good. So here's what we're going to do. I'm taking you to the next village. You're going to hide there. Stay undercover. Then I'm going to get Reed."

Lucy squinted. "Reed?"

Turk adjusted his plan. "I'm going to get the others. Wolfgang and Turk."

"Okay..."

"Be strong, LB. We're gonna get through this."

He stood over the soggy leaves and looked to the sky. Another flash of lightning played across black clouds but there were no visible stars, no moon. No way to map a course or determine direction.

He would simply head away from the village nearest Samir's house. Put the soldiers to his back and find a place to conceal Lucy. A barn or an abandoned house. Find some food and something to store rainwater in.

And then?

The question hung over his neck like the blade of a guillotine, because he didn't have an answer, only an objective.

Find Reed Montgomery. Find the team.

"Come on, LB," Turk said. "Time to roll."

Something soft and cold touched Turk's palm and he looked down. It was Lucy's hand, slid right into his, fingers wrapping tight and squeezing. She looked up and a little of the shine returned to her eyes.

"Fear no evil," Lucy whispered. "Fear no evil."

Turk returned the squeeze. He offered a confident nod he didn't quite feel. Then he led Lucy into the dark.

23

Capitol Hill
Washington, DC

Senator Matthew Roper of Iowa was a shark, and he could smell blood in the water from two-point-six miles away, at 1600 Pennsylvania Avenue. Standing in the middle of his sprawling senate office with the doors closed and the bustle of the capital building shut out, Roper's tie was torn loose and his jacket abandoned across the back of his desk chair. He faced the wall where a flat-screen TV played news reels of the same materials over and over again.

The bomb in Azerbaijan. The Russian presidential press conference. A feeble attempt of White House press secretary Farah Rahman to dismiss Nikitin's allegations as utter nonsense. Another day of spiraling on Wall Street while OPEC jacked up fuel prices. Heartbreak at the fallout of the Baton Rouge terror attacks, panic from sea to shining sea.

It was chaos, pure and simple. Catastrophe. America stood on the precipice of a third world war, and she knew it. But what Senator Matthew Roper, chairman of the senate select committee on intelligence, knew was that nobody could be feeling that pain more than the fractured Trousdale administration. With Maggie Trousdale herself slowly recovering from liver transplant surgery and acting president Jordan Stratton floundering to extinguish one wildfire after another...the writing was on the wall. America couldn't expect the White House to pull her through the fire. They were woefully underequipped and overwhelmed.

For Roper, that was the best news he'd heard in months.

The door opened, admitting a clatter of noise from the marble halls outside along with Roper's chief of staff, Jim White. A diminutive man with a face only a mother could love, White was overweight, balding, and showered so infrequently that Roper often had to evict him from his office on charges of body odor pollution. White was grimy. He was repulsive.

But much like Roper, White was a shark, and always had been. He loved nothing more than the taste of political bloodshed, and for that reason alone Roper would carry him right to the top, BO and all.

Roper waved a hand and White shoved the door closed. The noise dampened. Roper mashed the mute button on the television remote and actually chuckled. He couldn't help it.

"They're cooked, Jim. It's like a smoker turned down low. Just gonna keep chugging until it's time for dinner."

"Assuming we aren't nuked to death in the meantime." White's voice was a nasal whine, predictably cynical. It was another habit that annoyed Roper, but he couldn't deny that White was usually correct in his cynicism. Certainly, he'd been correct when he predicted that president-elect William Brandt would renege on his promise to grant Roper a cabinet position in exchange for his efforts on the campaign trail.

Brandt had indeed reneged, leaving Roper hanging out to dry. Three years later when Brandt's VP was dismissed in a cloud of corruption and disgrace, and Governor Maggie Trousdale of Louisiana was nominated to replace him, Roper had been the single member of the US Senate to vote against her confirmation. It was spite, nothing more. When Brandt was killed only weeks later and Trousdale took his place in the Oval Office, Roper almost regretted his decision to alienate the rookie executive.

Almost. It turned out that Trousdale was every bit as insufferable as Brandt—worse, perhaps. And she was also a lame duck with an expiration date printed across her forehead. The deluge of disaster that mired her presidency like axle-deep mud reinforced for Roper that he was right to distance himself.

Now Trousdale was crashing toward her second election cycle with enough baggage to crush an elephant. Even *if* she survived the transplant, she was damaged goods. The field was primed for another candidate—a strong, confident candidate with leadership experience—to fill the gap.

Somebody like, say...Senator Matthew Roper of Iowa.

"Relax, Jim. You think too much. Nikitin is just pushing the envelope, per usual. And who can blame him? The Trousdale admin is about as scary as a kitten with a ball of yarn."

Roper took his chair and popped a stick of gum into his mouth. The fragrance of spearmint helped to fight Jim's stench.

"Save the campaign talk, Senator," White scoffed, taking a seat across from him. "You've already got my vote."

Roper waggled a finger. "Now Mr. White, I'm sure I don't know what you're talking about. I'm fully focused on the business of the nation right now."

White rolled his eyes. "Listen, something's come up. An opportunity, perhaps. But we've got to be crazy careful with it, trust me. This one's molten hot."

Roper squinted. "What sort of opportunity?"

"Well, not so much an opportunity. More of a...line of inquiry."

"Explain."

"I was on the phone with Kirk Phelps. You know, congressman from—"

"Delaware, I know. Brown-nosing little punk. What about him?"

"Brown-noser's an understatement. The dude would flatter Adolph Hitler if he thought it would get him a free bratwurst, but people like that. Phelps hears things. Keeps his ear to the ground."

"So what did he hear?"

"Something from the Health Resources and Services Administration, actually. A little nugget about our friend James O'Dell."

That got Roper's attention. He ignored the BO, leaning across the desk. "What about him?"

"Seems O'Dell paid a visit to Director Nightcloud last week. Off the books, but the secretary—she's sleeping with one of Phelps's aides—claims that it was a confrontational meeting. Some shouting involved. It's all speculation, but the secretary thinks O'Dell was trying to pressure Nightcloud into manipulating the organ donor priority list. Giving the president a little bump, as it were."

"Did she?" Roper couldn't contain the anticipation in his voice.

White shook his head. "No. Doesn't look like it. I did some checking, the list was good. Trousdale received a transplant in order of priority."

"So...you have nothing."

"Nothing concrete. Just a curiosity. I got my hands on the donor file for Trousdale's liver. It was a guy from DC, some convicted sex offender who lived by himself. Dude offed himself with a handgun, blew his brains all across his couch. Six hours later, Trousdale is rolled into surgery."

Roper didn't bother to ask how White had gotten his hands on the police report detailing the suicide in question, let alone a highly confidential medical record detailing the identity of an organ donor. As a shark, White had his ways. It was best for Roper to know as little as possible.

"I still don't see the opportunity, Jim."

White twiddled his thumbs, staring at nothing in particular. Roper cleared his throat. White held up a hand.

"It's just an instinct."

"I need details, Jim."

"Well, remember how former CIA director Victor O'Brien was set to testify about alleged corruption within the Trousdale administration?"

"Of course I do. I was chairing the committee."

"And then he wound up dead..."

"Drowned in his swimming pool, drunk as a skunk."

"So says the police report."

"Right. And I spoke with Director Purcell at the FBI. Tried to spark a second investigation. It went nowhere. What's the point?"

"My point is, people seem to have a way of dying when it's most convenient for Maggie Trousdale. First a witness, then an organ donor? And right before that organ becomes available, James O'Dell, the president's longtime bodyguard and rumored lover is witnessed pressuring Nightcloud to bend the rules in Trousdale's favor. Sounds desperate, don't you think? Makes you wonder."

Roper squinted. He scratched a cheek and unpacked the puzzle...then slowly shook his head.

"It's thin, Jim."

"I know. Very thin. But my gut says there's something there—enough to take a deeper look. I want to hire that guy from Baltimore. The one with all the parrots."

"The PI?"

"Right. He's discreet. I'll have him start with this supposed suicide. Should be easier to dig into that than the O'Brien thing. If he could pin James O'Dell to the scene of that pervert's so-called suicide..."

Roper chewed the gum in silence for a full minute, and this time White didn't interrupt. At last Roper spit the wad into his trash and nodded.

"Proceed. But keep it quiet—dead quiet. This is the kind of thing that could easily fly back in my face."

White stood, unleashing another sour wave of BO as he did. "Have I ever let you down?"

White left the room, and Roper looked back to the TV, still kicked back in his chair. The broadcast was now reporting on the march of Iranian troops headed north toward Azerbaijan—tanks, light infantry. Everything Tehran needed to join the melee. For a moment it was enough to drown thoughts of James O'Dell and the prospect of skewering the Trousdale administration once and for all. Instead Roper couldn't help but picture the twin mushroom clouds that had broken the atmosphere in the past two weeks and wonder...

Would there *be* another election?

24

Somewhere in Azerbaijan

Strickland had stopped shouting. Reed wasn't sure when the change occurred, because the dehydration was getting to him. He was fading in and out of consciousness, with something that may have been a dream or a hallucination in between.

Reed saw Tennessee—which was strange, because if he was honest, he hated Tennessee. Not the state, just Nashville. All the concrete and tall buildings. The crowds and the cramped restaurants that Banks loved so much. Reed had never wanted to live there, but for an aspiring music artist like Banks, Nashville was the golden city of opportunity. The gateway to her dreams of performing glory.

Maybe that was *why* Reed saw the twin-spired "Bat Tower" when he closed his eyes. The winding Cumberland River. Nissan Stadium. It wasn't *his* place, not in and of itself. But it was the place where Banks was, the woman he would give anything in the world to hold just one more time.

He remembered storming out on her. Remembered avoiding her calls. Remembered the blanket of debilitating depression that consumed his mind and left him unable or perhaps unwilling to answer her pleas for emotional connection and open communication. It was like a drug state. An all-consuming sensation that had mired his brain in enough concrete to prevent any chance of unravelling the psychotic mess that was his life.

It was all his fault. Of course it was. The marriage trouble, his inability to interact with his own son, his difficulty in enjoying all the glitz and glamour of a thriving American metropolis. Call it PTSD or just a wrecked sense of self...did it even matter?

Now he was here. When he opened his eyes he saw blackness. The tormentors had left, leaving the lights off. Reed still swung from the chains, feet inches off the floor. The heavy cap was back on his head, forcing his chin down. His arms ached so badly they didn't ache at all. He couldn't feel a thing. It was all a blur of flashing, spinning illusion.

Was he even awake?

"Are you with us, Prosecutor?"

Ivan Sidorov's voice rasped from down the hallway, so dry it was difficult for Reed to discern the words. Or maybe that was simply his blood-clogged ears—they were both stopped up thanks to a face-beating by one of the Azerbaijani thugs sent to interrogate him. If he worked his jaw the blood cracked and crumbled, some falling out of his ear, most remaining in place.

"I'm here," Reed whispered.

Ivan coughed, and from down the hallway somebody moaned softly. It might have been Corbyn. Reed still couldn't hear Strickland, and that worried him. He couldn't recall exactly what his last memory of the pilot was. He thought, maybe...Strickland was singing. Yes. That sounded right. "America the Beautiful," wasn't it? Screamed like a heavy metal song, broken by laughs and shrieks so morphed together that they sounded the same.

"Strickland!" Reed coughed, fighting to twist his face toward the general direction of the door.

No answer.

"Strick!" Reed called again.

"He is gone, Prosecutor," Ivan said. "He went out like roaring Russian bear. The motherland would have been proud."

Reed blinked, eyes burning. He gritted his teeth and felt the pain again, ripping through his shoulders and down his spine. Almost overwhelming.

Spitting more blood out of his mouth, he shook the chains, struggling to find solid footing. It was useless. He'd been hoisted too high off the ground.

"Save your strength," Ivan counseled. "This is not over."

Not over. Reed couldn't imagine much more. Not because he couldn't handle it, but because the Azerbaijanis seemed to be losing patience. He remembered that. They beat him harder, screaming questions loud. Getting flustered and reckless.

"They are amateurs at this," Ivan said, as though he had detected Reed's thoughts. "They apply too much pain and not enough time. The body shuts down. It is easier to resist this way. They should slow down."

"Sage advice," Reed croaked. "Any for me?"

That brought out a dry chuckle, then a horrific racking cough. The prison grew quiet again. Reed licked his lips and croaked: "Wolf?"

Long pause. Reed repeated the call.

"Here." The voice was distant and weak, but it brought a little warmth to Reed's blood.

"Corbyn?"

"Here." Corbyn's voice was different than Wolfgang's. Not just weak, but sort of broken. It sounded as though she were speaking through a waterfall. Perhaps she was crying.

"Strickland?" Reed tried again.

No answer. The prison drifted into bitter silence, and Reed fought to lift his head against the weight crushing down on his skull. It was a superhuman effort. He managed only an inch, then gave up, winded again.

Seconds passed into a minute, or maybe an hour. Reed closed his eyes and thought of Nashville and how he would have traded both legs to be back there again. Not to stay...he didn't deserve to stay.

Just to hold Banks one final time. To say how sorry he was. To make it right.

"Do you think..." Ivan began, then broke off. He coughed again. "Do you think the big guy made the call?"

Reed's eyes opened. He thought of Turk and Lucy, rushing out of that valley as the Azerbaijanis closed in. A last hope of contacting Washington with intelligence that would contradict Makar Nikitin's outlandish accusations—and maybe, just maybe...trigger a rescue effort.

"If I know him at all," Reed whispered, "Turk will find a way."

25

Langley, Virginia

Deputy Director Silas Rigby was finally calling it quits. After a forty-three-hour shift punctuated by catnaps on the couch in his office, he was past due to check in at his Arlington apartment. Cleves, the thirteen-year-old tabby cat who had been his companion since senior year of college, was well cared for by a neighbor who kept more routine hours, but Rigby still wanted to check up on him.

Even more, he wanted to check up on a hot shower, a TV dinner, and at least six hours of sleep in his own bed. With luck, he could slip in quietly without alerting Anne—the generous neighbor who looked after Cleves. Rigby suspected that Anne had a crush on him, and if he had anything resembling a personal life, he wouldn't have minded. She was cute and made him laugh, even if she talked a little too much.

But with radiation spreading across two continents, luxuries such as romance felt like a distant fantasy at best. He'd be content with the TV dinner and the shower. Cleves was companion enough.

Rigby grabbed his jacket from the back of his chair and steered his mouse toward the computer's power menu. A full shut-down, per security protocol. His cursor had just opened the correct menu when the familiar chime of an incoming email burst through the computer speakers. Rigby winced and almost clicked the mouse anyway. One more email could wait.

At least, that was his rationale until the preview banner popped across the top right-hand corner of his screen, announcing the sender and a subject line. It was from one of his deputies, specifically the officer in charge of the civilian-facing division of the CIA responsible for gathering tips from the general public. The subject line read *Azerbaijan Daily*, which meant the email would contain a summary of all civilian tips gathered from the tip line throughout the day.

There might be a dozen, or there might be a few hundred. Typically, Rigby wouldn't review any of them as a matter of logistical necessity. He didn't have the time. But the moment the bomb detonated in Azerbaijan, Rigby had directed his deputy to send him a daily summary of all tips collected from that part of the world, with highlights to mark anything that might actually represent usable intelligence.

It was clutter, mostly. A waste of time. But Rigby had learned the hard way that the smallest details, observed by the most unlikely informants, could change the entire tide of a complex operation. It was his job to manage those operations.

Therefore, it was his job to review the intelligence...even when he was overdue for a shower and longing for his own bed.

Rigby settled back into the chair and opened the email. The structure was exactly the same as the previous three days, which made it simpler for him to review. His eye caught on a few highlighted items. Most were reports from distant, unproven CIA informants who were very early on in the grooming process. The content of their reports was simplistic and generally things the CIA already knew—troop movements, reserves being called into action, etcetera. Nothing game changing.

Rigby reached the bottom of the report and breathed an unconscious sigh of relief that nothing would keep him for another hour in his grimy clothes. He scrolled back up, ready to close out of his email.

Then he stopped. Something caught his eye—a seven-letter word amid a three-line paragraph. A meaningless report the deputy hadn't even seen the need to highlight, even though it came directly from Azerbaijan. The word was *Turkman*, and the moment Rigby saw it, his heart leapt. He scanned to the top and read quickly.

0947 EST, INBOUND PHONE CALL, NUMBER UNKNOWN. SPEAKER, IDENTIFYING AS "TURKMAN," CLAIMS TO BE AGENCY OPERATIVE STRANDED IN AZERBAIJAN. NO IDENTIFYING ID NUMBER OR CODE. CALL RULED ILLEGITIMATE.

Rigby had barely finished reading before he was snatching up the phone, speed-dialing the deputy. He could tell by her sleepy voice that she was in a similar mode as himself, ready to clock out, but she answered.

"Sir?"

"Entry number eighteen. Who took this call?"

Brief pause. The shuffle of papers and the clack of a keyboard.

"Uhm...civilian call line...looks like it was an R. Spielman."

"Do we have any other details?"

"Just what I sent you. It was a short call. I can send you the recording."

"Do it. *Now*."

Rigby hung up. The next email arrived four minutes later. He pressed play on the file. The connection was distant and distorted, but the voice was impossible to misidentify. Rigby had never met the speaker—not in person—but he'd listened in on plenty of phone calls.

He knew *exactly* who spoke from the other side of the world.

"Rufus Turkman. Look, I don't have time to explain. I need—"

"What's your officer ID?" The CIA phone agent cut Turkman off.

"I don't have an officer ID. Didn't you hear me? I work for SAC. I'm off the books. I need to speak with—"

"I'm sorry, sir. If you worked for SAC you'd have a direct contact line and an agent ID."

Rigby gritted his teeth, overwhelming frustration crashing over his body in a tidal wave. The phone agent's response was perfectly logical. Completely expected. Per protocol, in fact.

But it was wrong—completely wrong. Rufus Turkman didn't have an ID because Rufus Turkman did not exist. Not even to the knowledge of most of the Special Activities Division. The entire existence of the Prosecution Force was so secret that Rigby's own deputies didn't know the names *Reed Montgomery* or *Rufus Turkman*.

Another logical decision...but now it was costing Rigby.

Punching out a quick pair of commands—one to print the original email, the other to forward the call recording—Rigby snatched the printout from his desktop printer and exploded out of the chair. Ten seconds later he was on the other side of the executive floor, barging through Director Aimes's glass door as she beckoned him in. She was halfway through the recording he had forwarded, face flushing red. She smacked the space bar to pause the audio.

"They're *alive*," Rigby said.

"Do we have a contact? Some way to call back?" Aimes demanded.

Rigby stopped at her desk. He held up the printout, shaking it triumphantly.

"We've got a sat phone number."

26

Goranboy District, Azerbaijan

The house was really more of a hut—maybe a fishing cabin from a bygone era now long abandoned to the moss and rot of crushing time. Situated a half mile off the road overlooking a small lake, Turk found it by raw instinct, marking a sunken roadbed visible only as a vague impression leading off an Azerbaijani two-lane and into the hills. He followed that roadbed with Lucy riding on his back, fighting through brush and drifts of rotting leaves before he finally reached a speck of a clearing with the one-room cabin slouching in the middle.

The roof was metal and rusted. The walls constructed of rotting lapboards with a window blown out. The door was locked, but a single application of Turk's boot busted it open. Inside he found creaking wood floors and two empty cabinets. A pair of chairs standing next to a dusty table, and two twin-sized beds parked in the rear, mattresses full of rat holes.

There was no food in the cabinet, just a few filthy dishes. The sink faucet squeaked when he turned it on, and no water came out. Even when he closed the door, wind still continued to whistle through the busted frame.

But for all that, the cabin was the best place Turk had found to park Lucy since fleeing Samir and Zahra's house. It was mostly dry, and safely out of sight.

It would have to do.

"Sit here," Turk said, settling Lucy into one of the chairs. It creaked. She wrapped her arms around herself and glanced around the room, sharp eyes examining every detail before returning to Turk.

Lucy was coming back—Turk could feel it. Progress was agonizingly slow, but she now made easy eye contact, and the whispered repetitions of the twenty-third Psalm had faded away. She still didn't seem to know where she was, but somehow she felt...calmer.

"Wait here," Turk said, holding up a finger. Lucy nodded, and he departed the cabin. Back down the sunken roadbed, a mile down the two-lane to an apple orchard he'd observed during their trek. He vaulted the fence and landed amid knee-high grass, searching amid the trees for late summer fruit. It appeared that a harvest had recently taken place, because most of the apples were gone, and many lay crushed by heavy tires at the base of the trees. After twenty minutes Turk had filled the tail of his shirt with three dozen survivors, and he turned back to the cabin, consuming four along the way.

Dumping the fruit across the table, Turk wiped an apple clean with his shirt tail, then offered it to Lucy. She hesitated a moment, seeming perplexed. He made a chomping expression and extended the apple again.

Then it clicked. Lucy snatched the fruit and sank her teeth into it. Juice dripped down her chin as she devoured it, munching right down to the core and immediately reaching for a second.

Turk left her with her dinner and turned his attention to his pockets, sifting through the contents as he struggled for the next step in his plan. The sat phone was down to two percent battery life, and without the phone charger or an outlet to plug it into, he would be without communication altogether in the very near future.

The only other items that remained were his pocketknife and the Zigana 9mm in his waistband—the weapon that had slain Samir.

Turk ran his hands through his hair, squeegeeing out water and taking a different sort of inventory.

Next steps. Leaving Lucy in the cabin with the apples, he would head toward the next settlement and...what? Interrogate random soldiers? Turk had done so before, in Iraq, and knew exactly what a waste of time that sort of strategy could be. Low-level soldiers almost never know anything useful, and besides, Turk didn't speak any more Azerbaijani than he had when he first arrived in this place.

So how to find Reed? How to plan an extraction?

Stress boiled up in his chest, as hot and searing as before. He rolled the pocketknife in his hand and backtracked to the beginning, to the moment the Azerbaijani military overwhelmed the Prosecution Force.

They're dead, Turk. They're dead and you know it.

The thought cracked through his brain and he drove a fist into his leg. Lucy looked up from her fourth apple but didn't say anything. Turk closed his eyes and focused on his breathing.

He couldn't leave. Not until he knew for sure. It wasn't even an option. So how to know for sure? Maybe he should call the CIA again. Try the public access line...

The chime broke his focus. A harsh trill from the satellite phone as it vibrated in his lap. Turk's eyes snapped up and he lifted the device, scanning the tiny LCD screen. There was no caller ID, just a long phone number he didn't recognize. Country code: USA.

Looking instinctively toward Lucy, Turk opened his mouth but wasn't sure what to say. Lucy didn't say anything either. She just sat with a half-eaten apple in one hand, juice dripping off her chin. Turk made a gut call and mashed the green button.

"Hello?"

The connection was distant and distorted. At first Turk heard nothing. Then a voice he recognized reached out to him from the other side of the planet.

"Turk? Is that you?"

Turk sat bolt upright, his fingers tightening with it around the phone. "Director?"

"Don't say my name," Aimes said. "This line isn't secure. We got your message."

Turk's mind wound quickly backward to Samir's house and his frantic call with the useless CIA phone agent. It had only been a few hours prior, but it felt like days. Already he couldn't remember what he had said.

Better to say it all again, straight from the top.

"This phone's about to die," Turk said. "Listen carefully. The Russians are responsible for the bomb. They trucked a nuke out of Georgia and into Azerbaijan. We intercepted them, but it was too late to stop the blast. The device was marked as American, stamped with an American flag and *USA*."

"You saw them deliver it? In person?"

"Affirmative. Russian Alpha Group—a dozen of them."

"Are they..."

"Dead."

"Right. Okay."

Turk shifted the phone to his opposite ear. He'd indulged Aimes long enough. "I need help. The team was fractured. Reed, Wolf, the others—they all fell into Azerbaijani hands. We need to find them, *now*."

"Hold on, Turk. Slow down. Where are you?"

"I don't know. Someplace in northwestern Azerbaijan. I can't read the signs."

"That's okay. We'll trace this call. Are you alone?"

"I've got Lucy. She's badly shell-shocked. She needs medical. I need QRF, whatever you've got. I need an extraction plan and a strike team. I need you to *find* Reed."

Long pause.

Turk's blood boiled. "Are you hearing me?"

"That may not be possible, Turk. You've got a war erupting about a hundred miles north of you, and the Iranians are deploying toward southern Azerbaijan. You're at ground zero. We'll do what we can to get you out, but—"

"I didn't *ask you* to get me out! I asked you for QRF and Reed's location. Are you freaking hearing me?"

Turk's voice rose to a shout. Lucy sat bolt upright and didn't blink. When Aimes returned to the phone her voice was as placid as ever.

"I heard you, Turk. Now I'm communicating the realities of the situation. I don't have a genie in a bottle. I—"

"Then you better *find one*, dammit! You shipped our butts over here to do your dirty work, and now we're up the creek without a paddle. This is my *team*. Do you understand me? My *team*. I don't give a rat's ass about your realities. If you want another *scrap* of intelligence out of this hellhole, you better find Reed. Do you understand? *Find him*."

Another long pause. Turk's heart hammered. Then Aimes spoke six simple words. "Stay put. I'll call you back."

The call cut off, and Turk slammed the phone into his leg. He ran both hands through his hair and stared at the floor, feeling just as helpless as the ants crawling slowly toward Lucy's fallen apple cores.

Scrambling for the prize...and hopelessly out of reach.

27

Zagulba Palace
Baku, Azerbaijan

President Elchin Rzayev finally made contact with Moscow at 1:13 a.m., local time. To be more accurate, it was Moscow who made contact with him. Baku had reached out to the Kremlin dozens of times since the bomb detonated, and had received no response. As Russian troops massed at the Red Bridge border crossing and Azerbaijani defense forces rushed north to confront them, Rzayev's perspective of Moscow's intentions grew irreversibly darker.

He'd never trusted Nikitin. Despite the greasy warmth the Russian president projected as he worked to "rebuild" the bridges burned by his predecessor, Rzayev smelled a snake. He expected a double cross.

He just never expected *this*. A nuclear blast and a gathering Russian army breathing down his neck.

"Mr. President, I have President Nikitin on the line."

"Put him through," Rzayev barked, guzzling coffee. He hadn't slept in nearly two days, and he knew the fatigue was catching up with him, but he didn't actually feel sleepy. How could he? The future of his entire nation hung in the balance.

"Elchin, good morning." Nikitin's voice was smooth and relaxed, not at all reflective of the desperate situation boiling between the two men. It was enough for Rzayev to slam his coffee cup down.

"Makar! What the hell are you doing? We have called all day. Your embassy has stonewalled—"

"I must apologize for the delay," Nikitin said. "We were sidetracked with security measures, as I'm sure you can imagine. Such a tragedy erupting so close to our borders—"

"You were not too sidetracked to hold a press conference, Makar! Not too sidetracked to deploy a full *army* to our borders and send Russian war planes into *our* sovereign airspace."

"Yes, about that. I'm glad you mention the planes. I must confess I am deeply disappointed in you, Elchin. Those aircraft were deployed to intercept the American weapon headed south into your country. I would have thought after so many years of mutual trust that you would have hesitated before murdering my pilots."

"Hesitated?" Rzayev couldn't believe his own ears. "You are committing acts of *war*, Makar. We responded accordingly, and we will continue to do so. Whatever game you are playing, I swear if you move so much as one boot across Red Bridge, we will *annihilate you*. Do you understand me?"

Nikitin didn't answer. Rzayev's heart hammered so loudly in his own ears that he couldn't be sure, but he thought the Russian president was sipping tea. When Nikitin at last spoke again, his voice was as calm as ever.

"Precautions, Elchin. Nothing but precautions. The security of the region is our top priority, which includes your security, of course. My men will not proceed south of Red Bridge. Not unless you call for assistance."

"Call for assistance? How about I call for a retreat? If you are Azerbaijan's friend, withdraw your troops. We are not under duress. We do not require assistance!"

"Elchin, be reasonable. Your country is the victim of a nuclear attack. The Americans are conspiring to bring division and chaos to the region. We must not fall victim to their manipulations."

Rzayev's blood boiled. "Manipulations? I find it difficult to concern myself about the monster on the other side of the planet when there is a monster breathing down my neck. If you want to accuse the Americans of bombing us, we require proof."

A theatric sigh. "Very well. Of course we have proof. I wanted to speak with my allies before dropping the bomb but—I'm sorry. That was a terrible metaphor. If you so desire, we will release our evidence."

"I *do* desire. Immediately."

"Very well. I'll make it so. And Elchin?"

"*What?*"

"I am your friend, even if you do not see it. I pray that someday you will."

Makar Nikitin hung up the phone and sat for a while, staring at it. The office around him was perfectly silent, even though he was not alone. His right-hand man, the so-called *Ghost of the Kremlin*, Anton Golubev, sat across from him. Recently returned from the front lines, it was Golubev who had overseen the successful—and almost overnight—occupation of Georgia. In context of the sprawling, mired Ukraine conflict, the seizure of Georgia felt like a fever dream.

That was the difference between brute force and venomous cunning.

"Did he mention Iran?" Golubev asked.

Nikitin shook his head. "Not once. The man is blinded by our movements. The Iranians will be on his southern border before he even knows what's happening."

Golubev grunted, but neither man celebrated. It was still much too early. The stage was set, yes, and the actors in position. The script rehearsed and perfected to every last detail. The supporting cast on standby, ready to follow Moscow's lead.

And yet...

"What is it, Makar?"

Golubev was one of the few in Nikitin's cabinet who ever addressed him by first name, a mark of their extensive history clawing their way from the ashes of the Soviet Union to the very heights of Russian federal power.

And now, the *next* empire. Not a soviet one. But an iron one.

"We are missing something," Nikitin said. "Something very small. I can sense it."

Golubev bunched his lips. The two men sat in silence for several minutes. Then Nikitin shook his head.

"It is no matter. The show must go on. Rzayev is demanding the release of our evidence concerning the bomb."

"Right on schedule," Golubev said. "Should I give the order?"

"Yes. Publicize the files. But let's make it a one-two punch...knock the Americans off balance just a little more."

"What did you have in mind?"

"The Chinese," Nikitin said. "It's time for our squinty-eyed friends to put some skin in the game. Tell them to push a button—whatever button they please. Enough to shake Washington."

Golubev stood. At last he smiled.

"We are here, Makar."

Nikitin looked up. Slowly, he returned the smile. "Yes...we are. At last."

28

Langley, Virginia

Rigby never escaped Langley. From the moment he and Aimes hung up with Turk, the crushing gears of the CIA dragged him back into another endless shift. Phone calls were made. Rigby tasked an investigative team to tap all available Azerbaijani intel outlets and search for the captured American operatives. For an hour he sprinted back and forth between his office and Aimes's, mining every available resource in search of a single scrap of evidence which could substantiate Rufus Turkman's outlandish claim—that Russia herself was behind the bomb.

"Do you believe it?" Rigby asked.

Aimes was poring over a series of satellite photographs taken of Azerbaijan in the moments preceding the nuclear bomb. There had been air activity in the region during that time. A plane—likely the SAC jet she had originally deployed the Prosecution Force on—had gone down. There was a fire. Indications of a gunfight, which supported Turk's narrative.

But no proof of Russians. The photographs were far too blurry.

"I know *we* didn't do it," Aimes said. "Have you heard back from any of our Baku plants? What are the Azerbaijanis thinking?"

"I'm still waiting for an update," Rigby said. "It's chaos over there. We may need to be patient."

Before Aimes could answer, her phone rang. She mashed the speaker button. "Yes?"

"Ma'am, I have the State Department on the line for you. Secretary Gorman is requesting a brief call."

Aimes's gaze locked with Rigby's. They both frowned.

"Gorman? Now?"

"Yes, ma'am."

"Put her through."

Aimes shifted the photographs aside and motioned for Rigby to shut her office door. She left the phone on speaker mode.

"Good evening, Secretary. What can I do for you?"

"Director, I'm sorry to call at this hour. I just got off the phone with the Russian embassy. Their ambassador is announcing the release of Russian intelligence files concerning the Azerbaijan bomb. The *proof*, he called it."

"Proof of Nikitin's claims?" Aimes asked.

"So he says. I've only just begun to review the files myself. I thought you'd want a look."

"Very much so. Thank you."

Aimes reached to end the call. Gorman caught her first. "Director."

"Yes?"

Gorman's voice lowered. Rigby leaned in to listen.

"We aren't the only ones the Russians are disseminating this information to. They're broadcasting it to all of our allies, and they're threatening to curtail diplomatic relations if we don't...explain ourselves, I guess. I don't think I have to tell you what a precarious position this puts us in."

"What are you asking me, Madam Secretary?" Aimes had a pretty good idea. She wanted Gorman to say it.

"I'm asking if we have any vulnerabilities, Director. Anything at all which I should know about before I try to confront this mess. And if it's all a scam, then I'm asking for proof. As rapidly as humanly possible."

"I understand. There's nothing that comes to mind. As General Yellin stated in the cabinet meeting, America does not manufacture this size of nuclear weapon. It's not even possible for it to be ours."

A brief pause. "Very well. In that case I hope the agency will be able to disprove Russia's claims."

"It's difficult to prove a negative, Secretary, but we're working on it. As fast as humanly possible."

Aimes terminated the call and Rigby circled her desk without waiting for an invitation. She opened Gorman's email, and after jumping through the necessary cybersecurity hoops, she accessed the attached file. Rigby found himself holding his breath.

The contents were written in English, but that hardly mattered, because most of those contents were photographs, not text. They depicted grainy, surveillance-style footage of a cargo ship offloading a crate. The location was printed as Sochi, Russia, just north of the Georgian border. The ship was the *Ocean Titan*, an American-flagged container vessel registered to Portland, Maine.

The photographs played like frames in a comic strip. The crate left the port and was followed by various security cameras across Sochi. It entered a warehouse and disappeared. Several hours later, per the time stamps, a truck rolled out with vague shadows of men seated behind the wheel. The plate was clearly visible and was traced south into Georgia exactly thirty-two hours before the Russian invasion.

The camera views continued. Toll booths. Security checkpoints. The crate wound southeast to Kutaisi. It was there, according to supporting notes, that a security inspection was finally conducted. The next photographs were in full color, supplied by the Georgian government.

One wall of the crate was removed. A large, stainless steel box was exposed, nondescript in appearance, with the American flag and the letters *USA* stamped into it. According to the file, the Georgians classified the cargo as "machinist's equipment." Then the truck was released. Hours passed as the Russian invasion of Georgia consumed Tbilisi.

Then one final photo—the same truck, the same plate, time stamped for only hours before the Azerbaijani bomb blast. Chugging southward, passing through another toll booth. Pointed toward Red Bridge.

"This is unbelievable," Aimes muttered.

"It's..."

"Way too clear," Aimes finished.

"*Way* too clear," Rigby echoed. "It's like a storyboard, start to finish. Security cameras at every angle, just happening to catch the license plate and direction of travel. Not once in my career have I seen an intelligence file this complete."

"It's fabricated," Aimes said. "Every bit of it. If Turkman is right, the Russians put that crate on that ship for the very purpose of crafting this narrative. They took the photos themselves, including that absurd shot from the Georgian security inspection."

"Some security inspection," Rigby said. "They open the crate and snap a picture, but never bother to determine the actual contents?"

"It's phony," Aimes said. "But it's also an impossible point to prove with Tbilisi under Russian control. The Georgians can't even locate their own president."

Rigby withdrew from behind the desk. He rubbed his eyes, fighting to focus his mind. The weariness was getting to him. Thoughts he knew should be simple were requiring Herculean effort to process. One glance at Aimes, and he knew his boss was experiencing the same deadlock.

What does this mean?

"We need hard proof of Turkman's claims," Rigby said. "It's the only way we can wiggle our way out of this. Britain and Israel may never actually believe that we planted a bomb over there, but crap like this could be convincing to the fence riders."

"India," Aimes said. "Brazil. China and Iran. Skeptics and rivals Russia can manipulate."

"Exactly," Rigby said. "And they will. One hundred percent."

Already Aimes was reaching for the phone.

The sat phone rang for the second time two hours after the first. Turk snatched it up, conscious of the battery life displaying an ominous one percent. The device sipped power while on standby, which was a miracle, but he knew the battery would drain quickly while conducting a call.

This had to be quick.

"Hello?"

"Turk, it's me." Aimes's voice was clearly recognizable, and she made no further effort to clarify her identity. "I need you to listen closely. We—"

"Where's Reed?" Turk demanded. "Did you find Reed?"

"No. Not yet. We're working on it. Now I need you to listen. We've received evidence from the Russians that the bomb in Azerbaijan was one of our own. So they claim. I know you said—"

"Russian Alphas," Turk growled. "I told you. A dozen of them in a truck."

"Right. And we believe you. But we need proof—yesterday."

Turk squinted. The exhaustion and hunger were playing tricks on his mind, but he thought he understood where this conversation was headed, and he could barely believe it. Anger boiled in his stomach, and his fist closed over the top of the table where Lucy still sat.

"*Reed Montgomery*, Aimes. *Kirsten Corbyn, Wolfgang Pierce, Ivan Sidorov, Kyle Strickland*. That's what I need to be hearing from you, right now!"

"Don't use my name, Turk."

"What name? Dr. Sarah Aimes, Director of the Central Intelligence Agency? *That name*?"

Dead silence. Turk kicked his chair back, rising to his feet.

"You listen to me, you paper-pushing bureaucrat. If you want evidence, you *find my team*. Do you understand me? I couldn't care less what Russia is up to. That's *your* problem. You want my help, help me. Okay?"

Another lengthy pause. Turk pulled the sat phone away from his ear, half expecting that Aimes could have hung up.

Not yet. The call log ticked on, a minute twenty and counting.

He returned the phone to his ear. He breathed a little more evenly. "Please. I'm begging you. I need you as bad as you need me."

"We're going to locate your team, Mr. Turkman. We're working on it now. But we need you to meet us halfway. If Russia is able to convince the world of a lie, that's the predicate to World War Three. Do you understand? We won't count bodies by the thousands, or the millions. We'll count them by the *tens* of millions."

Turk gritted his teeth. He understood what Aimes was saying. He simply couldn't afford to care. He couldn't turn back the clock and somehow prove what he already knew to be true. Aimes was asking for a silver bullet that simply didn't exist.

But if she believed it existed...

"Reed took pictures," Turk said. The lie burned as it left his lips, but he didn't stutter. He pressed on. "Just before the bomb went off, while it was in the truck. Reed took photos. There were Russian Alphas there. We interrogated the driver. There's a video."

He stopped short of detailing a bloody confession. It might be a bridge too far for Aimes to believe. Maybe he'd already gone too far.

"Where are the files?" Aimes asked.

"Reed has them."

Silence filled the line. Turk waited.

"Are you lying to me, Mr. Turkman?"

Turk opened his mouth. He stopped. Then: "So what if I am? Your options are the same. Reed Montgomery is a witness. Every member of my team is a witness, and I swear to you, if you help me get them out, we'll find your evidence. Whatever it takes. Okay?"

Turk looked to Lucy. She was fixated on him, huddled in her chair next to a pile of apple cores. She didn't speak. She didn't so much as blink. But there was recognition in her eyes. Understanding.

"Stand by," Aimes said. "I'll get you a location."

Then she hung up.

29

USS Sampson
Arleigh Burke Class Guided Missile Destroyer
Taiwan Strait, South China Sea

It was a hot night. The sun had set late in the day, sinking over China as *Sampson* made her way south from US Fleet Activities Sasebo, on the Japanese island of Kyūshū, toward that 108-kilometer sliver of water running between the western shore of the Republic of China and the eastern shore of the *People's* Republic of China. It was a one-word differentiation that made all the difference in the world, and this was far from Petty Officer Third Class Herbert Walter's first trip through the strait. During his eighteen-month assignment as a culinary specialist aboard the *Sampson*, Walter had often stood aboard the starboard deck of the 509-foot destroyer and enjoyed a cup of black coffee while facing westward, not nearly close enough to the Chinese coast to see it, but easily able to imagine it.

Even though the entire purpose of *Sampson*'s presence in the strait was that of signaling America's stalwart commitment of defending ROC independence, Walter had never felt the tension in this place. In fact, it was one of the more peaceful spots the Navy had ever taken him, at least in principle. Hot, yes, but Walter liked to be hot. It reminded him of his hometown of Biloxi, where beautiful Rose and their newborn son, Herbert Jr., anticipated a Christmas reunion. Walter had yet to meet his son. The video calls and the snapshots were all that kept him connected to what felt like another world, so far away Walter had to keep promising himself that it was real.

Even so, it was an honor to serve his country. Serving it in a place such as the South China Sea, where the mission of displaying naval power was so clearly important, inflamed his natural patriotism. He knew there was chaos back home, both from terror attacks and now from the instability overseas.

No doubt China knew about that chaos and instability, also. Maybe they would use it as an opportunity to test the resilience of the most powerful navy the world had ever known. If so, they would find a crew of disciplined sailors aboard the USS *Sampson* only too happy to respond—well fed with the grub from Walter's galley.

Slurping coffee, Walter enjoyed the burn in his throat as a hot breeze tugged against his fatigues. From the aft deck of the *Sampson* he looked dead westward, his back to the ROC, his face toward the PROC. It was too far away to make out any lights along China's southeastern shore, but Walter knew they were there. He wondered if young families waited in small apartments for men like him to return from their own deployments.

A different nation, a completely inverted set of values. But the same dance.

"Nice evening, eh, Walter?"

The voice rang from over his left shoulder. Walter straightened instinctively, falling into attention as the *Sampson*'s skipper, Commander John Ulysses, appeared out of the darkness, his own coffee mug in hand.

"At ease, Walter. I'm just taking in the view."

Walter relaxed—a little. He knew Ulysses better than most, having served from time to time in the officer's mess on fill-in duty. The skipper was an amiable fellow by all reports. Strict, but not overbearing. The men liked him. *Sampson* ran well under his command.

Stepping to the railing, Ulysses drank coffee and sighed. For a while neither man spoke, just facing west toward China. Maybe thinking the same things. Maybe thinking about nothing related. Walter's thoughts drifted toward his son...and Rose.

Christmas. One hundred thirty-two days away...and counting down.

"They're watching us, you know," Ulysses said.

Walter squinted. "Begging your pardon, sir?"

Ulysses gestured with his mug. "The Chicoms. Every vessel that passes through the strait, they've got their eyes on it. Even had an attack sub trailing us earlier today. Stupid thing was rattling and clanking so loud we could hear it coming from ten miles away."

Ulysses laughed. Walter studied the skipper's eyes and noted that the mirth didn't reach them. He looked...strained.

"It's important, what we're doing here," Ulysses said, turning to Walter. "We're the tip of the spear, you know. First line of defense."

"Aye, Commander."

Ulysses lifted his mug. Both men drank. Ulysses yawned.

"Well, I'm gonna get some shut-eye. Thanks for everything, Walter. I hear good reports about you. They say you fry a hell of a pork chop."

Walter grinned—both because it was true and because he never tired of hearing it. "Thank you, sir."

Ulysses stepped off, and Walter looked back to the sky. He raised his coffee, thinking of the pork chops he would cook for Herbert Jr. and Rose that Christmas. He swallowed bitter black. He saw the glint on the horizon—so far away he thought it was a star, at first. Then an illusion.

What happened next was anything but an illusion. A piercing whistle rent the air, so loud and shrill it would have brought a grown man out of a coma. Walter's face snapped toward the bridge on instinct as the whistle rose, then fell. A split second later a voice barked through the ship's public address system.

"*General quarters! General quarters!* All hands, man your battle stations. Set material condition *zebra* throughout the ship."

The voice cut off and Walter's heart slammed inside his chest. The coffee fell to the deck and shattered as *Sampson* swung into an aggressive right turn, bow slamming through the waves on its way westward. Walter slipped and caught himself on the railing, fighting back to his feet. The whistle repeated and the commands followed it. He found his footing, and then he was running forward. Down through a hatch, sliding along the handrails with his heels held up. Through one watertight door after another, the metal rooms surrounding him an endless din of shouting voices and pounding feet.

He was headed for the galley. No longer as a cook but now as a member of the *Sampson*'s standby damage control team. Specifically, Walter was a member of a firefighting team. The moment he reached the galley he would be tugging on fire clothes and unwrapping hose. A self-contained breathing apparatus—SCBA—would prepare him to charge into any corner of the ship, ready to extinguish flame the moment it erupted.

All that was muscle memory. He didn't even have to think about it. Instead his mind was frozen on his last memory before the general quarters alarm shattered the night—that flash of light over the horizon.

What?

Walter reached the galley and broke through the door just as eardrum-busting thunder exploded from someplace overhead. It was a snarl, perfectly endless, a vibration that ripped down the length of the ship as a Phalanx CIWS close-in weapon system opened fire on an invisible target, dumping fifty rounds a second. Walter covered his ears and staggered, again picturing that flash, and this time understanding.

Missile. It was a missile.

"Walter! *Battle stations!*"

The voice broke through the din of the Phalanx and Walter's eyes snapped open. His chief petty officer stood three paces away, already dressed in fire-retardant gear, pulling hose from a wall closet. He beckoned. Walter's mouth fell open and he staggered forward.

He made it only a step before something like the sound of a giant's fist slamming into a refrigerator exploded from the starboard hull of the *Sampson*. Walter felt it only a split second before unbelievable heat swallowed him. He was flying backward. His skin was on fire. His body slammed into solid steel.

Then all was dark, and Petty Officer Third Class Herbert Walter entered eternity.

30

The White House

Stratton was entering his second hour of uninterrupted sleep when knuckles crashed against his door. Sitting upright in the guest bedroom of the White House residence, he scrubbed sleep from his eyes and checked the clock.

It was midnight, on the dot.

"What is it?"

"Emergency call from the Pentagon, sir."

Stratton swung both feet onto the carpeted floor and lifted the receiver from the nightstand. He signaled the caller to proceed with a single word, then listened in raptured silence to a curt report communicated in the most direct English. When the speaker was finished Stratton simply hung up. The exhaustion remained but the sleepiness was long gone, his body charged with a fresh wave of adrenaline as he reached the shower. Three minutes in the cold was enough to further push his mind into full operational mode. He dressed in jeans and a White House polo, then he was jogging through the bedroom door and down the steps toward the West Wing, a pair of Secret Service agents flanking him, Jill Easterling at his side.

"We just received reports of a full Chinese air deployment over the strait, sir. I have the Pentagon ready to brief you in the Situation Room."

Stratton held up a hand, acknowledging the comment and forestalling further updates. He didn't want to know the ancillary material, he only wanted to know the key points—and what action he would be advised to authorize.

Only the SecDef waited in the Situation Room. Right on brand, Steven Kline had arrived at the White House early and stood upon Stratton's entry. Stratton waved him back into his chair and took his own, looking down the length of the table to view a panel of additional cabinet members available via video call—National Security Advisor Nick West, Secretary of State Lisa Gorman, and—of course—Chairman of the Joint Chiefs, General John David Yellin.

"What happened?" Stratton said, pouring hot coffee from a carafe. He'd already been briefed on the situation in the Taiwan Strait, but he wanted the update a second time right from the top.

"Thirty-eight minutes ago Chinese aircraft fired anti-ship weapons at the USS *Sampson*, sir, a guided missile destroyer." Kline answered the question, his voice clear and didactic. "She successfully defended against at least two missiles, but was struck by a third. Damage was catastrophic. The ship was lost, along with roughly a third of her complement. About a hundred and thirty men."

Stratton bit back a curse, looking to a display screen which mapped the location of the USS *Sampson*'s demise. It was dead center in the Taiwan Strait, roughly equal distance between the ROC's western shore and the PROC city of Xiamen.

"What have we done for the survivors?" Stratton said.

General Yellin took that one. "We've already deployed three additional guided missile destroyers to the scene, sir, along with rescue aircraft and a wing of Navy F-18 Super Hornets. The Chinese have deployed forty-eight fighter craft to the region but are holding just west of the *Sampson*'s wreckage."

"Beijing?" Stratton addressed the question to Lisa Gorman. He couldn't help but notice that she looked like a ghost—black bags beneath her eyes, no makeup. Hair held back in a ponytail that stretched the lines running through her forehead.

"I just got off the phone with the Chinese ambassador," Gorman said. "Beijing claims that the *Sampson* entered Chinese territorial waters and made aggressive maneuvers toward one of her domestic shipping vessels. They fired in defense."

"Like hell they did," Yellin growled. "The *Sampson* wasn't anywhere near Chinese territorial waters. She was ninety klicks off the coast!"

"There weren't any nearby surface contacts, either," Kline added. "Certainly no domestic shipping running under *Sampson*'s guns. This was an unprovoked strike, Mr. President. The only way this could have happened within Chinese territorial waters is if you acknowledge their claim of Taiwanese ownership."

Stratton ran a hand over his face, still staring at the screen. Feeling every ache, every tired muscle sagging under the weight of the world.

Now the decision.

"This is about Russia," Easterling said. "Beijing is watching Moscow bully us, and they're adding to the storm. Seeing how weak we are."

"I agree one hundred percent," Yellin said. "They're testing our strength. The only logical answer is to authorize a full, tactical military response. I've already assembled a list of possible targets, including the Chinese air base where their planes deployed. We can launch from the three guided missile destroyers en route to the strait. They'll be within range in under an hour."

Stratton squinted, struggling for a moment to keep up. "Wait. You want me to strike the *Chinese mainland*?"

"That's where they launched their fighters, sir. It's precedent to hit the thing that hit you, and will send the clearest message. With our air cover in place and the *Ronald Reagan* on standby to reinforce, they won't be able to stop us. I estimate a fifty percent on target ratio. More than enough to flatten their air base."

Stratton's gaze pivoted to Kline, expecting an objection. A clarification. Some sort of additional comment. The SecDef said nothing, hands folded over the tabletop. Not even Gorman—usually a hawk for diplomacy over lethal force—voiced an opinion.

"I agree with the general, sir," Nick West said. "We can't afford to look weak on this one. It wasn't an accident and it was completely unprovoked. If we don't defend our own naval assets, the Chinese will be storming Taiwan by the end of the month."

Stratton looked back to the screen. He fixated on the red X where *Sampson* had gone down—where over one hundred brave United States sailors had lost their lives. Their bodies weren't even cold yet. Intelligence on the strike was as shallow as a mud puddle.

A mainland strike?

"No," Stratton shook his head. "You are not authorized. I don't want another move made until we have absolute, certain intelligence on what happened."

"Mr. Vice President," Kline began, "this isn't the time for indecision."

"It's not the time for reckless action either, Mr. Secretary. You want me to fire on a sovereign nation when we don't even know for sure who fired at us—"

"We know *exactly* who fired at us," Yellin broke in. "And we know exactly where they came from."

"But we don't know *why*," Stratton pressed. "This could have been rogue action from an overzealous fighter pilot, and now Beijing is forced to stand behind it. Flattening their air base could lead to an open naval battle by lunch time—total war by dinner. No, General. You do *not* have permission for a strike. I want concrete, absolute intelligence. I want a public statement from Beijing, and I want more than a bullseye to shoot at. I want a full, strategic plan, or we're not launching a thing."

From the video call screen the general visibly bristled. Cheeks flushed, shoulders bulged. "Mr. Vice President, it is incumbent upon me to inform you that you are making a catastrophic mistake—"

"And it's incumbent on *me* to keep us out of a world war! That air base will still be there if and when you prove your point, and we'll wipe it out of existence. That's the final word on this matter. Am I understood?"

Yellin said nothing. Kline filled the gap. "You're understood, sir."

Stratton turned to Gorman. "Get Beijing on the line. I want to speak directly to Chen."

"He's out of the country, sir."

"All the more reason. Tell him to bring Nikitin to the call. I'm sure we'll find something to chat about."

31

Langley, Virginia

Eight a.m. found Director Aimes still in her office, poring over reports of the Chinese missile strike against the USS *Sampson*. She hadn't received a call from the White House, but that didn't surprise her. The Pentagon would be heading up the intelligence report on this one, as well as the recommended response.

But there was still work for the CIA to do. Aimes still had to switch gears away from the Caucasus and toward the South China Sea. The implications were already unthinkable. Chinese aggression toward the ROC—Taiwan—had gathered from distant storm clouds into a constant, boiling thunderstorm over the past few years, hanging just off the coast, always threatening to make landfall. Beijing wanted her rogue territory—and the invaluable microchip manufacturing that it contained—back under her control. She was willing to use force to make it happen, and she had force to use.

All the PROC needed was an opportunity, and with America reeling from terrorist attacks and a faltering economy, Russia making massive territorial moves in the Caucasus, and Iran seemingly rallying to support them...it wasn't difficult to read the tea leaves. The meeting between

Nikitin, Chen, and Kazemi had been a productive one. A brand-new axis of evil was forming right before her very eyes.

"Hey, I may have something."

Aimes looked up to find Rigby standing in the door, a tablet computer in hand. She waved him in. He closed the door and set the tablet on her desk. It was a digital map of Azerbaijan, with two Xs marked across it—one in the northwest, and one just outside the capital city of Baku.

"What's this?"

Rigby pointed to the first X, the one in the middle of nowhere. "This is Turkman's location, in the Goranboy District. The backside of nowhere, essentially. Rural mountain country with sporadic agriculture."

"And this?" Aimes pointed to the second X.

"That's the sight of an Azerbaijan State Security Service outpost thought to contain an underground prison and interrogation center. We've monitored it for a number of years in connection to various accusations of human rights abuses and illegal detainment of foreign nationals, but none of those nationals were Americans, so..."

"So we let it go."

"Right."

"What brings it to our attention now?"

"Reports from our assets in Baku indicate that a truck arrived at the SSS facility under heavy guard some five hours after the detonation of the nuclear weapon in northern Azerbaijan. Two hours later, President Rzayev himself made an appearance at the facility, and has made at least one additional appearance since. Further, this fellow..." Rigby tabbed the tablet's screen to a picture of a dark Azerbaijani man with a thick beard. "Colonel General Yusif Hasanov has arrived at the facility and stuck around. We don't keep close enough tabs on Azerbaijani SSS activity to say for certain whether any of these events are true outliers, but—"

"But they definitely appear so," Aimes finished.

"They do. And with five missing American operatives in Azerbaijan, you have to wonder."

Aimes tabbed back to the map and pointed to the gap between the two Xs. "How far?"

"One hundred fifty miles as the crow flies. Farther by road, and those roads are infested by Azerbaijani soldiers moving north."

"Do we have any operational assets in the region?"

"You mean black ops? No. Closest team is in Baghdad, and they're not exactly optimal for this kind of mission. A better bet would be a JSOC team. SEALs, ideally."

SEALs. Aimes might have laughed if the situation weren't so dire. There was a zero point zero chance that Steven Kline was authorizing any sort of JSOC mission into Azerbaijan's capital city based on the hunch of the CIA's deputy director. Even if the agency could somehow confirm that Reed Montgomery and his team were held hostage in that SSS facility, there was still the question of diving headfirst into the middle of a developing war zone with so many other threats demanding the Pentagon's attention.

The ugly truth was that Reed Montgomery was expendable. That was the reason Aimes had signed him on in the first place and tolerated his reckless and costly tactics. The Pentagon didn't even *know* about the Prosecution Force.

This was the price of Reed's hefty paychecks.

"Notify Turkman," Aimes said. "He's free to pursue the lead if he so chooses."

Rigby squinted. "We're not going to back him up?"

"We can't back him up, Silas. We have neither the resources nor the justification. Even if I could pull a team out of thin air and put them on a chopper for Baku, how would I sell that to the White House? We're talking about a country that is convinced we just nuked them. Now Americans are landing in their capital gunning down their state security? No go."

Rigby nodded. Considered. "So…"

"So they're on their own, Silas." Aimes looked back to her computer. Her voice softened. "They're on their own."

32

Goranboy District, Azerbaijan

The satellite phone rang for a third time just as Turk was drifting off on one of the rat-gnawed mattresses. He sat bolt upright, snatching the Zigana from his side and pointing it toward the door, breath whistling through his teeth, chest heaving.

From the bed next to him Lucy sat with her knees pulled up to her chest, wide green eyes fixated on him. She said nothing, but she lifted a hand to point toward the phone where it lay on the floor. Turk's gaze locked on it, and he lowered the handgun. Placing both feet on the floor, he answered the call.

"Hello?"

"Mr. Turkman it's…well. It doesn't matter who I am. I'm calling on behalf of the company."

The company. A euphemism for the CIA about as paper thin as Turk's patience. He didn't recognize the voice. It was male and relatively young.

"What do you have?" Turk said.

"We may have a location for you."

"Reed?"

"Possibly. Our intel is…speculative."

Turk wanted to punch something. He removed the phone from his ear and checked the battery readout. The device now read zero percent. The battery symbol blinked. He didn't have time to bicker.

"I'm out of battery. Hurry."

"It's outside Baku, in the subdivision of Qobu. Do you have something to write with?"

The only thing Turk had was his pocketknife, but the floor beneath him was plenty dusty. He clicked the blade open and prepared to scratch into the hardwood.

"Go."

The voice on the phone read out a series of coordinates. Turk scraped the blade across the planks. He got down the final number and jumped straight to the next question.

"Details."

"It's an SSS building—State Security Service. Secret police, essentially. There's an outer fence and multiple armed guards. You can expect heavy internal security."

You can expect.

Turk didn't like the sound of that. It was indicative of a "sucks to be you" situation.

"Where's the QRF?"

Pause. "We don't have it, Mr. Turkman. I'm sorry."

"You don't have it? Are you kidding me?"

"We did everything we could!" Now the voice on the phone snapped. "Believe me when I tell you that I'd be there myself if I could."

"Gee, thanks, I'm all warm and fuzzy."

A patient breath. "Look. There's a caravan of Azerbaijani civilians moving southeast toward Baku along the R-9 highway. They're fleeing the bomb site and the Russian army. It should offer you cover. I'll give you a phone number—my direct line. Once you get to Baku you can call for satellite surveillance. We'll help in any way we can."

Satellites.

"Why don't you give me a knife for my gunfight?"

No answer. Turk didn't regret the sarcasm. He looked to the door and imagined a cross-country trek to an unknown compound heavily guarded by Azerbaijani secret police. The whole mission reminded him of North Korea, but at least in North Korea, Turk had Reed by his side.

"How far?" Turk said.

"Three hundred twenty klicks by highway. You'll need a—"

The phone cut off. Turk checked the screen. It was black.

The battery was done.

Throwing the phone into his lap, Turk buried his face in his hands and tried not to scream.

No QRF. No positive location. No resources of any kind.

And now a dead sat phone.

"Are you going?"

Turk's gaze snapped up, finding Lucy seated in her chair, facing him. She was still pale-faced, still trembling a little. But the defensive, deer-in-the-headlights look was gone. There was some clarity in her eyes. It was as though she saw him for the first time in days.

"Yes," Turk said simply.

Lucy nodded. The room fell quiet. Then she stood. "Me too."

33

Makhachkala, Russia
On the Caspian Sea

The team assembled at sunrise, arriving at the abandoned dockside warehouse one at a time until all twelve were present. They parked their vehicles inside, rolling the doors closed. Nobody spoke as rifle cases were lined across tabletops and gear was distributed.

Plate carrier vests. Arsenal Strike One handguns and Vityaz-SN submachine guns. Flash-bangs, fragmentation grenades, night vision goggles and infrared optics. Two RPG launchers. Secure communications equipment with subdued earpieces. A designated marksman's rifle, and two AEK-999 general purpose mobile machine guns.

It was enough firepower to lay down a presidential compound, and the men wielding those weapons knew how to do exactly that. Most of the equipment was the same as that used by Spetsnaz or Alpha Group, but these men were neither. Not officially, anyway. They were something else. Something much less defined, but every bit as lethal.

As the sun rose out of the Caspian Sea, one man cranked up a radio while another fired up a barbecue grill. Preparations continued while steaks sizzled. The confines of the warehouse flooded with the odor of sweat mixed with the cooking meat, and still, nobody spoke.

There was no need to. These men weren't friends. Outside of training, they barely knew each other, and that was okay. What else was there to discuss besides: *How will you spend your money?* That money wasn't yet in the bank, anyway.

Better to focus. Get to the finish line alive.

Ten minutes past ten a.m., a cell phone rang, and the de facto leader of the group accepted the call. He stepped away from the others, approaching the door and looking out over the glistening Caspian Sea. A freighter drifted by, heading south toward the next major city on the western bank—Baku.

"Da?"

"Green light." Anton Golubev's unmistakable voice growled the order, unleashing a spike of adrenaline in the team leader's chest. "Wait until dark. The boat will be there. We're sticking with extraction point alpha, as planned. Do you have any questions?"

The team leader grunted in the negative, and Golubev hung up.

It was almost time.

34

The Oval Office
The White House

Beijing chose the worst possible tactic as it concerned Stratton's vanishing hopes of de-escalation—they ignored Washington's calls, flatly declining to connect the acting president with their own president, Chen Lei. Easterling pressed, and Gorman harassed the Chinese ambassador with threats of immediate American retaliatory action, but the Chinese narrative remained as inflexible as iron: The United States breached Chinese coastal waters with a warship, and China responded accordingly.

The ball, effectively, was in Washington's court, and Stratton's options for something less than a full missile strike were evaporating before his very eyes.

"The *Ronald Reagan* is in position northeast of Taiwan, sir, ready to launch air cover for a missile strike. Guided missile destroyers *Milius*, *Higgins*, and *McCampbell* are within range for a full strike. We can have a hundred birds in the air before there's anything they can say about it."

General Yellin's update barked over the speakerphone with the energy of a pit bull yanking against a chain, just begging to be cut loose. Stratton didn't have the benefit of the Situation Room screens displaying the exact location of each ship, but the strategy had already been explained to him in detail.

While the three destroyers launched cruise missiles against the Chinese air base responsible for the attack on *Sampson*, the *Ronald Reagan* air corps would dissuade any additional Chinese aircraft from attempting additional anti-ship strikes or encroachments on the fleet. Coupled with the note that SecDef Steven Kline had slipped him, notifying him of the USS *Rhode Island*'s position only two hundred miles off the Taiwanese coast, an arsenal of twenty Trident ballistic missiles nestled in her hull, and the message was clear. America was ready to give a lot better than she got.

But Stratton wasn't there yet.

"Hold, General."

"Sir, I must strongly—"

"I said *hold!*" Stratton hung up as Secretary Gorman appeared in the Oval Office, rushing with the urgency of a woman who had a tiger by the tail.

"Sir, my office just connected with President Rzayev. He's requesting to speak with you."

"Who now?" Stratton squinted. He recognized the name, but the chaos of the night was getting to him. He was having difficulty switching gears away from the crisis in the South China Sea.

"President Elchin Rzayev, sir. President of Azerbaijan. Baku just called. With your permission, I'd like to sit in on the call."

Easterling appeared in the doorway and Stratton snapped his fingers, motioning for her to enter and shut the door behind her. Gorman lifted her cell phone and gave an order to one of her deputies. A moment later a red light blinked on Stratton's desk phone.

The two women sat. Stratton inhaled a long breath. He mashed the speaker button.

"Mr. Vice President, I have President Elchin Rzayev for you. Would you like a translator?"

"Does he speak English?"

"Limited, sir."

"Put him through."

The speaker crackled. Even before he spoke, Stratton detected Rzayev's aggressive breathing boiling through the speaker. It sounded as though the man had his phone jammed up against his lips.

"Mr. President?" Stratton said.

"Who is this?" Rzayev's voice was predictably accented, his tone crackling like a bullwhip. Stratton remained calm.

"This is acting president Jordan Stratton of the United States. Thank you for calling, Mr. President. We have much to discuss."

"We have only one thing to discuss. Why did you bomb my country?"

Stratton settled into his seat. He remained calm. "We did not bomb Azerbaijan, Mr. President. The Russians are lying to you, and they're about to invade your country. The United States would offer you assistance—"

"*Assistance*," Rzayev spat the word. "We do not require your assistance. We require your truth."

"My truth?" Stratton squinted.

"Truth about what you have done! You must explain."

Stratton looked to Gorman. Her face was impassive, offering no guidance. He returned to the phone.

"Mr. President, America has done nothing inside your borders. This bomb was not our—"

"You *lie*!" Now Rzayev screamed. "You *lie to me*! I know about your people. Your soldiers."

Stratton squinted, genuinely confused. "What?"

"I have them, Mr. *Acting* President. They are here, and they are witness to your treachery. If you cannot tell me the truth, perhaps they will."

"What are you talking about?"

"Azerbaijan is not the puppet of Moscow," Rzayev said. "And we will not be the puppet of Washington. Now I will find the truth...one scream at a time."

The phone went silent. Stratton sat up. The operator came back on the line.

"I'm sorry, sir. President Rzayev has left the call."

Stratton hung up and looked immediately to Gorman. "What the hell is he talking about? What soldiers?"

Gorman shook her head. "I don't know, sir. This is the first I'm hearing about this."

"Could be more Russian misdirection," Easterling said. "Another attempt to compromise our international image."

"The Russians haven't reported on it, though," Gorman said.

Stratton replayed the call in his mind, examining each statement. The emotional velocity of Rzayev's accusations. And then he reached a conclusion.

"It doesn't matter. Rzayev is a dog in a corner and he's lashing out. Our chief concern is still China."

"With respect, sir...that could be exactly the position Russia wants us to take."

Easterling's point was valid, but it didn't change Stratton's mental math. The conflict in the Caucasus involved neither the United States nor a direct ally of the United States. It was a problem—a huge one—but a US destroyer lay at the bottom of the South China Sea with over a hundred brave souls aboard. Stratton had stalled on a response with good reason.

He could only stall so long. The greatest country on earth could not tolerate being yanked around.

"Notify the Chinese," Stratton said, addressing Gorman. "They have until one p.m. Washington time to explain their unprovoked attack, or we *will* respond...with lethal force."

35

Goranboy District, Azerbaijan

The thunderstorm finally dissipated an hour after sunrise, and Turk and Lucy departed the cabin, proceeding on foot through the woods alongside the two-lane until they reached the next Azerbaijani village. This was smaller than the first, where Turk stole the satellite phone, but it was no less chaotic. Empty storefronts and abandoned houses lined the streets, with the last of the villagers piling meager possessions into sagging sedans, ready for the flight southeast for Baku.

Away from the Georgian border and the tidal wave of Russian soldiers gathered behind it.

Standing at the edge of the tree line with residual rain still dripping from evergreen needles, Turk surveyed the village while watching Lucy out of the corner of his eye. She had changed over the past several hours. The progress was so slow that he barely noticed at first, but even since leaving the hut in the woods, he'd observed Lucy's mind slowly focusing around the present.

She remembered him. She called him by name. She walked without assistance and no longer hugged herself. She still seemed vaguely confused about the particulars of their situation, and he frequently had to remind her how and why the Prosecution Force wound up in Azerbaijan.

She couldn't remember the plane crash, the bomb, or the gunfight in between. The last memory she could clearly articulate occurred nearly five days prior, back in Tennessee. Lunch at a sandwich shop. But she accepted the facts Turk fed her without objection or question, the keen edge of a sharp mind growing sharper by the minute.

"We need a vehicle," Turk said. "Food and medical."

"They're taking those things," Lucy said, lifting her chin toward the last of the villagers. It was a family of four, and the children appeared to be twins. The parents were young—younger than Turk—and clearly terrified. The Lada sedan they had packed their life into looked ready to burst at the seams, so rusty Turk couldn't tell what color it was. He saw food. He saw blankets and a first aid kit. All things they needed...

"We can't," Lucy whispered.

Turk shook his head. "No. There's some other way."

The Lada pulled away in a cloud of dark exhaust fumes and the flooded gravel street fell quiet. Turk watched it go and mapped out a path to the house the family had just abandoned. It was small, but there was no way its entire contents could be packed into the car. He and Lucy could at least fill their stomachs and maybe find some dry clothes before—

"Do you feel that?" Lucy looked up, eyes widening with trepidation.

Turk felt nothing. He looked over his shoulder, following Lucy's line of sight, and still couldn't sense it.

"What?"

Lucy held up a hand. Turk focused.

Then he felt it. His brain told him it was distant thunder, but the soldier's instincts in him spoke to another reality—a much more deadly version.

Tank.

"Down!" Turk hissed, pressed Lucy over the shoulders.

The two of them buried themselves in the underbrush at the tree line, and five seconds later the first armored behemoth appeared. It was a Russian T-90 design, but it wasn't a Russian tank. The flag printed on the camouflage body panel was that of Azerbaijan, and the vehicle was trailed by two heavy trucks and a Cobra armored vehicle similar to the one Turk had infiltrated while stealing the sat phone, only this was a multi-door model complete with a machine gun turret.

The tank reached the village's main street and rattled to a stop at the intersection. The two trucks fanned out and stopped behind it. The Cobra pulled up at the outskirts of the village only fifty yards from Lucy and Turk's position. Neither of them moved, keeping low to the ground and breathing in slowly.

Then the tank hatch popped open. An Azerbaijani soldier appeared in full uniform, a helmet draped over his head with the chin strap unfastened. He shouted to the trucks, a grin spread across his face. In short order both trucks burst open and fully two dozen soldiers bailed out. Four men appeared from the inside of the Cobra, hats cocked back on their heads, pant legs sticking out from the tops of their boots, gear not quite fitting. They were overweight, awkward. And looked entirely too happy.

"Reserves," Turk whispered. "Emergency troops."

"What are they doing?" Lucy asked.

Turk held up a hand. He watched as the Cobra troops leaned AK-74 rifles against the front bumper of the vehicle. One unzipped his fly and pissed on the beefy all-terrain tire. The others headed toward the now abandoned village, calling out to their companions in their native tongue. Exchanging jokes. Laughing.

Then they entered the abandoned houses, and Turk gritted his teeth. The laughter rang louder. The guy who pissed on the Cobra rushed to join his friends. Glass busted and soldiers ran in and out of doors, their arms full of abandoned property from the recently evacuated civilians.

Electronics. Clothing. Food and beer. One particularly hefty guy in his late thirties appeared with an arm load of lingerie, burying his nose in it and guffawing.

"They're sacking their own town!" Lucy hissed. The disbelief in her voice betrayed her ignorance.

Turk muttered between his teeth: "Welcome to war."

The pillaging continued, moving gradually toward the heart of the village. As the voices grew dimmer, Lucy tugged Turk by his torn and bloody sleeve. She jabbed a chin toward the abandoned Cobra.

It stood with doors open, engine ticking as it cooled, rifles leaned against its front bumper. Lucy cocked an eyebrow.

Turk indulged in his first smile in days. "I like the way you think, LB."

36

The Kremlin
Moscow, Russia

Mikhail Orlov arrived at the Kremlin for the second time in as many days, his nerves hanging by a thread. He'd talked himself up to this point based on greed alone—the unquenchable desire to live the life his country had always deprived him of. Call it socialism, or communism, or a dictatorship, or a democratic federation...it was all just lipstick on a pig, in the end. Orlov was a practical man. He knew how the rich became richer while the poor ground through life hand-to-mouth.

He also knew how to beat that system, the same way the oligarchs beat it. Certainly, Orlov would never be even a fraction as rich as an oligarch, but he could use their same methods. He could cheat. Steal. Deceive. Play the game from beneath the table. The problem, of course, was that just like with the oligarchs, that sort of behavior came with dramatic risks. Now that Orlov was yet again penetrating the inner sanctums of Russian power, those risks were growing by orders of magnitude.

Death would be the best possible option if things went sideways. A more realistic and terrifying reality would be capture, transport to Siberia...

and the long slow winter of misery that would follow. Not just the natural kind, but the *Russian* kind.

Orlov scanned in at the security kiosk and cleared the metal detector. His purpose was the same as before, carrying messages from the military wing of the Kremlin to the executive wing. He'd pulled some strings to arrange the assignment. The documents beneath his arm were destined for none other than the crown jewel of the entire governmental complex—the Russian version of the West Wing.

And the executive office of Makar Nikitin.

The ornate fixtures and wall hangings of this portion of the Kremlin were unrivaled by the remainder of the complex. Everything was dark and rich, the carpet itself so thick it compressed beneath Orlov's every step. He was conscious of cameras staring down at him from the corners of each room, guards standing at multiple checkpoints, who inspected his ID and again asked his purpose.

His purpose was none other than to place the sealed folder beneath his arm into the hand of the Russian president. It was a task Orlov had never before completed, but none of the guards seemed unfamiliar with the protocol. They directed him around corners and down a long hallway to a massive white door framed by golden trim. With each step Orlov took, the cortisol already churning through his chest redoubled in strength. His hands began to sweat, his head pounded. He felt a little dizzy, almost as though his soul were fighting to detach itself from his body. It reminded him of taking LSD during his teenage years. That radical, floating sensation.

And just like with LSD, fear mixed with excitement to form a deadly cocktail that consumed his entire being. As he placed a hand on the president's office door, it didn't *feel* like his hand. For a moment Mikhail Orlov froze, uncertainty sinking his legs into concrete. His heart hammered, images of imagined gulags deep in the Siberian wilderness churning through his head.

What would they do to him? Stand him in front of a firing squad?

No. The torment would be much, much worse than that, and it would last far longer. Days, maybe weeks. Nikitin's people would carve him apart, extracting every last detail of his betrayal before finally releasing him to the embrace of death.

He couldn't do this. He had lost his mind, let the money get to him. It wasn't worth it.

Orlov looked down the hall, ready to turn back even though turning back made no rational sense. He hadn't technically committed any crime, at least not on this particular trip. He could deliver the file, duck his head to the president, return to his dusty desk in the forgotten corners of the military wing...

Orlov's thoughts trailed off as he noted the camera staring down at him from the end of the hall, its black lens like the glossy eye of a crow. In a strange way, that token of authoritarian control dampened his fear. It added fuel to the fire of frustration that had led him to this point in the first place—the fire of greed, also. He pushed through the door.

The president's ceremonial office was ornate and sprawling, with high wingback chairs, a fireplace, and more of the same golden wall fixtures as the hallway. There were paintings. A stag head mounted to the wall from one of Nikitin's Siberian hunting trips—supposedly, at least.

None of that mattered. Orlov wasn't bound for the president's ceremonial office but for Nikitin's practical one, which connected to this room by another door. He turned. He walked. He stepped through into a much smaller, simpler space with a smaller desk. An open laptop, no photographs on the walls. Only a few chairs and a window overlooking *Krasnaya Ploshchad*—Red Square.

Makar Nikitin wasn't there. The chairs sat empty, but there was a cup of black tea resting on a saucer next to the computer, and it still steamed. From beyond another doorway, Orlov observed a sound like running water, a trickle and a long sigh. Yellow light leaking from beneath the door.

It was a private restroom. Nikitin was inside. Orlov could hear him. This was his chance.

Adrenaline fueled his body, swamping the fear as Orlov pivoted the desk to face the computer. He wasn't sure what he was looking for—anything that could shed light on the nature of Chen Lei and Ali Kazemi's visit to the Kremlin. Communications, perhaps. Emails?

The computer was unlocked. Orlov memorized the layout of windows as Nikitin had left them and used the touchpad to skate through them. There was a Western news website displaying updates from America translated into Cyrillic. Details about a crumbling economy, a flailing White House. None of that interested Orlov. He proceeded to another tab, which was a porn website. Nikitin had a video paused halfway through.

Orlov hurried past. There were more noises from the bathroom. The flush of a toilet. The clink of a belt. Orlov reached an email pane and tabbed through messages. He didn't have time to read them all. He didn't have time to—

Orlov's attention snagged on the top message. It was sent by Nikitin, dated and timed for six hours prior. The recipient was a man whom Orlov knew by reputation only, but that reputation was more than enough to chill the blood in his veins.

Anton Golubev. The Ghost of the Kremlin. The president's fixer.

Orlov's gaze snapped toward the bathroom door as a sink faucet hissed. He looked back to the email. He read the last message, blinking in disbelief. He read it again. The faucet cut off and paper towels tore. Orlov's heart hammered. His body descended into deadlock. He couldn't move. He could only stare at the email as his mind screamed over and over again.

Go! Go now!

Footsteps tapped. Orlov snapped into gear. He closed out of the email pane, instant terror flooding his mind as he realized that it was the wrong move. Nikitin had the pane open but minimized. Why had he closed it? What was the correct arrangement of window panes?

No time. It was too late. Orlov abandoned the computer and moved quickly around the desk, standing just inside the office entrance as the bathroom doorknob rattled...then Makar Nikitin himself stepped out.

Orlov had never seen the president in person. He was slightly shorter than he appeared on TV, but somehow no less imposing. Broad shouldered, wearing dress slacks and a white tank top that exposed impressive gym muscles, Nikitin looked like the poster boy for Russian strength. The iron in his dark glare certainly didn't hurt. It was enough to amplify the existing stress coursing through Orlov's body as he snapped to attention.

"Good morning, Mr. President. Dispatch for you from General Shirov."

Nikitin extended a hand. Orlov passed him the sealed envelope. Nikitin flipped it over and stuck his finger beneath the seal. Orlov didn't move. Once more his legs felt frozen in concrete, his heart pounding so loud he was certain Nikitin must hear it. A dreadful long moment dragged by. Nikitin tore the envelope open. He stopped. Looked up. Raised both eyebrows.

Orlov swallowed. "Thank you, Mr. President."

Then he turned. He was out the door breathing hard, forcing himself not to sprint across the executive office. Back into the hallway, through the checkpoints, his head going light. The email flashed across his mind and his hands trembled. He fumbled his secure access card at the exit of the executive wing and stooped to scoop it off the floor.

The windows. You didn't arrange the windows.

Would Nikitin notice?

The answer came like a death blow, shrieking from an invisible alarm system concealed in the ceiling. A piercing wail, followed by the crackle of radios. Voices in Russian barked commands. Orlov retrieved the card and looked over his shoulder. There was a guard post twenty yards behind him. Two men dressed in black suits, manning the checkpoint. One held a radio against his ear, squinting.

Then he looked dead at Orlov and snapped a command to his partner.

Orlov's body launched into high gear—fight or flight mode, and as guns appeared from beneath the suit jackets, he knew fighting was no option at all. The card slid through the scanner and a green light blinked. The plexi-glass door opened. He barreled through as leather-soled shoes smacked the floor behind him. A voice called his name, demanding that he halt.

Orlov wasn't halting, not for a second. He sprinted down a flight of marble stairs toward a main exit that broke out into Red Square. As he dashed across the flagstones, he looked up toward the window of Makar Nikitin's private office. The sunrise glinted against the glass, but Orlov imagined that he saw the president standing there, pointing. Shouting into a phone.

From behind him the doors of the Kremlin burst open and the shouts of the guards called after him—more than two men, now. *Hands up. Stop where you are!*

Orlov didn't stop, and the guards opened fire. Handguns popped and bullets zipped over his head. Orlov reached the street and stretched out, tearing his jacket off and throwing his body ahead. He turned at every intersection, weaving through downtown Moscow as the hounds nipped at his heels. He couldn't see the guards. He didn't know how far behind him they had fallen. The gunshots had stopped, but now he heard sirens, which meant patrol trucks.

He couldn't outrun the patrol trucks.

Turning south, Orlov reached an outdoor farmer's market that served the governmental district. Stalls of produce, dairy products, and fresh baked bread lined the street, with a throng of civilians gathered around them. Late summer breeze filtered through his dress shirt and stung his lungs as Orlov buried himself in the crowd, shoving past a businessman with a sack of apples and a pair of teenagers pushing a trolly loaded with artisan cheese.

Phone. Orlov needed a phone. He had to contact the Agency, *immediately*, but Orlov had left his own cell phone in the secure locker at the entrance of his office, per standard protocol. With the sirens growing louder in his ears, Orlov's gaze swept the congestion of people and settled on a young mother pushing a baby stroller. She was shopping loaves of golden brown bread with a smartphone held to her ear. She didn't see him coming. She was helpless to resist as he shoved her into the bread stall and snatched away the phone.

She screamed. Orlov sprinted on. He hung up on her phone call and jabbed in the emergency contact number the Agency had given him by memory—eleven digits, a European number. The phone rang. Orlov reached an intersection and ducked into an alley. His heart hammered so hard he could barely stand. He slouched against a wall and gasped.

"Hello?"

"It's Blackjack!" Orlov's voice cracked with panic. "I'm compromised. I need help!"

"What? Calm down. What happened?"

The voice was that of the man Orlov had met in Muzeon Park. The American contact with the fake St. Petersburg accent.

"I made a mistake! They're onto me. I need you to get me out!"

"Where are you? What did you do?"

From the farmer's market a chorus of commanding voices shouted in harsh Russian. People scrambled. A siren rang louder.

"I got into his office!" Orlov choked. "There was an email. The president—the Azerbaijani president. Nikitin is going to kill...wait. *Help me!*"

Orlov's last words erupted like an exploding volcano as the phone fell from his hands. The Russian FSB agent appeared at the end of the alley, gun drawn. Orlov turned and dashed for freedom, hurtling around abandoned produce crates.

He made it only ten meters before the other end of the alley was closed off by the armored side of a patrol truck, blue lights flashing. The door was flung open. Another FSB agent dropped out.

Then the gunshots rained in like horizontal hail.

37

R-9 Highway
Azerbaijan

The looting soldiers in the village never noticed the departure of their Cobra armored car. Turk gathered the abandoned rifles and climbed behind the wheel as Lucy clambered into the front passenger seat. There was an ignition switch on the dash, similar to that in a Humvee. The engine chugged to life, and an automatic transmission backed them away from the tank and the empty trucks.

They returned to a two-lane and Turk kept the pedal mashed into the floor while Lucy fiddled with a GPS unit mounted to the dash, expanding the map it displayed. The Cobra was brand-new and featured all the latest technology. Upgraded suspension muted the ruts and bumps in the road much better than the '90s model Humvees Turk had used in Iraq. The motor was strong, hurtling them along at eighty kilometers per hour with ease as wind whistled through the roof-mounted gun turret. There were food stores in the back seat—bad military rations and canteens of water. Lucy found a couple of abandoned camouflage caps and jackets, also, stripped off in favor of plate carriers and helmets. They each tugged them on, pulling the hats low over their ears. Then Lucy found a cell phone charger and jammed one end into a port built into the dash of the Cobra. The opposite end fit into the sat phone. A few moments later the screen illuminated. The device was charged.

Lucy pointed to the GPS. "Right at the next intersection. We'll intercept the R-9 highway in ten klicks...I think."

Turk didn't question the ambiguity of the statement. The GPS displayed all its data in Azerbaijani, making it nearly impossible to read the directions. But the blue line and the arrow were clear enough, and the distances were all in standard Latin numerals. Turk kept his foot on the gas and roared past a pair of armored troop carriers headed in the opposite direction. They passed him without a hint of opposition or question. They climbed a hill, and Turk laid on the brakes as a valley spilled out before them.

And there was the caravan. The CIA's intelligence was spot on—tens of thousands of Azerbaijani civilians clogged both sides of the highway, crawling steadily southeast as Cobra armored cars cleared paths for military vehicles to churn toward the battle lines in the opposite direction. It was organized chaos at best, with very little in the way of structure. Furniture and boxes of personal items were tied to the roofs of sedans and small vans. Midsized trucks were loaded down with so many humans that their beds sagged almost to the ground. The sun baked down on the scene, reflected by dusty windshields, and Turk completed the mental math in mere seconds.

"This won't work," he said, shifting into park. "Much too slow."

Digging a pen out of a storage compartment between the two seats, Turk rotated his forearm and recorded the coordinates the CIA had given him from memory. Nearly ten minutes passed while Lucy fought with the GPS, struggling to identify the right commands to enter a destination by latitude and longitude. When she finally succeeded she copied the numbers off Turk's arm, and the GPS paved a blue line right across the middle of Azerbaijan, joining highways and back roads, empty fields and valley floors into the most direct possible route for an all-terrain military vehicle to reach its target.

"One hundred ninety klicks," Lucy said. "We'll skirt the highway and evade the caravan, but..."

But we're twice as likely to be stopped, Turk thought. *And we'll only be a little faster.*

There was no need to voice the obvious. He reached for the shifter and yanked it into drive. The Cobra clung to the pavement as they headed down the side of the hill, turning off a few thousand meters prior to the R-9 highway and striking out across an open field. They would connect with a two-lane in four kilometers.

Then turn east toward Baku and the black site. Progress would be decidedly slower than highway speeds. It would be dark before they reached their destination.

Maybe that was a good thing.

"When we reach the city..." Turk hesitated. "I can drop at the outskirts. If you can blend in with the refugees you should be safe until the CIA can get you out."

Lucy's bright green eyes snapped toward him. It was a look he hadn't seen in days. The haze was gone, that dead-eyed look of shell shock. Lucy still appeared ready to drop, crushed by the abuse of their present circumstance. But her mind had returned.

"Not a chance. I'm with you to the end...It's what I signed on for."

Turk wanted to argue. Maybe it was chivalry, or sexism, or tradition. A natural defense against dragging a woman into certain death. But in his gut, he understood just how helpless the mission ahead would likely be. He could use all the help available.

"Fear no evil," Turk said softly.

Lucy looked back through the dusty glass, settling into her seat. "Fear no evil."

38

The White House

Stratton never returned to the guest bedroom of the White House residence. There was no point. With the deadline he had imposed against China churning steadily closer—and still no hint of remorse from Beijing—the eventuality of military action now felt like an inevitability. The best he could manage was to block out the Oval Office for short periods, catching catnaps on the sofa with directions for Easterling to only wake him under select circumstances.

One of those circumstances was an emergency call from either the Pentagon or Langley, so when the desk phone rang and he rubbed sleep from his eyes, he already knew what to expect.

"What is it?"

"Sir, we have CIA Director Aimes for you. She says it's urgent."

"Put her through."

When Aimes's voice came online, none of her usual deference was present. She cut right to the chase, a woman with a job to do.

"Sir, I've just received intelligence out of Moscow that I think you should know about."

"Do we need to meet?"

"No, sir. We can handle this over the phone. The agency had a long-term asset deep inside the Kremlin, somebody we trusted. He called in an emergency report twenty minutes ago."

"*Had* an asset?"

"We believe he's dead, sir. The Russians caught him."

"So what was the report?"

Brief pause. Aimes seemed to be considering her words. Then she simply spilled it. "The asset claimed that Nikitin has authorized an assassination of Azerbaijani President Rzayev. Moscow has deployed a black ops team."

"*What?* How do we know that?"

"Details are limited, sir. The call was cut short."

Stratton's mind churned, temporary confusion rapidly giving way to a possible explanation for the madness just communicated to him. With Russian troops gathered on Azerbaijan's northern border and Iranian troops on the southern, the stage was set for a complete invasion. A long, bloody conflict that would inevitably result in Azerbaijan's defeat...

But that could take months. If the West interceded the way they had with Ukraine, it could take even longer. A mired, grinding, costly war.

"We still haven't located Georgian President Meladze, sir. The Agency believes that the Russians may have eliminated him prior to occupying the country."

"And now they'll do the same with Azerbaijan," Stratton finished.

"It seems so."

Stratton ran his fingers through disheveled hair and stared at the floor. He'd always considered himself an intelligent person, and both his college GPA and his performance in politics supported that viewpoint. But he was running out of brainpower. China, Russia, Iran, the economy...he couldn't handle it all.

But he was going to have to, especially if Russian and Iranian armies were allowed to merge over the ashes of Azerbaijan and pivot west toward Turkey...and NATO.

"Have you spoken with the State Department? Have we notified Baku?"

"No, sir. You were my first call."

"You're at Langley?"

"Yes, sir."

"You know the drill. Conference call in twenty. I'll be in the Situation Room."

"Understood."

Stratton hung up. Stepping to a mirror, he straightened his hair and tucked the polo shirt he was wearing into his slacks. The shirt was embroidered with a Chicago Bears logo, and as his eyes caught on it he remembered how simple life had been when he was a young senator conducting a ceremonial coin flip for the Bears' season opener at Soldier Field.

He could still hear the crowd cheering...but those cheers were starting to dissolve into something darker, and more desperate. Not anticipatory chants, but cries. Screams.

Fear.

Acting President Jordan Stratton was the only thing standing between those crowded stands and the prospect of total destruction.

39

Azerbaijan

Traversing the breadth of a country scrambling toward war was easier than it should have been. Turk kept his foot on the gas as the Cobra topped hills and forded rivers, churning at times through orchards and fields of wheat, at other times hopping up onto paved highways speckled with civilian cars and occasional military vehicles.

The route was over two hundred kilometers long, and due to the rough terrain and frequent obstacles, it consumed just over four hours. Yet during that entire span, nobody stopped Rufus Turkman. Nobody so much as challenged him. The civilians scurried out of the way at the sight of an oncoming military vehicle, and the other Azerbaijani Defense Force vehicles seemed preoccupied with their own missions. If there had been an alert broadcast about a stolen Cobra, nobody was heeding it.

Soldiers were headed north. Civilians were headed south and east. It wasn't until Turk powered the Cobra to the top of a final ridgeline and looked down into a sweeping valley that reached all the way to the Caspian Sea that he finally shifted into park and threw his door open.

It was hot in Azerbaijan. Sweat streamed down his back and stung his eyes as he dug through the back of the vehicle. There were further rations, medical equipment, cases of ammunition, and spare magazines for the AKs. A pair of abandoned helmets, a bag full of porno mags.

And, at last, a pair of field glasses. Turk dug them out and circled to the nose of the Cobra. The engine chugged next to him as he raised the binos to overlook the valley. The bulk of downtown Baku was visible as a glimmering white speck, reflecting early evening sunlight from a hundred thousand panes of glass. The Caspian Sea shimmered beyond, and multiple thick highways wound their way between sandy white mountain ridges, carving up desert on their way into the capital city.

There were open quarries. Small lakes. Sprawling subdivisions. The terrain was brutal, consisting of rough wasteland foothills bereft of trees, with shale-covered slopes that fell toward narrow valleys crisscrossed by two-lane roads.

Approach from this point forward would be much riskier than before. Turk could no longer avoid the roads. The hillsides were too steep to manhandle, and besides, the Cobra was down to an eighth tank of fuel. Unless he found more, he was now resigned to charge straight ahead.

"We should wait for dark," Lucy said pensively. "Scope out the facility and map a route of escape. Maybe secure another vehicle...an aircraft."

"I can't fly," Turk said, still looking through the binos.

"Right. But Corbyn."

Turk lowered the glasses. He looked sideways at Lucy, an implication in his face that he didn't need to voice. Lucy nodded once.

"Show me on the GPS," Turk said.

The two of them returned to the Cobra, and Lucy zoomed out on the little military GPS mounted to the dash. The coordinates provided by Langley indicated a point on the map southwest of downtown Baku, near a suburb called Lokbatan. The terrain there was barely visible as Turk looked back through the binoculars—it was arid, dusty, dry. And carved up by more quarries. Not many structures were visible, but then again, it was still ten klicks distant.

"It's rural," Lucy said, confirming his initial instincts. "The compound rests south of Baku's outskirts, about two miles from the shoreline. If we had a boat, we could exfiltrate that way..."

Lucy trailed off, zooming out on the map again. Turk assumed her trail of thought and reached the same conclusions—the same problem.

There were no safe places that bordered the Caspian Sea. To the south lay Iran. To the north lay Russia. The only other two options were Kazakhstan and Turkmenistan—countries Turk knew nothing about, and neither one of them was particularly close. A couple hundred miles by boat, if not more.

"The Iranians have a navy," Turk said. "So do the Russians. Even if we escaped the Azerbaijanis, we would be sitting ducks in the Caspian Sea. It's not an option."

"So we're back to an aircraft," Lucy said. "Maybe Kirsten or Kyle can still fly."

If they're alive.

Turk lifted his gaze toward the horizon, pivoting to look over his shoulder. The sun hung maybe ninety minutes above the western horizon, descending slowly toward Armenia. After dark the valley below would be lost, consumed by the thick shadows that would fill every gap between distant city lights.

It was a tangled mire of roads down there. An imperfect escape path, but better than the air, and better than the sea.

"We escape by land," Turk said. "It's the only option. Even assuming we have an operational pilot, and even if we found an aircraft, there's no place we can go quickly enough to avoid an Azerbaijani fighter jet. Our best bet is to wait for cover of darkness, breach the facility, and evaporate into the night. Hit the hills and get off the roads. Go it on foot, if necessary. Wait for the CIA."

Turk lowered the binoculars and chewed his tongue, reviewing the plan quickly enough in his mind to skate right over the one thousand possible pitfalls it promised.

Suicide mission. He knew it in his bones. He could put on a brave face and sketch out an extraction strategy as though he were planning a grocery trip, but there was very little chance that anyone would be leaving that valley alive. The odds were too far against them. There was no possible route of eventual escape.

Turk looked down to Lucy standing next to him, her auburn hair torn by the wind, and their gazes met. Lucy offered him the faintest hint of a smile, and that one expression said it all.

She was thinking the same. And she was okay with it.

"We could use a diversion," Lucy said.

Turk grunted and returned to the binoculars. He mapped the general location of the compound—it was still too distant to actually see—and then swept southeast along the shore. Then north...then slowly east.

He ratcheted to a stop, gaze fixating on a different sort of compound visible about one kilometer west of the GPS coordinates Langley had given him. It was fenced in—he could tell by the gleam of guard towers posted at each corner. The contents were too far away to see in detail, but the general shapes were there. Massive black blobs that looked a little like grain silos, only they were flat-topped. Eight of them in total.

Running along a highway just outside the fence line were a number of shining objects, long and caterpillar-like, creeping slowly toward the compound...and then back out of it.

Gas trucks.

It was a fuel depot.

Turk lowered the binos. "Hey, Lucy...was there any C4 in the truck?"

Lucy ducked her head through the door of the Cobra and shifted around. A moment later she emerged with a grunt in the affirmative.

"A brick. About three pounds. Why?"

A slow, vengeful smile crept across Turk's face. He turned back for the Cobra.

"Dial Langley," Turk said. "We've got our diversion."

40

State Security Service Black Site
Baku, Azerbaijan

President Elchin Rzayev arrived at the compound just as the sun was fading in the western sky. The thunderclouds from earlier that day had finally moved eastward over the Caspian Sea, but the roads were still wet and the ground soggy.

As he stepped out of the back of his armored car and looked northwest toward the distant Red Bridge border crossing where Russian troops had massed by the tens of thousands, Rzayev's mind skipped away from Moscow, around the globe, to another enemy.

America.

Tensions between Azerbaijan and Russia were nothing new. Alpha dogs don't like alpha dogs, and the same is true of dictators. Rzayev hated Nikitin for his bullying, entitled tactics. It was always the same story with Russia, just a different century. He trusted the Kremlin just as far as he could throw it. Every word out of Nikitin's mouth was almost guaranteed to be twisted.

And yet...the Americans. At least three of them were *here*, and Rzayev still didn't believe that the five prisoners he held constituted a NATO reconnaissance team. The bomb was real. And whatever happened next between

Baku and Moscow, Rzayev desperately needed to know the truth about Washington's involvement. The days had dragged by and Rzayev's prisoners hadn't broken from their unified narrative. At least one of them was dead. The SSS had failed completely in extracting intelligence from the others.

Time was now up. Rzayev had arrived at the black site for one very specific and simple purpose—to break the Americans, or slaughter them trying.

An armored door admitted him to a block building occupied by camouflaged soldiers with the letters "DTX" stuck to their plate carriers, submachine guns swinging from one-point harnesses. Halls were paved in concrete, doorways opening into sterile offices stocked by Soviet-era metal furniture. Everyone stood to attention as Rzayev passed, but nobody addressed him. They all knew why he was here. They all knew it was a sign of their failure.

At the bottom of two flights of stairs lay another hallway. Colonel General Yusif Hasanov met Rzayev at the end of that hall, standing next to a closed door with his face pressed into grim lines. He saluted Rzayev, but Rzayev didn't bother to return the gesture. He pointed to the door.

"Open it."

"Mr. President...before we go in."

"What?" Rzayev's voice snapped like a bullwhip. Hasanov stiffened, chin held up.

"The smell is very bad. There is a mess. Please consider allowing me to move the prisoners into a more suitable—"

"I'm not afraid of a little blood, Yusif. A fact you would be well advised to remember. Open the door."

Hasanov's lips bunched. He paused only a moment longer. Then he nodded to the sentry standing next to a solid steel door with a heavy latch holding it closed. The sentry lifted the latch. Hasanov gestured forward. Rzayev stepped through the doorway into a dark, dank room paved in concrete and framed by the same.

The colonel general hadn't exaggerated—the smell was unbelievable. Blood, rotting flesh, burning hair, human excrement. It all swirled together into a choking cocktail so smothering that Rzayev could hardly breathe. He gritted his teeth and jerked his head to Hasanov. The colonel general snapped a command, and a light switch popped. Overhead fluorescents hummed to life, bathing an expansive room in a flickering yellow glow.

The room was rectangular, stretching out with individual cells standing like horse stalls in rows to either side. There was a drain in the floor about halfway down the length of the cells, and blood ran into it. As Rzayev passed one particular cell about halfway down the room on his left, he observed a body sitting slumped in a chair.

It was a man...or it had been a man. Mid-thirties. Well built. With his head rolled sideways, his mouth hung open. All his teeth were gone, scattered over the floor along with a number of his fingers. His shirt was shredded, his skin filleted with cuts and swollen by burn marks. Both kneecaps were smashed.

He was...obliterated.

Rzayev stopped. He eyeballed the man, then turned a glare on Hasanov. "You did this?"

"He was loud, Mr. President. He would sing. He was inspiring the others. I thought it best to—"

"Stupid fool," Rzayev snapped. "This is not how you break soldiers."

Fast-walking down the length of the prison cells, Rzayev passed through another steel door and entered an empty block room about ten meters square. It was dark, but another jerk of Rzayev's head triggered the pop of a second light switch.

More fluorescents flickered to life. A muted groan was matched to the rattle of a chain. Yellow glow revealed four more bodies hanging from shackles, their toes suspended inches off the floor, their wrists bound together. Three were men. One of those men was missing a prosthetic leg—Rzayev knew, because the item rested on the floor nearby, covered in blood. They had beaten the man with it.

The other two men were big, white, and dark-haired. One had a face like an Easter Island head, all chunky with a giant nose. The other was handsome, or might have been. His face was so brutalized it was difficult to identify his features. His chin hung. Blood seeped from his lips. He made no effort to look up as Rzayev entered.

The final prisoner was a woman, dark-skinned with dark hair. Very pretty...or, like the handsome guy, at least she had been. She'd been flailed, her shirt ripped to shreds. Judging by the condition of her pants, she'd also been raped.

Rzayev gritted his teeth. He snapped his fingers.

"Lower them. Put them on the floor."

"I'm sorry, Mr. President?"

"You heard me!" Rzayev's voice exploded off the walls, echoing back on the small party. Three SSS soldiers scurried to operate the winches. One by one the four prisoners hit the floor.

They groaned. They cried out as tender limbs struck concrete. They fell sideways and backward.

They didn't get up. They didn't fight back.

"Who raped her?" Rzayev asked.

Hasanov looked blank. "Sir?"

"Who raped her?" Again Rzayev's voice thundered.

"I...believe it was one of my men."

"Shoot him. Immediately."

Rzayev broke away from the SSS leader and approached the second big guy. Not the ugly one with the busted nose. He wanted the handsome one, the one he'd spoken with before. The *American*.

Squatting alongside the prisoner, Rzayev inserted a finger beneath the man's chin and forced his face up. Swollen skin was blackened by bruises and dried blood. Breath rattled between cracked lips. Dark eyes met his.

And glared defiance.

"You understand me, American?" Rzayev spoke in English. The American made no sign, but Rzayev saw the glint of recognition in his eyes.

"I wish to apologize for the rape of your friend...and the death of another. My men were overzealous."

No response.

Rzayev grunted. "We are not so different, you and I. There is a warrior in your eyes. I too am a warrior, and you must understand...a warrior cannot back down until the mission is complete."

The American made the first indicator of a response. His lips pursed. He choked on a cough, then spat. Blood landed between Rzayev's feet. The president didn't so much as flinch.

"Now I will tell you," Rzayev continued, "that I am not like my men. I am not here to grind you to dust. I am here to strike a bargain...one warrior to another. You will tell me who you really are and what you know of this bomb that struck my country. Then I will give you medical care and food. You will be healed."

Rzayev let the carrot hang in the air. Gave it time to sink in. Then he revealed the stick.

"Otherwise, I will execute your team. One at a time. Very slowly. Their fate will be so much worse than the man we have already killed, and you will witness it. Because I am a warrior, and I cannot quit until my mission is complete."

Dead silence. Rzayev stared into those dark, angry eyes and waited for a sign of the wall coming down. Reason taking over. A desire for self-preservation and the preservation of his team overcoming his own relentless dedication to resistance.

Seconds ticked closer to a minute. Nothing changed in those eyes—but something did change in the room. It began as a low, rustling cough, similar to dry leaves skating over concrete. Rzayev barely noticed at first, but then the sound grew louder. It came from his right—from the man with one leg—and it wasn't a cough.

It was a laugh. Soft at first, but gaining in momentum. It was joined by a deeper rumble from the big guy, the one with the Easter Island face. Then the woman joined. All three were laughing, curled up on the ground, quaking with pain.

But not giving an inch of ground.

The American in front of Rzayev spat again, this time striking the president in the gut with a mixture of snot and blood. A wicked grin stretched across his face that never reached his eyes.

"We are a NATO reconnaissance team," the American snarled. "The bomb was Russian. Now do your worst, you pig."

41

The Situation Room
The White House

Be advised: Turkman on site and deploying.

Aimes read the message as she departed her government sedan and stepped into the West Wing. She resented the car ride and the visit to the White House as much as ever, but she couldn't deny the necessity of it for this latest meeting of the security council.

Aimes needed to be on site. She wanted to view faces, read reactions. Push her point across no matter what it took. There were some gaps technology simply couldn't bridge.

Pocketing the phone, Aimes pictured Rufus Turkman alone in Azerbaijan and breathed a silent prayer on his behalf. She didn't know what had become of Lucy Byrne—Rigby's message hadn't mentioned her. Whatever the case, the odds of Turkman surviving the next four hours on the other side of the world, let alone reaching or rescuing the missing Prosecution Force, were something less than microscopic.

He was going to his death...and in some small way, Aimes felt that she had sent him there.

"Right this way, Madam Director. The acting president is waiting."

An aide guided Aimes down stairs she knew too well, past the watch room, into the meeting chamber of the Situation Room. The conference table was already crowded by members of the security council, but Aimes's slot was saved. She settled in just as Secretary of State Gorman hung up a phone.

"No go, sir. We can't get Baku on the line."

From the end of the table, Jordan Stratton sat with a Chicago Bears polo stretched over aging gym muscles, his face pointed toward the screen at the end of the room. That screen didn't display anything in particular—just a map of the Caucasus—but the little red and green marks of advancing Russian and Iranian ground forces were more than enough to hold a person's attention.

"All right, Aimes," Stratton said. "Take it from the top."

Aimes didn't bother to rise from her chair. This meeting was much less formal and much more focused than any regular cabinet meeting she had ever attended. Most of the security council wore casual clothes—golf shirts, loose blouses, even gym wear. This was an emergency meeting. Straight to the point.

"Four hours ago the Agency received word from an undercover indigenous asset, codenamed Blackjack, working deep inside the Kremlin. Blackjack contacted us under duress, and his full report was cut short. We believe he was terminated by the Russians. However, just before ending the call, Blackjack stated that he had intercepted evidence indicating that the Kremlin—and specifically President Nikitin—had deployed black ops assets to Azerbaijan for the purpose of assassinating President Elchin Rzayev."

No gasp, no hint of shock circled the table. Everybody already knew why they were there, even if the details had escaped them. Aimes proceeded.

"Efforts to reestablish contact with Blackjack have failed, reinforcing our belief that the asset was lost. We have since orbited our attention to the Caucasus, acting on the assumption that Blackjack's information is accurate, and put ourselves in the shoes of would-be Russian assassins. If you'll direct your attention to the screen..."

Aimes lifted a laser pointer, and the map of the Caucasus region zoomed to focus over the eastern half of Azerbaijan, with the Russian border clearly marked in white just above it.

"You're looking at the Republic of Dagestan, a Russian holding and part of the Federation's North Caucasian Federal District. Its capital is Makhachkala, a city of about half a million people resting on the Caspian shore about two hundred fifteen miles northwest of Baku. I'm bringing Makhachkala to your attention because five hours ago the Agency was alerted by the Automatic Identification System used by all maritime shipping that a Russian freighter departed Makhachkala, bound for Baku. Supposedly this freighter is carrying industrial machine parts. However, given the current state of diplomatic affairs between Russia and Azerbaijan, all shipping with the exception of this single freighter has ceased, and our efforts to produce receipts for the purchase of these machine parts have yielded no results. In fact, it would seem that the Port of Baku has no record of an incoming shipment of any sort."

"You were able to get through to the Azerbaijanis?" That was Gorman.

"Not directly, no. We..." Aimes hesitated.

"You hacked their database," Stratton said. "We're all adults. Proceed, Madam Director."

Aimes returned to the screen, grateful for the subject's dismissal. She used her laser pointer to mark a spot about three-quarters of the way between Makhachkala and Baku.

"The vessel in question is the *Caspian Voyager*. She's a small ship of about six thousand gross tons. Currently she is here, about fifty miles off the Russian coast, pointed south for Baku. At present course and speed, we expect her to arrive within the next three hours."

Aimes lowered the pointer. Nobody said anything. National Security Advisor Nick West removed his glasses and squinted at Aimes.

"Wait. Just exactly what are you implying?"

Aimes inhaled. Stopped. She hated the word *implying*, but she wouldn't gaslight the man.

"The Agency believes that if Blackjack's intelligence is legitimate, it may be possible that a Russian black ops team is sneaking into Baku aboard the *Caspian Voyager*, with intentions of assassinating President Rzayev."

Dead silence. West leaned back in his chair and folded his arms. He looked sideways to SecDef Kline, who also made no comment. Gorman was fixated on the screen. General Yellin's shoulders stiffened beneath a tight US Army T-shirt, but he remained quiet.

At last it was White House Chief of Staff Jill Easterling who broke the ice.

"They're gonna cap this guy?"

Aimes concealed a smile at Easterling's slang-laden question. She was as educated as anybody else in the room, but Jill knew when to cut to the point.

"That does seem possible," Aimes said. "Since the Russian invasion of Georgia, Georgian President Meladze has been AWOL, and the agency now believes him to be dead. It's possible—although completely unconfirmed—that Russian operatives removed Meladze prior to their so-called 'special military operation' into Georgia. That theory is substantiated by the bizarre reports that Georgian Defense Forces were under standing orders to comply with invading Russian ground troops. Hardly a shot was fired until the Russians had already reached Tbilisi, which indicates that the Russian military somehow successfully penetrated and sabotaged Georgian military command."

"So you think they're going to do the same with Azerbaijan?" Kline asked.

"Killing Rzayev wouldn't have the same effect as eliminating Meladze," Aimes replied. "Russia's military intentions at this stage are brutally clear—the Azerbaijani military *will* fight back, even if Russia maintains their propaganda about securing the region against nuclear threat. But without Rzayev it's likely that the core of Azerbaijan's government would struggle to stabilize. Rzayev is a dictator, plain and simple. There would be a power grab following his death. Predictable chaos. Russia could easily exploit such chaos in the interest of a much quicker, more decisive military campaign."

Aimes was now so far outside the realm of *know* and so deep into the forest of speculation that her very stomach was quaking with nausea, but she held herself together. If any of her implications were true—even partially—the results could be disastrous.

"Okay," West said, tapping his glasses against the tabletop. "I think I know, but just for the sake of clarity, allow me to ask: Why do we care about this when the Chinese just sank one of our warships?"

All eyes pivoted to the national security advisor. General Yellin actually started coming out of his seat. Stratton's hand shot up, stopping him.

"Calm down, General. It's a valid question. Madam Director?"

Aimes returned to the screen. She zoomed out. She motioned with the laser pointer—not to Azerbaijan or Russia, but to Iran.

"We care because nearly one hundred thousand Iranian ground troops, supported by armor and mobile artillery, are churning northwest toward the Azerbaijani border as we speak, with many more on the way. Those troops could be in position to strike southern Azerbaijan by the end of the week, which would be bad, but from a tactical point of view it's not altogether logical. Azerbaijan has maintained territorial claims over portions of northwestern Iran for years, but with Iran being the much bigger fish of the two, those claims have gone nowhere. We have little reason to believe that Tehran has any express interest in seizing Azerbaijan. It makes much more sense that the Russians would want to reclaim portions of the old USSR."

"So why the Iranian movement?" West asked.

"Turkey," Kline interrupted, leaning over his table. His face grew taut. He pointed at the map. "Turkey lies on the Armenian border. If the Russians annex Azerbaijan with the support of the Iranians, two armies merge, with nothing save Armenia standing between themselves and eastern Turkey—a *NATO* member state."

Aimes lowered the laser pointer. "We already know that Supreme Leader Kazemi met with President Nikitin and President Chen of China earlier this week. We can assume an alliance may have been formed. If Azerbaijan becomes an open highway for Iranian troop movement, there's nothing to stop Iranian and Russian armies to converge on Turkey, directly threatening NATO."

"And while we're distracted by the Chinese, there won't be much we can do about it," Kline finished.

"They'll have us by the balls," Yellin growled. "And it won't stop there. Iran doesn't give a rat's ass about Turkey. They want Iraq—and more than anything, Israel. We're talking systemic, viral war inside of mere weeks."

"It's even bigger than that," Gorman said. "If Russia attacks Turkey, we'll be compelled to respond, per NATO treaty. Israel will want help also, as will Iraq."

"And *Taiwan*," Kline said. "The Chinese won't miss an opportunity."

Brief silence. Easterling whispered a curse. "So we're talking about world war, here."

"Almost overnight," Kline said. "All while our economy is on the brink of major recession and the loss of the Panama Canal has our Navy hamstrung."

"We've got to hit them first," Yellin said. "Strike before they find their footing."

"Strike *who*?" West said.

"The Chinese, for a start! Mr. Acting President, the deadline passed nearly two hours ago. Beijing has made no statement justifying their actions beyond their flimsy accusation that we breached their territorial waters—which is blatantly *false*. The world is watching. If we don't respond, we have no reason to expect any of our enemies to back down. They'll be emboldened. We punch China first, then we deal with Russia and Iran."

"Did you not hear a word the director said?" West interjected before Stratton could respond. "Russian-Iranian intentions are *speculative*."

"Would you rather they became a reality?" Yellin barked.

"Enough!" Stratton smacked the table. His blood was up. Aimes could see it in his face. Cheeks flushed, eyes a little red. He hadn't slept.

None of them had.

"You're all right," Stratton said. "We have to act, but not on speculative intelligence. Madam Director, we need hard confirmation, as soon as you can get it. If Russia has deployed a team to assassinate Rzayev, it's in our interest to stand in the gap. Dictator or otherwise, Rzayev may be the last roadblock between Russia and a direct challenge to NATO."

"Understood, sir. We'll do our best."

"Now, Secretary," Stratton pivoted to Gorman. "I don't care what you have to do. Send carrier pigeons if you must. I want contact with Baku, I want contact with Tehran, and I want contact with Moscow. If they won't respond, the gloves *will* come off. Make that brutally clear."

"And Beijing, sir?"

Gorman voiced the question everyone was thinking. Aimes's heart rate accelerated a little as she faced Stratton. The acting president sat tall, despite the crushing pressure on his shoulders. He inhaled once. Then he looked to Yellin.

"They've attacked our country. They've ignored our warning. *Hit them.*"

42

Absheron District
Azerbaijan

Nightfall descended over Azerbaijan, and Rufus Turkman was ready for action. With four devices strapped together into one giant wad roughly the size of a softball, Turk couldn't find the remote detonation hardware he would have preferred in the back of the Cobra. The C4 itself seemed to be an afterthought—something an Azerbaijani soldier had slung into the back of the truck as he rushed out of an armory.

The best Turk could find was an old-school blasting cap with a lengthy coil of fuse—like something from an old western movie. Designed for use with dynamite, not C4, Turk knew from experience that the blasting cap would still produce enough kinetic energy to detonate the modern explosive, assuming he shaped the charge correctly. The bomb would still go *bang*...the only question was whether or not Turk could haul ass out of the blast zone before it did so.

"Can you reach the pedals?"

Turk clambered into the passenger seat of the Cobra, shooting Lucy a sideways look. She sat behind the wheel, a wadded-up military duffel bag jammed behind her hips to bring her legs closer to the pedals. The seat was racked all the way forward, bringing the wheel into her lap. Her toes barely touched the accelerator.

"I can reach just fine, thank you." Lucy's reply carried a little salt—a little sting. It was enough to bring a smile to Turk's face.

Her old self was coming back...one slow second at a time.

"Drive, then."

Lucy shifted into gear, and Turk cradled the bomb in his lap. The detonator and fuse wire were both curled inside his cargo pocket, rendering the C4 perfectly safe even during the bumpy ride out of the mountains and toward the fuel depot. Lucy already knew the route—they had mapped it out with the aid of the unidentified voice whose number was stored in the sat phone's call log.

The voice didn't like the plan. Turk didn't care. He wanted a route of ingress and a separate route of egress, which the voice was able to map out with the aid of a CIA spy satellite. Further, the voice promised to maintain overwatch via that satellite for the duration of the mission—although what good that would do, Turk had no idea. The image would likely lag, and even if Langley did manage to observe something useful via their eye in the sky, Turk's only form of communication was the sat phone...slow and unwieldy while engaged in a gunfight.

As if on cue the phone buzzed, and Turk mashed the answer key.

"What?"

"We've got you on screen. It would help if you could beacon the truck somehow...put something on its roof for us to track it by."

"Why don't I do a strip tease for you while I'm up there?"

"I'm trying to help, Mr. Turkman."

"Help me with QRF, or stop calling. I've got work to do."

Turk hung up. He bit back a curse and noticed Lucy giving him side-eye.

"What?"

"I was just thinking...you're a lot like Reed."

"Is that a compliment?"

"Do you want it to be?"

This time Turk didn't spare the curse. He pointed at the black road ahead. "That way. Let's move."

Lucy scooted forward in the seat and jammed her foot against the gas.

43

They drew within half a mile of the fuel depot before Turk waved Lucy off the road. They were running without headlights, and thus far only civilian vehicles had passed them. Nobody challenged them—why would they?

The situation was the same as before. Azerbaijan was at war, and they were driving a war wagon.

"Remember," Turk said. "Sixty seconds after the blast, then you drive to the crossroads. You wait sixty seconds, and then if I don't show up, you split. Got it?"

Lucy nodded. Her mouth opened. She stopped.

"What?" Turk said again.

"Do you...want to call your wife?"

Turk's stomach descended into knots. His eyes stung. It was a question he'd already evaluated, and then relegated to the basement of his mind. Battlefield focus was a fickle thing, a trained instinct. Turk knew that the moment he heard Sinju's voice from the other side of the planet...

No. It wasn't an option. He would see her again. He had to keep telling himself that.

"Crossroads," Turk repeated. "Sixty seconds from the blast, wait sixty seconds. Not a moment longer."

"Got it."

Turk turned, cradling an AK-74 with three spare magazines jammed into the cargo pockets of his pants. Lucy called out once more.

"Turk!"

He looked back.

"God be with you."

The words warmed his blood more than Turk expected. He nodded once, then he was lost in the darkness, and Lucy was growling away in the Cobra.

The arsenal of gear Turk and Lucy had captured from the Azerbaijani military had been irregular and incomplete. Turk wore a camouflage jacket and a matching cap, and he cradled a rifle. The only body armor he'd found in the Cobra was much too small for him, and he'd left it behind. The Zigana was his only sidearm, jammed into his belt without a holster.

There was no chest rig. Only two fragmentation grenades and a smoke grenade, and they rode in an undersized backpack along with the explosives and one bottle of water. It wasn't anything close to a proper loadout, but nothing about this situation was ideal. The best Turk could do was charge ahead, picturing his team buried inside that black site...and hoping.

One man against the world, with a highly competent but still shell-shocked former assassin as backup, and nothing even remotely resembling QRF on the horizon.

I'll see them again. Turk pictured Sinju with beautiful baby Liberty riding in his arms, and he pressed forward into the dark.

The space between the roadbed and the fuel depot consisted of a rocky field that might once have been agricultural but was now too sandy to be of any use. Dust rose around Turk in a cloud as he leaned low and kept the AK pressed into his shoulder. The lights of the depot guided him like a beacon, two klicks away, dragging slowly closer. The line of trucks was still there, most of them military in appearance, but several civilian.

He would have to select a tank removed from the column of trucks waiting to be filled. There was a risk that those tanks would already be empty, and therefore useless, but the alternative was to murder a couple dozen Azerbaijani soldiers.

The ambient glow of the security lights grew brighter as Turk neared the compound. He reached the perimeter fence without detection, three hundred yards removed from the entrance of the compound and the line of trucks approaching the gate. The fence itself was chain link, ten feet tall but without any barbed or razor wire at the top. Turk had searched the Cobra for wire cutters and come up empty handed. Instead he simply slung the rifle over his back using the two-point strap, then commenced to climbing.

His heavy body dragged against the chain link, shaking flimsy poles as he shinnied straight to the top and slung a leg over. He was still mostly concealed in shadow, glancing left toward the busy center of the compound every few seconds to ensure that nobody had detected his intrusion.

There were a dozen or so workers running giant fuel pumps to fill the tanker trucks, but they were all preoccupied. The three or four visible Azerbaijani soldiers standing guard were also distracted, looking inward and toward the gate—not toward the perimeter.

Turk's boots struck hard gravel on the interior of the compound and he automatically swung the AK back into his shoulder. He picked a target—a black fuel tank fifty feet across and twenty feet high, standing like a squatting giant in the dark. It was on the outside of the compound, farthest from the soldiers and the trucks. As Turk drew alongside its hulking metal side, he lifted a rock from the ground and tapped it against the exterior wall.

The resulting *ping* was dense and didn't echo—the tank was at least partially full. Squatting in the dirt, Turk withdrew the explosive from his backpack. He hadn't bothered to split the C4 into multiple wads. One concentrated blast would do the job, rupturing the side of the tank and unleashing a surge of fuel. It was unlikely that the C4 itself would ignite the petrol, and the flame of the fuse would be extinguished by the blast. Turk would need a secondary flame, removed from the first, but close enough to ignite the resulting fumes.

The wad of C4 rested against the base of the tank, and Turk piled gravel against it to hold it in place. Then he inserted the detonator, double-checked the fitment, and trailed the fuse across the gravel, five feet to a slight depression. Turk checked his watch and confirmed that he was right on schedule before dipping his hand back into his backpack for the second half of his mechanism—a gallon jug of raw gasoline taken from the Cobra.

The jug gurgled as Turk dumped the gas across the gravel, creating a five-foot-wide stain. He dumped the empty can into the midst of the wet spot and retreated twenty feet, eyes up, rifle slung across his chest. The tension coursing through his body was at an all-time high, a battle-ready blend of adrenaline and necessary nervousness. It was a cocktail that had kept Turk both alive and lethal for dozens of engagements, and now kept him zeroed in on the task at hand.

He reached into his pocket and withdrew a damp pack of Azerbaijani cigarettes and a cigarette lighter, both taken from the Cobra. Only one smoke remained, and he pressed it between his lips. The lighter came out next, and he ground it with his thumb.

His hand trembled, and Turk shook it to drive back the nerves. He wasn't afraid, but the combination of the battle-ready cocktail and overwhelming exhaustion was getting to him. The lighter produced nothing but sparks. He ground his thumb again. Still sparks. He shook the lighter and looked through the translucent case to check the volume of butane contained within. It was empty, and then his thumbnail scraped over a crack in the plastic. The lighter had been drained—it wouldn't ignite. Turk padded his chest and pockets for another means of flame, sudden anxiety joining the adrenaline.

What had he been thinking? He hadn't even double-checked the lighter?

"*Salam!*"

The voice carried from the shadows beyond the tank. Turk's gaze snapped up and his hands fell instinctively to the rifle. An Azerbaijani soldier stood just inside the fence, fifty yards away...smoking. He lifted a hand in a wave and called out again.

"*Sənin sigarətini yandırmaq istəyirəm?*"

Turk froze. He didn't respond. The Azerbaijani was smiling, blowing smoke through his nose. He poked the cigarette back between his teeth, his rifle hanging loosely from a shoulder strap, then advanced.

Turk dropped the busted lighter and placed his right hand over the grip of the AK. The Azerbaijani continued to smile as he approached. He lifted his chin toward Turk's military cap, perhaps identifying the rank insignia embroidered onto it, and threw a sloppy salute.

Another blast of smoke through his nostrils. Then he extended the cigarette, orange tip first. He nodded encouragingly.

Turk slowly removed the water-damaged smoke from his lips. The crinkled tips touched. Turk's gaze passed over the soldier's shoulder to the fence line thirty yards away. The sign there was printed in Azerbaijani, and Turk couldn't read a word of it, but the symbol of a cigarette covered over by a circle and an X was pretty much universal.

Turk's cigarette ignited. He drew it back with his left hand, still holding the AK by its grip with his right. He nodded his thanks and inhaled. The smoke was sour, the tobacco ruined by rainwater that had yet to fully dry.

But it burned. Turk breathed out. The Azerbaijani grunted and pulled on his own cigarette. The man seemed perfectly relaxed, not the least bit suspicious. His gaze had passed over Turk's jacket and the name tape printed there, but he hadn't seemed to notice the mismatched combat pants Turk wore.

"*Dəli gecə,*" the soldier said with a shake of his head. "*Siz ehtiyatdasınız?*"

Turk sucked on the smoke again, bringing the tip of the cigarette to a blistering hot orange glow. The sour smoke filled his lungs. He hesitated. The soldier raised both eyebrows, waiting for an answer. His head rocked. He seemed to notice the backpack for the first time. He squinted.

Screw it.

Turk flicked the smoke with his left hand the same moment as he rotated his hold on the AK with his right, releasing the grip of the rifle and grabbing it by the base of the stock instead. The butt of the weapon arced up, riding at the ends of the two-point sling just as the cigarette arced through the air like a tiny amber missile...and landed right in the middle of the gasoline-soaked gravel.

A rush of flames lit the night, glinting off the soldier's confused and panicked eyes a split second before the butt of the AK struck him dead in the forehead with the force of a kicking mule. His eyes rolled back. His body went limp. Turk's gaze snapped toward the flames and he noted the C4 fuse burning a yard outside the inferno. The gasoline fire had lit it, all right. It had burned fully two feet of fuse in an instant, slashing precious time out of Turk's calculations.

Momentary panic rushed his body as the soldier collapsed to the ground unconscious. Turk looked to the fence and almost made the dash, but guilt held him back. Squatting, he grabbed the guy by the chest rig and jerked him away from the flames. Turk could feel the heat on his face. Sweat drained into his eyes and he thrashed toward the fence, the heavy Azerbaijani dragging along behind him like a dead animal.

Ten more yards. Turk couldn't see the fuse through the smoke. An alarm rang from the far side of the compound, and voices shouted. Turk reached the fence and dropped the guy at the base, fifty yards removed from the fuel tank. It wasn't far enough—not nearly far enough. But it was all Turk could do. He couldn't haul the unconscious soldier over the fence, and he didn't have time to hack a hole through.

Grabbing the wire, Turk yanked himself up. His heart thundered as he caught a glimpse of his watch and realized he was now thirty seconds behind schedule. The interaction with the soldier had cost him. He reached the top of the fence and threw a leg over. From someplace behind, a voice shouted an alarm, and Turk instinctively looked over his shoulder just in time to catch the orange blink of muzzle flash from an AK. Rifles cracked. A bullet whizzed over his head. He dropped off the fence and hit the outside of the compound with a heavy grunt.

Back on his feet, Turk sprinted for safety, again checking his watch. He'd calculated for eighty seconds of fuse. Two feet were burned off, slashing the total burn length by about twenty percent, which meant—

Turk never had time to finish the calculation. The thunder of the C4 detonation was loud, ripping through the night like an artillery blast, but it had nothing on the earth-shaking explosion of raw fuel catching flame a split second later.

Turk half flung himself, half fell into a ditch as the night sky illuminated with a brilliant glow of bright orange. He buried his face in the mud and didn't even try to look back as the ground convulsed beneath him like an earthquake. The roar of it was louder than gunfire in his ears, driving concussive shockwaves through his chest. He twisted in the mud and looked over one shoulder, squinting in the light...

Just in time to catch the second fuel cell going up in flames. And then the third. It was a chain reaction, and there was no stopping it. The tanks were too close together. Flames reached toward the sky as an alarm screamed and soldiers ran like ants, fleeing the gate. The next fuel cell exploded, sending a truck hurtling into the air like a toy.

The entire depot was going up in flames, right before his very eyes.

44

SSS Black Site
Baku, Azerbaijan

The scream echoed against the prison walls, a protracted shriek that erupted from Corbyn's throat with the explosive energy of a detonating RPG. Reed writhed on the ground and fought to face his waylaid pilot, but the heavy boot of an Azerbaijani soldier kept him pressed down, crushing against his sternum and driving the air from his lungs. The hiss of a blowtorch intensified, and Corbyn screamed again. Reed could see the flames out of the corner of his eye, working their way up her legs, slowly toward her waist.

"Let her go!" Reed choked, jerking against the boot. The guy crushed down, and the last of Reed's worthless demand left his throat as a choking hiss of disrupted breath.

Rzayev himself stood over the torturers, watching impassively as the torch did its worst on Corbyn's unprotected skin. He held a pistol against his leg, eyes glassy and cold. Reed thrashed, and Rzayev tilted his head.

The torch was pulled away, but Corbyn continued to quake with pain. Reed twisted his head sideways to face her and saw tears streaming down her face, eyes bloodshot, lips quivering.

Rzayev cocked the pistol and stepped behind Corbyn. He placed the muzzle against the back of her trembling head and looked dead at Reed.

"I will ask one last time. Who *really* sent you?"

Reed didn't answer. His gaze flicked from Rzayev down to Corbyn. The pilot trembled with pain. Her gaze turned hard.

"We are a NATO reconnaissance team—"

Rzayev's boot struck Corbyn in the spine, ramming her against the concrete and driving the breath from her lungs. He bent, jamming the pistol deep into her skull. His teeth gritted. Spit sprayed Reed in the face as Rzayev bellowed.

"*You lie!* What are the Americans planning?"

Reed met Corbyn's gaze. For a long moment, he measured the pain in her eyes. The fear. It was almost enough to break him—to send him spiraling down a vortex of confession, or at least a vortex of alternate lies. Something that might protect Corbyn without playing into Russia's hand.

But no. The iron in Corbyn's face hardened. Her lip curled, and she shook her head. Just once.

Reed turned back to Rzayev. "Go to hell, pig."

Rzayev's cheeks flushed crimson. His jaw locked. His finger dropped over the trigger.

"Have it your way, American."

Reed looked back to Corbyn. Their gazes met, and Corbyn offered him just the hint of a tormented smile. Her eyes closed.

Then the ground convulsed with a distant, bone-jarring explosion. It resounded from outside the compound, someplace above ground. A throaty boom that rattled mortar from the concrete walls and sent Rzayev stumbling. The blast had barely finished before it was followed by another, and then a third. Two blasts went off at once, pounding the ground and filling the air with the voice of angry thunder. Rzayev's men shouted and closed around their president, pulling him away from the walls. Voices shouted into radios. No answers came.

The lead officer called to Rzayev in Azerbaijani, and the president holstered his pistol. His men shoved him toward the door, boots pounding. A final blast ripped through the compound, farther removed than the first five, but no less violent. Reed looked in the direction of the disturbance, his view blocked by a blank concrete wall. His chest ached as he gasped for air, his hands burning from the zip ties binding his wrists behind his back.

Then he closed his eyes in resigned defeat, because he knew that sound. There was only one thing on earth that made it—detonating fuel, likely from a depot.

The Russians had arrived.

45

35,000 Feet above the South China Sea

With his head bent toward the canopy, US Navy Lieutenant Michael Nash could easily see all three guided missile destroyers bearing southwest into the Taiwan Strait, frothy white trails stretched out behind them. They were little more than bricks on his radar, specks in the midnight silence, but the destructive capability housed beneath each of their decks was more than enough to level multiple city blocks.

Inside the cramped confines of the FA-18E Super Hornet's cockpit, that sort of destruction was all academic. All theoretical. But with a full loadout of six AIM-120 AMRAAM missiles and two AIM-9 Sidewinders mounted to his jet's wings, Nash knew something about destructive potential himself. He'd just never experienced the so-called "real thing."

"Heads up, everybody." Captain Mark "Rudolph" Pollard—a call sign gifted in honor of his perpetually red nose—said over their tactical UHF, or ultrahigh frequency. Nash looked instinctively toward the empty black sky ahead and his blood pressure spiked. He knew what Rudolph was about to say even before he said it. He could sense it, and the knowledge sent a tremor down his spine.

"We just got word," Rudolph continued. "We are golden days. Repeat, we are golden days. Mission is a go."

Nash's fingers flew as he and the sixteen other Super Hornets spread out over the designated umbrella zone. Their Offensive Counter Air mission, or OCA, was simple—sweep the airspace above those three ships so that the sailors below could dispense their deadly payload...straight toward China.

Nash couldn't help but glance down again toward the hulk of the USS *Milius*. The vessel was just a dot, a black speck through his night vision cueing and display that he could easily have missed if he wasn't looking for it. But then that speck flashed brilliant green. Hot light flooded the ocean near the *Milius*'s bow, and Nash tracked the flight path of the launching Tomahawk cruise missile as it reached two hundred feet of altitude before arcing westward. The bow of the *Milius* flashed again and again. Thirty missiles in total, and the USS *Higgins* and the USS *McCampbell* fired just as many. A veritable shotgun blast of one-thousand-pound high explosive warheads screaming toward the Chinese coast at over five hundred miles per hour.

Death on the wind.

"Badman, deploy!" Rudolph's voice sounded choppy over the frequency-hopping UHF radio, pounding inside Nash's helmet. "Here they come."

Nash looked down at the Situational Awareness page on his MPCD, and his chest tightened. They were coming all right. Dozens of them.

Chinese fighters—inbound.

46

The Situation Room
The White House

"We're underway!" Yellin spoke as he hung up a phone. The screen at the end of the room blinked, switching instantly away from Azerbaijan and transitioning to the South China Sea.

There were markers—three American warships entering the Taiwan Strait, with fifteen more, including the USS *Ronald Reagan* hanging back by a hundred miles. A wall of little green dots marked the path of cruise missiles zipping across the strait toward the Chinese mainland, and as Stratton watched, his stomach descended into knots.

He looked to Easterling. She said nothing. He looked back to the screen.

"We've got Chinese fighters inbound, sir." Admiral Dan Turley, chief of naval operations, was next to speak. "Chengdu J-20s, about twenty of them. They're headed straight for our Super Hornets."

"We're outnumbered?" Stratton asked. He thought he recalled Yellin mentioning a deployment of only thirty US fighters.

"They don't stand a chance," Yellin scoffed. "We've got three destroyers with two dozen surface-to-air birds each. They're walking face-first into a buzzsaw. Enjoy the show, Mr. Vice President."

The comment may have been in poor taste, but Stratton could see the white-hot rage burning in Yellin's eyes, the same as Turley's and every other military officer in the room. They'd lost people—good people. The sailors of the *Sampson* had been ambushed and slaughtered. This wasn't a question of balancing the scales, this was a question of obliterating them altogether.

"Remember, General," Stratton said. "Your boys don't fire unless the Chinese engage. I want equalization, not escalation."

Yellin made no reply, but Stratton detected the rigid tension in his shoulders. The man looked ready to explode. He fixated on the screen, just like every other person in the room, and watched as the dots drew nearer. Red Chinese Xs and green American circles, with blue arrows marking the path of the cruise missiles.

Yellin's desk phone buzzed. He snatched it up before the chime even completed. He looked to Stratton.

"The Chinese are attempting to engage the missiles. We've got to take them."

"What are their odds, Admiral?" Stratton skipped over Yellin and spoke directly to Turley. Of the two, the admiral seemed calmer.

"Not better than twenty percent, sir. Their jets are flying too high."

"They could be faking," Yellin interjected. "They could be prepping to fire on our planes."

Again, Stratton looked to Turley. The admiral nodded once. "That's possible, sir."

Back to the screen. Stratton chewed his lip. He pictured a world at war, flames consuming every city, ballistic missiles decorating every horizon. Warships and aircraft and so, so much bloodshed.

If the Chinese were in earnest, that reality was unavoidable. But what if it was all a mistake? A rogue action, prompted by Russian harassment. Stratton could flatten the airbase that had deployed the aircraft which sunk the *Sampson*, and that could be the end of it. An eye for an eye, a tooth for a tooth.

But if he escalated...

"Hold, General."

Yellin slammed down the phone with visible frustration. He stood up.

Lip twitching. Face flushed red. Another brutal five seconds ground by. The phone rang again. Yellin nearly tore it free of the receiver. He spun on Stratton.

"They're firing on us!"

Stratton's heart sank. A sickening cloud closed around his mind, blocking out the sun. The hope.

But with that cloud was something else, something the general had radiated all night—rage.

Stratton gave the order. "Let 'em have it!"

47

35,000 Feet above the South China Sea

Lieutenant Michael Nash had only ever faced China's fifth-generation stealth fighter from the secure confines of a simulator. His actual air combat maneuvering training had only involved head-to-head dogfights with other US or NATO fighter jets. Even after training against TOPGUN-trained adversaries in the skies over Guam, he felt ill-prepared to go up against the best pilots Beijing had to offer.

But it was getting real, and it was coming quick—at over eight hundred knots of closure.

From out of the black, a morass of twenty contacts appeared on Nash's scope—already inside forty miles—fading in and out as their radar-absorbing skin and electronic countermeasures wreaked havoc on the Super Hornet's electronically scanned array radar. But they were all Chinese. Of that, Nash was certain. And based on their closure, they were all fighters.

They're coming in hot.

"Weapons yellow," Rudolph reminded. "Do not engage unless fired upon."

Unless fired upon. Nash wasn't aware of what convoluted politics were at work on the far side of the globe, but he was pretty damn sure he was about to be fired upon. The Chinese had already sunk the *Sampson*, and even now ninety cruise missiles were screeching toward their airbase in retaliation. This wasn't a show of force or a minor skirmish. This was war.

Nash sucked down oxygen from the onboard generator as he rocked the weapon switch to select one of the six loaded AIM-120 AMRAAM, or advanced medium-range air-to-air missiles. His radar struggled to provide a stable track file to engage, but he was still too far away for one of the two AIM-9X Sidewinder infrared-guided missiles on his wingtips. Twenty miles remained between the American Super Hornets and Chinese Chengdus, but that gap was closing fast. Nash's heart hammered, sweat trickling down his spine despite the subzero temperatures outside his canopy. He breathed deep and reminded himself why he was here, why he'd joined the Navy in the first place. What it meant to be the very tip of the spear.

Bring it.

"Smoke in the air!" A shrill call cut through the chatter on their tactical frequency. Nash's face snapped instinctively to the left—it was Banshee, so named for the tone of his voice. He flew over two miles off Nash's left wing, one of four jets making up the wall of Super Hornets streaking toward the Chinese.

"Vampire! Vampire! Vampire!" Rudolf called. "Showtime, target lead group!"

Anti-ship missile. The Chinese were firing on the destroyers.

Nash's blood boiled hot in sudden outrage, enough to drown his nerves. He pushed his thumb down on the weapon-select switch to call up one of his Sidewinders. Immediately, a low warbling tone filled his helmet as the seeker, but he ignored it as flashes of light drew his eyes up to the horizon. In horror, he realized that *all* of the Chinese fifth-gen fighters were pumping anti-ship missiles into the trio of guided missile destroyers crushing through the Taiwan Strait.

It was the same trick they had pulled against *Sampson*, but this time Nash was there to keep them from getting away with it. The anti-ship missiles were fire and forget—the destroyers would have to try to shoot them down. Meanwhile the Super Hornets would make sure those Chinese planes never fired on an American vessel ever again.

"Showtime One One engaging north lead group," Nash's division lead called. "Showtime One Three, target south lead group."

"On it," Nash replied.

With practiced muscle memory, Nash pushed his throttles into afterburner and rolled left. The Super Hornet lurched forward, and he glanced over at Banshee to make sure the younger pilot was still in position as they streaked toward the Chinese left flank where the Chengdu fighters had scattered. But it was impossible to miss the Phalanx CIWS close-in weapon systems on the destroyers far beneath them, opening up on the incoming missiles and whipping ropes of fire across the night sky. One anti-ship missile after another broke apart into balls of fire, falling victim to a wall of lead.

There were still so many missiles left in the air, but there was little Nash could do about them. He had to focus, now.

He had to dogfight.

Rolling level, Nash zeroed in on the smut-black prey littering the horizon, visible only under the glow of their own afterburners as they scrambled to flee.

Big mistake.

"Showtime One One, Fox Two!"

Nash glanced over his right shoulder and saw the plume of a missile leaving his division lead's jet. He castled up on his stick and used his night vision cuing and display to guide his own radar on a fleeing Chengdu. He slaved his missile's seeker to its hot exhaust.

The low warbling ring was replaced by a high-pitched squeal.

Good tone.

The sweat was gone now. The nerves faded under a dump of adrenaline and focus, honed by thousands of hours of training and anticipation. This was the moment. The tip of the spear was crashing toward the enemy.

The target was well within the Sidewinder's launch acceptability region, but the tone flickered as the Chinese pilot maneuvered to shake his tail. Nash added afterburner—the Chengdu was fast, capable of reaching speeds as high as fifteen hundred miles per hour, but the Super Hornet was no slouch. Nash saw the number in his helmet-mounted display top out at Mach 1.2, and he squeezed the trigger.

"Showtime One Three, Fox Two!"

The plane twitched as the heavy Sidewinder fell away from his right wingtip. A flash of fire, and then it was gone. Not Mach 1.2, but Mach 2.5. The Chengdu had no chance of outrunning it, only breaking the seeker's lock.

"Come on...come on..." Nash whispered as he stared at the fading glow of the Chengdu's hot exhaust. The missile had disappeared moments after leaving the rail, but he knew the gap was closing. "Any second..."

Suddenly, the Chengdu pitched up into an aggressive climbing maneuver as dozens of flares fanned away from the jet to spoof the Sidewinder's seeker. Nash watched with frustration as the infrared countermeasures fell away from the red of the Chengdu's exhaust.

But then he saw something else.

From the darkness, the flares illuminated an object streaking into the fifth-gen fighter. The two met, and flame erupted through the clouds.

"Hell yeah!"

His celebration was momentary and died in a wash of icy cold. Nash had taken his eyes off the other retreating fighters for only a few seconds, but those few seconds had been too long. Over the low warbling tone of his second Sidewinder seeking another target, a more pressing sound drilled into his brain. His radar warning receiver had detected a radar lock, and he twisted his head, instinctively looking for the offending enemy.

No time. Bug out!

From all around him flashes of orange illuminated the sky—missiles streaking and detonating, afterburners dumping. Their tactical frequency was alive with desperate shouts and broken curses from each division. Showtime. Javelin. Tempest. Fury. Euphoria mixed with white-hot rage as two Super Hornets vanished from Nash's display at once. He nosed his jet hard down just as the tone for a radar lock changed once more.

Weapon launch.

"Showtime One Three is defensive!"

The Chengdu J-20 was right on his ass. Nash couldn't see it, but he could feel it. The Chinese pilot had leveraged his plane's stealth capability against the FA-18E's weaknesses and had maneuvered into Nash's control zone when he wasn't looking. It was check, and it might well be checkmate if Nash didn't pull a rabbit out of his hat.

The Higgins.

Nash saw the ship far beneath him, churning through the torn waters of the strait with Phalanx guns still blazing and surface-to-air missiles launching at regular intervals. He made a split-second decision and rolled inverted, then yanked the stick back into his lap while dumping out flares of his own. He strained against his narrowing vision and caught sight of the Chinese missile arcing delicately through the air as it sailed past his jet.

Don't shoot me, Higgins!

The Super Hornet streaked toward the ocean as the Chinese pilot fired another missile. Nash had dodged the first with a lot of skill and a little luck, but now he needed more luck than skill. He leveled off four hundred feet above the water, half a mile off the *Higgins*'s starboard side. No longer worried about being targeted by a heat-seeking missile, he pushed his throttles into full afterburner and imagined the invisible weapon streaking down toward his jet. A mile. Then half a mile. Closing hot, racing at nearly twice his own speed. Nash repeatedly slammed his fist against the red switch on his left canopy rail, dumping his Super Hornet's entire load of chaff and flares at once. Fragments of aluminum and glass fibers exploded from underneath his jet, reflecting the brilliance of the infrared countermeasures and forming an instant cloud as a last-ditch effort to throw off the missile.

Nash pulled hard right and streaked away from the *Higgins* as the missile struck the chaff cloud and just kept going. The radar-guided weapon was following him, racing past the *Higgins*'s starboard side and about to turn into the Super Hornet.

Then one of *Higgins*'s Phalanx guns thundered, and Nash saw its rope of fire stretch out behind him like a whip, generating a brief flash of orange. He gasped inside his oxygen mask and looked over his shoulder, elation rushing his bloodstream as the screaming tone in his helmet disappeared. The missile was gone, obliterated at forty-five hundred rounds per minute. A second later another flash of orange burst from the *Higgins*'s bow, and a surface-to-air missile raced into the air. Nash looked over his shoulder as the trailing Chinese fighter blew into a million pieces.

And then he heard another sound—Rudolph's screaming voice drowning out everything else around him.

"Break right, Nash! Smoke in the air!"

It was too late. Nash never saw the incoming fighter or recognized the blaze of hot missile exhaust. But he reacted to Rudolph's call on instinct, rolling right and again trying to rip the wings off his jet. His hand never dipped toward the ejection lever, even as his mind accepted that he was already out of time.

Lose sight, lose the fight.

The missile raced in. Perfect stillness enveloped the Super Hornet's cockpit.

And then everything went white.

48

Absheron District
Azerbaijan

When Turk picked himself up out of the ditch, nothing was left. The fence, the fuel cells, the trucks, the pumping station, the soldiers. Everything was erased from memory, consumed by dust and flames that lit up the sky as bright as day. The fire was so hot that it singed the unshaven beard stubble on his face, scalding his exposed skin. Turk spat out grit, ears ringing as he surveyed his surroundings for signs of life.

He could have spared himself the trouble of dragging the unconscious soldier to the fence. That guy was history—likely burned to ash, as were his buddies. The distraction had worked better than Turk had imagined. Possibly too well. One exploding fuel tank had ruptured the next, and the next.

Now it was all gone, and a quick glance at his watch confirmed what Turk already suspected. He was *way* behind schedule.

Turning up the hill, Turk flung himself ahead with the backpack slamming against his spine and the AK riding in his arms. The Azerbaijani military cap was gone, blown away by the blast, but the jacket remained. He navigated left, over the top of the hill and onto the road. The pre-selected rendezvous point was one kilometer distant. Lucy was scheduled to depart in five seconds. He would never make it.

Turk ran anyway, hurling himself ahead as the glow of the blasts slowly dimmed behind him. Sirens rang, and a few klicks to his left, headlights hurtled along a highway. First responders, or perhaps Azerbaijani military. He looked to the sky as jet engines shrieked overhead, no doubt responding to the perceived threat of high-level bombers dropping guided weapons.

Nobody suspected a redneck from East Tennessee. The thought was enough to bring the hint of a smirk to Turk's face, but the elation didn't last long. Ahead he saw the intersection, and Lucy still sat there. The headlights of the Cobra gleamed, and he stretched out harder, winded but not stopping. The exhaustion no longer mattered, and neither did the pain. Adrenaline and the consumptive drive of a bred warrior had taken over. He couldn't stop if he wanted to. He reached two hundred meters to the Cobra and lifted his arm. The Cobra's lights flashed once, clicking off and then back on in recognition. He reached the passenger-side door and flung it open, piling inside.

Lucy sat on the front edge of the driver's seat, eyes wide as she gazed toward the distant glow of the decimated fuel depot. Turk collapsed into the seat and breathed hard, also looking back to review his handiwork before facing Lucy. When he did, a split second of panic washed through him at her widened gaze. He hadn't even considered the possibility that the sound and concussion of the blast might cause Lucy to relapse into shell shock.

He needn't have worried. A slow grin spread across Lucy's face and she uttered a single word.

"*Wow.*"

"Drive," Turk said, returning the grin. Lucy yanked the shifter and planted her toes into the gas. The wheels spun, and the nose rocketed around, pointed northeast toward Baku. In seconds the glow of the burning depot faded as the distant lights of downtown Baku grew on the horizon. Turk's destination lay between the two, a dark spot near the coast where the secret operations of the Azerbaijani SSS proceeded under the cloak of secrecy.

"What next?" Lucy panted.

Before Turk could answer, the satellite phone clipped to his chest rig rang. He yanked it up and mashed the answer button. That nameless male voice from the other side of the globe crackled with something between shock and anger.

"Was that you?"

Turk ignored the question, crashing straight ahead to one of his own. "Don't worry about that. Did it work?"

Pause. Static rang through the speaker. Lucy reached the top of another hill and Turk motioned her to the side of the road. She pulled off and he piled out, bringing the binoculars with him.

The SSS black site lay in the bottom of the next dusty valley, outlined by security lights with the Caspian Sea to its right, empty mountain foothills to its left, and downtown Baku some ten kilometers directly ahead. The facility sat alone, just the way the nameless voice on the phone described, and Turk didn't need an update from the satellite phone to know that his ploy with the fuel depot was working.

He could see it working in real time. A convoy of Cobras, tanks, and armored troop carriers were all converging on the spot, moving away from the black site.

"They're taking the bait," the voice said. "Our view of the black site is obscured by clouds, but we've monitored it for the past four hours and haven't seen any reinforcements."

"Approximate occupancy?" Turk asked.

Pause. "We really have no idea. We haven't monitored it long enough to say."

Great.

Turk held the sat phone with one hand and the binos with the other, surveying the complex. It was too dark to make out details. Too distant to properly inspect the layout. There could be ten men or a hundred inside. Lawyers and priests or spec ops soldiers.

This was the very definition of flying blind, but Turk knew in his very bones that he couldn't afford to wait.

"I'm going in," Turk said. "Enjoy the show."

"Mr. Turkman, we would advise you to wait. We're monitoring ongoing developments in the region. In another few hours we may—"

"In another few hours my friends may be *dead*, jackass!" Turk snapped. "Call me when you're sending QRF. Turkman out."

He hung up. He returned to the Cobra. Lucy sat behind the wheel, engine still running. She raised her eyebrows in a question.

Turk leaned against the Cobra's doorpost and poked his head in. He didn't say anything for a long moment. Then he spat into the dirt.

"So you believe in God?" he asked.

"With all my heart."

"You believe He's here?"

"Every moment."

"You know how to reach Him?"

"Been reaching Him all day."

Turk nodded. Looked over the rise. Looked back to Lucy.

"If you stick with me, you just might meet Him in person."

Lucy smiled. It was a gentle, confident smile. "I'm ready. Are you?"

Turk sucked his teeth. He inhaled a long breath. Then he dodged the question.

"Here's the plan."

49

It wasn't an ideal plan. In fact, it wasn't much of a plan at all. It was simply brute force, violence of action, and reckless speed all swirled together into one deadly cocktail.

Turk marked the gate of the complex from the hilltop, and then Lucy drove. She wore the plate carrier, which was too small for Turk and too big for her. An AK-74 and a med kit waited in the seat next to her, and there was a handgun strapped to her hip. As she smashed her foot into the accelerator and Turk emerged through the Cobra's gun turret, he could hear her reciting the twenty-third psalm.

It sounded like a song, gentle and melodic, so calming that it soothed Turk's ragged nerves. He planted his feet on the floor of the Cobra and racked the charging handle on the massive swivel gun mounted to the roof. It was a CANiK M2 QCB, a Turkish knockoff of the M2 Browning .50-caliber machine gun Turk knew so well. Belt fed, firing at over five hundred rounds per minute, it was a weapon of absolute devastation in the right hands.

Turk's were the right hands.

"Straight for the gate!" Turk called. "Right through the middle."

The Cobra left the dirt and struck the two-lane asphalt road leading to the black site. With headlights switched off, the beast ran like a silent wolf toward the gate, undetected until they had closed within a hundred yards.

Then, at last, the alarm bells rang. A siren from someplace beyond the fence. The flash of a spotlight flicking over their front bumper. The appearance of silhouettes in the guard towers standing either side of the entrance. A blink of muzzle flash.

Turk engaged, pivoting the CANiK and mashing the trigger. Hellfire thundered from the muzzle, the belt of ammunition rolling through the receiver as he obliterated first one spotlight and then the next. Silhouettes collapsed inside the towers and wood splintered into the air.

Then the Cobra struck the gate. It was constructed of solid steel, covered in welded wire with an automatic hydraulic opening-and-closing mechanism mounted to one side. Enough to stop a sedan, probably, but not a heavily armored attack vehicle moving at sixty miles per hour. The hydraulic mechanism shattered, the gate exploded open, and the Cobra crashed right inside.

Now the muzzle flash gleamed on every side. Lucy mashed the brakes and the Cobra slid to a halt right outside the main building—a block structure three stories high, painted desert tan, with a steel door for an entrance and no windows. The gunfire came from outside it, camouflaged Azerbaijani SSS guards rushing to engage the Cobra from guard houses and auxiliary structures.

The CANiK spun easily on a greased mount, firing in short bursts that cut men down like dry cornstalks. AK rounds pinged off the armored gun shield and whizzed past Turk's head, but none found their mark. It was all too fast, too sudden. In seconds a dozen bodies lay twisted across the ground, gun smoke hanging in the air like a cloud, Turk's ears ringing. He swung the gun back around, over the nose of the Cobra, pointed straight at the heavy steel door that guarded the building's entrance.

The next burst of fire was sustained, a five-second blast of .50-caliber destruction that shredded the door around its locking mechanism, riddling the frame with half-inch holes, and blasting the latch into the darkness beyond. The CANiK fell silent with barrel smoking, and Turk slid out of the turret. The interior of the vehicle stank of sulfur, a gray haze obscuring his vision as Turk retrieved his rifle and turned for the door.

"Man the gun. If backup arrives, you have my blessing to split."

He turned for the door, but Lucy wasn't headed for the turret. She clambered out of the front seat and joined Turk on the bloody concrete outside, an AK-74 looking like a rocket launcher in her small hands, medical pack slung by a strap over her back.

"Lucy—"

"Blessed be the Lord, my rock, who trains my hands for war."

Turk thought it was a Bible verse—it sounded like a Bible verse—but he didn't have time for a Sunday School lesson. From inside the shattered door, voices boomed out. Feet pounded. Turk jerked his chin.

"Go left!"

Lucy sprinted toward the far side of the door, plate carrier sliding on her shoulders as Turk fired twice to blow out security cameras. Then his back was against the wall, the blown-out door to his right. Inside, the footsteps neared. Voices barked in Azerbaijani. The panic was imminent.

Turk pulled a grenade from the undersized backpack. The ring fell over his finger, the pin snapped out. He looked to Lucy. She nodded once.

Turk flung the grenade through the blown-out door latch.

50

Langley, Virginia

Silas Rigby abandoned the executive floor of CIA headquarters in favor of the buzzing operations center nestled deep in the heart of the compound. His old stomping grounds, and now his field of dominion, he stood in the elevated office overlooking banks of desks, computer screens, analysts, and case officers as the full might of America's intelligence wing managed multiple crises around the globe.

In the Taiwan Strait, the battle raged on. The Chinese had deployed twenty fighter jets, and the pilots and sailors of the United States Navy were busy mopping up the last of them. American casualties ranked in the low double digits, not counting the losses aboard *Sampson*.

Too many for Rigby, but his focus for the moment drifted thousands of miles west of the South China Sea to a battlefield where far fewer American lives were at stake, and yet the implications could be so much more costly.

From the desk in front of him a phone buzzed. Rigby snatched it up, and the case officer on the other end proceeded with her report devoid of any formalities, as trained.

"Confirmation on the *Caspian Voyager*. Vessel is emerging from beneath cloud cover two miles north, northeast of Baku international port. Flying Turkmenistanian flag, appears to be making dock."

"Air surveillance?" Rigby asked.

"ETA nine minutes."

"Assign to primary display."

Rigby hung up. On the large screen stretching the length of the room, a pixelated image of sweeping mountain terrain appeared, slowly clarifying as the signal was refined. The image was black and white, taken from an altitude of forty thousand feet using the cutting-edge night-vision and infrared enabled camera technology aboard the mighty Northrop Grumman RQ-4 Global Hawk—compliments of the United States Air Force. In the bottom right-hand corner of the screen, a clock counted down the time to arrival over the Caspian Sea—eight minutes, eighteen seconds. A heck of a long flight from northern Iraq, complicated by the necessity of skirting Iran, flying through Turkey and Armenia instead. Now the Global Hawk was almost on site, ready to orbit high above sovereign territory while searching for confirmation of Blackjack's claims.

The phone buzzed again. Rigby lifted it, already confident who was calling.

"Sitrep." Aimes was just as direct as Rigby had trained his case officers to be.

"Drone almost on site," Rigby said. "Will feed you updates as we have them."

"Russian military action?"

"Still static on the border. Iranians closing to within two hundred kilometers of Azerbaijan."

Aimes hung up and Rigby replaced the phone. He slurped an energy drink and monitored the screen. The Global Hawk was passing over downtown Baku, rising to its maximum altitude of sixty thousand feet to avoid detection by Azerbaijani radar. The clock had run down inside of five minutes, and before long the drone would need to descend again to break cloud cover and obtain a clear picture of the *Caspian Voyager*.

This was likely a suicide mission for the drone, but what was a petty two hundred million dollars?

"Come on..." Rigby whispered.

From the far side of his overwatch office the door burst open, and one of Rigby's senior officers appeared with a printout grasped in one hand. His face was flushed, his breathing up. He approached without comment, thrusting the printout into Rigby's hand.

It was a satellite image taken of a remote structure surrounded by foothills and desert. Rigby recognized the building layout in an instant—it was the Azerbaijani State Security Service black site south of Baku. The one he had directed Rufus Turkman to.

"What's this?"

The case officer didn't answer. He simply pointed to a spot in the image, behind the primary building, at what appeared to be an open-faced garage. The tail of a vehicle poked out. An SUV? The image was monochromatic, so color was impossible to confidently determine. Rigby squinted, drawing the image closer to his face.

Then a chill ripped down his spine. "This is Rzayev's SUV?"

The case officer nodded.

"When was this taken?"

"Twenty minutes ago, sir. We missed the SUV on first pass."

"Rzayev is *in* the compound?"

"Yes, sir. We believe so."

Rigby lowered the printout. "And Turkman?"

"We're fighting cloud cover again. I'd need the drone to re-task to be sure. But we just detected light flashes through the haze. Muzzle flash. We think he's infiltrating now."

51

Absheron District
Azerbaijan

The fragmentation grenade detonated with a thunderclap and screams rent the space beyond the steel door. Turk clamped his AK into his shoulder and pivoted on his heels, yanked the door open, and lead with the rifle.

"On me!"

Lucy fell in behind, and then they were crossing the threshold into a hallway still choked with grenade smoke. Bodies littered the floor—five of them, lying in twisted heaps with rifles tangled across their chests and blood spraying the walls. Turk swept his rifle with five quick twitches of his trigger finger, delivering headshots into every skull before any one of the survivors could reach for a handgun. His ears still rang, his heart thundered, but Turk was dead focused. The taste of the gunpowder and blood on his tongue was so familiar he didn't even register it. He only saw the hallway ahead, illuminated by the flicker of fluorescent lights mounted to a suspended tile ceiling. The place was like a hospital, but no doctors were present.

Only messengers of death.

Dropping his rifle, Turk exchanged it for an identical AK-74 model with a full magazine, a mounted weapon light, and a reflex sight. Then he was headed forward again, unleashing a double-tap to the chest and a single to the face of the next guy who appeared around the corner. He wasn't even armed, but Turk didn't have time to hesitate. Lucy moved directly behind him, sheltered by his body with her own rifle suspended in steady hands. The hallway terminated in a T-intersection, and Turk swept both ways.

More hallway, connecting to rooms that looked like offices. Doors stood open and from overhead the alarm siren continued to wail, now mixed with blinked red lights.

"Which way?" Lucy asked.

Turk had no idea. He'd been to places like this before, many times. Black site centers used for the detainment, interrogation, and sometimes torture of terror suspects. Usually there was a prison block or "cage" where the detainees were kept. Separate offices for the CIA specialists on site, and further barracks for any military personnel.

But that was the American setup. This was clearly different. Thus far everything Turk had seen indicated an administrative environment. As he hurried down the hallway clearing one small office after another, momentary anxiety entered his mind.

What if the team was being kept in an auxiliary structure? Some hole off to the side—

His thoughts cut short as Lucy shouted from behind him. "Door!"

Her voice was instantly drowned out by the snarl of a submachine gun, something light and fast. Bullets skipped down the hallway and pinged off doorframes. Turk and Lucy dove into opposite offices and the hail persisted, unrelenting. A drum magazine, Turk thought, and a reckless shooter.

Standing at the edge of the doorframe, he looked across the hallway to Lucy. She squatted inside the opposing office, rifle clutched to her chest, no hint of fear in her face.

"Grenade?" Turk called.

Lucy shook her head. "I can't see! I think it's a stairwell."

Stairwell.

Turk edged closer to the door, rifle raised. He measured the tempo of the gun and knew the shooter would need to stop soon. The barrel would overheat. The magazine would run dry.

Sure enough, the gunfire paused. Turk jabbed his boot into the hallway, instantly retracting it. The pause in fire had been a trap, just as he suspected. The next burst of fire riddled the floor and wall near his position. A voice shouted in Azerbaijani.

Turk pinpointed the source of the sound, rifle held into his cheek, measuring his breaths. The next break was coming, and when it did...

The gunfire broke off. This time, Turk didn't bother with the fake. He rolled straight into the hallway, already opening fire even before the holographic sight mounted to the AK fell over the open doorway fifty feet away. It was on the left side of the hallway, a slice of open blackness with a moving shadow beyond. Turk's rounds ripped through the gap and a scream burst down the hallway. He sprinted, still firing. Lucy close behind him. They reached the door and Turk kicked it closed against the protruding muzzle of an H&K MP5 just as the shooter behind opened fire. The gun snarled, blasting fire into the hallway directly between Turk's legs. He closed his shins, pinning the weapon in place, then he reached into the backpack for the next grenade.

Pin pulled against the charging handle of the AK. Spoon released. He snatched the door open and dumped the weapon.

Another shout from inside, mixed with a desperate cry. The sound of the grenade bouncing against metal steps. The pound of rushing feet.

Then the blast, loud and pronounced, pounding against the door. Bodies slumped and Turk kicked the door open. He led with the rifle, clicking the weapon light on and repeating headshots against three camouflaged men stretched along the stairway. Bloody weapons littered the steps. The light cut a swath of illumination into the pitch darkness below.

Revealing a staircase—leading down. Into what?

Prison.

"This is it," Turk said. "You ready?"

Lucy lifted the rifle. Turk headed down over the bodies.

52

SSS Black Site
Baku, Azerbaijan

First came the pound of a .50 caliber, mixed with the crushing roar of a heavy vehicle. Reed heard it from someplace far above, echoing down the ventilation shafts that pumped fresh air into the pit. He cocked his head back, gasping for breath as he lay on the floor. Still bound. Still bleeding. Still choking on the stench of Corbyn's burned flesh.

But he was alive, and he tasted blood on the air. The .50 caliber was slightly confusing, because Reed didn't think Russians used .50 caliber weapons. Typically they used AEK-999s, chambered in the ubiquitous 7.62x54 World War One–era cartridge. That cartridge sounded different from the blare of a Browning .50 caliber. Sharper and faster.

Were they not Russians?

The next sound dashed any hope Reed maintained of a miraculous American rescue. It was a far more familiar sound than an AEK, even more familiar than the thunder of a Browning fifty. This wasn't a thunder at all, but a chug.

AK fire.

Reed gritted his teeth, forcing himself into a seated position against the wall. His head spun. His mouth was so dry it felt like packed sand. Each thought required focus, tuning out the pain in his own body mixed with Corbyn's agonized moans.

Rzayev was gone. So were the rest of his security detail. They had exited the prison, and even now that detail might be engaged in repelling the oncoming invaders. One side or the other would prevail, in time. Did it really matter which?

Both sides would return to kill the Prosecution Force. What remained of this battle was likely the last chance Reed would ever have to save his team.

"They're coming." Ivan's voice was hoarse. He breathed through his teeth to Reed's left.

"Anybody got anything sharp?" Reed asked.

Wolfgang answered in a hiss so weak Reed barely understood it.

"R...rock."

Reed looked. In the dimness of the overhead lights, he made out Wolfgang lying on his side, bloody and broken, his bound hands twitching as he slowly worked his wire tie bonds against something dark and jagged.

Reed gritted his teeth. Rolled slowly onto his stomach. And wormed his way toward Wolfgang.

53

Langley, Virginia

"Positive ID! We have positive ID!"

The next phone call Rigby took carried an intensity rare among the iron professionalism of the operations center. It was a young officer, maybe his first time managing a mission like this. The nerves and excitement had overcome him.

But for all that, he wasn't wrong. Even as Rigby stood in the overwatch booth monitoring the display screen at the end of the room, he knew the kid was right. Positive ID indeed, straight through the lens of the Global Hawk.

The *Caspian Voyager* never made port in Baku. She dropped anchor one mile off the coast while the drone circled overhead at thirty thousand feet, tracking her position with difficulty through cloud cover. It was dark in Azerbaijan, necessitating the use of night vision and infrared technology.

In the end, it was the infrared that served the CIA most. A heat signature was witnessed departing the container ship. A small red dot that grew brighter as the temperature of the heat source increased. It moved rapidly away from the *Caspian*, headed inland. As the drone focused and zoomed in, additional heat signatures could be distinguished.

Twelve men, Rigby determined. In a fast boat, headed toward shore.

He mashed the hang-up button on the office phone and hit zero for the operator. A woman picked up immediately.

"Sir?"

"Get me the director, ASAP."

54

Absheron District
Azerbaijan

The stairway proceeded downward for two flights, a metal structure that switched back on itself. Dull lights mounted into the wall provided illumination, and long before Turk made the first turn, he knew he was on the right path. He could hear the pound of boots someplace nearby, pounding against concrete. The hiss of voices. The drip of water splashing on concrete—or maybe it was blood, running from the men he'd just slain.

The next sound he detected barely registered in his ringing ears. His mind made sense of it just in time, a sharp *click*. The sound of an AK selector lever switching from safe to fire.

"Back!" Turk swept his arm around, driving Lucy against the wall as muzzle flash blazed from the darkness at the bottom of the stairs. A hiss of bullets zipped between the steps, pinging off their bottoms and striking the walls at random. The open slot between the switchbacking flights of stairs was alive with gunfire, blocking any chance of Turk leaning out to shoot back.

"Grenade?" Lucy called. Turk patted his chest.

He was out. There was nothing left save the single smoke grenade. He pulled the pin anyway and kicked the device into the gap. It fell. Somebody shouted as the grenade popped. The gunfire ceased.

Turk leaned over the gap and dumped his magazine, spraying lead all the way to the bottom of the stairwell. Screams echoed back at him, but Turk couldn't see the bodies. The bottom of the shaft was choked by thick gray smoke, reflecting his weapon light as a wall of gray.

The AK clicked over an empty chamber and Turk shucked the mag. His heart hammered as he ratcheted in the next, and then he was headed down again, into the smoke. Sucking in a deep breath and running. He could no longer tell if Lucy was following. Her footsteps were lost in his ringing ears. He penetrated the cloud and kept moving, nearly falling over the first body. He double-tapped the guy in the face, then he was on to the final landing, lungs ready to burst, eyes flooded with defensive tears.

"On your right!" Lucy shouted the warning, and Turk threw himself instinctively left. Orange starlight blinked, accompanied by the pop of a handgun. Before Turk could pivot his rifle toward the threat, Lucy had engaged. A chatter from her AK, and the guy was down. Lucy ran past Turk with her rifle held into her shoulder, both eyes open, lips moving in measured recitation.

"The Lord is my light and my salvation—whom shall I fear?"

Turk fell in behind her, lungs ready to burst. They rounded the corner and reached a door. One impact of his boot, and Turk knew it was locked. Solid steel, framed by additional steel and concrete.

"Step back!"

Turk moved to the side of the doorframe and planted the muzzle of the AK against the latch assembly. Designed as an upgrade over the slow and heavy 7.62 rounds that fed the AK-47, Turk knew that the ammunition blazing from his AK-74 was very likely steel core, a favorite of the Russians who produced most of it. Steel core ammunition was designed to penetrate body armor, which meant it might punch through the door and blow out the lock.

It might also explode in his face. Turk pressed the trigger anyway, three quick pulls that broke the locking mechanism into jagged shards. He kicked the door again, and this time it hurtled open. Fresh air lay just around the corner, but with it an additional storm of gunfire.

Turk yanked back from the door, squatting and padding his chest on impulse even though he knew he was out of grenades. He was down to the rifle and sidearm.

"Bodies!" Lucy called. "Turn on your light!"

It took a moment for the direction to clarify in Turk's mind. He swept his rifle back toward the steps and clicked on the light. The smoke was beginning to dissipate, rising up the stairwell, and the light painted ghostly images of the dead Azerbaijani SSS soldiers spread around the floor, coated in blood. Lucy danced over them with agile ease, locating a grenade and tossing it Turk's way. He pulled the pin and slung it through the door. They each ducked and covered their ears. The weapon detonated with a thunderclap and a shriek. Lucy tossed him another, and the process repeated.

Four grenades down the hallway in rapid succession was enough to silence the gunfire and bring Turk back to his feet. He left the weapon light on and pivoted the corner. The first soldier appeared writhing on the floor, his rifle abandoned, his face shredded by shrapnel. Turk put him down, crashing ahead down a hallway littered by shreds of bloody clothing. Each body received a skull shot, then Turk reached the terminus of the hallway.

Two doors. One led left, the other led right. Both were steel. Both were locked.

But the one on the left was locked by a heavy deadbolt. The one on the right was secured by an electronic locking mechanism with a card key reader. Turk looked to the corpse lying at the base of the door and found the corresponding key card attached to his belt by a lanyard. He was dressed like the other SSS soldiers but lacked the body armor or rifle. He carried only a sidearm, the patches on his arms written in Azerbaijani and unreadable to Turk. But the message clear.

He was a jailer. The room beyond was a prison. Turk snatched up the keycard and flashed it across the reader. The mechanism beeped. A green light blinked.

Turk raised his rifle and reached for the door handle.

55

The gunfire from outside the prison grew louder by the second as it drew inevitably deeper into the underground reaches of the black site. Reed had refined his initial identification of an AK type rifle into an AK-74, or more likely an AK-12. A modern Russian battle rifle chambered in the "poison bullet," 5.45x39mm.

More confirmation of the inevitable. Nikitin's troops had arrived.

Wolfgang had given up on the rock. There wasn't enough light for Reed to determine whether Wolfgang's efforts in breaking his bonds had yielded any progress, but it didn't much matter. Wolfgang was spent, utterly and totally. The demons who had beat him with his own prosthetic leg seemed to take special pleasure in Wolfgang's abuse. He seemed barely conscious as Reed slid next to him and lowered his wrists toward the rock. The jagged edge tore into his forearms as he fought to obtain the right angle. The wire ties were thick, not the household kind but the industrial sort. Every twitch of his arms sent so much pain radiating through Reed's body that he could barely keep himself upright. Ivan—also bloody and rasping—edged closer to Reed and used his shoulder to help keep the Prosecutor upright.

"I always knew Americans would be the death of me." Ivan laughed.

Reed gritted his teeth, inclined to ignore the Russian, but even more inclined to embrace a distraction from the pain.

"Those aren't Americans, Ruskie. You're about to die under Russian rounds."

Ivan had no comeback for that. Reed wiggled the bonds a little harder against the rock. From the far end of the prison cell, someplace on the other side of one or more doors, a loud bang rocked a hallway.

Then another. A third. A fourth.

Grenades.

There was no longer any doubt in Reed's mind. He wouldn't die at Azerbaijani hands. Whoever was coming down that hallway wouldn't be stopped. Violence of action was on their side—Reed was almost impressed. The best he could hope for was to free himself, drag his body to the far side of the room just inside the door, and wait for the point man to enter.

Reed would trip him. He would bash his skull with the same jagged rock now wearing on his bonds. He would fight to protect his team until his very last breath.

The first wire tie snapped, and a little strength entered his exhausted body. Reed worked his wrists harder, leaning back against the wall, heedless of the pain. It no longer mattered. It would all be over so soon. He might as well bleed—give it all. Go out in style.

For Corbyn. For Wolf. For Strickland.

The second tie broke and Reed pulled his arms from behind his back with a muted cry. His muscles constricted and ached, his shoulders so sore he could barely lift his right arm. He tumbled onto his side and couldn't fight the natural tears of pain that slipped down his cheeks. His wrists were coated in blood. His hands shook.

From the ground next to him Ivan grunted.

"Help me."

Reed gritted his teeth against the agony and rolled. He found the rock and rested his shoulder against Ivan's, pinning the big Russian against the wall. Then he went to work, even as the gunshots in the hallway switched from deadly bursts to even more menacing pops.

Execution shots. Eliminating the wounded before leaving them behind. These guys were smart and experienced. They understood combat.

But maybe they had one final lesson to learn.

The first tie broke. Reed leveraged the rock and twisted, using it to stretch the second tie instead of cutting it. Ivan screamed through his teeth, but the tie broke. Both men fell to the floor. Outside, Reed heard a door open on groaning hinges. Boots struck the concrete, headed their way down the long haul of torture chambers the team had so recently occupied.

"Door," Reed hissed.

The two of them attempted to stand but couldn't make it. Reed hit his knees and crawled instead, blood dripping from his lip, vision wavering. He was so dehydrated that he could barely swallow. It was all he could do to chart a straight course for the door, the rock in one hand. He went left, and Ivan went right. The Russian had located another chunk of concrete and in the dim light of the flickering overhead lamp his face stretched into a wolfish snarl.

Reed reached the wall and propped himself up just inside the door. His plan was simple—he would wait until the point man had crossed the threshold, then he would stick his left leg across the soldier's path and attempt to trip him. With luck, the man would go down. Reed would grab his plate carrier and follow him to the floor. He wouldn't get more than two strikes with the rock before the next guy in line shot him.

Very likely...he wouldn't even get one. But he would try.

Outside the door the footsteps drew nearer. They had slowed. The oncoming soldiers were clearing each of the prison cells as they advanced toward the room at the end of the hall.

Covering their bases. Clearing their corners. Surveying the gore of Strickland's mutilated body and moving straight ahead.

Professionals.

Reed's hand tightened around the rock. His teeth clenched. From outside the door the footsteps stopped. A latched lifted.

Reed made eye contact with Ivan, and the Russian nodded once. They both raised their rocks.

56

The Situation Room
The White House

"Skies clear. The Chinese are retreating."

From the end of the table, Yellin stood with his iron gaze fixated on the screen. He hung up a phone and turned to face Stratton.

"We lost six of our pilots. The destroyers are unscathed."

"Chinese killed?" Stratton asked.

Something like vicious satisfaction crossed Yellin's face. It wasn't joy. It wasn't even glee.

It was dark triumph.

"Seventeen killed," he said. "They couldn't take the heat."

Stratton nodded once. His attention pivoted to Admiral Turley.

"Dan, can the *Reagan* spare another wing?"

"Already taking air, sir. We've also deployed Joint Strike Fighters from the *America* and the *Tripoli*. Thirty aircraft in total. We'll maintain total command of the strait while our boys land and refuel."

"Lock it down, Admiral. If the Chinese so much as send up a kite, I want it shot down. The strait is *ours*."

"Understood."

The admiral turned back to his phone and Stratton ran a hand over his face. The tension boiling in his gut extrapolated ninety minutes of stress into what felt like eight hours of exhaustion. But this wasn't over. Not even close.

Six pilots.

"Lisa, where are we with Beijing?" Stratton said.

"Radio silence, sir. I can't even get through to the embassy."

"Not acceptable. They just killed six good Americans. If you can't get them on the phone, we'll put troops on their embassy doorstep. Make it happen."

Gorman simply nodded. She was back to her phone. Everybody was on the phone. The map at the end of the room displayed the Taiwan Strait with markers for each of the warships deployed to the region.

Nearly two dozen in total. The three Arleigh Burke class destroyers churning just northwest of Taiwan were depleted of missiles, but they would hold the position until additional warships arrived. The *Reagan* would reinforce them with air cover in the meantime.

And lurking a few hundred miles off the coast—and a few hundred feet beneath the surface—was the USS *Rhode Island*. A different kind of missile boat, with a different kind of mission. A last resort.

Beijing's eye was blackened. Hopefully Chen would have the good sense to step back.

A phone hit its cradle and from the left side of the table Director Aimes rose. She pivoted to face Stratton.

"Sir, a moment?"

Stratton rose from his chair and stepped automatically for the coffee bar in the back corner of the room. He noted Aimes tilting her head toward Yellin on her path to join him. The two cabinet members met Stratton at the coffee bar. Aimes kept her voice low as Stratton stirred creamer into a dark roast.

"There's been a development in Azerbaijan. We may have a situation."

"The Russians?" Stratton asked. His voice was flat.

"Yes, sir. In a way."

Stratton looked up. "In what way?"

"The Russian armed forces at Red Bridge are staying put. No movement.

The Iranian forces seem to be slowing also. But we've just confirmed the entry of a special operations team from the *Caspian Voyager*. The Global Hawk deployed by the Air Force surveyed a fast boat streaking toward the Baku coast. At least twelve men on board."

Stratton raised his coffee. He blew on the surface, processing one step at a time.

Twelve men. Was Nikitin out of his mind?

"We've got to stop them, sir." Now it was Yellin who spoke. "Elchin Rzayev is no friend of America, but if the Russians find a way to take him out, there will be little to nothing standing between them and a full occupation of the Caucasus. We've already seen what happened in Georgia with a missing president. A dead president would be even worse."

"I agree with the general," Aimes said. "There's also the very real possibility that Russia finds a way to frame us for Rzayev's murder. It's not logical, but with the world teetering on the edge of war, logic is inconsequential. It could be just enough to put our allies in a tailspin while Moscow and Tehran carve up territory."

"And threaten NATO," Yellin added.

Stratton lowered the cup. He still hadn't taken a sip. His mind churned through the information, calculating the variables of hostilities in the South China Sea joined with the vulnerability of a NATO state only a hop, skip, and a jump from Baku.

They were right, both of them. America couldn't afford to manage split conflicts. China's threat was by far the more pressing. Azerbaijan needed to take care of Azerbaijan.

"What are our options?" Stratton addressed the question to Yellin. "Is that drone armed?"

"Negative, sir. Surveillance only."

"Missile strike?"

"Would only work if we have a positive ID on the Russian location. Even in that case, launching missiles on Baku could easily be misinterpreted by the Azerbaijanis. We could wind up in an even worse state than if Russia blamed us for an assassination."

"So what about a team? How quickly could you get boots on the ground?"

Yellin pondered. His lips bunched. He shook his head.

"Not quickly enough. Our nearest assets are in Iraq. Six hundred miles by air, skirting Iran. The absolute soonest we could drop paratroopers over Baku would be...maybe four hours. And that assumes we can evade Azerbaijani's missile defense systems. It's a lot harder to sneak in a C-17 than a high-altitude stealth drone."

"These Russians are in Baku now? They know where Rzayev is?"

"He's at a State Security Service compound south of Baku," Aimes said. "We don't know if the Russians know, but it's logical to assume. We're talking minutes, not hours."

Stratton set the cup down. He spoke through his teeth. "So again I ask—what are our options?"

Aimes and Yellin exchanged a look. The director's voice lowered to just above a whisper.

"I may have one idea, sir. A...team."

"On the ground?"

"Affirmative."

"Near the compound?"

Pause.

"In the compound."

Stratton squinted. His mind ratcheted back to the day before. The phone call with Rzayev. All the bluster.

"We've had people there all along," he said, anger crackling into his voice.

Aimes held up a hand. "It's two operators. They're going after their teammates. They just entered the facility. They may already be dead, but if not..."

"We ask them to hold the fort," Yellin finished. "Protect Rzayev...whatever the cost."

57

Absheron District
Azerbaijan

The door opened with a bang. The point man crashed in like a dump truck, heavy boots slamming the concrete. Weapon light blazing across Corbyn's and Wolfgang's limp forms. Finger curled around the trigger of his AK-74. Reed saw him as a hulking shadow, much bigger than the average soldier, moving with far greater precision.

But still headed dead into Reed's path. He shot his left leg out and the boot of the soldier caught on it. The guy stumbled, grunting. The rifle pivoted right, toward Reed's face. Blinding light obscured Reed's vision as the soldier fell. He shouted, shoulder striking the concrete. The muzzle of his rifle fell over Reed's chest, but the soldier didn't fire. Reed launched himself away from the wall with everything he had left, shoving past the rifle. Landing on the guy's stomach. Raising the rock.

"Reed, *don't!*"

The voice was shrill and female, ringing from someplace behind him. A small hand landed on his shoulder and pulled him back. The speaker wasn't strong enough to stop his forward momentum. Reed's left hand landed on the point man's sternum, pinning him down. His right hand rose with the rock. He saw the vague outline of a face in the darkness. He started the swing.

Then the butt of a rifle crashed down across the side of his head. Not hard enough to knock him out, but plenty hard enough to throw him off-balance. Reed tumbled forward, missing the soldier's face and landing on it instead. The rock flew out of his hand. Bright weapon light played over his shoulders. From beneath him, hot breath blasted against his chest and a voice choked.

A voice he *recognized*.

"Dammit, dude! I'm trying to save your ass."

Reed's hands found rough concrete. He pressed himself up as the body beneath him wriggled free. The weapon light spilled over his shoulder as a petite figure circled him. Reed saw the face, and his heart jumped into his throat.

"Turk?"

Turk spat dirt out of his mouth, still stretched out on the floor with his rifle trapped under him. He offered a wry grin.

"Didn't think I'd leave you down here, did you?"

The grin was the best thing Reed had seen in days, but it wasn't enough to overcome the crushing weight of exhaustion consuming his body. He toppled sideways onto the concrete, gasping for air. Turk scrambled to his knees and another weapon light cast around the room.

"What the hell..." Turk breathed. "Are they alive?"

Reed managed a nod. "I think so."

"Stand by the door," Lucy said. "I got it."

Turk retreated obediently to the door, rifle at the ready as Lucy passed from one limp body to the next. When she reached Corbyn, a subdued gasp escaped her throat, but she said nothing. Moments passed as cloth tore and Corbyn let out a wretched cry. Lucy dug through her medical pack and slathered something from a foil envelope over raw flesh. Corbyn screamed.

Three minutes later Lucy returned to the door, now stripped down to a tank top.

"Wolf is unconscious. Corbyn is badly burned. She's lost blood. I treated the wounds the best I could with what I have. They need a hospital —ASAP."

From the floor, Reed focused on each breath, now overcome by the pain he had successfully blocked out for days. There was something about the hope of an unexpected rescue that ironically underscored the desperation of the situation.

"Please tell me you have an extraction plan," Reed rasped.

Turk appeared at his side, hands passing down Reed's arm to measure his pulse. The big Tennessean was filthy. Dark bags hung beneath his eyes. His face was bruised. He looked like he hadn't slept in days.

But he was in better shape than Reed by far.

"What if I told you I planned to wing it?" Turk asked, repeating the grin. This time it didn't quite reach his eyes.

"I'd tell you to make passionate love to yourself," Reed said.

From the back of the room, Corbyn choked a barely audible laugh. Turk squeezed Reed's arm.

"I've got an armored vehicle and a path into the hills. I also arranged a distraction. Should still be working. All we gotta do is get up two flights of stairs."

"Is that all?"

"Suck it up, Marine. No room for motards in this world."

Reed wanted to smile but he couldn't manage it. When he closed his eyes it was all he could do not to drift into blackness. He licked his lips.

"Strickland," he whispered, opening his eyes again.

Turk nodded. "I know."

Reed's jaw tightened. Sudden rage entered his chest, hot enough to numb the pain. He forced himself up on his elbows. Turk helped him into a seated position.

"What about the president?" Reed asked.

"President?" Turk squinted.

"*Rzayev*," Reed spat. "He's here. And he's *mine*."

58

The words had barely left Reed's lips before gunfire exploded from down the prison hallway. Turk's head snapped up and he kicked instinctively for the steel door. Ivan was faster, slamming it closed as bullets struck the steel. The chatter was faster than an AK, some kind of submachine gun snarling from about thirty yards away.

The second door. The one standing opposite to the entrance of the prison. It was locked, and Turk had opted to bypass it in the interest of momentum. Now that felt like the dumbest decision he'd made since embarking on this Hail Mary rescue attempt in the first place.

They were pinned in, and what was worse, if whoever was shooting at them managed to reach the main prison door and bar it shut, they would be permanently trapped.

"Open the door!" Turk shouted, scrambling to the frame. "They'll lock us in!"

Ivan understood. So did Lucy. While she moved to drag Reed out of the way, Ivan scrambled to his knees and pulled the door back. Bullets whizzed inside, smacking against the far concrete wall and blowing out the overhead light. Turk swung out from the doorframe anyway and engaged with his AK, dispensing measured shots back toward the prison's outer door at the far end of the cell block.

He wasn't a moment too soon. Under the glare of his weapon light he identified a figure rushing for the door, firing from the hip with a submachine gun. The guy reached the door and was shoving it closed just as Turk's next shot split his head open and sent him toppling backward. His body fell in the path of the door, temporarily blocking it, but he wasn't the only shooter. Additional muzzle flash lit the darkness in the hallway beyond, matched with the desperate shouts of a terrified commander…or maybe, a president.

"Give me a gun!" Reed's voice was hoarse as Turk retreated back into the room to reload. The Prosecutor sat propped against the wall, bleeding from his lip, arm shaking as he extended it. But Turk didn't argue. He drew the Zigana from his hip and tossed it. Lucy passed her own sidearm to Ivan, then the four of them turned for the door.

"There's another room just outside the cell block," Turk said. "We gotta get past it to reach the stairs. Every second wasted is more time for them to call reinforcements."

"Grenade?" Reed asked.

Turk shook his head. "Fresh out."

Reed leaned his head around the door jamb, drawing immediate fire. The chatter was as rapid as before. Small-caliber rounds pinged off cell doors and ricocheted off the floor, buzzing toward the ceiling. It was a maelstrom. Impossible to break through.

And yet they had no other choice.

"Oorah," Reed said with a sarcastic smile.

"*Oorah!*" Turk repeated. Then he was swinging out from the wall, engaging the first muzzle flash he saw even as hot lead zipped past his rib cage. The guy went down and Turk sprinted into the prison hall, heedless of the risk. Blind to the fear. Simply running, making it halfway to the second door before the next storm of gunfire erupted.

Turk dove right, passing into a prison cell and slipping on a bloody floor. He crashed down as bullets pinged off the doorframe and whizzed overhead. Turk rolled, struggling back to his feet.

Then he froze. There was a body spread out across the ground next to him, burned and filleted like a butchered animal, his face so mutilated that it was barely recognizable. But Turk recognized it, just the way he had the first time he cleared this room.

It was Kyle Strickland. Turk's stomach tightened and a little of the rage he'd seen in Reed's eyes entered his own bloodstream. He was back on his feet, circling to the hallway. Holding short as the voice of Lucy's AK was joined by the pop of handguns—cover fire. The burst lasted four seconds, long enough to silence the submachine guns. Then Reed's voice erupted down the hallway.

"Go!"

Turk exploded out of the cell and turned right. The AK rode at his shoulder. He engaged as a shadow appeared in the gap of the main prison door. A shriek ripped against the concrete walls. He reached the door and slammed his foot against the steel, kicking it open far enough to allow him passage. A pistol snapped from someplace ahead, but Turk ignored it. He cleared a pair of bodies and found a soldier leaned against the wall with blood gushing from a chest wound. One hand stemmed the blood flow while the other shook like a stop sign in a hurricane as he brandished a pistol. Turk shot him twice in the face.

The body slid sideways and Turk passed it, crossing the hallway, headed toward the second door. It was no longer closed, now standing open a few inches as terrified voices shouted from beyond. Turk's light played across the gap and drew another burst of automatic fire. He switched the light off even as Lucy's soft footsteps closed behind him. Turk slid against the wall and twisted to ram his rifle muzzle through the door. He clamped down on the trigger without aiming, spraying the room beyond. Lucy fell into a kneel and covered him as he kicked the door open. The light snapped back on. The first guy—another soldier—went down with a double-tap to the head. Turk crossed onto more bloody concrete. The LED beam of the weapon light revealed an underground file room, populated by metal cabinets and desks. Brass lay everywhere, joined by another body.

Then a pistol snapped from the back of the room. Orange starlight temporarily blinded Turk. A bullet struck his left arm, tearing through flesh but not quite disabling him. He bit back a scream and tumbled sideways. Lucy engaged, firing twice. The pistol fell silent with a muted shriek. Turk pressed ahead, clearing a desk and circling toward the back of the room. He reached a Zigana pistol lying on the floor, its grip coated in blood. Another desk lay beyond, and Turk detected the outline of a shoe.

Not a boot—not like the soldiers. This was a dress shoe. Leather soled. Trembling as he cleared the desk and pointed the weapon light downward.

A man lay there, and he wasn't a soldier. In place of battle dress, he wore black slacks and a black jacket. No tie. A pale face with wide eyes, mouth open, hands extended in a desperate plea. He shouted in English.

"Don't shoot! I am the president!"

Turk put a boot in the guy's sternum, driving him to the ground with the muzzle of the AK jammed into his face.

"Drop your weapons! *Hands in the air!*"

The president complied, both hands shooting up as Lucy reached the desk.

"Search him," Turk snapped.

Lucy slung her rifle and hit her knees. Patting the guy down, she produced a wallet, a cell phone, and chewing gum. No weapons.

"Take this." Turk handed his rifle off and grabbed Rzayev by the shirt collar, hauling him up and ramming him against the desk. Pens and documents scattered, and Rzayev shrieked. Turk backhanded him across the face.

"You did this?" he demanded, pointing toward the prison.

Rzayev quaked, blood running from his lip. Turk struck him right in the nose, hard enough to shatter it. Blood erupted. Rzayev shrieked and Lucy put a hand on Turk's arm.

"Turk, don't!"

Turk wasn't listening. His fingers sank around a wad of Rzayev's shirt and he turned for the door, dragging him across the hallway and through the prison door. Rzayev kicked, hopping over bodies, helpless to resist as the big Tennessean pulled him all the way to the room at the end of the hall and threw him down at Reed Montgomery's feet.

"That him?" Turk barked.

Lucy arrived with the rifles, and weapon lights played across Rzayev's terrified face. He held up both hands, a plea ready on his lips. It never left his throat. Reed Montgomery was broken, dehydrated, starved, and half beaten to death, but as Turk watched, his old battle buddy rose to his feet. Staggering at first. Choking.

And then grabbing Turk's AK from Lucy's grasp and slamming the buttstock so hard into Rzayev's gut that he projectile vomited, right there on the spot. Reed nearly fell. He threw the rifle aside and extended a hand.

"Knife!"

Lucy interceded again. She crossed in front of Turk and reached Reed.

"Don't do this, Reed! It won't help you."

Reed wasn't listening. He shoved Lucy to the ground, and then Ivan arrived. He grabbed Rzayev by the hair and yanked his head back. The president flailed, and Ivan crushed his right arm with a heavy boot.

"You like to play torture games, little man?" Ivan choked. "We will show you Russian way."

"Reed, wait," Turk said. "We can use him. We'll barter our passage out of the country."

"To hell with that," Reed retorted. "This pig *filleted* Strickland. He burned Corbyn half to death. He's dying right here. Give me a damn knife!"

Turk reached into his pocket. The only blade he had was his two-inch pocketknife. Not much of a weapon, but in Reed Montgomery's hands a beach ball could be hellish misery. He hesitated once more, and Reed tired of waiting. He stumbled to his knees next to Rzayev and punched him in the groin, sending the president into another violent convulsion. Vomit spewed from his lips again. Reed grabbed the AK and detached the magazine. It was solid steel, half loaded with 5.45mm rounds. The first blow smashed Rzayev's teeth and tore his cheek. Lucy was back on her feet and grabbed Turk.

Even as his stomach tightened, Turk held her back.

"No," he said.

Lucy fought...but not very hard. Turk stepped back, eyes clouding with tears as Reed struck again. Not aiming for the face, but the shoulder. Hard enough to bust bone. He wasn't going for the kill—he was going to make this pain last.

Lucy shook Turk's arm. He ignored her, teeth clenching. He wasn't angry at Reed. He wasn't even angry at Rzayev. He was angry at himself. He should have been here. He should have prevented this somehow.

"Turk! The phone."

Lucy's voice finally broke through. Turk blinked and recognized the chiming sound. He found the sat phone clipped to his belt, coated in blood but still operational. He mashed the green button.

"You got QRF yet?" Turk demanded.

The voice that answered wasn't the unfamiliar male but a very familiar female. It was CIA Director Sarah Aimes herself.

"Mr. Turkman, this is Director Aimes. Can you hear me?"

The signal was distorted, no doubt struggling with the layers of earth and concrete overhead. But connecting nonetheless.

"I hear you. Where's my extraction?"

"We'll get to that, Mr. Turkman. Right now I need you to listen very carefully."

Turk plugged his opposite ear as Rzayev shrieked. He squinted as Aimes rattled through a prelude. It didn't make sense. He questioned her twice. The context perplexed him. The geopolitics felt tangled and irrelevant.

But one part of the message rang through loud and clear—twelve Russian commandos, armed to the teeth, headed his way.

Turning back from the hall, Turk caught Reed's arm just as the bloody AK mag was cocked for a skull-crushing blow. Rzayev was a bloody mess, flesh torn, nose gushing, teeth missing. One shoulder was definitely busted. Ivan had dug both thumbs into the president's eyes hard enough to burst blood vessels. The guy looked like something out of a horror film.

"Stop!" Turk barked.

Reed's arm jerked, but didn't fall. Hateful eyes snapped toward Turk. Reed tried to wrestle his arm free. Turk was tired and battered, but in far better shape than Reed. He wrenched the magazine away and thrust the sat phone into Reed's bloody hands.

"It's Langley," Turk snapped. "They want him *alive*."

59

The Situation Room
The White House

Aimes put the phone on speaker as the voice of Reed Montgomery crackled from the far side of the planet, breathless and heavy with pain. There was no point in keeping the situation clandestine anymore. The national security advisor, the SecDef, and all the others...they might as well know. This was a global situation. An emergency situation that required less nuance and more brute force.

Anyone's concerns over the legalities of Aimes's decision to deploy a team into Azerbaijan could be debated at another time.

"Mr. Montgomery, you're on with the acting president."

"Can you hear me, Reed?"

Aimes was surprised to learn that Stratton not only was familiar with the personage of the Prosecutor but had actually met him following Maggie Trousdale's attempted assassination. Stratton didn't ask questions about how the Prosecution Force had come under the control of the CIA or why he had not been informed. More discussions for later, no doubt. Right now every breathless member of the security council listened in silence as Reed's voice cracked. He was panting. He sounded half alive.

"What do you want?" Reed said.

"Reed, it's my understanding that you and your team are currently being held at a black site outside Baku?" It was Stratton who spoke.

No answer.

"Reed, we know President Elchin Rzayev is there. Do you have him?"

A spitting sound. "Was just about to crush his skull. If you'll excuse me."

"Wait!" Stratton half rose out of his chair. He held up a hand, as though Reed could see him.

"Reed, I need you to listen to me very carefully. It is *imperative* that you do not kill Rzayev. As we speak, Russian and Iranian troops are prepared to smash through Azerbaijan and seize the Caucasus region. Within weeks their combined force will be in position to threaten NATO via Turkey. We're talking about the prelude to World War Three here. Do you understand me? We need him alive. He's the only roadblock in Russia's path."

"You think I give a damn about that?" Reed choked. "He tortured my team! He killed one of them. I've had more than enough of your puppet string politics, you prick. This is what war looks like!"

Stratton's lips clamped shut. He exchanged a look with Aimes, then with Easterling. Neither of them spoke. For once the entire room was still. Stratton's voice lowered.

"Reed...I will never understand war the way you do. It's not possible. I will never understand what you've sacrificed, or how badly it hurts. I can never fill that void. If I were in your shoes...I would kill this man with my bare hands."

Tension around the table escalated palpably. Secretary Gorman leaned forward as though she were about to interject. Stratton shook his head.

"You've given more to your country than any man ever is obliged to sacrifice," Stratton continued. "I'm standing here safe and secure *because* of people like you. And I have no right to ask anything further. But..."

A long pause. Stratton stood from the chair. He leaned toward the speakerphone. "I'm asking you anyway, but I also have a duty to protect our people. To make difficult choices. The choice I'm forced to make is between saving an evil man or permitting an infinitely more evil war. It's not black and white. It's not sugarcoated. It's blunt reality. I *need* Elchin Rzayev alive, for as long as possible. I need him calling the shots and resisting Moscow. Do you understand?"

The phone fell silent for so long that Aimes thought Reed had hung up. She couldn't even hear his breathing. Nobody in the Situation Room spoke or so much as budged. A sense of breathlessness consumed them all, as though the oxygen had been sucked out of the room.

Come on, Aimes thought. *Be a hero, just once more.*

"What do you want from me?"

Reed's next question was flat and lifeless, but it was enough to revive the security council. Relief washed over Stratton's face. He nodded to General Yellin, and the chairman of the Joint Chiefs stepped right in.

"Son, this is General John David Yellin. I'm deploying a C-17 with forty Ranger paratroopers and accompanying air support out of Iraq as we speak. ETA to your position is eighty minutes. The aircraft have to circle Iran and come in over Armenia. The two things I need from you are simple. First, I need you to get President Rzayev to order his air forces to *not* engage our aircraft. The C-17 and accompanying fighter jets must be allowed to pass."

A soft snort from Reed. "And the second?"

"I need you to keep him alive, son. Hold off the Russians until we get there. Then we're going to get you and your team out—you have my word on that."

Another long pause. Aimes thought she detected the murmur of voices. A discussion was being held, perhaps a debate. She thought she heard somebody curse in Russian. Ivan Sidorov, no doubt.

"So you just want me to hold off a dozen Russian commandos for eighty minutes? Wounded and unarmed?"

"President Rzayev's security detail will assist," Aimes chimed in. "Along with whatever military assets he can summon."

"I don't think so," Reed snapped. "They're all pretty *dead*, at the moment."

Aimes lowered her face. Stratton rejoined the conversation.

"Reed, nobody said it would be easy. But that's why we're not asking somebody else. The commandos have already entered Baku and we have every reason to believe they have full knowledge of Rzayev's location. I won't hold you up any longer. Let Rzayev use the sat phone to communicate with his air force. The Rangers are on their way...I promise."

A second passed. Then Reed Montgomery simply hung up, leaving the Situation Room once again blanketed in chilled silence.

60

Absheron District
Azerbaijan

Reed slumped against the wall, his body so weak he could no longer stand. Inside the dim confines of the underground prison, the outlines of Wolfgang's, Corbyn's, and Rzayev's bodies lay across the floor amid the dried puddles of blood. The place still stank of burnt flesh and gunpowder. It was a scent Reed knew so well it didn't even turn his stomach. There was nothing to puke up, anyway. He looked at the bloody sat phone in his hands, and then slowly turned to Turk.

"Eighty minutes," Reed whispered. The disbelief and disgust in his tone mixed with the rasp of a dry throat. Turk's face hardened.

"I begged for QRF hours ago. They wouldn't send it."

"They never do," Reed said. "Not until there's something they want."

He coughed, spraying blood over his arm and catching himself against the wall. Then he looked back to Rzayev. The Azerbaijani president lay quaking, his face covered in blood, his left arm shaking and his right arm completely disabled. Another twenty seconds and Reed would have snuffed his life out. The hunger deep inside Reed's chest to see him dead was so insatiable that he almost reached for the steel rifle mag again.

To hell with Washington. To hell with Azerbaijan. Kill this pig, get inside a truck, and run for the border...

Even as the thoughts coursed through his mind, they fell a little flat. He closed his eyes and he didn't see Old Glory. He didn't see the land of the free or the home of the brave. He didn't think of Nashville burning or American school children hiding from Russian rockets.

He simply thought of total war, a scenario he knew better than most men breathing. The worst possible thing. The greatest evil humanity could concoct. An eventuality that might well be inevitable, but if there was even a prayer of forestalling it...

"We're running out of time, Reed," Turk said. "What are your orders?"

Reed's eyes opened. He saw Rzayev again. His jaw locked and he departed the wall, crawling to the president. He knelt and grabbed the man by his now crimson collar.

"You been listening?" Reed said. The call had transpired over speaker. He knew Rzayev had heard. "A dozen Russian assassins are coming for *you*. Your security detail is rotting outside. The people in this room are your last line of protection. Do you understand?"

Rzayev did understand. Reed knew it by the abject desperation in his eyes.

"Please...I will do anything you ask."

Reed jammed the sat phone into his hands. "Contact your military. All American aircraft entering your air space are to be given *full passage*. No missiles, no fighter jets. No exceptions. Nod if you understand me."

Rzayev's head bobbed.

"Then you contact your ground troops," Reed continued. "Whoever is near Baku. We need them *here*, ASAP."

"They're all headed to the border," Rzayev said.

"Then you call the damn police!" Reed roared, slamming him to the ground. "You want to live, you *find* somebody! Understand?"

Rzayev choked. His fingers fumbled as he began to dial. Reed released him and staggered upright. The dizziness was overwhelming, but he forced it back with sheer willpower. He dug deep, right into that basement of resolve that had carried him through so many gunfights. So much carnage. He found a last ounce of resolve and used it to fuel himself. To deny the pain. To ignore the damage to his body and the convolution of dehydration and exhaustion warring to take him down.

He pushed it all back. He pretended it was all an illusion. He chose the warrior's path, one more time. Then he turned to Turk, even as Rzayev barked in Azerbaijani into the phone.

"We need a plan."

61

Al-Asad Airbase
al-Anbar Governorate, Iraq

"Go! Go! Go!"

The alarm bells had rung thirty-six minutes prior. The forty men of the United States Army's famed Seventy-Fifth Ranger regiment had been in showers, stretched out over cots, and crowded into the mess hall at the time, but they deployed with practiced ease. Boots slid on, plate carriers dropped over shoulders. Rifles, rocket launchers, mobile machine guns, and all the other little toys provided by Uncle Sam were rushed up the loading ramp of a dark gray Air Force C-17 Globemaster III, one of the largest and fastest cargo jets in US service.

Even as the jet engines warmed, the Rangers could hear the shriek of much louder aircraft taking air from Al-Asad's main runway—not cargo jets, but fighter jets. F-35 Lightning IIs, the Air Force's premier attack aircraft, now assigned to protect the Globemaster over the course of its 739-mile flight up through Turkey, skirting the Iranian border before turning east across southern Armenia and eventually through Azerbaijan to Baku.

Where those Rangers would hurl themselves into the blackness like so much debris, plummeting into the unknown with a mission that had yet to be fully explained. The details would be reviewed during the flight.

Right now their objectives were simple—get your gun. Grab your parachute. Get on the plane.

The hydraulics of the Globemaster's tailgate groaned as it slowly closed, locking the interior into a glow of night-vision preserving red. The hustle of the forty men inside was muted by the thunder of the engines as the C-17 taxied for the airstrip. Rangers found their seats and strapped themselves in, some swapping jokes or arguing about the football games from the night before.

Anything to calm the nerves of a sudden, unexpected deployment into a known combat zone three countries away.

"Listen up!" the Ranger major standing at the front end of the cargo bay screamed over the engines. Pretty soon, he wouldn't even be able to do that as the four giant Pratt & Whitney turbofans reached takeoff RPMs.

"There's a situation in Baku. Some CIA assets got themselves up the creek without a paddle...per usual."

A chorus of forced laughter.

"Russian commandos have been deployed to the region with the intention of assassinating Azerbaijani president Rzayev, currently under the protection of these CIA assets. Our job is simple. Drop in...and kick some ass. Hooah?"

"*Hooah!*"

The roar of forty voices answered the major just as the jet engines wound into an ear-splitting howl. The C-17 braced at the end of the runway, tense for action, brakes locked.

Then it was launching forward. Clearing the strip. Surging skyward.

Headed for Baku...and war.

62

The Kremlin
Moscow, Russia

They brought the body of the traitor, Mikhail Orlov, into the basement. Nikitin himself appeared, snapping angry questions at each of the FSB agents who were foolish enough to be caught too near him.

Who was the man? Why had he been in Nikitin's private office? Why had he been examining Nikitin's personal *computer*?

And most importantly of all—who was he working for?

The FSB didn't have any concrete answers, but the riddle wasn't a difficult one. There were only a few foreign entities who would have the motivation—or the balls—to engage in espionage right at the heart of Russian governance, and none of them were friendly. Whether Orlov had been paid by Berlin, Paris, London, or Washington, it mattered very little. The Germans, the French, the British, and the Americans all shared intelligence, and the email exposed to Orlov's view was a crucial one. The only real question was whether or not he had successfully communicated his stolen information to the West before FSB officers had gunned him down.

And the answer to that question came as an emergency report from the military wing of the Kremlin.

"American planes departing Iraq, Mr. President. Six fighters and one C-17 cargo plane. We think it's carrying paratroopers."

Paratroopers. Nikitin snarled a curse and hung up the phone. He looked across his office to Golubev, who had just arrived. The Ghost of the Kremlin looked as he always looked despite seventy-two hours without sleep. He was cold, pale, and perfectly calm.

"They know," Nikitin said. "The Americans know. They are deploying a response."

"That is not logical," Golubev said, sparing any formalities. It was a communication style Nikitin was accustomed to when nobody else was around. "Washington is not in good relations with Baku. We have led Rzayev to believe that the Americans are to blame for the bomb. There is no reason he would call them for help."

"Maybe he didn't call. Maybe they are deploying of their own volition."

"Also not logical. They would need emergency air clearance from Turkey and Armenia, to say nothing of the risk of being shot down by Iranian or Azerbaijani missiles. Why would they risk those men?"

"They *are* risking them, Anton. The planes are in the air! The Americans are not stupid. They are playing this game three moves ahead, the same as us. We have lost the element of surprise. They aren't thinking about Baku or Rzayev—they're thinking about Turkey. About *NATO!*"

Golubev remained calm even as Nikitin began to pace, his brow furrowed into a thundercloud, his hands clenched into fists. It was this very passion, expressed as calculated charisma, that had propelled Nikitin to the pinnacle of Russian governance, and would lead him far beyond it.

But just then it was clouding his head. He couldn't think clearly. He was so angry he wanted to break something.

Golubev acted on instinct, heading for the tea bar to retrieve one of Nikitin's favorite comforts. Black Russian tea. Golubev poured two cups. No sweetener. He brought his boss the glass and Nikitin accepted it without comment. The two of them sat on either side of Nikitin's executive desk. Nikitin chugged the tea, enjoying the burn in his throat.

The pain helped him focus. It sharpened him just the way the brutal physical training of the old Red Army and then the KGB had. His mind began to clear—slowly.

"Our ground team is ten minutes from striking," Golubev said, his voice calm. "Rzayev is holed up in some State Security Service facility...some interrogation black site. The American planes are still over an hour away. The math is not in their favor."

Nikitin snorted, still irritable. "Favor? What favor will there be when American ground troops are parachuting into Baku? We are not yet ready to directly engage Washington, Anton. It's too soon."

"Indeed. So I suggest we offer the Americans incentive to turn their planes around. Keep them out of the mix."

Nikitin squinted. "What did you have in mind?"

"We begin the invasion," Golubev said. "We cross the border at Red Bridge, deploy fighter aircraft into Azerbaijani airspace before the Americans arrive, and give our missile destroyers the go-ahead to fire on Baku—all at once."

Nikitin chewed his lip, contemplating. It wasn't the move he wanted. He'd always planned to cross Red Bridge, yes. And he also planned to fire on Baku.

But only *after* the Iranians were in position to support him. And *after* Rzayev was rotting at the bottom of the Caspian Sea.

Nikitin shook his head. "It is too soon. The Iranians are not yet ready. If we move now, the Americans may have time to intercede."

"They will have time, yes. But they won't use it. We have seen how this vice president, this Jordan Stratton, operates. He is timid. He holds his people back. It took him over twenty-four hours to respond to the Chinese attack on his warship, and even then he contented himself with a few slain pilots and a smashed airstrip. Two nuclear blasts in the past month, and he has yet to even declare an enemy. He will not move quickly against Iran. We have room to press our advantage."

Nikitin swirled the tea in his cup, gaze lost on the desk. Unpacking the counsel and waging war with his own uncertainties. Measuring the odds. Suddenly doubting himself.

Golubev leaned across the desk, staring Nikitin right in the eye. "This is the moment, Makar. Our strategy is sound. Our forces are ready. Do not allow the Americans to enter the mix. Stake your claim."

Nikitin looked up. His jaw tightened. He set the cup down and nodded once.

"Give the order. The operation begins."

63

**Absheron District
Azerbaijan**

"Pile the rifles in the corner! Grenades and spare magazines next to them. Bodies across the hallway."

Turk called commands while Lucy scurried across bloody concrete, gathering fallen AK-74s, Zigana handguns, and a trio of Uzi submachine guns with most of their ammunition depleted. Reed squatted at the base of the wall just outside the entrance of the cell block and sorted the gear, while Ivan dragged the bodies of dead Azerbaijani SSS officers into a bullet-stopping wall across the width of the hallway leading to the stairwell.

The strategy was simple—and it was far from ideal. Of all members of the Prosecution Force held captive by Rzayev's brutes, Ivan had escaped the most torture. Reed suspected that had something to do with the fact that he was Russian, and Rzayev's primary interest had been in breaking the Americans. Regardless, Ivan's legs had sustained less beating, and he was steadier on his feet. He would accompany Turk and Lucy to the top of the stairs, where they would establish a greeting party for the Russian commandos. A storm of fire, a few grenades thrown, and then they would fall back to the basement.

In tactical terms, barricading themselves inside the pit beneath the black site was the worst possible idea. Their back would be against a wall, there would be no way to escape. But on the other hand, it would also be impossible for the Russians to encircle them. They would have to approach down the stairway and into the hall in single or possible double file, allowing the Prosecution Force an opportunity to engage the enemy on their own terms.

Even more importantly than that, the basement offered Reed the best chance of keeping Corbyn and Wolfgang safe from the firefight to come. Neither of them was capable of defending themselves, but the block walls and steel doors would provide shelter from stray rounds or shrapnel. Corbyn's single job would be to endure her pain, a loaded Zigana in her lap, ready to unleash hellfire on the first enemy combatant who broke through that final door.

And Rzayev? Reed had a special arrangement for the brutalized Azerbaijani autocrat. After allowing him time to make phone calls to his air forces and to what military units lay close to hand around Baku, Reed had Turk drag Rzayev into Strickland's cell, dropping him directly adjacent to the mutilated body of the American pilot. It was a safer location than the exterior hallway—although not as safe as Corbyn and Wolfgang's position. Reed didn't care. If the Russians got past him, he wouldn't expect an unconscious man with one leg and a scalded pilot with a single handgun to defend Rzayev. In that event, the Russians had earned their prize.

"My men are coming," Rzayev panted. "Ground soldiers from Baku. They are fifteen miles away...they will be here!"

"You better hope so," Reed growled, leaning against the doorframe. Turk put his arms around Reed's back, offering support, and together they stepped out into the cell block. The cell door closed and latched. Rzayev whimpered, and Reed flatly ignored him as Turk helped him out of the prison, back into the hallway now barricaded by human bodies—a mix of SSS soldiers and Rzayev's personal protection detail. All dead men, now forming a four-foot-high bullet-stop across the width of the hallway. Turk guided Reed onto the floor, and Reed lifted an AK into his lap. He leaned his head against the cold concrete behind him and panted.

Every part of him hurt. His head spun. He wasn't completely sure that he would be able to shoot straight.

But he would give it everything he had.

"I hear tires!" Lucy's voice called from the top of the stairwell just as Turk hefted his own rifle. Reed looked to the steps and for the dozenth time in the past hour he cursed himself for being weak, for being mortal, for sitting here in the dark while his friends ran to the sound of the guns.

It was grueling to feel so useless, but no matter how badly he wanted to, Reed knew he couldn't get up the steps. Even if Turk carried him, it would only result in further danger for the team when it was inevitably time to fall back.

"Try not to shoot me on my way down," Turk said with a sarcastic grin.

"No promises."

Turk squeezed Reed's shoulder and turned for the human barricade. Reed caught him by his sleeve.

"Turk."

The big Tennessean turned back. Reed opened his mouth, then stopped. He wasn't sure where to start, whether it be with an expression of guilt or regret. Not only for bringing Turk here—for dragging him into this entire mess. But for ignoring Turk's counsel against this entire mission in the first place.

Turk had said it didn't feel right. That they weren't ready. Reed had pressed ahead. Now Strickland was dead and, before the next hour expired, the rest of them might be also.

But no. None of that mattered. Not really. Not to a soldier like Turk. He wouldn't want to hear apologies. He didn't have time for them.

So Reed said the only thing left to say. What he should have said from the start.

"Thank you."

Turk nodded slowly. He lifted his free hand in a sloppy salute.

"Stand fast. I'll be back shortly."

Reed winced as he pulled the charging handle on his AK. It slammed home with a snap, unleashing further pain from his left ear. The drum was busted, just like the rest of his body.

"Save some for me!" Reed shouted.

Turk dropped to the far side of the wall of bodies. He turned that sarcastic grin back on Reed.

"No promis—"

Turk's voice was cut short by a sudden blast of thunder. As distant as the rumbles Reed had heard before, but somehow sharper. And not just one blast, or even a half dozen. These blasts persisted, one after another, the ground shaking so hard that mortar dust rained from the concrete walls. Reed and Turk both looked upward on instinct, the reality of what was happening sinking in by the third clap of thunder.

"Rockets!" Reed shouted.

Turk said nothing. He simply dashed for the base of the stairs. Another three seconds later and he was gone, boots pounding up the steps as the voice of an AK-74 opened fire overhead.

"*Contact!*"

It was Ivan. Reed braced himself against the wall and pivoted the muzzle of his rifle toward the steps.

64

The Situation Room
The White House

"Cruise missiles! The Russians are firing on Baku!"

SecDef Steven Kline hung up a phone and exploded out of his seat. Shoving an aide out from behind a computer, his fingers flew over the keyboard. The screen at the end of the room presently displayed a map of the C-17 and accompanying F-35s crossing into southeastern Turkey, but with a few clicks of the computer mouse, Kline restored the video feed streaming in from the Global Hawk drone still circling high over southeastern Baku.

Only it wasn't Baku as Stratton remembered it. Now the dark city was illuminated by fire, white-hot spots erupting across the drone's infrared lens as one missile after another plummeted to earth across a four-mile swatch of city outskirts. The targets seemed to be entirely military—clusters of trucks, Cobra armored vehicles, a trio of tanks, a depot of warehouses surrounded by high fencing. They all went up in smoke and flame as the hail persisted.

"We've got movement at Red Bridge," Nick West called, holding a phone to his chest. "The Russians are invading."

Stratton stood from his chair, fixated on the drone feed. It shrank into a corner of the screen and the tracking map returned. Joining the markers that displayed the progress of the aircraft, however, were additional markers in northwestern Azerbaijan right on the Georgian border.

Red Bridge.

"Where the hell are these missiles coming from?" Stratton demanded.

"Gotta be naval," Yellin said. "Those blasts are too small to be ICBMs."

"Do we have eyes?" Stratton pressed.

"Working on it, sir." That was Aimes. Like everybody else, she held a phone to her ear, hunting for answers. Stratton's gaze snapped back to the seven dots blipping over southeastern Turkey, and he read the displayed ETA. Still forty-eight minutes—and that was without a compelled re-route.

"They saw us coming," Kline growled. "We forced them to escalate."

"I've got eyes on the Caspian Sea," Aimes said. "We've got five Buyan class corvettes firing from eighteen miles offshore."

"Kalibr cruise missiles," Yellin said. "Eight per ship. They're almost dry."

Sure enough, the flashes across the southwestern quadrant of Baku were subsiding, but the damage already unleashed was devastating. The entire region outside the SSS black site had been wiped clean. All the ground forces within reach of their beleaguered president had been wiped out of existence. The roads were smashed. Bridges blown into jagged chunks of concrete while buildings burned.

"We can't put our guys in there," Kline said. "It's too hot. Half of them will parachute right into bonfires."

"We don't have a choice," Aimes retorted. "My people need them now more than ever. There's no Azerbaijani contingency coming!"

"A dozen lives against forty Rangers and nine airmen, Madam Director. It's easy math."

"It's easy math when they're not your guys!"

"Quiet!" Stratton lifted a hand. He stood at the end of the table, gaze snapping between the oncoming aircraft and the devastation unleashed over Baku. Suddenly the progress of those seven planes no longer looked like a crawl. It looked like a sprint. They would arrive over the war zone in mere minutes.

Then what?

"Nothing has changed," Stratton said. "We still gotta make this work. General, what was your extraction plan?"

"It just got blown away," Yellin said, gesturing to the screen. "We were going to land that C-17 at an airstrip just outside the city."

"Can't you land those things on dirt?" Stratton asked.

"We call it an SPRO, Mr. Vice President. Semi-Prepared Runway Landing. There's nothing semi-prepared about missile craters. We'd need our guys to migrate to someplace else in the city."

And the Russians are coming.

Now Stratton was looking to Red Bridge. It was a couple hundred miles northwest of Baku, but a couple hundred miles was nothing if the Russians successfully penetrated Azerbaijani air defenses and took control of the skies.

"They're daring us," Stratton whispered.

"I'm sorry?" Yellin answered.

"Nikitin is daring us. He's pushing our buttons, expecting us to back down."

"With respect, sir, it's a great deal more complicated than that. We're talking about forty lives—"

"Send them in," Stratton said.

"What?"

"You heard me, General. The mission proceeds. Deploy the paratroopers and find a place to land that plane. You'll evacuate to Iraq afterward."

"Mr. Vice President, we can't guarantee the security—"

"Of what? Of the world? I'm well aware!" Stratton slammed a palm against the tabletop. "This isn't a game. If we pull back now, there's nothing to convince Nikitin that he can't storm the whole region. I want him looking down American rifle barrels before he presses that button."

Silence. Loaded stares passed around the room. It was SecDef Kline who spoke next.

"To be clear, sir, you understand that everybody aboard that C-17, not to mention the pilots of the F-35s, could be flying to their deaths. Forty-nine people."

Stratton looked Kline in the eye. And simply nodded.
"I do. Send them."

65

Absheron District
Azerbaijan

Turk didn't need Ivan screaming "*contact*" over and over to know that the Russians had arrived. He recognized the voice of their AK-12 rifles even before he reached the top of the stairs. Breaking through the open doorway, he caught Ivan's gaze just in time for the Russian to motion him down.

Turk dove, and the grenade Ivan had just slung detonated with an ear-splitting bang. Turk slid across a tile hallway and scrambled behind the barricade of metal desks he and Lucy had erected just beyond the entrance of the stairwell. Both Lucy and Ivan were dug in there, firing through built-in gun ports at the oncoming surge of black.

And it was a surge—Turk saw six men in a flash just outside the gaping hole that had once served as part of the black site's entrance. Somewhere during the cruise missile blasts, the Russians had applied enough plastic explosive to completely decimate a ten-by-ten chunk of blocks, exposing the smoky black night beyond. Ivan's grenade had landed only yards from the Russian commandos dug in at that makeshift entrance, but they had seen the weapon coming and scrambled for cover. Now the hail of bullets pinging against the metal desk barricade was ceaseless, each ricochet whining into the walls and ceilings as all three of the defenders were forced to lower themselves almost to the floor.

"They will use grenades next!" Ivan warned.

Again, Turk didn't need to be told. The pop of a launcher registered in his ears despite the thunder of gunfire. A moment later a canister landed against the outside of the barricade and detonated. The blast was so loud Turk rocked backward, instantly deafened. His head spun, his ears nothing but a dull ring. He caught himself on the floor and touched blood. Ivan's face was twisted into a horrific grimace, one hand clutching his left hip.

The hand was red.

Turk clawed his way off the floor, still dazed and deaf. He shoved his muzzle through the nearest makeshift gun port just as the grenadier reappeared around the corner of the torn-out wall. He clutched an AK-12 with an attached launcher. His hand closed around the launcher's grip, finger curling toward the trigger.

Turk shot him twice in the exposed neck and throat. The Russian pitched backward and the rifle fell. In an instant the force of gunfire pivoted to confront Turk's muzzle flash, and he yanked away from the hole.

"Grenade!"

Ivan pitched him a fragmentation grenade and Turk yanked the pin with a curled finger. Before he could throw it, Ivan shook him by the shoulder. His lips were moving, but Turk couldn't hear a thing. His ears were registering only a dull ring. Ivan mimed with his hands, gesturing an overhand throw and shaking his head. Then miming a side throw. He pointed to the ceiling.

Then Turk understood. The ceiling was too low. Ivan's last grenade had bounced off it and landed short. Turk would have to rise out from behind cover of the barricade and toss sideways to have any hope of reaching the door.

Ivan predicted the move and shouted something to Lucy. Together the two of them closed on the barricade and poked rifles through, unleashing a storm of cover fire as Turk erupted from behind the piled desks. His head and shoulders cleared cover, and he looked down a gun-smoke-clouded hall to the blown-out wall. Russian commandos dug in on either side of the gap had withdrawn to shelter from Ivan and Lucy's withering fire. Bullets pinged off the concrete and blasted dust into the air, clearing Turk's path. He released the spoon. Counted once—one one thousand.

Then he threw and kicked his legs out from beneath him at the same moment. The grenade left his hand and he never saw it land. He struck the tile floor instead. A split second passed. Then a distant *bang!* registered through his ringing ears. Turk clawed his way upright and looked through the nearest gunport to see smoke clogging the entrance. A dead Russian lay stretched out in a pool of blood, his rifle jammed beneath him. Others moved like shadows outside, evading Ivan and Lucy's persistent fire, retreating from the gap. In a moment they were gone, leaving their two slain comrades behind.

Turk withdrew and swapped the mag on his AK, breathing hard and still unable to hear. The world seemed to swim around him, but the lack of auditory input mixed with a flood of adrenaline had heightened his other senses. Most notably his sense of taste...and smell.

Diesel fumes.

Turk's tongue passed over his lip and he looked through the gunpoint, back to the blown-out wall. In the smokey darkness outside, a pair of headlights gleamed, small and circular like cat eyes. They looked vaguely familiar, but in the moment Turk couldn't place the memory. Then the front bumper of the Cobra armored truck Turk himself had driven up to the front door of the compound erupted through the smoke, driving straight into the gap and crashing over busted blocks. From the roofline of the vehicle, movement broke through the smog—a twitch of a long black barrel.

"*Move!*"

Turk hurled himself sideways, catching Ivan in the shoulder and throwing him straight into Lucy. The CANiK machine gun mounted to the roof of the Cobra erupted into dim cracks that sounded something like popcorn snapping inside a microwave. Turk felt the bullets whistling overhead, ripping straight through the flimsy metal barricade and striking the concrete wall behind. There was no longer any safe place to rise above a crawl, and the machine gun was working its way rapidly downward toward the floor.

"*Go!* To the stairs!"

Turk shoved, but Lucy and Ivan didn't need to be told. They both clawed their way toward the open stairwell door as the top half of the makeshift barricade collapsed behind. The corner of a desk landed on Turk's calf and he let out a shriek. Lucy looked back and he waved her ahead. He rolled, jerking the leg, breaking it free. His pants leg and the skin beneath it tore. The CANiK paused, probably run dry.

Turk wouldn't wait for the gunner to reload. He wriggled free of the desk and hauled himself to the door. Ivan extended a hand and dragged him through just as the snarl of small-arms fire returned. Turk's chin struck the concrete and his head went light. Ivan rolled him over and together with Lucy they dragged him onto the landing at the top of the stairwell. Lucy was shouting something, pointing to Turk's leg. He still couldn't hear.

Ivan took over. Hauling himself to his feet, the Russian staggered, almost toppling. In his massive right hand he carried three more grenades, the last of the supply they had brought with them to the top of the stairs. Ivan pulled all three pins at once with a snatch of his right hand. Then he was staggering through the door, stepping into the open. Turning.

"*Ivan!*"

Turk called the warning. It was too late. Ivan slung the grenades with an awkward backhanded toss of his left arm, losing his balance halfway through and stumbling on an injured right leg. His face, so badly blackened by bruises and abuse, now washed light purple. He twisted to throw himself back into the stairwell but couldn't get through fast enough.

The first bullet caught him in the leg. The second in the arm. Ivan pitched forward and landed on top of Turk as the three grenades went off in unison. The breath left Turk's lungs as his head rocketed backward into the concrete. He tasted blood and gasped for air. Ivan was writhing on top of him, screaming in his ear, long sweaty hair slapping him in the face.

But Lucy was on her feet. Even as Turk shoved Ivan off to the side, Lucy was headed to the door. She fought it free of Ivan's boots and slammed it shut, shoving the metal chair they had hauled to the top of the stairs beneath the doorknob. It was a terrible locking mechanism and would be easily defeated under the right pressure, but maybe it would be enough to buy them some time.

"*Come on!*" Turk couldn't hear the words, but he read Lucy's lips. She grabbed him by the arm and jerked. Turk fought to his knees and passed her his rifle. Ivan still lay on the floor, bleeding from two separate wounds. The Russian was struggling to fight his way into a seated position, but he couldn't make it. The loss of blood and the shock of the pain were taking over. He was already battered and malnourished. This was a bridge too far, even for a man made of Soviet iron.

"Go!" Turk said. "Get down there!"

Then he grabbed Ivan by the arms and yanked him backward. They hit the stairs at the same moment, Ivan jerking with each bump toward the bottom. Turk didn't have time to worry about Ivan's loss of blood or whether or not he was actually dragging a dead man. He yanked Ivan's bulk through the middle landing and pulled him on toward the bottom. Lucy met him halfway down the final flight of stairs and assisted in jerking Ivan onto smooth concrete. Turk dropped his wounded comrade and snatched his rifle from where Lucy had left it, leaning against the wall. He looked up, between the flights of stairs to the landing at the top.

He couldn't hear the thunder of boots or a battering ram pounding against the door, but he could see the metal stairs shudder with each jarring thunder against the chair.

The commandos were coming.

66

The Kremlin
Moscow, Russia

"The American's are not turning back." Golubev's voice snapped as he hung up a phone. Nikitin had left his inner sanctum of an office and now stood in the Operations Center. Above the stretching oblong table, mounted to every wall, digital screens displayed the situation as it unfolded. Some were drone feeds, some satellite feeds, some simply maps that marked the progress of Russian troops surging into Azerbaijan.

It was a night raid, and it was progressing perfectly. Cruise missiles from a flotilla of corvettes in the Caspian Sea had rattled Baku, smashing any military assets within quick response range of President Rzayev's location while also distracting Azerbaijani military officials from the larger threat—those seventy thousand Russian ground troops and accompanying armor now crashing through the Red Bridge border crossing.

The Azerbaijanis, despite having days to prepare, were anything but. The savage force of artillery fire that rained from the sky shattered their ranks and drove them into a retreat within twenty minutes. The fear sank in. The Russian veterans with months of Ukraine campaigning under their belts were unfazed.

And yet...the Americans had not turned back.

"Where are they?" Nikitin shoved his chair aside and circled the table. A military aide directed his attention to a singular screen on the right-hand wall. A map of the entire region, each country displayed as a different color. The red triangle arcing over the center of the map had just crossed into Azerbaijani airspace. It was pointed at Baku, clipping along at a measured and relentless rate.

Seven planes.

"Are they blind?" Nikitin demanded.

Golubev held up a hand. He was concentrated on his phone again, listening. His face distorted into a dark scowl. He hung up.

"That was the embassy," Golubev said. "The Americans are declaring their flight to be a humanitarian mission and are demanding passage. They are prepared to defend themselves."

Nikitin snarled a curse and planted his fist against the wall, still staring at the screen, estimating time.

The Americans were thirty minutes out from Baku. Forty, tops, unless derailed. There was no part of Nikitin that believed anything about the mission was humanitarian. The contents of that C-17 were unknown, but Nikitin had little reason to believe the aircraft would be dumping water bottles and food stores.

Jerking his head, Nikitin drew Golubev from across the room. He lowered his voice to a dull growl.

"Where are we with Rzayev?"

"The team has made contact at the SSS black site. They are encountering heavy resistance, but making progress. Local Azerbaijani defense forces were decimated by the missile strikes. We should have a body within minutes."

Nikitin's teeth sank into the inside of his cheek. He chewed until he tasted blood, once again enjoying the razor's edge of focus that pain offered.

"Can we engage the Americans?"

"In the air?"

"Correct."

Golubev hesitated. He shook his head. "We could try. The Azerbaijanis have concentrated their air defenses on the northern border. We would have to evade them first."

"They aren't moving to block the Americans?"

"No. Not yet."

They're dancing together. The Americans have taken control.

"Put up a dozen of our best pilots. I want the Americans shot down."

67

Absheron District
Azerbaijan

From behind the wall of bodies, Reed braced himself over a dead SSS soldier's stomach, cheek pressed into the stock of his rifle, fixated on the bottom of the stairs as Turk, Lucy, and Ivan crashed to the bottom. The clamor overhead had been almost ceaseless. Grenade blasts, rifle chatter, and then the unmistakable thunder of a .50 cal in full action.

Reed braced himself on one knee and gritted his teeth against the pain —not only the physical agony but the mental anguish of watching his team crash to the floor.

He saw blood. He wasn't sure who was wounded. Ivan didn't get up.

"Come on," Reed growled. "Get to the wall!"

The gunfire had paused overhead, but Reed thought he heard footfalls. He dropped his left hand off the fore grip of the AK and wrapped it around the string running beneath a corpse's neck. It ran down the length of the hallway, thirty yards to the base of the steps and then up to the first and second landings. Connected in four places, each at crucial segments of the stairway.

Thump.

A foot landed against a barred metal door. Voices shouted. Turk struggled to his feet, dragging Ivan behind him. The big Russian wasn't dead—Reed could detect the tension in his body—but he was clearly incapable of moving under his own power. Reed's weapon light revealed a ghastly pale face twisted with pain as Ivan's body slid over bare concrete, Lucy walking backward behind him with her rifle covering their retreat.

From the top of the stairs the boot slammed again, and this time the door burst open. Reed heard it as a metallic crash and panic rushed his chest.

"*Move!*" Reed scrambled against the bodies, forcing himself to his feet with one hand still clenching the string. Lucy grabbed Ivan with her free hand and together she and Turk hurtled down the hallway. Ivan screamed but did his best to kick along with his feet, aiding progress. They reached the halfway mark just as a blaze of automatic gunfire lit up the stairwell. Bullets flooded down it, pinging against metal and ricocheting off concrete blocks. Two whizzed overhead as Lucy and Turk ducked.

Reed braced himself against the bodies, almost falling. He released the rifle, wrapping his left hand twice more around the string. Drawing it taut.

Lucy reached him. Reed wrapped his fingers around her forearm and yanked, propelling her over the top of the wall and into meager safety beyond. Lucy fell with a thud, then Turk reached the wall and bent to heft Ivan.

But it was already too late. The Russian commandos had cleared the stairwell with their deluge of fire, and now they were headed down. Boots thundered on metal. Voices shouted.

"Down! Down!"

Reed called the order and yanked the string. It required more than one pull, but he could feel the *pop* as each subsequent grenade pin popped loose. Four weapons in total, each affixed with wire ties to key points of the stairwell structure. Three brutal seconds passed as Turk dove over Ivan. A boot appeared on a metal step just beneath the hallway ceiling, and Reed hefted his rifle.

Then the grenades detonated, one after another in four ear-splitting blasts. Smoke and shrapnel exploded through the doorway and whizzed into the ceiling. Screams echoed and at least one body fell, including the

Russian whose boot had just appeared. He was writhing, clawing at his stomach as blood spurted out. Reed snatched up his rifle and shot the commando twice in the head as the creaking screech of metal on metal signaled the total collapse of the stairs.

Turk was back on his feet, heaving Ivan. Reed extended a hand, but Turk didn't seem to notice. The stairs completed their collapse with a metallic crash, but Turk didn't so much as flinch.

He was deaf—blood ran from his ears.

Reed left his position and grabbed Ivan, dragging the Russian over the top of the wall of bodies. Blood ran from Ivan's left arm and his right thigh. His face was chalky pale, but more than wounded he looked angry—overwhelmingly outraged.

"Give me a gun!" Ivan shouted. "Put a gun in my hands!"

The Russian hit the ground, then Turk was over the body wall. Reed slammed his closed fist against Turk's, signaling that both were on the same page, then he turned back to the doorway. Hefted the rifle, bumping his weapon light to illuminate mangled metal and a pair of dead Russian commandos.

The grenades had worked better than anticipated. The stairwell was nothing but a hollow shaft with a pile of metal stairs piled awkwardly at the bottom.

But the fight wasn't over. It wasn't even started. From the top of the shaft Reed heard the voices shouting orders, making adjustments and preparations.

They were still coming.

68

The Situation Room
The White House

"Russians in the air!"

The declaration came from General Albert Porter, chief of staff of the Air Force. It was his planes streaking into Azerbaijan. His C-17 and wing of F-35s.

"How many?" Stratton demanded.

Porter remained calm, working his computer. He projected a map over the room-end screen. "At least ten, sir. Possibly twelve. Radar is unclear. They're fifth-gen stealth fighters."

"Time to intercept?" Yellin demanded.

"Unclear. Fifteen minutes, perhaps."

Stratton looked to the clock chugging steadily downward beneath the C-17's tracking chart. The Rangers were still twenty-six minutes out from the drop zone. A lethal eleven-minute gap.

Forty-nine lives.

Yellin made eye contact, a question on his face.

"We proceed, General," Stratton said. "If those Russians arrive I want you to blow them out of the sky."

69

Absheron District
Azerbaijan

The snap of ropes against concrete was Reed's first signal that the Russians had found an alternative path down the stairwell. Crouched behind the stiffening forms of four SSS soldiers, he'd turned his weapon light off, focusing the front sight post of the AK dead in the middle of the black doorway thirty yards distant.

Two feet to his left, Turk crouched in a similar position. The blood was drying on his cheeks, but he periodically flexed his jaw as though he were trying to clear his ears. Behind them Ivan growled Russian curses while Lucy packed gauze into his wounds. Her arms were so coated in blood she looked like a body-painted superfan ready for a football game with a red-themed team. Nearby, her rifle waited along with a spare for Ivan and a loose pile of loaded magazines.

For the moment the strange stillness consuming the hallway felt like the perfect calm inside the eye of a hurricane. It seeped into Reed's brain, working past the physical torment of his broken body and unleashing carnage on his psyche. He focused on the opening to the stairwell and watched as the black spot wavered and twisted like a mirage, shifting sideways. Dancing.

He blinked, and it drew back into focus. His own hot breath stung his lips as he shifted the rifle, waiting and watching for the first body to appear.

The Russians would fast rope straight into a wall of lead. Certainly, they knew that. But they were coming anyway, for the same reason that Reed had jumped aboard a plane and rocketed into this pit of hell without a second thought.

It's what soldiers do.

Turning back to Turk, Reed's eyes stung and he felt a sudden weight of hot lead in his gut.

"There's something wrong with this mission. I can feel it in my blood."

It was Turk's warning from just before he and Reed had separated, back in Tennessee. Before Reed had charged ahead, boarding a plane for Azerbaijan, and Turk had lagged behind.

"I won't go. I won't watch you destroy this team."

And yet, in the end...Rufus Turkman had turned up in Azerbaijan anyway. Not because he believed or didn't believe in the mission...because *that's what soldiers do.*

Reed poked Turk in the arm. The big man spun abruptly, battlefield instincts overcoming his rational sense as he reacted like a compacted spring. Reed held up a hand, calming him. Then he lifted that hand slowly to his face and brushed his lip. Miming like Turk had food stuck to his face.

Something between a scowl and a grin clouded Turk's face. He shoved Reed in the chest, knocking him off-balance before lifting a middle finger. Reed caught himself, grimacing in pain. Turk didn't apologize. Reed regained his feet and tried to laugh.

He couldn't. The pain was too deep. Not only because Turk had been right...but because Turk had turned up, willingly throwing himself in the grinder for his team. Even when he knew better.

Reed made eye contact with his battle buddy. The big Tennessean was smiling now. For a long moment neither moved. Neither blinked. Reed thought Turk's eyes were misting over a bit...or maybe that was his own. He swallowed the lead in his stomach...the guilt. The self-loathing.

He extended a free hand and Turk clasped it, pulling them together into a hug. Reed's face mashed into Turk's shoulder. He smelled sweat, BO, and blood. But he didn't mind. He squeezed his friend around the back and held the embrace for a long moment.

Then each of them turned back to the human wall, re-shouldering their rifles. A flash of green marked the passage of glow sticks falling down the stairwell. They landed amid the bodies, illuminating the black ropes that hung down from overhead. Then those ropes flicked, and a small silver item plummeted from the top. It pinged off mangled stair metal and popped. Gray smoke streamed out, flooding the base of the stairwell.

Reed calmly rocked his face against the stock, refocusing on the front sight post and seeing it clearly. His breathing calmed into measured, regulated waves. He placed his finger on the trigger.

70

40,000 Feet over Western Azerbaijan

"Viper One to Vulcan—be advised, I have twelve bandits bearing north-northwest at one hundred twenty miles and closing. Probable Flankers."

From the left-hand seat of the C-17, Air Force Captain Jeff Taylor's blood ran cold. He looked instinctively through the windshield of the giant cargo craft, searching a pitch-black sky as though he expected to see the oncoming fighter jets.

Flanker—the NATO callsign for the Russian fifth-generation Su-35 fighter jets. A direct rival to the F-35 Lightning IIs now flanking the Globemaster...except Taylor only had six escort fighters. Had Viper One just said *twelve*?

Taylor keyed his mic. "Copy that, Viper One. Reconfirm bandit count, over."

"That would be twelve, Vulcan. An egg carton full of the little devils."

Viper One sounded completely unfazed by the announcement, but Taylor knew the young lieutenant had to be overwhelmed with adrenaline. You could train and train and train...but how many modern American fighter pilots actually expected to experience nose-to-nose combat with a technologically advanced enemy?

Glancing to his cockpit display, Taylor confirmed the distance to the DZ —the drop zone. Nineteen minutes, maybe eighteen if he pushed the Globemaster to its limits. An Su-35 cruising at Mach 2, or about fifteen hundred miles per hour, would clear one hundred twenty miles in under five minutes.

Not good.

Taylor exchanged a glance with his co-pilot. The guy was a little pale, but otherwise the nerves were invisible beneath years of training.

"Viper One to Vulcan." The young wing commander's voice returned to Taylor's headset. "Be advised, Eagle's Nest has authorized preemptive deadly force within a twenty-mile radius. I'm going to leave you with Vipers Five and Six while I break off with Two, Three, and Four to roll out a welcome mat. Recommend you dump on a little fuel and move your fat ass."

That brought just the hint of a smile to Taylor's face. He thumbed the mic.

"Don't have too much fun, Viper. See you at the DZ."

"Copy that."

Taylor looked back out of his glass in time to see four members of his escort breaking left. Their tails illuminated in a flash of hot afterburner... then they were gone. Vanished into the black. Leaving him with two fighter jets...and forty-two lives on board. Plus his own.

"All right, Mac. Let's see what the old lady can do." Taylor placed his hands on the power levers and ramped up his engines.

71

**The Situation Room
The White House**

From the basement of the West Wing, Stratton listened to the communications between the wing commander and the officer in charge of the C-17, and he couldn't help but marvel at the relaxed calm in each of their voices. He knew it was artificial on some level. No man could charge into the teeth of probable death and not feel at least a *little* fear, but these men were flatly ignoring it…and charging on.

"Get them on the big screen," Stratton ordered.

General Porter's aide made it happen, transitioning the largest screen from a display of Russian incursion into northern Azerbaijan to a zoomed map tracking the progress of those four F-35s screaming toward a wall of Russian Su-35s. A three-to-one fight, but you wouldn't have known it by the continued calm in Viper One's voice as he issued commands to the three other pilots. Authorizations, engagement protocols.

A "welcome mat," the kid had called it. Stratton would have smiled if his body wasn't so alive with chemical anxiety.

"Time to engagement?" he said.

"Two minutes," General Porter replied.

Stratton's hands closed around the edge of the desk. Nobody moved in the room. All eyes were fixed on the screen as green triangles drew steadily closer to the red. Seconds dripped by like water from a slow-leaking faucet. Stratton reminded himself why he'd sent these young men into combat.

No. Not into combat. Into an early grave. He wasn't a fighter pilot and he didn't need to be to understand how this math—

"Smoke in the air!" Viper One's announcement broke his practiced calm, erupting as a shout. Stratton closed his eyes and listened as the commands kept snapping. The F-35s banked. Their own missiles flew. Another twenty sounds ground by before Viper One screamed, "Eject, Carter!"

Then one of the green triangles vanished from the map. Stratton's arms began to tremble. He forced himself to watch the screen as the voices faded. The three remaining pilots were in full concentration mode. Two of the red triangles had disappeared from the screen. The rest seemed to be swarming.

Then Porter erupted in a thundering curse, exploding from his chair. His right hand slammed into the table and his wide eyes fixated on the screen. The LCD blinked, and in a flash a wall of yellow triangles appeared out of nowhere, screaming in from the east and headed straight for the aerial battleground.

"The hell is that?" Stratton demanded.

"The Azerbaijanis, sir! *Hot damn*, they're joining the fight!"

72

**Absheron District
Azerbaijan**

Within seconds of the first Russian soldier dropping to the bottom of the stairwell, Reed was as deaf as Turk. He and his battle buddies opened fire at the same moment, shooting through the smoke and ventilating the shadow of a man beyond. A scream signaled rounds on target, followed by silence.

A momentary victory. But a short-lived one.

Within seconds the creak of metal and the bump of bodies announced the arrival of more soldiers headed down the ropes. Reed measured his shots, no longer aiming but simply putting rounds downrange through the smoke—right to left, left to right, Turk moving in an opposing pattern.

There were more shouts, followed by a muted cry. But Reed couldn't be sure if any of his shots had been fatal. What he did know was that the Russians had dug in behind the bodies of their comrades, and within seconds they were returning fire. He couldn't see the muzzle flash—it was shrouded by smoke. He couldn't hear the gunshots, either. His hearing had descended to dull, meaningless ringing. But he knew the gunfire by the twitch and jerk of the bodies stacked up in front of him. By random splashes of cold blood and the chips of concrete raining from off the walls.

Dropping behind the makeshift wall, Reed dumped an empty mag and caught a replacement from Lucy. Ivan had dragged himself to the barricade and was shooting one-handed with his rifle resting atop a dead man's face. Ivan shouted something through the smoke in booming Russian. Reed caught the words as vague and distant, like the burbles of fish in a tank. It was meaningless too him, but by the bloody grin stretched across Ivan's face, he could guess that the shout had been a taunt.

Returning to the wall, Reed was just in time to duck as a rifle-fired grenade landed at the exterior base of the flesh barricade. A moment later it detonated, loud enough to be heard through the ringing. The bodies shuddered. Gore sprayed against the walls. Then Reed was back over the top, ratcheting the AK to full auto and dumping the magazine into the smog.

The barrel was piping hot. His left hand scalded as he gripped the fore stock, his lungs so flooded by gun smoke that his head went light. A vague shadow moved through the thinning smog, and all three of them swept their rifles in that direction. The guy doubtless wore body armor, but twenty rounds later it wouldn't have mattered if he were made of steel. He went down, and now Reed could see the muzzle flash. Blinks of orange breaking through fading gray as bullets clipped over his head and zipped past his arm.

Reed reached back for another magazine and Lucy dropped it into his palm. As he ratcheted it into the rifle, her hand closed over his arm. She pulled. He looked back.

Lucy held up three more mags, shaking them in a clear signal. Reed nodded once and looked back.

Then the next rifle grenade landed. It arced only inches over Reed's shoulder and raced toward the wall. The world descended into slow motion as his head snapped backward. His gaze passed over his shoulder. He watched the little metal canister land and bounce. It spun on the filthy concrete. It rolled toward him, only seconds from detonating.

Lucy moved first. She threw herself sideways, those spiderlike reflexes that had made her such an absolutely lethal assassin once again taking command of her body. She landed on her side. Her right hand wrapped around the grenade. She twisted, hurling it sideways. Reed ducked and the weapon sailed back over his head.

It made it only a yard over the wall before detonating. Shards of metal ripped through the air and blasted the wall. Crimson sprayed Reed's body and he looked back to see Lucy's face contorted into a grimace, both hands wrapped around her gut.

"*RPG!*" Turk's shout was so loud Reed detected it through his swimming head. A heavy hand wrapped around his arm and yanked Reed sideways. A blast of smoke clogged the air. Reed felt the concussion even before the fire exploded across the full width of the hallway. The rocket-propelled grenade landed at the base of the human wall and detonated with a thunderclap. Bodies—and pieces of bodies—erupted into the air. Blood drenched the walls and Reed hurtled backward, slamming into Turk as Turk slammed into concrete.

The world spun. Reed choked on smoke. He was vaguely conscious of bullets zipping past his ears. He looked to his hands and saw red. He looked to Lucy and saw red.

Then Turk's heavy hands wrapped around his shoulder yanked him backward. Reed lurched and passed through the open doorway into the cell block. Turk dragged him, dumped him, then he was gone. Reed saw him as though in a dream—the big man turned just outside the doorway and clamped down on the trigger of his AK, dumping auto fire one-handed toward the oncoming commandos even as he grabbed Lucy by her jacket and yanked her to safety. Just as he reached the doorway, Turk flinched, agony crossing his face. He stumbled. Started to fall.

Reed was on his knees. Rifle abandoned, head floating. He no longer felt a thing. All the pain was drowned beneath an avalanche of sheer rage. He threw himself back to the door and caught Turk as the big man fell. Lucy was with him. Ivan was behind, worming along on his stomach. Reed dug his fingers in and snatched backward. Blood ran off Turk's neck and into Reed's mouth. Reed wrenched, kicking and sliding, pinned down as Turk fought to get up.

They cleared the door. Ivan dragged his body through, aided by Lucy. Reed kicked at the door, fighting to ram it closed. His boot made contact, but the door wouldn't move. Ivan's leg was still in the way.

"*Ivan!*"

The Russian twisted, fighting to relocate his gunshot leg.

Then another Russian appeared in the doorway like a black wraith. Dressed head to tow in combat gear, helmeted with a mask stretched across his face, an AK-12 pivoting downward straight toward Turk's back.

Reed snatched his leg back, already knowing he was too late. He kicked at the door again. Then the Russian commando jerked the same way Turk had. He stumbled. Red appeared, gushing from his face and his throat in a trio of holes. He fell backward. Reed kicked the door and it slammed closed. The automatic latch fell into place, the obliterated mechanism on the outside helpless to open it.

Temporary stillness fell down the prison shaft. Reed collapsed, gasping for breath. Writhing in pain. The world spun, and he twisted his neck to look up the hallway.

Kirsten Corbyn stood there, propped up against a prison door, the Zigana pistol extended in one arm. She made eye contact with Reed, then collapsed to her knees, dropping the gun. A split second later a voice barked beyond the door, and a heavy foot fell.

Turk picked himself up, clutching his own shoulder and offering Reed a moment to breathe. Both men looked to the door as it shuddered in its frame, dust erupting from gaps in the concrete.

The Russians were only seconds from breaking through.

73

500 Feet Over Baku
Azerbaijan

"*Hook up!*"

The command ripped down the line of forty standing Rangers, a signal that after eighty minutes of laborious flight time, the moment of truth had almost arrived. At the front of the right-hand stack, Corporal Duncan Sanders unclipped the static line hook from his reserve parachute's carrying strap and snapped it onto the heavy steel cable that ran the length of the C-17.

Heart thumping, body alive with pre-jump jitters. He always felt them. He never admitted to them. He never let them stop him from hurling his body out of a perfectly operational aircraft into a perfectly uncertain battlefield.

"*Check static lines!*"

On the next command Sanders proceeded with practiced routine to inspect the length of his yellow static line, searching for damage of any kind from the hook-up point all the way to where the strap disappeared over his shoulder. Satisfied, he waited for a tap on the helmet from the man behind him, confirmation that all his parachute gear was in correct order and ready for deployment.

All clear.

"*Check equipment!*"

As Sanders's hand ran beneath his helmet chin strap, confirming a positive connection, he looked to the jump door standing closed only two yards in front of him. A man-sized opening in the side of the Globemaster that would facilitate a leap into empty air.

A moment that would send his stomach hurtling into his throat.

"*Sound off for equipment check!*"

Starting at the tail of the C-17 and proceeding forward like a line of toppling dominos, each soldier shouted "*Okay!*" and slapped the man in front of him on the rib cage. When Sanders's shoulder was slapped, he shouted to the jumpmaster: "*All okay, jumpmaster!*"

Sanders instinctively dug his toes into the floor of the Globemaster, his body knowing what came next as clearly as his mind did. The jumpmaster advanced to the door. The big man rotated the latch, and in another moment the door rolled upward, admitting a hurricane blast of chilled night air that rammed Sanders so hard he almost stumbled backward.

Here we go.

"*One minute!*"

The three-lensed signal light mounted to the wall switched from red to yellow. A rowdy roar rose from the crowd of forty lethal men—the best their country had to give. The razor's edge of the largest battle ax the world had ever seen. Ready for the jump.

Ready for war.

Sanders's heart continued to hammer as he faced the open blackness. He thought of Maria, the Mexican American girl from Austin that he hoped to marry. He remembered their last night together. How she got a little drunk and finally admitted that she loved him too.

"*Thirty seconds!*" The jumpmaster faced Sanders. "*Stand by!*"

Sanders's stomached lurched. Cortisol entered his bloodstream. Then, along with the lead Ranger in the left-hand stack, he stepped forward just the way he had dozens and dozens of times before. He released the static line, handing it off to the safety, and advanced to the door. He turned to face the short jump platform that jutted out from the side of the bird like the plank of a pirate's ship.

"Have a nice jump, kid!" The jumpmaster shot Sanders a wink. Sanders never had a chance to reply. He never saw the signal light on the wall flick from yellow to green. He simply felt the slap of the jumpmaster's hand against his shoulder, accompanied by the shout: "*Go!*"

Sanders moved without thinking, acting on pure muscle memory. He passed through the open jump door, reaching the jump platform and continuing as though that little ledge lasted forever. His leg muscles bunched. The roar of the wind stole the breath from his lungs, and then he hurled himself off the end of that platform and into the unknown.

74

**The Situation Room
The White House**

"Rangers deploying!" General Porter called. "We made it to the drop zone."

A breathless sigh of relief circled the table, mixed with momentary clapping. At the end of the room, Stratton was still on his feet, monitoring his only link to the brutality unfolding on the far side of the world.

The Russian fighter pilots were dead—all twelve of them. Only one of the American fighters had survived, and at least eight of the Azerbaijani pilots were also sent spiraling to the earth in smoke and flame.

But the heroes behind those sticks had done their job—they had protected the C-17 all the way to the end, and now the giant plane was dumping her lethal cargo right onto the black site.

Too late? There was no way to be sure. Aimes had tried calling Turkman half a dozen times. Radio silence was the only answer.

"What's the plan, General?" Stratton's next question was addressed to Porter.

"We've identified a stretch of highway about six miles south of the drop zone," General Porter said. "It appears wide and long enough for the Globemaster to touch down. The Rangers will be advised to collect their target and retreat to that objective."

"Six *miles*?" Stratton asked. The moment he looked into Porter's eyes, he regretted his tone. The strain in the old general's face was absolute.

"It's the best we could do, sir. Maybe they can find vehicles. Viper Two is headed to rendezvous with Vipers Five and Six. They're all equipped with limited air-to-ground capability. They'll provide what cover they can."

"And the Azerbaijanis?" This time it was Yellin who interjected. The question was addressed to nobody in particular, and nobody answered.

Stratton simply looked back to the screen, now displaying the feed of the Global Hawk surveillance drone still circling high overhead, and watched as green parachutes dropped slowly toward the ground.

75

**The Kremlin
Moscow, Russia**

"We lost them all." Golubev's tone was no more personally invested than if he had been discussing spoiled fruit, but there was edgy focus in it nonetheless. Nikitin flicked his hand, directing for the display to change from the devastating dogfight over northern Azerbaijan to the American paratroopers now descending dead over the black site in Baku.

How did the Americans know? Nikitin had moles so deep inside Elchin Rzayev's government that he knew when the Azerbaijani president was taking a piss, let alone his constant location. But how had the Americans determined the site of Rzayev's distress? It would have been logical for them to parachute over the Presidential Palace, or any number of Baku's governmental buildings.

Nikitin had missed something—something small, but crucial, just the way he had feared. And now he was caught between a rock and a hard place. Churning forty miles off the Azerbaijani coast was his flotilla of five corvettes, but they were exhausted of cruise missiles and relatively useless to engage either the Rangers or the C-17 cargo plane now circling for a landing on a nearby Azerbaijani highway.

Option two would be to deploy more Su-35 fighter jets to engage the three remaining American F-35s, then bomb the black site into oblivion. But that wasn't an option for two reasons. First, the Azerbaijani air force had now swarmed the whole of northern Azerbaijan. It was a defeatable presentation, but there was little chance of Russian air power penetrating that barrier before the American Rangers completed their objective.

And secondly, even if Russian fighters somehow *did* reach the black site, how could Nikitin confirm that Rzayev was killed?

No. He had no other options now. He had to stick to the original plan.

"Press the ground attack," Nikitin said. "Do not inform our team of the American paratroopers. I want a photo of his body—*now*."

76

Absheron District
Azerbaijan

Reed knew the latch would never hold. It was solid steel, and heavy, but it was designed to keep prisoners *inside*, not to keep intruders *outside*. Even with the shattered electronic mechanism that operated the latch, it was only a matter of time before the oncoming Russians deployed enough brute force to simply knock the entire door down.

A shaped charge would do it. Another RPG, perhaps. Then Reed and what remained of his fractured team would face the end.

But damn—they weren't going down alone.

Besides Corbyn, Ivan was now in the worst shape of those members of the Prosecution Force still conscious. Turk dragged him into the mouth of a prison cell, positioned him against the wall, and put an AK-74 with half a magazine of ammunition in his hands. Reed sat across the hallway, using an open prison cell door as cover. He was squatted into an easy shooting position, rifle pointed at the open door. Turk would take a position directly opposite. Corbyn and Lucy were dug in at the end of the hall with the Uzis and the remaining 9mm cartridges in Corbyn's Zigana.

When that door burst open, the first man through would meet a wall of lead. The second and third would equally bite the dust. After that...

Reed breathed a long sigh, his aching body so numb it was difficult to hold the rifle steady. Every muscle sagged. He wanted to simply collapse onto the hard floor, no longer caring what happened to him.

But he *did* care about his team. He had brought them to this place. Certainly not against their will. Every one of them knew what they were getting involved with from the start. But Reed still felt the culpability of a leader who could have made better choices. Who could have somehow, some way done things differently. Fought harder, run faster. Kept them from the inevitable.

"Were we really that bad?" Turk said. His voice was a croak that Reed barely heard through his shattered ears. He blinked, momentarily confused, then twisted to face his battle buddy.

"Huh?"

"The gym," Turk clarified. "Were we really that bad at coaching fat rich guys? I mean, I'd give it another go."

A dry smile crept over Reed's face. He met Turk's gaze, and his eyes blurred. From ten feet apart, crouching behind doorframes, Reed couldn't help but feel an overwhelming wash of déjà vu. He'd been here before, so many times.

Iraq. Louisiana. South America. North Korea. And now...what was this place called?

Reed's mind blanked. He couldn't remember. He knew it started with an A. He knew it was someplace south of Russia, a place he'd never before been.

Did it even matter?

"I'd give it another go," Reed said.

Turk smiled, although Reed wasn't sure that he had actually heard the comment. Blood still ran from the big Tennessean's ears. He winced as he stepped across the hallway and settled into a shooting position alongside Reed. He shouldered the rifle without comment and breathed evenly, fixating on the door.

Reed turned his face away, blinking to clear the tears. From beyond the door he could hear the Russians moving. They were calling orders and pounding occasionally on the doorframe.

So it would be a shaped charge, then. *Good.* The door would come down all at once. The soldiers would run in soon after. Better to get it all over quickly.

"Turk," Reed said.

He put a hand on Turk's arm, and Turk's head pivoted. He raised an eyebrow. The sarcastic smile returned, weaker than before, but still sincere.

"Don't say it, Montgomery. Don't you ever say it."

Closed fists touched, and a hot resolve surged into Reed's chest. It wasn't enough to bring him back to one hundred percent, not even close. But it was enough to go out strong.

From the back of the hallway, Lucy called softly through Reed's ringing ears. Just loud enough to be heard.

"God is our refuge and strength, a very present help in trouble. Therefore, we will not fear though the earth gives way."

From outside the door, boots pounded as soldiers retreated. Lucy continued.

"Though the mountains be moved into the heart of the sea, though its waters roar and foam, though the mountains tremble at its swelling…"

The footsteps ceased. An eerie stillness settled over the prison block. Reed pressed his face into the stock of the rifle and curled his finger around the trigger.

Lucy said: "The Lord of hosts is with us."

Then the charge detonated, and the door exploded inward.

77

"Shots fired, basement!"

Corporal Duncan Sanders circled the nose of the bullet-marked Cobra attack vehicle and reached the giant hole blown into the block wall of the black site facility, leading the left-stack entry team. Night vision goggles painted a clear view of the battleground ahead, a green laser marking his point of aim as it danced across bloody blocks and several bodies clad in black Russian commando gear. Sanders and the point man on the right side of the Cobra lit those bodies up with full-auto discharges of their M4A1s, not waiting to see if they were already dead. Not taking any risks.

Sanders boots reached the edge of the entrance, and a familiar wave of anxiety cascaded over him like a waterfall—the absolute terror of the void ahead.

Nobody knew what lay inside this building. What combatants, explosives, collapsing walls and ceilings, bursts of poison gas...

And yet again, it didn't matter. Sanders bottled the fear deep in his stomach and hurtled ahead anyway, crossing the fallen blocks and penetrating the facility. With four Rangers at his back and five more to his right, the remainder of the forty-man incursion team was already circling the building to establish a security perimeter. On the lookout for trouble, whether it come from air, sea, or land.

But not Sanders. He was part of the door-kicking detachment—the room clearers. The most dangerous element of any operation, and he was there for it. Born for it.

Hurtling ahead into it.

Brass casings littered the floor amid shattered glass and additional bodies clothed in all black. The Rangers lit them all up, dumping lead regardless of whether the corpses twitched or lay rock still. As they progressed through the room, they mapped the progress of a bloody firefight that led directly into a hallway. Grenade signatures marked the walls, and a stack of mangled metal desks bore the clear signature of an RPG blast. The launch tube lay abandoned on the ground. Muddy boot prints led the way to an entrance with a plastic sign that indicated the shaft beyond as a stairwell.

It was from that stairwell that the gunfire Sanders had previously detected belched upward—the chug of Kalashnikov-type rifles, mixed with the frantic pop of a handgun.

Sanders reached the door and pivoted around it, leading with the M4. The green glow of his night vision illuminated a stairwell, just as he expected, but there were no stairs. They'd collapsed—or been blown apart—and now lay twenty-five feet below at the tail end of dangling black ropes.

Sanders didn't hesitate. He probably should have. There could be anything from a bomb to the muzzle of a minigun waiting at the base of that stair shaft. But did it matter? American lives were slipping steadily closer to eternity with every brutal second that passed, and Duncan Sanders hadn't been born to think twice.

Feet to the wall, rifle slung, gloved hands riding the rope. He went down flanked on either side by two of his brothers from Fort Moore. They kicked off the walls and cleared the drop in under four seconds, finding purchase on the mangled metal of collapsed steps. A body lay there—another black-suited guy with a Russian AK-12 trapped under his rib cage, his features twisted into a death grimace. He took two rounds to the face anyway, Sanders's boot slipping on bloody metal as he caught himself on the wall. Then he was dropping back to solid concrete, rifle rising into his chest just as his NVGs illuminated a picture of his first target.

Two of them, actually. Men in black kneeling outside a steel-framed door, thirty yards distant, rifles held into their chests, point of aim directed to Sanders's right down an invisible hallway.

Sanders and the private to his right fired at the same time, green lasers dancing, muzzle flash blinking bright green through the NVGs. Bullets stitched a reverse failure drill pattern—two in the pelvis, just beneath the body armor, and one to the head as the targets toppled. Both Russians collapsed sideways toward the floor, their screams broken short as the head shots administered instant death.

"*White light!*" Sanders called.

The three Rangers thumbed weapon lights, bathing the end of the hallway in an overwhelming cold glow that illuminated a tangled mess of mangled bodies—dozens of them, torn and shredded by an explosion that left the walls dripping with blood. They weren't Russians, but they weren't hostages, either. These bodies wore uniforms.

Azerbaijani SSS soldiers?

American M4A1s thundered again, riddling the corpses as the Rangers closed on the end of the room. Sanders was first in line, and he pivoted toward the next doorway. His rifle swept across it, green laser beam racing down a fifty-foot hallway littered with more bodies. White light flooded the space, so bright it drove the shadows out of every corner. The stench that assaulted his nostrils was overwhelming—flesh and gun smoke and rot. Sanders choked, but he didn't stop.

Three Russians remained, and every one of them stood over a bloody survivor stretched over the floor. One with a rifle pointed down, another with his boot crushing into a petite woman's stomach as he snatched a knife from his chest rig. The third swinging his rifle backward like a club, butt stock arcing downward toward the unprotected skull of a man whose face was already so beaten and bloody he looked like raw meet.

But the rifle never fell. Sanders and his companions opened fire together, still advancing down the hallway, brass pinging off the concrete walls and raining over a gory floor as lead tore through unprotected pelvises and faces. All three Russian commandos jerked standing, guns and knives falling as death swallowed them in a split second.

They were down, and Sanders was running. He passed the first prison door and cleared left, sweeping NVGs over a horror scene. Blood, flesh, and the stench of burned skin. No people. The next room was the same. His companions moved down the right-hand side of the hallway. Sanders advanced toward the next cell, then stopped cold.

This one wasn't empty. It contained two bodies—one of them so mutilated it was barely recognizable as human. Half filleted, half skinned, half burned to a crisp. Twisted and mangled, and most certainly dead.

The second...not so much. Sanders hauled the door open and rocked his NVGs up, deploying his weapon light again. Blazing white illumination poured straight into the face of an average-sized guy with a very average set of smashed, bloody features. Dark skin. Torn suit slacks and a ripped blazer. Wide, terrified eyes.

President Elchin Rzayev.

———————

"Net call, Trailblazer, all secure." Sanders called into his throat mic. "*Jackpot*. Coming out, south side."

78

The Situation Room
The White House

"Jackpot!" General Yellin exploded out of his chair as confirmation of Rzayev's rescue crackled through the Situation Room speakers. Grainy video feed, accentuated by night vision technology, circled the globe to bring the tense security council a view from a pit of hell.

A view that, in Stratton's mind, did much more to condemn the Azerbaijani president than excuse him. The piles of bodies. The gore. The mutilated figure of a man now completely unrecognizable in the prison cell next to the petrified president. But for all that, Rzayev was alive, and the forty Army Rangers deployed to rescue him had seized control of the black site facility without suffering a scratch.

"Multiple tangos down, five hostages recovered, plus one body," the Ranger point man reported. "Extracting now."

The camera bounced again. The soldiers moved. Stratton tilted his head, directing Vice Admiral Garret Price, Commander of the Joint Special Operations Command, to kill the audio. He stared at the screen a long time, a hotter and deadlier rage than he'd ever before felt rising in his gut. It was worse than the fear and uncertainty of an attempted presidential assassination. Worse even than what he felt after witnessing the terror attacks in Tennessee in Louisiana.

It was worse, because Stratton now saw the big picture.

"General, I want the names of the pilots we lost. And I want to know the moment those Rangers are back into secure air space."

Yellin nodded. "Yes, sir."

Stratton pivoted to Secretary Gorman. His voice came out as a snarl. "And I want the Russian president on the phone. Not his ambassador. Not his underling. I want *Nikitin*."

79

The Kremlin
Moscow, Russia

The American military operation at the SSS black site was as clear on the Russian display screens as it no doubt was to the Pentagon halfway around the globe. Nikitin watched as a Russian surveillance drone fed him crystal-clear pictures of American paratroopers—airborne Rangers, his advisors said—landed around the black site, seizing full control within minutes. He couldn't be sure of what happened once those soldiers vanished inside the building. The drone was deaf to gunfire, and unable to penetrate concrete.

But he could guess. The mathematics of the equation were brutally simple. Twelve against forty—assuming all twelve of his commandos still lived, which now seemed unlikely. The Americans would seize control of the building, they would survey its contents. Only one of two possibilities remained.

Either they found Elchin Rzayev alive and managed to rescue him, or they found him dead...in which case they knew Russia had killed him.

Nikitin forced back the tremor at the back of his skull that shook him like an earthquake. He shouldn't *feel* disappointment. The invasion of northern Azerbaijan was going far better than expected, despite the fact that Azerbaijan still maintained control of the skies. By dawn, Russia would have penetrated fifty miles inland and have the Azerbaijani Defense Forces in full retreat. The sheer volume of artillery fire was too great for them—they weren't battle hardened the way the Russians were.

The skies would be resolved in due time, also. As Russia progressed along the ground, surface-to-air missile trucks would give the Azerbaijani pilots second thoughts about bombing his troops. Russian pilots would arrive. Dogfights would swing in the favor of the experienced and technologically superior.

In truth, all was going far better than anticipated. Within weeks Azerbaijan could fall under the full control of Moscow, bringing precious oil reserves and strategic positioning into Nikitin's grasp. And yet it didn't feel like a victory, because one thing *had* gone wrong. One thing that Nikitin had banked on. One thing that he had spent *years* working toward—leveraging, manipulating, calibrating.

It was the Americans. They had *not* backed down, scurrying for cover as he had hoped. Far from it, they had actively engaged themselves in the fight, moving with speed and precision that defied his estimations of the current administration. Even though their relative impact on the region was minimal, it was the spirit of the thing that bothered him most.

America was not broken.

"Mr. President?"

The military aide spoke to Nikitin's right, his tone reflective of a repeated question. Nikitin straightened slowly from the table, still fixated on the screen, then pivoted his gaze.

"Our corvettes are equipped with surface-to-air missiles. If you give the order, we can move them into range before the Americans take off. We may have a shot at their transport plane."

A shot.

Yes. Nikitin had heard that before. A shot at many things. But what would be the fallout?

"No," Nikitin said. "Let them depart. Do not fire."

"Mr. President?" This time it was Golubev who spoke, using Nikitin's formal title in front of his generals.

"You heard me, Anton!" Nikitin screamed. "Stand your men down. Focus on the Azerbaijanis. That will be all."

Nikitin spun, exploding out of the war room and marching down the hall. He tore his tie free and slung it to the carpet, not stopping until he was inside his private study. Door locked. Headed straight for the tea bar. But he didn't want tea—he tore the cabinet doors open and located the vodka. One large glass and a healthy pour. He drained it and filled the glass again before reaching his desk.

The phone rang. He mashed the speaker button.

"Block all calls—"

"Mr. President...it's the White House."

Nikitin froze, his finger hovering over the *End Call* button. He breathed, smelling the liquor on his own breath. He looked to the door, half expecting Golubev to appear.

No. The door was locked. Nikitin settled into his chair. Sipped vodka.

"Mr. President?"

"Put them through," Nikitin growled. He set the glass down. The secretary confirmed his connection with the White House. Acting President Jordan Stratton was on the line.

"You have a hell of a lot of nerve, Mr. *Acting* President, to deploy American warplanes into a sovereign airspace and engage Russian pilots!"

Vodka sprayed from Nikitin's lips as he spoke, his body now trembling with exploding rage. He slammed the glass down, ready for the comeback. The accusations about Rzayev. About Russia's incursion into Azerbaijan. All of it.

But it didn't come. The line was perfectly quiet. Nikitin checked the display, wondering if he had failed to connect. The connection was active.

Just when he was about to speak again, Jordan Stratton's voice carried from the far side of the world. Not shouting. Not demanding. Perfectly calm, and ice cold.

"It was you, wasn't it?"

Nikitin frowned. "What?"

"It was you all along. The attempted assassination of President Trousdale. The fiasco in Venezuela. The terrorist attacks in Tennessee and Baton Rouge. Both nuclear bombs—Panama and Azerbaijan. It was all you."

A sharp chill ran down Nikitin's spine. He sat frozen, temporarily deadlocked. It wasn't like him to be caught off guard, but this was the last thing he expected Stratton to say.

"You've been working to undermine us for a long, long time," Stratton continued. "To compromise our economy. Our administration. Our very society. Anything to take the biggest player off the board before you made your ultimate move...a third world war."

Nikitin's teeth clenched. He leaned in close to the phone. "You are a coward and a fool. You know nothing of what you speak. Tomorrow when the West reads of illegal American military operations not only in Azerbaijan but in the Taiwan Strait, we will see who the villain is. We will see how *great* is this so-called 'Free World.'"

Dead silence. The rage boiled up in Nikitin's chest like magma bubbling out of a volcano. Ever hotter, moving ever faster. He wanted to punch something, to break his own desk in half.

Stratton's next words were harder than his first—like razor-sharp titanium slicing out of the phone speaker.

"You want to dance, you thug? Here I am. Let's *dance*."

And then the White House hung up.

80

The Oval Office
The White House

Stratton hung the phone up so hard the plastic cracked like a gunshot. Inside the quiet Oval with late afternoon sun fading behind the curtains, nobody moved.

Easterling was there, seated across from him. So were Aimes, Gorman, and Yellin. But for once, none of them spoke. They waited while Stratton clenched his fist around the arm of his chair, still fixated on the phone, working out all of the restrained rage he had bottled up during the two-minute phone call.

The calm was forced, the clarity calibrated. He could tell by Nikitin's tone that the Russian president was far less collected. The American military operation had been a curve ball. It had caught him off guard.

It had thrown him on his ass.

Stratton looked up, making eye contact with Yellin. He didn't need to voice the question.

"Our boys just crossed into Armenia," Yellin said. "Not home free yet... but looking good."

Stratton simply nodded. He didn't speak. He glanced at the portrait of

George Washington framed on the wall over the mantel. He gritted his teeth.

"Communicate with the Pentagon. I want war plans on my desk by tomorrow morning. A full strategy to confront Russian and Chinese aggression."

"Understood, sir."

Gorman held up a hand. "Sir, with respect, there's still a diplomatic option—"

"Michael P. Scoresby," Stratton said, cutting her off. "Douglas R. Peck. Angela J. Doles. Michael T. Nash. Jeremy Q. Fisher. Fifteen hundred bodies in Baton Rouge. A few dozen more in Tennessee. Tens of thousands in Panama."

Stratton stopped. He was speaking in a growl, even though he hadn't meant to. The point rang loud and clear.

"We're finished playing games, Madam Secretary. Our next diplomatic protocol comes from the muzzle of a rifle."

Gorman's lips parted...and simply closed. She ducked her head. Easterling took the floor, a question ready.

Then everybody turned as the door at the far end of the room suddenly clicked open. A squeak heralded the turn of a wheel. From down the hall an aide called in confusion.

"Madam President?"

And then Muddy Maggie Trousdale appeared through the door, rolling in a wheelchair, her body propped up by pillows, her face so ashen white she looked nearly dead. James O'Dell stood behind her, manning the chair. Two nurses hurried to keep up, one pushing an IV pole, the other pleading with James to stop the chair.

He wasn't stopping. The moment Maggie entered the Oval, the room fell deathly still. Everyone rose from their chairs. Stratton circled the desk, something between dull shock and horror tightening his gut as he locked eyes with Maggie.

He'd seen her in rough shape before—many times, in fact. But never like this. Maggie appeared as a ghost, her lips blue, her skin clinging to cheekbones that looked so much sharper with the loss of ten pounds. She slumped in the chair, fighting to hold herself up. Fighting even to breathe.

But she wasn't down. Stratton knew that the moment she flicked a hand at O'Dell, directing him to excuse the nurses. Both women objected—James O'Dell didn't give them the time of day. As soon as they were gone, O'Dell closed the door, and once again the room was still.

Stratton opened his mouth. Maggie spoke first.

"What the hell have you gotten us into?"

81

35,000 Feet over Armenia

The cargo bay of the C-17 was as familiar to Reed as his own bedroom. The howl of the engines, the smell of hydraulic fluid, the beat of the wind outside. It all blended together into a background buzz that somehow soothed the mindless tension in his body.

Laid out on a stretcher with Army combat medics toiling around him, Reed enjoyed the slow drip of morphine into his veins and the numbing buzz it brought. Despite the dulled pain, he felt about as wrecked as he ever had. None of the medics as yet had updated him on his specific medical prognosis.

Reed didn't care. He was alive, and for the most part, so was his team. They had escaped the jaws of death once again...all except Strickland. If Reed closed his eyes he could still hear the fearless pilot's taunts as he deliberately drew focused attention to himself, throwing his body into the gears of torment to save his team. It wasn't the first time Reed had seen faultless sacrifice in a moment of tremendous need, but no matter how many times he was witness to that level of courage, he couldn't ever imagine himself not being awed by it.

Kyle Strickland was a hero in the truest sense of the word. And pretty soon, he would be a hero avenged.

"How's it hanging, boss?" The voice was gentle, a little melodic. A little high, maybe, thrown off pitch by Reed's still-ringing ears. Lucy appeared at Reed's elbow, with a glassy look in her eyes that told him she had also benefited from a solid dose of morphine. Of the entire team, she was the only one still on her feet, and by every appearance she shouldn't be. Bruises and bandages decorated her exposed body like a patchwork quilt. Her shirt bulged around her stomach where another wad of bandaging covered over a nasty bullet graze.

Yet she wouldn't lie down. If Reed wasn't so doped up, he might have scolded her.

"I'm fine, LB. You should sit."

Lucy shrugged, and Reed followed her gaze as it passed across the occupants of the plane, a mixture of sleeping Rangers and survivors on stretchers. One stretcher was covered over by a sheet. Another had its occupant handcuffed to the rails.

It was that occupant that Reed found himself fixated on. Elchin Rzayev avoided his gaze. The president had avoided everyone's gaze. He looked like a whipped dog, his face bandaged from Reed's beating, perpetual tears leaking out of his left eye. Tears of shame and self-loathing, Reed hoped.

"Are you going to kill him?" Lucy asked, voice so soft Reed could barely hear it over the thunder of the jet engines. He looked away from Rzayev. He didn't answer.

Lucy settled onto the edge of Reed's stretcher with a tired sigh, her body so light he barely noticed the difference. She looked at her hands, then closed her eyes. Her lips moved without a sound. Reed watched for a while, unwilling to break her focus. When at last Lucy opened her eyes, she noticed Reed staring at her with a little start, as though she'd forgotten he was there.

"It was Scripture?" Reed asked.

"What was?"

"The words you said, in the prison. Just as they blew down the door."

Lucy squinted. Her eyes drifted across the tail of the plane.

"*The Lord of hosts is with us,*" Reed repeated.

Lucy blinked. She nodded. "Yes...right. Psalm forty-six."

Reed's mouth closed. His jaw tensed. But he didn't say it. Lucy caught the expression and shrugged apologetically.

"It's just something I do when I get stressed. It helps."

"Sure," Reed said.

Lucy laid a hand on Reed's arm, offering him a gentle squeeze. She started to speak, then stopped.

"There's a reason," she said at last. "A reason for everything. A plan. I can tell you...when you're ready."

Reed said nothing. Lucy eased off the edge of the stretcher. She forced a smile and mumbled something about getting some shut-eye. As she stepped away, Reed's head rotated back toward Rzayev. This time, the president's face also twisted. His right eye was covered over by bandages, but his left eye locked with Reed's. And didn't blink.

Deep in his chest, the heat Reed had felt before returned and redoubled. Harsher than before, burning sharper. It was stronger than anger, more consumptive than rage. It spread into his blood and reached every extremity, like the slow seep of the morphine...but not nearly so friendly.

Reed stared until Rzayev quaked and turned his face away, then Reed closed his own eyes.

He didn't know about a reason. He didn't expect there to be a plan. The one thing he did know was that his battle wasn't over—not even close to it.

Not until the last of these savages had answered for every last drop of innocent blood.

FULL DARK
THE PROSECUTION FORCE THRILLERS Book 9

The stage is set, the battle lines drawn. War has arrived.

After a brutal operation in Azerbaijan, Reed Montgomery and the battered Prosecution Force barely have time to breathe before they're pulled into the opening act of a third world war. Russia, Iran, and China are acting fast and violently to tighten their grip, bent on global supremacy.

For the Prosecution Force, stopping the inevitable feels impossible. But wars are won one battle at a time, and the next fight isn't on the battlefield—it's in the halls of power. India, the world's second-largest military power, stands at a crossroads, teetering between Western allies and Chinese threats. And when the CIA uncovers a covert Chinese operation designed to pull India into the enemy's grasp, the White House is left with no choice: intervene or lose a critical ally.

Now, deep in the streets of Kolkata, Montgomery and his team have their orders—sabotage the Chinese operation, no matter the cost. But the Prosecution Force is beat up, undermanned, and walking straight into the lion's den.

They have no reinforcements. No second chances. Just a world on the brink of war—and a fight they refuse to lose.

Get your copy today at
severnriverbooks.com

ACKNOWLEDGMENTS

It truly takes an army to bring a book like this from concept to completion to publication. As many hours as I invest into each page, there are a plethora of people who have worked just as hard on their own specialties to make this book the very best it could be. In no particular order, I wish to extend special thanks to...

Jack Stewart, Naval aviator, TOPGUN graduate, and fellow thriller author for all the advice and expertise regarding the Navy fighter pilot scenes in this book. I literally could not have written them without you! (Find Jack's novels at severnriverbooks.com)

Jason Kasper, US Army Special Forces veteran and fellow thriller author for all the expertise and fact-checking on the Ranger scenes featured in this book. Again, I couldn't have made these scenes authentic without his support. You rock, dude! (Find Jason's novels at severnriverbooks.com)

Cate, Andrew, and the entire production and editorial team at Severn River Publishing for their relentless support of my novels and belief in me as a writer. I go to work every day knowing that I have a team of experts at my back who are as dedicated to the success of my books as I am, and I simply cannot overstate how much I appreciate them.

Gary Bennett, the voice of Reed Montgomery and the Prosecution Force for his faithfulness to the series, relentless dedication to the craft, and patience with all the foreign pronunciations I make him learn. You're an absolute rock star, dude!

And finally, last but never least, my dear wife, Anna, for the decades of support, love, friendship, laughter, patience, and companionship. I'd be a bum in a shack without you.

—Logan

ABOUT THE AUTHOR

Logan Ryles was born in small town USA and knew from an early age he wanted to be a writer. After working as a pizza delivery driver, sawmill operator, and banker, he finally embraced the dream and has been writing ever since. With a passion for action-packed and mystery-laced stories, Logan's work has ranged from global-scale political thrillers to small town vigilante hero fiction.

Beyond writing, Logan enjoys saltwater fishing, road trips, sports, and fast cars. He lives with his wife and three fun-loving dogs in Alabama.

Sign up for Logan Ryles's reader list at
severnriverbooks.com

Printed in the United States
by Baker & Taylor Publisher Services